# SAVIOR'S DAY

*Other books by Alan A. Winter*

**Someone Else's Son**

**Snowflakes in the Sahara**

# SAVIOR'S DAY

## Alan A. Winter

iUniverse, Inc.
Bloomington

# Savior's Day

iUniverse books may be ordered through booksellers or by contacting:

iUniverse
1663 Liberty Drive
Bloomington, IN 47403
www.iuniverse.com
1-800-Authors (1-800-288-4677)

ISBN: 978-1-4759-8908-3 (sc)
ISBN: 978-1-4759-8906-9 (hc)
ISBN: 978-1-4759-8907-6 (e)

Library of Congress Control Number: 2013907980

Printed in the United States of America

iUniverse rev. date: 05/16/2013

"Alan Winter has anticipated a series of interconnected contemporary events that are terrifyingly believable in terms of our world today. Based on historical fact, he has written a tight, dynamic thriller definitely on a par with those appearing on the bestseller lists."

Olga Vezeris,
Visiting Lecturer for the NYU Publishing Institute, former editor Simon & Schuster/Pocket Books, Time Life, Grand Central Publishing, and Harper Collins.

# Chapter One

Jericho Glassman shrugged into the Israeli soldier's camouflage fatigues and assumed the dead man's post. A glance skyward. There was no sign that the thick overcast clouds would break up anytime soon. He was thankful for the grey veil of cover, assured that his presence had a better chance of going undetected.

At least he'd be safe for a while, and a while was all the time he needed.

Jericho snatched the telescopic sight he had hidden inside the AC condenser weeks earlier and jiggled it onto the mounting of the dead man's rifle. He couldn't believe his luck when he went unchallenged onto the roof the first time. He had scaled the stairs with the authority of belonging there, found the door to the roof locked which slowed him down in the time it takes to muscle open a stubborn jar, and then stood akimbo staring at the Wailing Wall. The Wall was a two thousand year old ochre-colored brick edifice built of Jerusalem limestone only a short sprint away.

"It must happen at the Wall," the Voices urged him. Commanded him. He had been hearing them from time to time, but in recent weeks, the frequency had increased. The Voices gave guidance. Comfort. They gave him strength when he needed it and greater focus.

It was time to set matters right.

Jericho did not challenge the Voices or ask, "Why?" He knew *why*. It started here, and it must end here. In Jerusalem. At the Wailing Wall. Where the Second Temple once stood. The logic was impeccable. The Voices were always right.

1

Now, an unexpected turn of events would enable him to complete his mission. Their mission. The Voices' mission for him. For without Jericho Glassman, what would happen to the world? Who would reset the balance back to *right*?

Standing there, with only time ticking between him and destiny, Jericho peered at the ancient stones first assembled by King Solomon, then destroyed by the Babylonians under Nebuchadnezzar more than five hundred years before Christ, only to be rebuilt at the behest of Cyrus the Great and completed during the reign of Darius the Great. It stood as a symbol of the Jewish people for another four hundred and twenty years until the Roman, Titus, squashed the Jewish uprising and destroyed the Temple for the last time some thirty years after the crucifixion.

Empire after empire, conquest after conquest, oppressive rulers and benevolent ones, Jericho's people survived. Somewhere along the way, the Jews lost control of their most important landmark, the Temple Mount. That was scheduled to change. It was part of the Voices' agenda.

"The Muslims have controlled it too long," said the Voices.

"What do you want me to do?" he asked.

He listened with rapture as they detailed each step. The Voices left it to Jericho to determine the time and place. The *what* and *why* were already decided.

It happened a few weeks back. It was a sunny day in Ashkelon, with blue skies and a gentle breeze coming off the water. Jericho was sitting at Fisenzone, a small restaurant at the marina. The waitress had just placed a coffee Americano, black, when he opened the Israel Post. There, staring back at him in bold, black letters was the missing piece needed to complete his mission.

*They* would all be gathered in same place.

Get to Jerusalem and the deed would be done.

He looked about, wanting to share the good news with the Voices. No need. They already knew.

Now, tucked low on the roof, peering through the telescopic mount, Jericho scanned white paper fluffs wedged between the ancient stones, messages to God exhorting His good will, praying for wealth or good health or some other meaningless wish. It was a ritual repeated millions of times by millions of souls seeking His favor. His forgiveness. His beneficence.

"They're all fools," mocked the Voices. Jericho agreed.

He didn't need the scope to see the rest. On a normal day, the routine never changed.

Men to the right; women to the left. A fence between them.

Prayer shawls. Headscarves. Black hats. Yarmulkes.

Short and tall. Light and dark-skinned. Young and old. They came by the busload, wheeled in chairs, hobbling on canes. Black frocks and paisley shirts.

Countless *bar mitzvahs* from America. Men circling a lectern that sported a Torah, the Five Books of Moses. Some with phylacteries wrapped around their left arm; a black box strapped to their forehead containing sacred prayers. A rabbi and a freshly scrubbed thirteen year old soon to become a man.

This and more, at the Wall, every day.

But not today. Today was special.

Jericho was the one they chose; the Voices anointed him.

The day at hand, getting this close to his penultimate goal had been child's play; escaping would take all his cunning. In minutes, his years of training and resourcefulness would be put to the test. And while Jericho was not a religious man – religion has been beaten and ripped out of him years back – he prayed for a steady hand and a clear shot.

The darkened skies hung low, an accomplice to the plan.

Jericho drew in a deep breath and then exhaled long and slow, squeezing a flicker of rising jitters out into the still air. Controlled chaos was in front of him, surrounded him, but for Jericho, the air was still. Even quiet. Nirvana would soon be at hand.

He drew in another steadying breath; his pulse dropped to forty-five beats per minute.

He was ready.

Cheers and shouting erupted across the Temple Mount.

The moment drew near.

While Jericho was not able to view the Man's progress, he was apprised of every solemn step the Man took. Twenty minutes earlier, an informant who had been an Army buddy, texted that the package had been plucked from the limousine and handed to him. The Man embraced it to his chest and began the walk of all walks that would be etched in history, perhaps the equal of when another, at another time, carried a cross on his walk.

But this walk was different. Glorious. Triumphant. The Man was bringing home the package.

Then a surprise to all: the Man made an unscheduled stop. Maybe it was to gather strength for what he was about to do? Maybe it was to contemplate all that it meant? Did he have doubts? Fear? Maybe they picked the wrong person.

Droplets formed on Jericho's upper lip. He told himself to wait, to be patient. Jericho waited for a text from a two-bit accomplice that the Man was on the move again. He waited. His palms grew slippery. With care, he wiped each on a pant leg, careful not to attract attention.

Maybe the Man was overwhelmed? Unable to continue?

The Voices wouldn't like that.

A vibration, a text, a glance, and the mission were back on track.

The Man now edged his way toward the Muslim cemetery. The graveyard had been installed there to prevent pious Jewish priests, forbidden from ever entering a cemetery, from passing through it and gaining access to the oldest gate of the city wall. To insure no such transgression could occur, Suleiman the Magnificent sealed the entrance with massive stones more than five hundred years earlier. It was sealed to prevent this day, but now it was open. A miracle in itself.

This Man holding the package is both pious and religious, and yet the cemetery he must walk through will not deter him. The Man turned left and made his way through the headstones at the foot of the Golden Gate that were forbidden to high priests. The Man was a high priest, but of a different kind.

Had it been another time, Jericho would have stepped back and pointed out the symmetry that was unfolding on the world's great stage in front of him. The Scriptures. History. Prophecies. A Holy Place. A Communion in God's Temple. His Temple. All had been in play once before…and then destroyed forever. Or so they thought.

Jericho would change all that, the Voices told him so. There was a time the Voices did not speak to him, a time when Jericho went his own way, not knowing his true mission. But then the Voices appeared and foretold of this day, and what he had to do. And when they told him, he knew why he had been so challenged, why the ones he loved had been snatched away, why he had been tested and tested, and then tested again. Jericho was chosen for his inner strength, and for his convictions. The Voices told him all this and more.

Jericho heard voices below. Everyday voices. He glanced down and permitted a slight upturn of his bluish lips. A quiver of a smile. How poetic. No, thought Jericho, poetic was not the word. Not by any stretch of the imagination.

Biblical, was more appropriate.

He might even take liberty with words, certain that some would come to refer to his mission as "Messianic."

With the benefit of time and hindsight, history might anoint this special day as apocalyptic. Witnesses would describe what they saw, what they were certain happened on this day. Some might get it right and be accurate historians; others would have their eyes play tricks on them. In time, they would see the truth because Jericho was there to guide them. The Voices told him that, too.

Cheers jackknifed his attention to the moment at hand. He stole a nervous glance behind him, to reassure himself that the dead Israeli soldier remained slumped behind the wire-reinforced skylight. Lifeless.

Jericho chastised himself for the time it took to turn his head, the brief lapse that a dead man could still be a threat to him. To Jericho's success. To the bidding of the Voices. To the Master Plan. The soldier was heavier than he thought. Stealing up the stairs, the soundless steps, and garrote around his neck…those were the easy parts. Dragging the heavy body proved tougher than he had anticipated. And wrestling the soldier's clothes off worked up quite a sweat. Jericho never liked to sweat. For him, it was a display of weakness, of yielding to elements not in his control. But everything was in his control now. Everything. Life. Fate. History.

All controlled by an index finger.

Jericho replayed in his mind what happen in the next moments, and then how he would escape this place. He anticipated no difficulties. With the soldier now a lump of decaying protoplasm, and with a clear path to the roof door, Jericho would slip down the stairs, slip from the building and blend into the chaos that would follow, chaos that he had caused.

And what chaos it would be!

Chaos the world never thought could happen because of every precaution taken to protect this day. To make it sacred and holy to all. Jericho was prepared to leap over the barbed wire in some off chance that the route down the steps was blocked. People had been known to survive high falls. Maybe he would be the lucky one today.

Others were targeted for death this day.

Not him.

But if becoming a martyr was necessary to accomplish his mission, Jericho was prepared to sacrifice his life in order to change the course of history for the rest of all time.

To correct the ills that had befallen his people. All people.

Reckoning was around the corner.

# Chapter Two

Across the dry and sultry way, on the Temple Mount, Zakkarhia ibn Mohammed shifted his weight. In preparation for this day, he had slipped into the Al Aqsa Mosque the day before, to pray as he had done countless times in mosques all over the world. Yesterday was different. When everyone left the mosque the night before, he remained. Zakkarhia had climbed into the tall minaret, curled up on his prayer mat, and had the most restful sleep he had known in years. And what years they had been from the time he left his family in Gaza, to his return as a prodigal son. So much had changed there. And not for the better.

Now this. His final mission.

The sanctity of this place on earth, what is now called the Temple Mount, was not lost to Zakkarhia. This is the very place where the angel Gabriel guided Muhammad through the eastern gate, known by Muslims as the Gate of the Prophet, to the Sacred Rock that was at the center of Solomon's Temple. Here, Muhammad performed his prayer-prostrations in the holiest of holy places, in the spiritual center of the world where Abraham, Isaac, Jacob, and, later, Jesus had also once prayed. Finished praying, Muhammad stood and then, guided by Gabriel, mounted his white steed, Buraq, and ascended through the celestial dimensions where he witnessed the delights of Paradise. He passed through the seven heavens to stand in the presence of Allah where, like Moses on Mt. Sinai, he received instruction as to the prayers his followers were to perform.

Muhammad was the messenger for Allah. So was Zakkarhia.

In a few hours, it would be Zakkarhia's time to reach Paradise, to make this his day of Resurrection...once he did Allah's bidding. His mission was doubly sweet, for it would also serve as the ambrosia of revenge. An eye for an eye.

Reverie aside, Zakkarhia needed to exercise caution and wait until the moment arrived, and to make certain that the caretaker of the mosque, the muezzin who called the believers to prayer, had left for the evening.

A click echoed from below. Metal against metal. Zakkarhia slumped against the cold wall. Though empty of worshippers, the Holy Shrine was sealed drum-tight. Now nothing stood in his way from fulfilling the mission that would gain him entrance through the Gates of Paradise.

Morning came. Secure in knowing that no one would be coming to the mosque that day due to the heightened security measures, he still tiptoed down from the minaret, voided in the latrine, and then unrolled his mat to pray. He prayed that his mission would meet with success. He prayed that the Infidel would leave his peoples' land. He prayed for his sister Aliah. He prayed to Mohammed for strength of heart and sureness of hand.

As the time drew near, he snaked his way back to the top of the minaret, ripped off the gray duct tape holding the parts to the disassembled rifle he had planted along the molding in the days leading up to this day, and assembled his rifle.

◆　◆　◆

Two gunman, one Jewish the other Muslim, from different backgrounds and different beliefs, shared much in common on this day. Both were driven. Both shared an overlapping mission.

Would their parallel universes coalesce into one?

Did a common bond link the two?

A common goal?

A common target?

Perhaps.

Had anyone sighted either of them from afar, they might have noted exposed weapons, they might have noted the direction each was aiming at, and they might have noted the obvious: Zakkarhia to the south, and Jericho to the west both pointed rifles at those gathered at the open area next to the golden covered, Dome of the Rock.

No one could be blamed for thinking the two worked in concert.

A team of assassins.

Double trouble.

But the outside observer would have drawn the wrong conclusion: neither man knew the other existed.

No matter. In a few short minutes, the world would discover who both were.

In a few short minutes, the world would discover their truths, truths they would all have to face. Consequences they would have to live with.

♦   ♦   ♦

Jericho screwed the rifle into a short, stubby tripod and planted it on the roof ledge, careful not to have it protrude and call attention. He examined the Zeiss telescopic sight; it was flush to the mountings and aligned to the barrel. He checked for parallax. He fanned the rifle from side to side, his eye glued to the site: the crosshair stood fast. He caressed the smooth metal, pleased that it would be dead-on at one hundred meters, and accurate enough beyond that for the task he needed. Even with the ring of security circling the world's most important leaders, no one would question an Israeli soldier's gun barrel poised at the ready.

The time neared.

Jericho lay prostrate, left elbow on the flat stone rimming the roof, gunstock against his shoulder, the barrel under the barb wired that encircled the building, finger on the trigger, pulse at a steady fifty-six beats. All that was required was the missing Element that would complete the Holy Pentacle. And that Element was approaching the

East Gate of the old city that was sometimes referred to as the Golden Gate or Gate of Mercy by Jews.

Jericho had once taken a city tour, where the guide described The Golden Gate as the portal through which Christ entered Jerusalem on Palm Sunday.

"Isn't this where Christ is supposed to return," Jericho asked.

"If you believe that he was the Messiah, then yes. But this portal is also important to the Muslims," the guide answered. "This is where the last Day of Judgment will occur when Mohammed returns to earth." The guide pointed upward. "Mohammed will sit on top and judge all those who pass through."

"Then if it is such an important spot, why is it sealed?"

"It can't be that important," answered the guide, "or the Muslims would have left it open. Don't you agree?"

◆　◆　◆

The fifth Element, or the Man as Jericho referred to him, was about to march up the stone stairs to deafening acclaim. All eyes would focus on the sacred pages of Israel's greatest treasure that had been lost for more than half a century that he would clutch to his chest; he was a father bringing home a child. The Element would edge his way to the gaggle of dignitaries already gathered on the Temple Mount, only meters from the Dome of the Rock and execute the transfer of the sacred papers.

The world anticipated this moment with irrational enthusiasm. After all, pages were pages, and words were words. How could sheaves of paper, parchment really, ancient as they were, command the collective hopes and prayers of the planet's more than seven billion? Though Jericho could not understand this human frailty to worship and pray to a God none could see, he cherished the fact that it gave him the chance to fulfill the Voices' wishes.

And as the fifth and last Element entered the Ring of Hope, The Man would complete the keystone to peace. The Man was the headstone quoin that made the circle whole. The Man carried the link that joined

Jews and Arabs into a ring of harmony, a ring that ended rocket launches and senseless killings, bus bombings, and generations of hatred. The Man was the link that ended neighbor fighting neighbor and he was the link to tear down fences that would no longer keep cousins apart since Partition was declared in '47.

The four other pillars, each Element so integral to life, stood ready to be made whole. They waited for the Man, the nexus who would connect them all in a link of peace and harmony.

Fire. Air. Water. Earth. Only the Spirit was missing.

The Holy Spirit, thought Jericho, had been responsible for more deaths than any army the world had known. Since the dawn of time, the Holy Spirit segregated, defined, empowered, enslaved, burned, killed, maimed, and tortured, all in the name of its righteous causes. The Crusades, the Thirty Years' War, the French Wars of Religion at the end of the sixteenth century, the Israeli War for Independence, the Second Sudanese Wars started in the 1980s that lasted more than two decades, the quarter-century long Lebanese Civil War and the worldwide jihad.

Ah, the jihad! Would it ever be different?

The formal protocol for this historic event had been plastered on CNN, in the Herald Tribune, the Jerusalem Post, Facebook, Twitter, and in every other form of news media, including both the Arabic and English-speaking Al Jezeera. For security reasons, news trucks with satellite dishes necessary to transmit the event live were congregated blocks away. They needed to snake black wires through extra-wide PVC conduits that extended through the streets to a single Israeli government feed parked outside the Wailing Wall. This truck, with its large cage platform worthy of overlooking Times Square on New Year's Eve, telescoped above the Wall, able to train its lens on the dignitaries assembled by the Dome of the Rock.

Schools turned on TVs or were glued to live Internet connections. Worldwide commerce slowed to a crawl. Drivers pulled off the road to listen to their radios. Parks were empty. Movie theaters interrupted shows with the live broadcast. The day-to-day actions of every man, woman, and child on the planet ceased so as not to miss this once-in-a-lifetime event.

Every second was orchestrated, every gesture, every spoken word would follow a script, except for the glitch named Jericho Glassman… and another named Zakkarhia ibn Mohammed.

The events were unparalleled in the annals of diplomacy.

The first step along this negotiated historic path had Israel removing all governmental agencies from Jerusalem, including the Knesset and the Supreme Court, in preparation for this ancient Biblical site to become an international city. Berlin had gone this route at the end of World War II when the Allies divided Berlin into four sectors: the French, British, Russian and American. Then came the siege of the city by the Russians. The airlift. The Berlin Wall. Separation. Communism. The Cold War.

This would not happen here in Jerusalem. Not now. Not ever. All because of the Fifth Element. This newly negotiated safe harbor, an ancient island older than the Torah itself, surrounded by a sea of Semites who spent centuries battling and killing each other, would now be administered by the United Nations, backed by the might of the US… leaving nothing for the Israelis and Arabs to squabble over.

The event would be triggered the moment Pope Lazarus II handed the missing pages of the Codex of Aleppo, considered by all the greatest Bible ever written, to the Israeli Prime Minister, Yehuda ben Moses.

Next, the Israeli PM would clutch the pages to his chest, kiss them, and then hand them to Professor Yussif Tawil, a leading manuscript scholar from Hebrew University, to authenticate. Once he verified them as the long lost missing pages, Tawil would insert them in their proper place within the ancient text while the Vatican choir sang Handel's "Messiah."

With these missing pages added to the ancient tome commissioned by the black-garbed Karaites in the early part of the tenth century AD, Professor Tawil, a Yemeni Jew by birth, would hand the book to the newly elected Palestinian president, Jabil Habeeb. The symbolism was lost on no one. It would be an Arab who, after the noted scholar reassembled it, would be the first person to hold the restored treasure in his hands. Not an Israeli. Not a Jew...but a follower of Muhammad.

Habeeb would hold the book over his head, bow to Mecca, bow to Medina, and then lumber to his knees, lower his head, and hold the great book out in meaty hands toward the Dome of the Rock before struggling to stand. He would next pass the Codex to the Secretary General of the United Nations, the honorable Naomi Soweto. She would utter a few words anticipated to be the equal of Neil Armstrong's, and then deliver the book to the U.S. president, Logan Rothschild. Rothschild would return the book to the Israeli Prime Minister.

It was fitting that one Jew would hand the greatest treasure of the State of Israel to another. It was also fitting that at that moment, Jericho would pull the trigger.

Once the Pentacle was complete.

◆   ◆   ◆

Across the way, hidden in a minaret that all thought safe, secure, and unoccupied, Zakkarhia ibn Mohammed took aim at an imaginary target in the open area meters in from of the protected structure erected to shield the international luminaries from the late morning sun. In moments he would fulfill Allah's wishes while carrying out his orders at the same time. The act was sweetened because it would also permit him to exact revenge to honor his dead sister. For his family. For Allah.

In moments he would put a hole through the madness centered around these absurd missing pages written on ancient parchment.

In moments he would extinguish the myth that anything could be holier than the Koran, Allah be praised.

◆   ◆   ◆

Gittel Lasker's arms ached. She stole a moment to let the Nikon 10x42 Monarch ATB drift downward, long enough to rub her red, tired eyes. No one would begrudge a few seconds. Protecting not only the

Israeli the Prime Minister but also charged with protecting the other dignitaries participating in this historic event was an ever-constant challenge. Gittel spent a lifetime in her country's service, but no event had the magnitude of this one. Super-vigilant was the catch phrase of the day.

Gittel scoured the buildings that rimmed the Wailing Wall, the tallest of which had direct sightlines to the Temple Mount. Army sharpshooters were assigned to the rooftops with specific orders not to reveal their whereabouts and under no circumstances to display their weapons. The last thing anyone wanted was a civilian looking skyward and feeling they were in a shooter's sights.

Her walkie-talkie crackled. She tilted her head and placed her finger on the earpiece. "All clear." She replied in kind.

She drew the binoculars upward when a glint of sun danced off something metal, metal that was not supposed to be there, not supposed to be visible.

"Eleven o'clock," she whispered into the microphone that coiled from her ear and hugged her cheek like a viper ready to strike. "I'm checking the rooftop above my station. Over."

# Chapter Three

Each assassin needed to wait for the moment to ripen before the seeds of their discontent would burst forth like flowers under a desert rain. Only these flowers were black, but they bled red. Unknown to each other, but kindred spirits in every sense, Jericho and Zakkarhia felt throbbing in their ears; their pulse echoed each second, bringing triumph so close they could taste it on their dry tongues and parched lips. Jericho slipped his finger off the trigger and wiped it dry on his pant leg; Zakkarhia swiped the sweat off his brow, the salt stinging his eyes.

Each focused, waiting for the moment that was ever so near. Both drew in a deep breath, held it a tick, and then exhaled a sour stream of air that slithered over their teeth. Their bodies tightened as a distant rumble turned into a crescendo of hallelujahs.

Pope Lazarus II neared.

Throngs jammed every square inch of hallowed ground leading to, and at the base of, the ancient Wailing Wall. The narrow streets leading up to it were filled with all who needed to be there. Many hung out of open windows straining for a glimpse. Though most could not see the Temple Mount, for it was elevated, they jockeyed to see one of the large screens that dangled outside building walls or from cranes erected to carry a live feed. No matter where one turned, tears of joy streaked the faces of every man, woman, and child, regardless of their ancient birthright or political beliefs, regardless of their skin color, or regardless if they sported a yarmulke or held prayer beads or rosaries.

15

Peace would soon be, at hand. Nations would not lift up swords against each other, least of all Palestinians against Israelis.

That's what the ancient Codex represented. Peace. Peace to the Israelis. Peace to the Palestinians. Peace to the Middle East. In turn, peace would spread to every other hotspot in the world including Iraq, Iran, Afghanistan, Syria, Sudan, Darfur, Mali, Algeria, and more. Peace to the world.

From his perch, Zakkarhia could see Pope Lazarus II dismount from a donkey at the gate that led into the old city, cradling a package wrapped in a royal purple cloth. The Pope stepped under the ancient archway and marched with purposeful steps toward the waiting assemblage. Unlike his predecessors who lived their lives in bulletproof bubbles, this Pope insisted that no bodyguards accompany him on this joyous event. He had to be free, unencumbered. He was every man and every woman. When the detachment of Swiss Army guards argued that no such thing would occur on their watch, the Pope stilled their objections with a scathing reprimand as to what it meant when the Lord's anointed emissary on earth made a request. The guards had no choice but to acquiesce. They were comforted knowing that the crack Israeli security team would protect every step the Pope took once he passed through the stone archway. His Holiness's safety was not at issue.

To the dismay of many, an army of laughing and singing, black-haired, dark-skinned children trailed the Pope by a mere step or two. Every few steps, His Holiness stopped to touch the head of one of the urchins; when he did, those chosen to protect him skipped a beat, praying they were just that: children.

The Pope passed directly under Zakkarhia. How easy it would be to pull the trigger now. End it all. Accomplish the cherished goal. But Zakkarhia was a professional; he would exert patience. Obey his inner strength and wait until the Pentacle was assembled in the designated order, praised be to Allah. Symmetry and order would rule; he needed to wait.

# Chapter Four

Nasser Albakree, the much-decorated general in the Palestinian Security Force, would leave nothing to chance. His charge was to secure the base of the slope leading to the east gate before the Pope rode a donkey down from the Mount and would enter the ancient city of Jerusalem. With his back to the limestone walls, he viewed each building in front of him, including the church, with grid-like precision. Methodically he combed doors, windows, and rooftops, his trained eyes seeking anything out of the ordinary. He did so without distraction, ignoring what the rest of the world was lapping up in its unquenchable thirst for both immediate news and history as it happened.

The world was in the moment. So was Nasser, but his moment was fixed in responsibility. Fixed in duty. Nasser had already searched a fruit cart, poking the barrel of his gun deep into the stacks of oranges. He caused an Arab woman to utter expletives that would shame a camel driver as she undid her baby's diaper to make certain it was not filled with C-4. As the seconds and minutes clicked by, he gained a measure of confidence that all would be right in his sector, that the Pope would be safe as he passed through the Holy Gate to fulfill his historic task.

Some would call it a task of destiny.

Nasser trailed the beehive of children buzzing behind the Pope as Lazarus II climbed the steps and reached the archway. Trailed by the papal Swiss Guard and two Mossad agents, the humble Palestinian wriggled through the children to get as close as possible for that moment when the Pope would transfer the long-thought missing pages of the ancient codex to the four notables waiting for him. Out of habit due to his security training, he scanned the buildings closest to the Temple Mount. He glanced past the Al Aqsa Mosque, content that at least one structure was empty and posed no threat.

It was then that his head jerked back; the snout of a rifle poked out from the minaret. He followed the barrel; a yellow stream ran down his leg.

◆　◆　◆

Jericho heard the cheers a split-second after Zakkarhia did. He knew it would only be minutes before the Pope climbed the stone stairs and passed through the ancient gate into view. The Pope would wave and his righteous image of happiness and joy would be beamed to the seven billion glued to televisions, radio or the Internet the globe over.

Never since Christ drew his last breath, had an event so changed the world.

Never in the two millennia since the Second Temple had been destroyed, had the Jews been given such hope.

Not even after the UN tried to repay the Jews for the six million dead by redeeming Biblical promises and voting for Palestine's partition in '47, had God's chosen children felt His love. They didn't feel it then, but they felt it now. For the first time in generations, they felt loved and safe. And not since Mohammed rose to Paradise from the Temple Mount, had Muslims around the world been given so glorious a reason to rejoice.

The agreement about to go into effect had been unthinkable since the Jewish state was first formed. Surrounded by hostile countries whose only goal was to drive the descendants of Moses into the Mediterranean, Israel's borders were sacrosanct. For the Israelis sacrosanct meant borders that would be defended at any cost and expanded when victory permitted them to claim more. Secure borders gave comfort, and it was political suicide for any leader to suggest otherwise. Secure borders would never be abandoned or compromised in anyway. Until now.

The missing pages changed all. The Israelis not only agreed to the concept of accepting the notion of an independent Palestinian State but agreed to help them form it and to give them financial and technical aid. The Israelis agreed to retreat from some borders and to cast aside past differences. The Palestinians were just as conciliatory.

In moments, history would set off on a new course. This course was plotted by the Trinity plus Two – The Pentacle – and endorsed by the billions of Jews, Christians, and Muslims the world over.

In fact, the brilliance of this plan was so simple, so exquisite, that no soul on earth doubted its genius and the glory to mankind that would follow in its wake. The rich would no longer turn away from the poor, the healthy from the sick, or the powerful from the meek.

The renewable resources of faith and hope would be rekindled in a rebirth of brotherhood and sisterhood for those lucky enough to be alive at this moment in time. Future generations would experience peace and prosperity unlike their parents and their parents' parents ever had.

◆　◆　◆

Everyone accepted this plan except two lone men pointing rifles at the ring of world leaders entrusted to initiate this blessed event.

◆　◆　◆

Zakkarhia drew in a deep breath as President Rothschild handed the Codex to UN Secretary General, Naomi Soweto. He timed the rhythm of his heart to pull the trigger between beats.

◆　◆　◆

Jericho focused with both eyes open, his dominant right eye peering through the scope.

The red laser tattooed his target. He modulated his breathing. He waited for the Palestinian President, Jabil Habeeb. Habeeb took the book from Professor Tawil and brought it to his lips. He bowed in the directions of Mecca and then Medina, two of the three holiest cities to the world's more than one-and-a-half billion Muslims. Then, with a grace that belied a man who walked with a cane and was challenged by even two small steps, he plunged to his knees in homage. With outstretched arms, he symbolically offered the book toward the golden Dome of the Rock.

♦ ♦ ♦

Zakkarhia had the patience of a sheepherder. He waited for the son of a Palestinian grocer to kiss the thick book. He stole a glance upward and noted that it was time. The sun, long blocked by morning clouds, began to peak out.

♦ ♦ ♦

The bells in all the churches in Jerusalem clanged that *the* moment had come.

Men, women, and children touched their prayer beads, their rosaries, and kissed the sacred books that they carried, giving thanks for what they were about to witness. To experience. To be part of living history. They would tell their children and their grandchildren and their great-grandchildren. There were only ticks of a clock left and they prayed to witness what all said could never be done. Would never be done. But they were there to see it with their own eyes.

And then it happened. Two shots rang out.

Pandemonium erupted. In the spit of a flash, soldiers rushed to form a tight ring around the Trinity plus Two.

It was too late.

Jericho and Zakkarhia each succeeded in hitting their mark, and history, as we know it, was changed forever. It was changed in a way that could not be quantified. It was changed greater than the thousand suns at Hiroshima.

The indelible, unchangeable, irrevocable act occurred on what would be forever known as *Savior's Day*.

# Chapter Five

His Holy Eminence, Cardinal Arnold Josiah Ford, head of the Catholic diocese of New York, shuffled past his startled parishioners of St. Patrick's Cathedral. Only moments earlier, he had their rapt attention balanced in the palms of his weathered, outstretched hands. He preached self-sacrifice. Make do with less. Suffer as the Lord Jesus did for his minions, and in so doing the world would be a better place for all the Lord's children. Black and white, yellow, brown, and red, we are all brothers and sisters.

They had heard it before, had come to expect it from him. His homilies were germs of kindness and wisdom, sprinkled with love. Like an orchid grower, the Cardinal nurtured his teachings to cajole the elegant beauty out of everyone. Not a simple man, Cardinal Ford.

It happened without warning in the middle of his homily. An inner voice "warned" him that a life was about to change. Not just any life, his life. Cardinal Ford tried to collect his thoughts. Was the Almighty Lord speaking to him? Speaking through him? Or was he delusional?

The silver goblet turned heavy in his hand. He struggled to raise it, to heft the water to his quivering lips. Droplets scatted across his parched tongue like mercury, not quenching, not even wetting. He struggled to swallow. He gripped the lectern in a vise-like grip, *or was it feather-light,* to steady the feint feeling washing over his body. A flash of worry crossed his mind. He must not let his congregants think he was having a "TIA" – a trans ischemic attack - or, worse yet, a stroke.

Was this how it happened? Numbness? Loss of body control only to succumb to eternal blackness?

Would he spiral to the floor? He held on tight.

It was that damned voice again. He had been hearing it more than he would ever admit. Absent divine intervention, it caused him enough concern to visit a neurologist at Cornell's New York Hospital. The MRI proved negative.

He didn't know which was worse. Had the doctor found a tumor, a mini-stroke, at least something, it would explain what he was experiencing. After a battery of tests, the report was unequivocal: nearing four score, Cardinal Arnold Josiah Ford had the heart and mind of man half his age. He could expect to live forever; at least that's what the young doctor had said. Harrumph. Didn't the wet-behind-the-ears physician know forever had a way of sneaking up on everyone doggoned fast? What do doctors know anyway? It was more frightening now that he received a clean bill of health; there was no corporal reason for hearing voices.

Yet they were there, again, and this time, quite emphatic.

Cardinal Ford was not a striking man by most standards. To look at him was to see a man with large hands and an even larger head; both were too big for his barrel-chested body that supported his narrow frame. He had craggy skin that was weatherworn like leather, with furrows that rippled across his brow, and wiry hair that was steel-wool gray, and cropped short. No bald shiny spot for him. His brown eyes were the one feature that drew people to him. Embraced them. Made strangers feel connected the first moment they met him. They were described as soulful. All-seeing. Beneficent. Soft to the point of being angelic. Yet all who met him, worked with him, and prayed with him agreed: Cardinal Ford was a giant of a man in the largest archdiocese in the United States, and that he was graced by the Almighty Himself.

A child of the Lord, in a figurative sense.

The leader of the Roman Catholics in New York looked across the sea of parted lips, across the field of raised brows, across thousands of eyes that beckoned for him to continue. Should he tell them about The

Voice? It was not many voices, only one. Always the same one. Clear and crisp. Not willowy and flighty so as to think a soft wind might be carrying words from afar. Whispering in soft hushes. Rather, it was strong, firm, and direct.

Cardinal Arnold Ford heard words and saw visions with disturbing clarity. These visions pained him. Scared him. He no longer wondered if they were real; he knew they were.

Ford shifted his weight, leaned forward. He made eye contact with a grey-haired man who had once colored his hair a light brown, only to have it appear orange. But that was a while ago. Now he was clad in a brown plaid suit that draped over this withered body that was being eaten alive by cells gone awry. The man met his gaze. A supplicant in search of hope. How many came to church only when the chips were down, when they couldn't bear life's stresses anymore? Were they praying for a miracle or just needed strength to continue? Regardless, they were here, in his church, expecting him to offer hope and a way to work through their troubles.

Ford knew this one. He owned a private limousine service. Came on the big holidays, missed all the Sundays…except this one. But today, he was a soul hoping that prayer would cure what an abandoned Whipple procedure couldn't, when the pancreatic surgeon discovered the metastasis while performing the surgery that would leave him with six months to a year. Enough time to get his affairs in order, to see his grandkids a couple of times more. Maybe even take a trip. The man's sentence was imminent. Ford had visited him in the hospital, urged him to pray. They prayed together. Somehow, by dint of willing it, the man was eking out a few extra days.

Their gazes held for a moment; the man nodded. Cardinal Ford was about to acknowledge him when the vision appeared before him; he stopped stone cold. There, floating above the congregation was a man dressed in a navy suit wearing a gray fedora. Ford saw the man as if looking through the old time, brass oculars, the kind that cupped around your eyes like goggles. A kinescope. The man flickered, scampering uptown, north, on Fifth Avenue, chased by a thug clad in black. Ford could see the grimace etched deep into the man's face. The labored breathing. Legs of molasses. Pain. Fear.

This was the Cardinal's second vision in as many weeks, and far more disturbing than the one before, which was enough to make him question his sanity then.

The first time it happened, Cardinal Ford didn't know what to think. How could he? He must be losing his mind. After all, when does dementia slip through the web of lucidity into an otherworldly state? No, he was certain this was it. There was no other accounting for this most bizarre event.

It was during a parishioner's confession, which he still administered in spite of the tolls on his time. He recalled chastising himself some minutes after it had begun; he was less than as attentive as he should've been. Life was complex at best; running St. Patrick's was formidable.

What? She said something that triggered him back. What word was it? Or was it a string of words, a phrase that brought back a memory? Maybe it was her look? Her caramel-colored skin and black hair that harkened him back to his early years in the priesthood. As a young priest, Arnold Ford followed his calling from church to church: Philadelphia to Chicago to Nairobi to Calcutta to the jungles of Peru. It was in Peru that he stayed in Iquitos, a sleepy city nestled at the crook of the murky brown Amazon River that sidled toward Brazil. Few there had electricity or running water. Most were barefoot. Clothes tattered. Yet he found happiness in their faces and hope in their hearts when they came to church each Sunday. Regardless of where or when, it was always the same: they would ask him to pray for cures or ways to escape their misery; to absolve them of their sins and to remove any roadblocks to heaven, for there surely was a better place that they'd be going to than living this hell on earth. This is where he learned the power of faith, his faith. But it was not a faith that went unquestioned. Ford had questions and he sought their answers.

Ford, ever the optimist, never wavered from giving hope and comfort to all. Yet in his deepest recesses, in his most private moments, he questioned the good he could ever do for the downtrodden and weary.

Was mere faith enough? And why was it that they transferred much of their faith to him, a simple man? Had he earned it? Deserved it?

How did priests do it year after year, decade after decade? Didn't they lose their own faith seeing mankind at his worst day in and day out?

Ford dug deeper. Ford used prayer the way a doctor used medicines, though he knew that not all medicines worked. But medicines did give hope. Ford had built churches in the jungle, saved children in Africa from dying of diarrhea, and had given a reason to live to those who suffered from the "Slims." By all measures, his time spent on earth had value, yet he was unsure of what that value meant. He was always unsure...and more so at this moment.

The reverie of things past faded as Ford turned his attention to the woman in the confessional.

Clothes rustled.

She cleared her throat.

Ford waited for her to speak.

Maybe she was waiting for him? What had she said? "How can the Lord's servant help you, my child?"

The voice quavered and became fractured, uncertain of how to start.

She stumbled. "Forgive me Father, for I have sinned."

And when he asked her to describe her sin, he heard an all too familiar story.

"What is your sin?"

Her voice grew. "Did you not hear what I said?"

At that moment the oak door to the confessional booth cracked open for the briefest second.

"I am the one who asks forgiveness, my daughter, for I have much on my mind and I lost some of your words. Forgive me, for I have committed the sin of not hearing you."

Awed by the Cardinal's confession to her she plowed forward, retelling how her sixteen-year-old daughter was caught shoplifting a designer handbag so she could sell it for drug money. When the daughter called from Riker's prison, the mother refused to post bail. Maybe a night in general lock-up would do the girl good, she said.

"Did I do the right thing, Father? I feel so guilty leaving her there overnight. To be among..." she paused, unable to say the words, and then managed to hurl out, "those people."

As she spoke, Cardinal Ford lifted the veil and peered through the brass latticework that graced the small window separating the two compartments. He glanced absently beyond her dark hair, and was surprised to see a little girl playing on the red velvet bench. The child wore a black jumper with a white blouse sporting blouson sleeves. He craned his neck when she lifted her foot and he could see white socks with the scalloped edges and the tops of black, patent leather, Mary Janes. The girl threw an imaginary ball in the air, catching it, and then throwing it up again. All the while, she smiled, baring teeth the size of tiny white corn niblets. Maybe she was five years old. Six at the most.

"Before I tell you about tough love and that what you did was right, I need to ask you why you brought your younger daughter into the box with you?"

The women's head jolted to her left and then behind her. Her lips moved, but no words came out. She searched up and then down.

"What is it my child? My question does not judge."

Ford saw the whites of her eyes. Her lids fluttered. Her head flitted from side to side. She turned chalk white. Confused. "There is no one in here with me, Father. I speak of my only daughter, the one who is sixteen," she whispered.

"I know what I see. There is another child in the confessional with you." His voice was firm with certainty. When the Cardinal described the little girl's clothing, the woman shrieked and fainted; her head crashed into the oak wall behind her. By the time Cardinal Ford yanked open the door to the confessional box, the little girl had scooted out. He glanced about; she was nowhere to be seen. Maybe she was hiding under a pew. No matter. He would find her once he felt the mother was safe to leave.

But that didn't happen. When the mother revived, first she screamed and then collapsed into heaving sobs. All Ford could do was pray for her recovery and for her to regain some semblance of self-control. As the seconds passed, he began to doubt himself. Did he really see a girl? The mother was so certain there was none, that she had only one daughter? Of course she knows how many children she has. So what did he see?

Beads of doubt formed on his upper lip. His skin grew moist. Clammy. Being unsure edged him toward a vortex of self-doubt. And self-doubt was no good for anyone, let alone the spiritual leader for millions of Catholics. For a soldier of the Lord Jesus Himself.

"Oh Father, that was my little Elizabeth. She was taken from me when she was five. Run over by a drunken truck driver. The clothes you described, that was the outfit she wore the day of her funeral. And she was always tossing a ball in the air. How could you know?"

From certainty to doubt to validation. Cardinal Ford was on his own rollercoaster of emotions.

"I did see her, my child. She was in the booth with you."

Rather than express shock or fear, a wondrous smile emerged across the woman's face. "This is the happiest day of my life, Father. I can now live in peace knowing that we will be united, again, and when it happens, it will be forever. And it fills my heart that my little girl is happy where she is." Then she took Ford's hand and brought it to her lips forgetting, for the moment, that her other daughter was locked in a cell at Riker's Island, and not happy where she was.

But Ford didn't forget. The next day, he called the Mayor and arranged for the girl's release in his recognizance. They spoke together, prayed together, and broke bread together. He found out why she stole; it was money for her dealer. He explained that self-medicating on drugs was not the answer to her problems, but healing first through self-love, and then the love of others, would make her stronger.

The girl understood. No one had ever taken the time to see her as a real person. To believe in her, but Cardinal Ford did. Ford called her mother, united the two and made arrangements for the necessary help that the girl required, that she wanted so she could heal.

That was last week.

Now, clenching the sides of the lectern, his flock perched on the edge of anticipation, eager for him to continue, the Cardinal had another vision. In it, the man in the blue suit was slowing down. Gasping for air. Heart pounding like the rapid rhythms of an express subway train barreling over tracks. Iron and steel. Fear etched across Ford's graying face, not the fear of a stroke or that he was losing his mind. He knew now that none of that was happening. At that moment, Ford's fear was for an innocent about to be harmed.

Without a word, the Cardinal unlocked his fingers, kissed the weighty gold crucifix that dangled around his neck, and stomped off the pulpit. He ignored the gasps and murmurs rippling through the congregants, and broke into a trot. Stoked by his vision, he motored down the red-carpeted center aisle with the ease and grace of younger man.

Hands reached to touch him; he never broke stride.

He would explain later.

They would understand that he had to intervene. To save this man.

In time, Ford would see more visions and know them to be real. He would learn to make peace with them and accept these visions as his gift for what they were. Who was he to question how God called out to him? Guided him to help others? More than any other time in his life, Arnold Ford stopped questioning life and the role he played in it. Clarity of vision had become his guiding light.

The organ played a pastoral hymn, out of sync with his movements. His arms churned. Ruby-colored shafts of light poured through the rose window above vestibule, half-pulling, half-guiding him to the bronze doors that lead out onto the steps and Fifth Avenue.

Outside, Arnold Ford, the first Afro-American Cardinal of a diocese in any American city quick-scanned the pedestrians strolling uptown. At his feet, teens with pierced brows, bellies, noses, and lips, milled about the Cathedral steps. He noted the red double-decker Big Apple Tour bus waddling by, the street vendors partially hidden in a mist of savory smoke laced with curry and cumin, the rollerbladers scooting past, the caravan of pedicycles toting passengers down the Avenue, the baby carriages wheeled by Caribbean nannies, and the tourists capturing digital images by the flashcard-full. Images that would soon be posted on Facebook or Instagram.

He edged down a step, searching for a glimpse of the old man. A sea of yellow cabs whizzed past the statue of Atlas shouldering the world in front of Rockefeller Center. Nothing seemed out of place. The sun shone brilliant, the city electric with life, and, in a Christian way, hope was in the air...save for the unfortunate soul in his vision.

Where was the man?

Paying no heed to an ailing hip he somehow forgot to mention to his doctor at his annual physical, Cardinal Ford, scatted down the remaining steps onto the quartz-studded sidewalk only to see a man scamper past the Cole Haan shoe store at the southwest corner of Fiftieth Street. It was the old man from his vision, who was skip-walking, limping, and dragging his left foot toward him. Pale-faced. Wheezing. The man clutched his chest. The grit to survive plastered across his face.

On another day, in another time, this was a race the man might have won. The race to beat the Grim Reaper. He had done it before, having outfoxed Arabs who attacked Jews in Syria during WWII; he made his way, once the conflict ended, to fight for the Haganah during the Israeli War for Independence. He had the scars to prove it. But not this time. There would be no escape.

The last sands were pouring though his timepiece.

With a practiced eye for detail, Ford noted the man's blue suit, the white shirt, and his striped bowtie, the uniform of the vanishing breed of European Jews who owned many of the stalls in the diamond district on Forty-Seventh Street.

Without a care for safety, the old man bolted across Fifth Avenue, angling toward the church. Horns blared, cabs swerved. Brakes screeched. The man lumbered forward.

Behind him and gaining fast, a younger, bigger man dressed in all black from head to toe except for a white starched shirt gave chase.

Sprinting in pursuit, he dodged oncoming cars and buses and crossed the wide boulevard. Both were now on the eastern side of the street. Ford saw everything in slow motion. The old man trying to cajole his legs to pump harder, and the young man dropping to one knee and taking aim.

This was the same moment in Ford's vision when he saw the man running and knew his life was in balance. Just because Ford saw it beforehand, did it have to happen? What could he do to alter the man's fate? If this were Hollywood, Ford could deflect the bullet with his palm or pulverize it with the gaze of his special powers. But this movie was real.

Ford made the sign of the cross. A shot rang out. Then a second. One hit a metal street sign; the other shattered a city bus window. The bus careened into a corner lamppost. Screams erupted. Bystanders fled. A proselytizer for "Jews for Jesus," stopped handing out leaflets and watched, mesmerized by the drama.

Cardinal Ford charged toward the old man, whose sad eyes conveyed what both knew: it was too late. Then, with a burst of energy, the old man charged toward St. Patrick's. Ford hurdled over strewn packages dropped when the first shot rang out and ignored the screams that erupted when the second caused the bus to screech out of control.

Unfazed by the tumult about, the attacker held his position and fired once more.

Ford tripped as the old man lunged forward. It was unclear from that distance that the third bullet hit anyone. A second ticked by. Then another. Heads peeked from behind cars and out of taxi windows, from behind the mountain of boxes strapped to a FedEx hand truck, from behind metal cubes with spring doors that offered brochures for courses at The Learning Annex. They all stared in horror.

Had His Eminence been shot? Did he sacrifice his life to save another?

No other shots followed. None were needed. The last had found its mark.

Cardinal Ford stirred. He could feel the man's faint heart beating under him. Ford peeled himself off the crumpled body and turned to locate the shooter, to face the assassin and urge him to lay down his weapon, but the man was gone. Sirens blared. A crowd formed around the old man and the priest. A timid medical student offered to help; he knew CPR, but the old man waved him away.

Cardinal Ford rocked back on his knees.

A pool of blood spread beneath the man; death was near. The two men, strangers only seconds earlier, were inches apart, connected by a power greater than life itself. Names were not necessary.

The old man knew it was his time; the last moments of his life were in the hands of a priest.

The irony didn't escape either.

"Take this." The old man shoved a laminated card into the Cardinal's hand. "It will bring you luck." His eyes fluttered. The Cardinal squeezed tighter, about to reassure him that help was on its way. Before he could, the old man implored him, his accent thickening, reverting back to another time, "Don't let those bastards get it."

Ford took the card. Their eyes locked, the creases of the old man's pale lips turned slightly upward and then his head dropped to side, his mouth slack in death. An autopsy would reveal that the bullet pierced his aorta. Ford wriggled out of his sash and cushioned the man's head onto the concrete. He said a benediction over the man and prayed for his soul to no longer be in pain.

With the help of someone behind him, the Cardinal raised himself to a standing position. Police and a city ambulance arrived and took control of the crowd. Efforts to revive the man on the sidewalk failed.

Ford was asked to step to the side and wait to be questioned as to what happened. While he stood in front of his church, he turned the three-by-five inch laminated card over in his hand. He tried to understand what was so important about a few words that cost a man his life, but could make no sense out of the Hebrew lettering.

Ford frowned. For a good luck talisman, this yellowed parchment left much to be desired. Who would want this? What magic could it hold? What story could it tell?

Ford held it to the light. Turned it. No hidden words. No tiny message. Little did he know that this snippet of ancient parchment was a critical piece from a larger puzzle. And this larger puzzle was so important to a fistful of people that they spared no effort, and apparently no life, in order to find all the missing pieces they could recover.

But to what end? Ford hadn't a clue now. How could he? He didn't read Hebrew and even if he could, he was not scholar enough to understand the implication of the words in his hand, or why words were important enough to take a life.

But everything has a meaning, he thought. The meaning may not be clear or apparent now, but it is there to be discovered. Ford had learned to wait for discovery. He knew that he didn't have to find the meaning of all things that happened, there were times when their meaning would find him. And this would prove no exception.

Unbeknownst to Cardinal Ford, but not surprisingly so, the prelate had taken a first step in a journey of discovery that would lead him into a maze of twists and turns that would change his life forever. As the mysteries of this laminated piece of parchment were unraveled, so, too, would the world order be inexorably altered.

# Chapter Six

"**W**hy was he running toward St. Patrick's? Witnesses sensed that the man knew you," said the NYPD officer assigned to investigate the homicide. "Did you?"

Detective LeShana T. Thompkins sat ramrod straight, knees together, at the edge of a gilded chair in Cardinal Ford's private office. The chair was upholstered in a deep burgundy pattern dotted by a constellation of miniature suns. A golden braid edged the fabric. Matching tassels of thick cord dangled from the cushion corners like bell ringers. She tapped answers into her yellow Trimble Rugged Nomad, the state-of-the art handheld that the NYPD was field-testing that linked all devices into a centralized server/data base. Like physicians with their tablets, NYPD cops in the field had access to reports, data banks, fingerprint identification, and more, in milliseconds instead of the unacceptable time gaps built around human effort.

LeShana's dark eyes skirted about the book-filled room, absorbing the arched ceiling that was crisscrossed with support arches designed to mirror cathedral naves. This was unlike any room in any church she had ever visited. In fact, no house of worship she was familiar with was as opulent as St. Patty's, and that included the church overlooking Rio that she visited on her honeymoon.

Her honeymoon was a relic of the past, like any knick-knack tucked on a shelf collecting dust. Her marriage? It was short-lived. Short of trust and short of good times. Wisdom dictated that cops shouldn't marry cops, even though they were drawn to each other because who better to understand a cop than another cop? Too many long nights, too many opportunities. Hard to be faithful, at least for *his* part of the bargain. No matter. In a way, she'd been thankful it didn't work because life has been simpler all these years on her own. Well, not alone. The best thing that came out of a bad marriage was her pride and joy: her daughter.

As she glanced about, she felt Ford's scrutiny, not the way normal men looked at her. LeShana knew she turned more than a few eyes each day. She had good genes: clear, mocha-colored skin, high forehead, hair that curled in waves if she let it loose, long legs, and ample body parts where they mattered. No, the Cardinal was looking at her in the same way he absorbed all of the *Lord's lambs*. Still, thought LeShana, the man was magnetic. She whistled under her breath. *Too bad that he's a man of the cloth.*

Maybe LeShana was uncomfortable being in the presence of the most visible Catholic leader in the United States? She had met her share of dignitaries over the years, and guarded many. There was that time when she had to guard the door leading to the podium at the UN General Assembly and Putin asked if she was having a nice day? Or when Tony Blair insisted on going to Times Square for a Nathan's hot dog. Desmond Tutu was the one who impressed her the most. And now Cardinal Ford. Now there are a couple of fine gents, she thought. Tutu and Ford; two peas in a pod. *Black-eyed* peas. She thought that funny, and cracked a smile.

LeShana lingered for a second longer over the gold-lettered, leather-bound books. Did he sense that in seconds of meeting him, she found the Cardinal…she couldn't even admit it to herself…appealing? Charming? Soulful? Maybe it was a father thing. Her mother and dad passed a while back, she of breast cancer, he of heartbreak and nicotine. But he was attractive, in a Sidney Poitier sort of way.

LeShana was not wrong feeling that she was being scrutinized with more than a casual glance. She wondered how he saw her?

For his part, Ford studied the detective's features. Creamy skin, a quick smile, and cornrow tresses, all assets that folded into a comforting manner. He wondered what her hair would look like if she let it down?

Cardinal Ford had been around cops before, lots of them. VIP funerals. Mayoral task forces. Ecumenical Councils guarded by a battalion of officers. But this one was different. She exuded a confidence that rarely crossed paths with public officers of any station. No, thought Ford, this woman intrigues. And that's where it stops.

Ford tented his fingers together as in the outline of a church spire, and finally answered her question of being familiar with the victim. "God delivered him to me. It's not for me to question why. It just happened."

Detective Thompkins wagged her stylus in the air as she arched back, still balanced at the chair's edge. "I don't mean any disrespect, but not everything happens due to divine intervention. Certainly not in this city, that's for sure. I see bad things happen here every day, your Eminence. Horrible things. And from where I'm sitting, the hand of God isn't behind any of them. Humans cause the suffering I see in the subways, on the streets, in the rat-infested apartments in Harlem and Bed Sty. It's people doing things to other people. If God Himself were involved, a whole lot of stuff sure wouldn't be happening and the world would be a lot better place. Are you sure you didn't know the man? Maybe you've seen him on the street before? Passed him walking outside? After all, you two *are* in the same neighborhood."

Ford was not interested in debating what he knew to be true, that every moment of every day is guided by the Divine and powerful hand of Lord Almighty. The Cardinal cocked his head and shifted his focus to her.

"You're a riddle," he said.

"What makes you say that?"

"An enigma," was all that he offered. Detective LeShana T. Thompkins made him curious in many ways, yet even he – a good judge of people – would underestimate. There was an edge to her to couldn't quite grasp. Not a sharp edge as in her manner, but in the perspicacity exuding from her eyes, in the authority in her voice.

She wanted to pursue his comment, but let it pass.

"There's a purpose to everything. Only sometimes, we don't know what that is. But the Lord does. He follows His divine plan for us." Ford leaned forward; she met his gaze. "Are you a believer, Detective?"

"With all due respect, what I believe in and what I don't believe in have nothing to do with this investigation."

"Oh, but it does, my child. It has everything to do with it. Don't you see that nothing in this life is random? That everything happens for a reason." She was about to tell him about all the children she had seen shot dead by random bullets gone astray, about innocents sipping lattés at an outdoor café only to be mowed down by an out-of-control vehicle, when he continued. "We're mere pawns in His master plan. We follow His orders and must accept tragedy with the good, disaster with beneficence. We can reason and question all we like. In the end, all answers come from the Lord, though we may not be able to understand them at the time."

"What I do understand, Your Excellency, is that I've heard of that propaganda before and I'm not buying what you're selling."

Nonplussed, Ford continued. "What about the stories in the Bible?"

"What about them? They're just stories passed down through the years. Told in caves and around campfires. They gave the people something to believe in, to give meaning to their miserable lives. Who wouldn't want to believe that there is a better place to go after your time on earth is finished? This hasn't been a wonderful experience for most. Especially for the folks during the Middle Ages. The Aborigines. The peasants around the globe. Hope is for the wretched. It gives them a shot at going to a better place after their time in this living hell is over."

Ford drew in a deep breath as he leaned back an inch or two. A concerned look gave way to a serene smile. "You're tainted by your job. What you see every day."

"Aren't you? You see bad stuff all the time. Doesn't it get to you?"

"I've seen all that you've seen and more. Don't dismiss His teachings so easily, Detective. The Bible is more than just stories. The Old Testament chronicles every word God ever spoke to man, either directly to him or through His prophets. Can't you grasp the magnitude of that?

Recorded thousands of years ago, it's a blueprint for how man should live. A primer for life. The way man should treat his neighbor, his family. What he should eat. How he should pray. How many times did I hear from a young couple struggling to raise a child that they wished their son or daughter had come with a handbook of instructions?"

LeShana smiled. Her mind skipped to her budding teenage daughter. "I sure wish they did. There's so much to know about raising a kid."

"I think there's a boy in my class who likes me," her daughter said one day.

"How do you know?"

"Becky Weintraub told me."

"And how does Becky know?" LeShana asked, knowing this day would come.

"Because he asked her if I like anyone."

"And who is this 'he'?" asked LeShana, arms crossed her chest. They were in the kitchen of their Brooklyn brownstone, preparing dinner one night.

"His name doesn't matter, he's just a boy."

"Don't pull that on me. You brought him up, said he liked you, but you won't give up his name? I'm not playing that game."

"Does it matter?"

"It does if you like him. If you are kind of, sort of, trying to find out what to do when you are alone with him. Yeah, it matters. What's his name?"

"Bradley."

"That's a start. Thank you for sharing that. Do you like this Bradley?"

"Not really. He's nice and all that, but I don't like him in that special sort of way," she said, her lids fluttering for emphasis.

"Then there's not much to talk about, is there?"

Now that her daughter's teenage years were here, LeShana made certain she knew where she was going and who she was with at all times. If she were supposed to be at a friend's house, LeShana would call the parent to ensure an adult was home. Everything said about raising a teenage girl was true...and then some.

"But that's just it, Detective. All of humanity *did* come with a handbook, with all sorts of rules and commandments to live by. The trouble is, most don't follow it. The consequence is evident all around us; we live in troubled times."

*Not my daughter.* She bared her white teeth. "Meaning no disrespect, Your Excellency, but believing in all them stories in the Bible is part of your job description. Not mine. For me, I believe in what I see everyday…and the Bible ain't got nothing to do with it. Not at all."

"This is not a matter of believing," Ford said, having heard sentiments like LeShana's many times over. "Believing leaves room for doubt." He touched his chest over his heart. "God's existence is something I know here," and then he touched his temple, "and here. Simply stated, Detective, God does exist."

LeShana wrinkled her brow, shaking her head. "I'm a bit more acquainted with the Bible, especially the Old Testament, than you'd think. This talking thing? God speaking to man? Other than a pipeline to Charlton Heston, God hasn't had a lot of speaking parts for a very long time. It gives me pause to wonder if they weren't all stories made up by desperate people to believe there had to be something better than what they found during their time on earth."

"It's all right not to believe in His Divine intervention. You're not alone. But I know it to be true because…" Ford hesitated. He wanted to tell her about the little girl in the confessional booth. He wanted to tell her that he saw the man running from the assassin before he stepped off the pulpit and trotted out to the street. He wanted to tell her so much more that would spark that sacred belief system lodged in everyone's DNA since the beginning of time.

Since the discovery of fire.

And at that moment, a voice told him it was all right to tell her.

"…God spoke to me during my sermon," Cardinal Ford said to her in a matter-of-fact tone, as if it were an everyday occurrence.

His statement did not stoke a flicker of surprise from LeShana. This was New York and what hadn't she seen or heard before? There were the ridiculous reasons for one person killing another. Aliens, the space kind, being blamed for cajoling someone to pull the trigger. Then there was the woman who Crazy-Glued her two-year old to the wall so she wouldn't move when she beat her. She heard about planes falling out of the sky on Y2K and then witnessed it really happen on nine-eleven. There was Nostradamus predicting the end of the world, and the Mayans picking their own date for the apocalypse. So much for that! When it came to organized religion, there was little that wriggled into LeShana's belief system.

"And what exactly did the good Lord say to you?" LeShana tapped away at her PDA, unfazed that God had given the Cardinal a "head's up" regarding a soon-to-occur homicide. She remained straight-faced as the image of summoning God as a witness in this murder case, needing for Him to raise his right hand and swear on the Bible, to tell the whole truth. She needed to twitch her head to scoot that picture out of her mind.

"That a life was about to change," Ford continued.

Unable to shake the image of God on the witness stand, she countered, "Being shot to death does have a way of changing someone's life."

"But maybe that's not what God meant. Maybe the Voice was referring to me. That I would be the one changed by this tragic event."

The room was sparsely furnished, yet rich in feeling. A polished mahogany desk, the chair she was sitting on plus another matching one, rows of books filling the wall behind the Cardinal. There were two pictures on the wall. One was of Pope John XXIII, with a beaming face, round, cutting the quintessential figure of the church's spiritual leader. The other was of Pope John Paul II, not when the one-time freedom fighter and actor was robust and straight-backed, a dashing portrait of masculinity and power, but one where he is hunched over and made frail by Parkinson's disease. Still glorious in a failing body. Holy and righteous.

Cardinal Ford's choice of pictures made the man all the more interesting. Every power office she had ever been in was unique to its occupant. Gilded framed pictures flanking high-backed chairs and over-sized mahogany or teak desks were not picked randomly. They were there to emote strength, to display a message of power and inspiration. And respect. Ford's choices said a lot about himself.

"With your permission, Your Eminence, I am going to concentrate on how the recently deceased's life changed. I am going to ask, again, did you ever see him before?"

"No. Not ever."

"Did you ever have occasion to go to the diamond district? It's only a few blocks away. Perhaps you saw him in his stall?"

"For me, those few blocks are as far as the moon. I've never ventured to either."

"Can you describe what he was wearing?"

"Didn't they show you the pictures? There was a police photographer snapping them from all angles."

"I've seen them, but I'm interested in your perspective. Would you say he was a religious Jew? Or was he secular? An every day sort of guy."

"Who knows what he believed in? He did dress in an Orthodox manner. Plain suit. White shirt. A gray fedora with a yarmulke underneath. There was a prayer shawl under his shirt."

"Wearing *tzitzit* makes him a religious man in my book."

Ford studied LeShana. "How did you know to call the prayer shawl by its Hebrew name? I only recently learned what it is."

"Excuse me, Your Eminence, this is New York. 'You don't have to be Jewish to love Levy's rye bread.' That's what the commercial always said back in the day. Who doesn't know what a bagel is? We're a city of cross cultures. We absorb religious, ethnic, and cultural differences like parched grounded soaking in rainwater. To outsiders, New Yorkers appear to be a mash of strangers. Aloof. Disconnected from each other. That we blend together in a cocktail we call, 'The City.' Nothing could be further from the truth. We know a lot about each other, including what religious items we wear under our clothes and what foods we eat on special holidays."

Ford eased back and pushed off the edge of his desk.

"I have something to show you."

He handed the laminated card the dead man gave him to Detective Thompkins. He studied the way her eyes moved across the Hebrew letters and noticed her lips moving. He saw her eyes widen and then, in a practiced motion, bring the card to her lips and kiss it. He was about to ask what she was doing when she spoke, her eyes filled with wonder.

"Do you know how special this is?"

"I don't read Hebrew," he answered. "How can you?"

She loved the incredulousness that filled his voice. As if it were a challenge to everything known to be true. That a fourth law of Newton's had just been violated. It actually gave her the giggles. She beamed.

*The only thing to assume…is nothing.*

"Just because I'm black, I'm not expected to be able to read Hebrew? Is that what you were trying to say?"

He opened his palms toward her. "You must admit it's a bit unusual."

"And I assume, Your Eminence, that if you dressed in civilian clothes and were in a different setting, you being able to read Latin wouldn't raise a brow or two?" The words dangled in the air, their impact seeping in. Then she added, "Being a black man and all."

"Touché. I know better than that. I'm sorry. Yet I must confess you do surprise me." He was pleased that his first impressions of her proved accurate. LeShana Thompkins was not ordinary in any sense of the word. In a short time, he would learn to use the word *extraordinary* to describe this detective sitting before him.

And that time was fast approaching!

"Strap yourself in, Your Eminence, Cardinal Arnold Ford, because that's not the only surprise I have for you, me being able to read Hebrew and all. I know your Eminence is busy, but if you can spare me some extra time, I need to share something with you."

"You seem so sure of yourself."

"Because I am."

"I've traveled the world, my child, and I have seen every wretched heartbreak man can cause to his fellow man. I've seen war and sickness, famine. Pestilence. There's little that can ever surprise me." He chuckled for the first time, not politely from the back of his throat, but from deep within. She sensed laughter for Ford was rare, something to be parceled out only when necessary, and cherished when it did occur.

"What do find so amusing?" she asked.

He shifted in his chair and hunkered down to get more comfortable; ready for the "surprise" she offered to share. "I have no reason to think your story will amuse, but instinct bubbled a humorous twist on this scenario. I can see the headlines in the Daily News: Detective Shocks Cardinal Ford with Fabulous Tale from the Almighty."

LeShana rolled her lips over her teeth edges, paused before speaking, then broke into an ivory smile, "That's not bad, your Eminence. Not bad at all. And closer to the truth than you can imagine."

"Oh?" Ford sat taller…this woman was serious, and he needed to be, too.

When LeShana finished not minutes but hours later, Cardinal Ford would be changed in ways he could never imagine. Nor could he fathom the integral part he would play in restoring this missing piece of parchment to its rightful place.

LeShana Thompkins was a remarkable woman.

# Chapter Seven

"Let's start with who I am, because then you will be able to understand what I'm about to tell you."

"You're a police detective, with the NYPD. You're black like me, and apparently you consider yourself a Jew. Or is it Jewess?"

"I'm a cop all right, but this story has nothing to do with what I am. As for Jew or Jewess? Take your pick, but I don't *consider* myself a Jew. I am one."

"I stand corrected."

"You're forgiven," said LeShana. "As long as you're willing to give me the time to tell this story. It's not about me, Your Eminence, it's a story about you."

This piqued him even more, but he said nothing. His eyes, displaying amusement, spoke legions. *Was she impudent? Brazen? Maybe she was just plain delusional?*

"It will be clear where I'm going in a few minutes."

Ford shrugged toward her, palms open, welcoming her to continue. He would not interrupt...as long as she engaged him with meaningful words. But how could she have any story of meaning about him? How could she know anything about him that he didn't know already? As archbishop, much had been written about him. Once he became a cardinal, considering it was in New York, every minute detail of his life had been dissected and regurgitated in magazines, newspaper pieces, and on TV.

Most knew that he had been adopted by Catholic missionaries, that while they could have picked a new name for him, they didn't, including his surname, so that he would always be linked to parents who loved him, and then raised him to love the Lord and do his bidding.

What did this detective know, *or think she knew*, about him? This was growing more curious by the moment.

LeShana drew in a big breath. "Let's set the record clear about me. My name has nothing to do with those attempts to shed a white slavery background and embrace our African heritage. Not the way blacks seem to make up names, change spellings, label kids with names that, while unique, brand them for life."

"You mean like LeDamien or Kaheesha?"

She nodded. "But not LeShana. My full name is LeShana T. Thompkins. LeShana Tova Thompkins."

"Your name means, 'Happy New Year.'"

"Who said you're not a New Yorker."

"And I do like rye bread."

"Corned beef with spicy mustard?"

"How else?"

*I bet with a cold beer!* She continued with a nod. "So, yes, my first and middle names make up the phrase that Jews say to each other on Rosh Hashanah. As a little girl, I hated my name. Then, as luck would have it, it was considered mainstream like those Ebonics names we just mentioned that shouted, 'We are of African ancestry.' Black names were in; white names were out. That's when the name 'LeShana' worked for me. And I did have an African connection, even if I was Jewish."

"Lesson learned…and I thank you for that. The next obvious question: how are you Jewish?"

"You mean, were my parents Jewish?"

He nodded.

"My mother was; not my father. He refused to convert."

'That doesn't exactly answer the question. Your mother was Jewish and she passed that heritage on to you. I understand that, but how was she Jewish? Was she born into it, or did she convert to it?"

"Can't you tell by looking at me?"

"What do you mean?" asked the Cardinal.

"Obviously I'm black, but my features are not typical of most blacks that are here. I have a broad forehead, a higher hairline, and a narrow nose." She turned so he could observe her profile. "See," she ran her index finger down her nose. "Straight, with narrow nostrils. These are typical traits of Ethiopians."

"Should I have known that?" he asked. "I did leave the country when I was only a few months old."

"You get a pass for that. Suffice it to say that if you know what you're looking for, it's easy to spot someone from Ethiopia. That's where my mother's from. She can trace her Judaism back thousands of years. She came here on a student exchange program and never left. She got a degree in accounting, but never could get a job using all her skills. She ended up a bookkeeper in a lighting store. One of the workers there was kind to her. They eventually got married and had me."

"And he wasn't a Jew?"

"My father was a nice guy. He loved my mother and she loved him, and it didn't matter that she was Jewish. There were other black Jews living in the community, so she didn't appear that strange to him."

"You and your mother weren't the only ones?"

"That's part of my story that I want you to hear."

"And this somehow comes back to me?"

"It does."

"I must say," said Cardinal Ford, "I'm at a loss to describe all that has happened this day."

*She wanted to add that it had nothing to do with God, but controlled herself.* "It's real hard to see someone die, Your Excellency. And me, on top of that, being so different and all."

"Admittedly, yes. Before you go on with your story, I know many, many, Jews. Most can't read Hebrew. If they can, they can't translate it. How can you?"

She squirmed a finger under her shirt collar and extracted a gold mezuzah, a good luck piece that contained a tiny sacred scroll inside it, passages from the Torah. "After my Bat Mitzvah, I continued going to religious school until I finished Hebrew High School."

"Was it like a yeshiva?"

"Not like an all-day religious school, but going to public school during the day and then Hebrew school afterwards, three times a week, was pretty intense. Rest assured it wasn't my choice. If I had my way, I would've been playing after-school sports or been on the debate team. But not my parents. They said I had to have a strong sense of who I was and where I came from. So I had to go to Hebrew school long after my Jewish friends cashed out from their Bar and Bat Mitzvahs."

"Was it that bad?" he asked.

"Let's say that I would never make my kid do it." *And my daughter wouldn't go, anyway.* She waved the laminated card. "Getting back to this. It's a passage from Writings.

**But I trust in You, O Lord;**
**I say, "You are my God!"**
**My fate is in Your hand;**
**Save me from the hand of my enemies and pursuers.**
**Show favor to Your servant;**
**As You are faithful, deliver me.**

Ford shook his head at her ability to translate what the passage meant. "That couldn't have been more prophetic. But why did these few words cost the man his life?"

"It was less about the words and more about the actual piece of paper. For one thing, the poor soul carried this as a good luck talisman. He most likely believed that as long as this was in his possession, not only would evil spirits be warded off, but that business would always be good."

"It's not even a religious symbol like a cross or the mezuzah you're wearing. Are you sure it was about the paper and not a robbery? Maybe it was some sort of grudge, or a business dealing gone bad?" Cardinal Ford was perplexed. Killings based on religion have occurred for thousands of years. Ethnic cleansing, as horrific as it is, still occurs. But this? One Jew killing another for a piece of paper made no sense. If the detective didn't sound as knowledgeable as she was, he would've thought her way off the mark with her yet-to-be-proved theory.

As if she could read his mind, LeShana mused out loud. "I've come across this sort of laminated parchment before. We'll run the investigation and check the man's background, his business associates, and look into the people who owed him money. Maybe he owed a lot of money? But I think I'm on safe ground telling you that this wasn't a religious killing. At least not in the way it appears…assuming that the shooter was really a religious Jew."

"I'm not following you, Detective. This appeared to be one Jew killing another. It didn't seem random, not like those shootings at movie theaters or university campuses by people gone crazy. This appeared methodical. I'm certain the old man was targeted on purpose."

"Without a doubt. And for the record, the perp was an alleged Jew. Until we catch him, the man firing a shot could be from anywhere in the world and might have used Hasidic clothing as a cover. Don't put it past Al Qaeda to have an assassin dressed like a Jew. They would do anything to promote their agenda. It's a great way to get close to a victim in this city, especially close to one in the diamond district."

They were both reminded of a robbery that wiped out a diamond merchant when the thieves gained access to a fourth floor office more secure than Fort Knox simply because they wore the garb of religious Jews. Jews, they weren't; thieves, they were.

"Their disguises gave them access where others couldn't penetrate, and they got millions to prove it," said LeShana.

She fingered the laminated parchment and stared out. She was seeing and not seeing at the same time. She snapped her head upright. "This was a robbery gone bad. The way I figure, the man wanted to rob the victim of this parchment. The old man didn't want to give it up. It meant a lot to him, and because it did, it cost him his life. That's what this is all about. Until the facts tell us the real story, this must be considered a hate crime," she said.

Ford reached for the laminated card; LeShana hesitated before handing it to him. He inspected it. The parchment was yellowed. He studied the script.

"These letters are not from some printing press; they're handwritten. This must be a one-of-a-kind. Like a Torah."

Ford knew that Torah's not only had to be handwritten by a trained scribe, but each stroke, every letter, had to be perfect. One mistake and the work had to be discarded...and not in the recycling bin. Pious Jews held that the written word of the Lord could not destroyed, but it had to be buried according to religious tradition. More than once, Cardinal Ford had attended a Jewish funeral only to observe religious books being placed in the grave on top of the deceased's coffin. A prayer was uttered and the books were buried alongside the deceased.

"You obviously know a lot about how a Torah is made and the respect we accord to the Lord's name," LeShana said, impressed with his knowledge, "and how we treasure our books and hold the written word sacred." She extended her hand, he handed back the laminated parchment. She held it upward, as if an offering. "This is beyond holy. If I'm right, this is a sliver from a spectacular ancient treasure that's been missing for a long time."

"How is it that you know so much about this parchment? And how did you even recognize it all?"

"I told you I not only went to Hebrew School, but I continued through Hebrew High School."

He stood. He had been sitting too long and grew stiff. Had she not been there and he was alone, he would have stretched the way a runner stretches, pushing against the wall, extending one leg back at a time. A couple of deep squats and twisting his torso left and then right. But he did not know this woman, though he was glad he had the chance to learn about her. It would not have been dignified or appropriate for the Cardinal of the New York Archdiocese to perform stretching exercises while being interviewed by a female detective.

He returned to his seat after walking to the window, peering past the curtain, then shuffling a few feet along the wall and back to loosen up.

"Detective, with all due respect, going to Hebrew School is not going to give you the knowledge you seem to exhibit. To say the breadth of what you know impresses me is an understatement. To say I am intrigued is also an understatement. Tell me how you know these things."

She glanced at her oversized Swatch watch with a frosty lime-green band. "You sure you have time for this?"

"I said I did."

"Then buckle your seat, Your Excellency, because you may be in for the ride of your life."

No matter how outrageous, he doubted this would be that spectacular. Yet, her manner of speech amused; he settled deeper into his chair, and beckoned her to continue. As she did, his astonishment turned from amazement to disbelief to such a degree that his secure universe, one that he had inhabited his entire life, one that was constructed by walls of tradition, knowledge and scholarship, one that he would even give his life to support and protect, now turned tenuous by this perfect stranger, a black New York City detective who spoke Hebrew, was Jewish, and had more information in her head than in all the books on the shelves that surrounded them.

How was this possible, as she told her story - a story that would soon become his story - that he had never heard about the Codex of Aleppo? He was learned, and knew about ancient and medieval manuscripts. And he knew much about the Old Testament. But not about this particular book.

How is that that he didn't know that black Jews existed? Not the ones from Ethiopia but those from right here in the United States? And in New York City to boot?

How is it that, after today's events, his life would change forever, with no opportunity to return to his cocoon of safety that gave him comfort?

*Was meeting this detective part of a greater vision or simply a random event that cost a poor unfortunate his life?*

How is it that on this day, LeShana T. Thompkins walked into his life? Did the Lord Almighty send her? Was she the messenger of His message meant for him? There was something to a Divine message, thought Ford; the key ingredient is to recognize it when it appears. The more she spoke, the more he could see a halo above her head.

It was a halo richly deserved.

# Chapter Eight

Zakkarhia ibn Mohammed grew frantic that he could not worm his way to the front of the chanting throng before the beloved sheik's car passed by. He dreamed of this day, of seeing the sheik close up. He had to be in front, he just had to! An experienced eye carved a path through a knot of schoolgirls and a cluster of aged three-legged fighters, some leaning on canes, others on Kalashnikovs. A wave of cheers erupted to his left signaling there was precious little time to squirm and twist his way to the front so he could face the entourage heading toward them. And would it be asking too much that if could get close enough, that the holy leader might turn his head and glance Zakkarhia's way?

Zakkarhia didn't know which was more of a blessing: to see the glorious Sheik Ahmed Yassin with his own eyes or to complete his training on how to launch Qassam rockets. Both gave him strength, praise be to Allah, to make every man, woman, and child in the Jabalya refugee camp proud that he, Zakkarhia ibn Mohammed, would help rid the Palestinians' sacred soil of the hated infidel once and for all. There was no nobler goal. Glory to the great *jihad*. Soon his people would have their own state.

It was two years ago. His father saw it differently. "Zakkarhia," his father would say, "you must get new friends. The one's you have are filling your head with nonsense. What do they know about *jihad*?"

"They know all there is to know about fighting our enemies. This is more important than anything else."

His father reached to pat his oldest firstborn's head, to make a gesture of peace. Tension between them had been increasing. Zakkarhia swatted it away, glad that he stung his father's feelings. "I am not a child anymore father." He was fourteen at the time and stretched taller to prove it.

"Only a child could cast away what our great Muhammad has taught us, that *jihad* means struggling in the name of Allah Almighty. You fight oppression; this is *jihad*. You tell the truth; this is *jihad*. You teach lessons from the Koran; this is *jihad*. Planning to kill for the sake of killing, waging war when no war is waged, this is not *jihad*. This goes against everything, Allah be praised, we were ever taught. These friends of yours, they are against everything the Koran teaches."

Zakkarhia flipped his hand in the air. The message was clear: the old ways must be discarded, pushed aside. If they had worked, his people would be free. He would not have to become a soldier or join the *jihad*. But that wasn't the case, was it?

"You are an old man, Father. What do you know of *jihad*? My *jihad*?"

His father raised his hand in anger, his nostrils flared. Zakkarhia held his ground and did not turn away.

"Anyone who can speak against the teachings of Muhammad is no son of mine. You, and others like you, are the reason we will never have peace. I don't know what path you will end up taking, Zakkarhia, but one day you will learn that the Israelis are not our enemy. Our own leaders, they are our enemy. They stoke fires that should never have been lit. They talk about crazy things and our people listen. They cause hardships and make our people suffer for no reason. Why?"

"I'll tell you why! They are right to want to cast the infidel out from our lands. They are right to call all Muslins to fight the Holy *jihad*," said Zakkarhia.

Zakkarhia's words burned deep. Tears streamed down his father's face. The man could not believe that this was his son speaking. No, these were the utterances of others. This was not the son whom he raised. This was not the son that he would walk through fire to save, to save his little sisters or his mother or his brother. But could he count on Zakkarhia to save him, the father who bore him? The father who taught him to be a man? Where did he go wrong?

Zakkarhia would never find the answers to his father's questions; the two never saw each other again.

◆　　◆　　◆

Now at sixteen, Zakkarhia was tall and sinewy. He had dark piercing eyes and a fierce pride. Even before his ill-fated break from his father, one that left him with no regrets, Zakkarhia had been a veteran of many Hamas campaigns. He graduated from chucking rocks at the Israeli soldiers to tossing Molotov cocktails at their tanks. His nerves of steel, his willingness to follow commands, brought quick attention to the more senior terrorist leaders. As the Intifada continued, word came down from inner circle of Hamas leadership, from Sheik Yassin himself, that in the months to come, their ring of terror would launch an attack on the Israeli cities that would drive the heathens into the sea once and for all.

Zakkarhia would be part of that attack. He would help deliver the crushing blows to rid his country of the hated occupiers; they would regain the territory that was taken from them. It would be nothing like Arafat's Fatah imbeciles who once sent a twelve-year old loaded with explosives through the Hawara checkpoint, south of Nablus, only to get blown up without killing any of the enemy along with himself. It was rightful justice to deny *that one* a place in Paradise.

The sheik's car drew near.

Zakkarhia ducked under the outstretched arm of a Palestinian soldier in time to see the black limousine ease around the corner toward the square. Cheers erupted from the people lining the street.

Paralyzed in a freak sports accident in his early youth, the sheik had been in and out of jails for most of his life. With each release, his stature rose. The time before this release, the sheik's glory ascended to the mythical. Attacks across the border increased, more rockets were fired at the Israelis than ever before, and youth like Zakkarhia begged to join the Intifada. They would do anything to be part of the Holy *jihad*.

That time, two years ago, the sheik's freedom was short-lived. His followers kidnapped two Israeli soldiers, killing one. Misplaced rockets were one thing, killing an Israeli soldier left no other option: swift, harsh retaliation that included rescuing the captured soldier.

In a stealth operation, the Israelis slipped into Gaza under the mask of night and kidnapped the sheik still in his bedclothes. Justice was swift; he was sentenced to life imprisonment without parole. No one was killed or injured and the raid went perfectly except for one thing: they did not find the captured solider. An informant told the Israelis the exact location where the soldier was being held, but the information was wrong. The informant would be dealt with afterwards, but the soldier? How could they leave without him? But they did.

Oh, Hamas protested and tried to get the UN General Assembly to sanction the Israelis for the unlawful raid, but all knew it was smoke. They had no credibility. But they did have that soldier.

Try as they may, all efforts to determine the location of the MIA sabra soldier failed. He would have to use his own cunning to survive, finding comfort in the fact that Israel never forgot its own. It may not be now, it may not be soon, but he knew that if it were possible, they would come from him...and when they did, he'd be ready.

At the same time, Sheik Yassin settled into the Israeli prison life that was akin to a first-rate vacation. He was able to update his own Facebook page using his smartphone, and request his favorite foods, which his family brought each time they visited him in prison.

Even though Sheik Yassin refused to acknowledge the State of Israel, he appreciated that his captors permitted him and his fellow Moslems to enjoy satellite Arab TV channels. And when it came to buying sweets and high-priced goods, every Muslim terrorist in the Israeli prisons received a salary from the Palestinian Authority... money Hamas dispersed redistributed from the US foreign aid to the Palestinian people.

"Yassin," called a guard one day, "save the scraps for us." The guard gazed through the barred window built into the cell door with hankering eyes as the sheik plowed through a filet mignon dinner. It was the same night after night, and the guard was jealous.

The sheik didn't acknowledge the prison guard, but it was known by everyone that he and the other prisoners ate better than the Israeli prisoners, ate better than the families of the victims they murdered, and indeed ate better than the guards themselves. And when it came to what they ate, they ate anything they wanted, whether it was part of their dietary laws or not. In the sheik's case, he often disregarded his physician's orders to curb his intake of rich foods high in cholesterol. It gave him immense pleasure to eat what he wanted and yet berate his captors every opportunity he could.

"How could you eat pork?" asked the guard, "It's Harām. Forbidden. You are angering Allah eating that."

This was one of the few occasions the sheik spoke to a guard, sipping wine that also was not permitted. "In here, everything is halāl," answered the sheik, returning to his dinner.

Unknown to the outside world, none of the Arab militants minded being arrested and sent to an Israeli jail. It was a paid holiday. The longer the sentence for some, the better it was. In spite of what most thought or the rhetoric they espoused, none were in a hurry to leave and rejoin their precious *jihad*.

The Israeli's endured the worldwide outrage for being aggressive when retaliating for rocket attacks on their settlements. No one was killed in the latest one; the damage was minimal. It was wrong for them to blast their way through checkpoints, march down densely populated streets, and arrest the sheik. But they did. They had to teach him and his followers a lesson; that those who preached the destruction of Israel and that there was nothing wrong in firing rockets into nearby settlements had to be stopped.

The Israeli Prime Minister went on national television; CNN broadcast the speech around the world. "On average, one thousand rockets are aimed and fired at Israel from Gaza each year. This amounts to three each day, every single day of the year. And they come at all hours. Let me be clear, Israel will stop at nothing to defend its citizens. Would the French, the British, the Russians or the Chinese tolerate such acts of war? Would they be expected to sit around and do nothing when their people are being shelled?"

The party line to the world was clear: only the Israelis are being attacked, not any other nation. No one has ever stepped forward to protect their small country and force the Palestinians to cease their constant barrage of missiles. Just as it has been throughout history, and in modern times, the Israelis could only count on themselves to protect their own people.

The clamor would die down. It always did.

But then the Israelis made a blunder of the highest magnitude. At least as far as espionage goes, it was a colossal mistake they would not live down for a long time to come.

It was September and the Israeli secret service, the Mossad, set up a covert action to assassinate Khaled Mashaal, a Hamas leader, by poisoning him in an open café on a street in Amman, Jordan. The hit was not clean. The Mossad agent responsible for the killing was captured when he tried to escape on a dingy from a coastal launch south of Petra.

"This is a courtesy call," Hussein said, getting through to President Clinton. "The Israelis have tried to assassinate an Hamas leader on our soil. We consider it an act of war."

"Did they succeed?" asked the President, his honey-smooth voice peppered with astonishment.

"Not yet. He's presently in a coma; we are trying desperately to save him. I am calling to ask you to intercede. To force the Israelis to give us the antidote to the poison they used."

"When it comes to this, they won't listen to reason."

"My dear President, make it clear to them that they have no choice. We captured one of theirs. Tell them we demand a prisoner exchange for the life of their agent…on the condition that Mashaal survives. "

The Israelis could have protested, but they didn't. Not this time. They secretly feared that Sheik Yassin, for all his lavish prison lifestyle, would die in their jail from any of the assortments of medical ailments that ailed him. The sheik had macular degeneration and was slowly losing his sight; he had damaged hearing from having been close to so many rocket launchings; and he had chronic tubercular bronchitis with lesions on both lungs. If he died in their custody, they would certainly be blamed for withholding medical treatment, be investigated by the Red Cross, scolded by the United Nations, and accused of letting the prisoner wallow in inhumane conditions. This was a classic no win situation they had come to ignore in the past...but not this time.

It was their screw up in Jordan, and they would pay the price: the sheik was included in the prisoner release and the Israelis could not control what happened next.

Well, not immediately.

No sooner had the Sheik been released with the other prisoners then he and minions of fellow inmates were driven in a caravan of busses to a soccer stadium outside Bethlehem. They had obtained the proper permits to hold a public meeting and there was little the authorities could do but watch and listen. A cheering throng of deliriously adoring followers met the Sheik, – fifteen thousand strong were rounded up on short notice – and praised him as a *mujahedeen*, a holy warrior. In spite of his good treatment in the hands of the Israelis, the sheik lost no time denouncing his captors and exhorting his followers to continue the holy *haj* against them.

"Let us be clear why I can stand before you today, liberated from the horrific conditions imposed on me and our fellow soldiers, may Allah be praised, by the infidels, by the invaders of our land. By the Jews who kill our sons and daughters."

An Israeli fighter pilot buzzed low, the engine roar deafening.

The sheik waited for the noise to recede. He pointed to the sky. "You see, my fellow jihadists, even now they try to prevent me from telling the truth, from speaking from my heart so you can follow yours."

The sheik went on to exhort his followers to attack Israelis every chance they could. While most Palestinians were peace loving, law-abiding, and hardworking citizens, there were enough disenfranchised by the system who could easily be stirred to action in this cauldron of hate.

Scores of terrorist attacks followed in the days and weeks after the sheik's release. Dozens of Israelis died in the aftermath, while hundreds of Palestinians were displaced from their homes, and known terrorist refuges were destroyed. While they had no problem eliminating the fomenters of hate, the Israelis made every attempt to spare civilian lives.

Rather than confine the Sheik to house arrest as they normally did, they let him move about without restrictions. At least they would have a better notion of where he was most of the time. The Israelis were giving the Sheik his slack, knowing that the proverbial noose around his arrogant neck could be tightened at any time.

The Sheik called for an attack on an Israeli outpost. A baby was killed.

And now Zakkarhia came to cheer his beloved sheik. The sky was blue. Cloudless. The Sheik sat protected in a bulletproof black limousine, inching toward the welcoming crowd in Gaza, cheering the latest damage Hamas rockets inflicted on the Israelis. He sat between his beloved son, Abdul Aziz, and his trusted advisor Ayoub Atallah.

The caravan crept forward.

The Sheik waved to the frenetic swarms. He felt secure with his people. His bodyguard, Tariq Kadah, brandished a machine gun from the front seat, the man's keen eyes searching every window and rooftop before they neared, looking for anything out of place that would endanger the Sheik, even though the limousine was bulletproof.

"See, Abdul," said Ayoub, the Sheik's advisor, "you fight the Infidel with every weapon you have. Never let them think for a moment that they control you. That they can tell you what to do or think." He waved his hands at the hollering people that lined the streets. "You have much to learn from you father."

"Let him be, Ayoub," said the Sheik. "He is still a boy."

"Not in the eyes of Allah. He knows his enemy, and if he knows his enemy, then he is old enough to be a warrior."

The driver eased off the gas pedal and turned toward the back, "There are hundreds waiting for you, praised be to Allah."

The Sheik nodded. "The more the better. Stop in the square and open the roof. I will give them what they want."

The car slid around the corner.

Cheers escalated to a deafening crescendo.

Zakkarhia raised his fist to the glory of Allah. He chanted and swayed in the sheer ecstasy of being in the presence of the great Sheik Yassin.

Then, like a snake that can sense a flicker in the air, Zakkarhia froze. There was a buzz in his left ear. He twisted ever so slowly, twisting to look over his shoulder; his inner radar dial spun to high alert. He scanned the rooftops searching for a hidden foe.

No gun muzzles sticking out.

No window curtains swinging from someone ducking back, avoiding detection.

He heard it again.

Now he was certain; there was no time to waste.

Zakkarhia stepped toward the Sheik's car, but was thrown back by a Palestinian guard. Zakkarhia lunged at the guard, grabbed the man's chin and jerked his head skyward, forcing him to focus on the impending attack. Zeroing in on the Sheik's car was an Israeli helicopter gunship. The drone grew louder and a sinking feeling filled Zakkarhia: the bastards were going to attack his beloved leader.

Zakkarhia screamed and shouted, but no one heard him; the guard was too slow to warn anyone.

The blast was deafening.

When the smoke cleared, the Sheik was no more, his son was no more, and the car was no more.

There were blood and body parts everywhere. Metal and glass from the limousine hurtled through the earth, slicing through men and women and children. Sirens wailed; many cried. Others were dazed, pounded into a stupor. Streaks of blood, shredded clothes. Smoke and fire. Broken glass.

Blackness surrounded Zakkarhia. He tried to move but couldn't. His legs were gone; at least he couldn't feel them. A crushing weight strapped him down. He tried to talk, but no sound emerged from his burning throat. He tried to move his arms, but they were pinned.

He blinked, uncertain if this is how the dead felt: weighted down, unable to move or talk or cry out for help, "Hey, I am here. I am still with you." But they weren't still with the living…because they were dead. Was he?

Other noises filtered through. He could twist his head slightly to the left. The right eye of the guard dangled from its socket; he already on the road to Paradise.

Not yet, thought, Zakkarhia, not me. I'm not ready.

Zakkarhia wiggled the fingers on his right hand and then the left. He lifted a shoulder off the cold ground high enough to edge one hand and an arm back an inch. Then he moved the other. More sirens. People in white coats.

"Here! Here!" he shouted. They couldn't hear him.

Then, in a burst of strength, he pushed with all his might causing the dead guard to roll off his head giving him more space to maneuver. He pulled his head in, tortoise like, and struggled to work his way free. After many failed attempts, he succeeded.

Exhausted, he got to his feet. He stared at the spiraling smoke wafting from what had been the limousine. He looked left and then right, at the shattered windows, and at the cracked and broken walls of the buildings that surrounded the square. He looked at the bodies being piled to the side and the doctors and nurses helping the wounded, making life and death decisions in an instant.

"Let me take care of that," said a young doctor. Zakkarhia could not decipher the man's accent, but for now, it didn't matter.

"I don't need anyone's help," Zakkarhia told him.

"They all say they don't need help," said the doctor, "you're in shock. You're bleeding from your forehead. Let me stop it."

The young doctor fished into a red First Aid bag and pulled out alcohol and an antiseptic soap to wash and clean the wound before sewing the pieces together. Zakkarhia smacked his hand away, not out of anger, but out of urgency. "Thank you, but no. I want a permanent remembrance of today, the day Sheik Yassim was killed by the infidels."

This was the day that Zakkarhia dedicated his life to revenge the Sheik's death. He didn't know how he would do it, but he would find a way. He sought training from the best...and in the end, he became the best at what he did: a *jihadist-killing* machine capable of carrying out the most complex and dangerous missions.

Zakkarhia made a career out of hate and revenge.

# Chapter Nine

J ust the day before an Israeli air-to-surface missile vaporized Sheik Yassim's limousine, Gittel Lasker received an urgent message to leave the broken chards strewn about the Canaanite burial chambers that had been discovered near the ancient seaport of Ashkelon. Like so many Israelis, Gittel was an amateur archeologist. She was in the middle of a fourteen-day leave when two Palestinian suicide bombers sneaked out of Gaza to detonate their bombs. They killed ten innocents in the seaside port of Ashdod, in addition to themselves. Gittel left the moment she heard; Ashdod was only about ten miles up the coast.

It could have been worse. More devastating. The leader of the Aqsa Martyrs' Brigade, Abu Qusay, bragged that the attack was aimed at the fuel storage tanks that bloomed like white metal mushrooms from the ground. Their goal was not only to cause a tremendous loss of life, but also show the Israelis that their infrastructure was vulnerable in the same way Israelis seemingly attacked the Palestinian camps whenever it pleased them. The Israelis were not the only ones who could destroy buildings and kill innocent lives with little regard for the generations of Arab families they ruined. Abu Qusay's people had done it before. They would continue to bomb targets with the goal of killing as many innocents as possible. Their goal? Drive all the Jews into the sea and reclaim their rightful ownership of Palestine.

Before the fires were even out, Israeli reprisal was not an issue of "if" it would occur; it was only a matter of which target. Reuters reported an Israeli military official going on the record, "Forces have assembled near the Gaza Strip and await orders as to what their targets will be. Bomb making facilities, the families of the suicide bombers, and Hamas leaders will be high on the list."

Gittel was assigned to protect the mourners in Ashdod. She made every attempt to blend into the background, to be unobtrusive to the grieving, but to make her presence visible enough so that those wanting to disrupt the solemn burial service would think twice.

Gittel stood in the blazing sun, scanning fences and trees, anywhere that a sniper could gain an advantage. She glanced at the mourners gathering around six freshly dug graves: a mother, father, mother-in-law, and three children. The waste of life was something she could never accept. And yet, as a citizen in a country that was in a perpetual state of war with its neighbors, she was hardened to death itself.

Death was part of life.

Her mind drifted to the day that she would be in mourning. Who would be first? Her father or her mother? Each had been through so much. Both families left Germany in the mid 1930s and emigrated to what was then Palestine, where Gittel's parents were born. When the War for Independence began, her father was too young to fight. Only eleven, he was put to work fixing guns that jammed after turning white hot from repeated use. School was not for him, and he dropped out, becoming a car mechanic, able to patch together anything with a motor.

Her father had just entered the army for his two-year military service when Egypt and Syria decided to gang up on Israel, blockading the Suez Canal in the process. With the permission and guidance from both England and France, the young state of Israel, waged war against the tripartite coalition of Egypt, Syria and Jordan.

Gittel's father made tank commander. His marksman's eyesight and ability to make engines purr were powerful assets to being an effective tank commander until he took a direct hit in the Sinai. That he was not killed was a miracle; that he only lost an eye was, well, not so bad considering what could've and should've happened to him.

The years passed. He met Gittel's mother, opened a car repair garage, and blessed the day that his seemingly infertile wife was not so infertile. A girl. Gittel Leah. Gittel was lavished every opportunity to succeed. She wanted to be an engineer, which was a natural offshoot of her father's mechanical abilities and was able to achieve that goal after her completing her obligatory military service.

There was also a boy born, Gittel's brother. She rarely thought of him. A mournful cry brought Gittel back to the present. Was it the cry from one standing at the graves or did it come from deep inside her?

Dozens crowded around the freshly dug graves, six rectangles side-by-side for one family. Scores stood behind them. No matter how many times the wails of grief pierced the air, no matter how many died during this Intifada, Gittel could never get used to innocents dying. Collateral damage during a planned attack was one thing, deliberately targeting and killing civilians, especially women and children, was the ultimate act of cowardice.

Gittel despised cowards.

"Did you lose someone?" The youth was fifteen. Sixteen at the most. He was broad-shouldered, a bit barrel-chested. He had coal-black black hair and already needed to shave every day. His dark eyes were hollow. Haunting.

He had folded his arms across his chest, hugging himself tight.

His lower lip trembled when he answered.

"I'm an orphan now." He pointed to the coffin furthest from where they were standing.

The youth wiped his eyes with his sleeve. He wore black pants spotted with caked dirt, and a white shirt that was ripped on the sleeve. A strip of black ribbon was pinned over his heart.

"My father. He was in the tool shed when it went off. He never had a chance."

"Why aren't standing over there? Next to him?"

"I don't know what to do." He turned to her, lost.

"Don't you have anyone else?"

He shook his head.

She reached out to touch his arm. "I lost my younger brother during the siege in the church at Bethlehem." He nodded, but she wasn't sure he heard her. "We are a nation of sufferers. Of perpetual mourners. There's not a soul in this country who hasn't been touched by senseless killings." She drew in a long breath. "As long as we are surrounded by our enemies, this is our destiny."

The youth plumbed Gittel's face, unable to find solace in her words. He would never get passed his father's death. He grabbed at the torn shirt fabric and yanked it like a parachute ripcord.

His sudden action surprised. He drew in a deep breath, the air replacing sadness with anger.

Gittel shifted a step back. The youth's eyes turned to burning coals. "There's nothing you can say that will make sense out of this madness. Our people forgive too easily. Every time something bad happens, we find a way of excusing it. Of forgiving our enemies who hate us."

"Forgiveness makes us better than them," she answered.

The youth scoffed. "So they can kill more of us? Drive us from our God-given lands. Lay claim to what's not theirs?"

He spoke with a maturity that was greater than his years. "Why are you so angry?" she asked. Trembling herself, unsure of how to comfort him, she reached out to touch his shoulder. She thought that maybe a bit of kindness and warmth would ease his pain. After all, the wound from the loss of her brother still oozed and, soon, it could be any day now, she'd feel the emptiness of no longer having parents.

He batted her hand away, snorting. "I don't want your comfort." The bitterness in his voice turned to anger. "I don't want anyone's pity or help. Our enemies fight fire with fire. They preach an eye for an eye. That will be the way I honor my father, not by trying to understand them and being better than them. Your way paves the road for more innocents to die." He swept his hand toward the graves and mourners. "*This* is from forgiveness and understanding. This is what compassion brings our people." Tears streamed down his face. "This is the stupid truth that we've been forced-fed for the years, and it killed my father. But me, I don't buy it any longer."

"Your brand of truth will get you nowhere. Not with our people, not with the Palestinians. Keep in mind that the world watches what we do. They hold us to a higher standard. We can't kill like they do without a reason."

Again, he pointed to the coffins. "Do I need more reasons than that?" He turned to her. "Did the world lift a finger to protect my father?"

He stood his full measure and squared opposite her. She squirmed under his gaze. The meek, sad boy of a few minutes ago was now transformed into a powerful youth. She was trained to notice pent up rage, and to note telltale signs like those he displayed. What she saw that day in Ashdod sent a chill up her spine. This one needed to be above the radar.

Their paths would cross years later, and she would recall his haunted eyes. True he wept when his father died. True he felt sadness. Something about him transported her back to a black hole in her own past, greater than the loss of her brother.

He would be included in her report. "What's your name?" Gittel asked.

"Yesterday, it was Moishe Schlamowitz."

"And today?" asked Gittel.

"Jericho Glassman." '

# Chapter Ten

S he was raw. A rookie. It was her first assignment. The outer perimeter was rimmed with soldiers. Everyone in the audience was frisked not once but twice. The ever-cautious Israeli security. Baby diapers opened and inspected. No exceptions. Her orders were clear: stand by the car door. Don't move. Scour the crowd even though everyone had been checked and double-checked. Leave nothing to chance. Assume that the worst could happen, and then protect against it.

Gittel had just turned twenty-four. After her compulsory two years of military service, she studied aerospace engineering at Tel Aviv University. As graduation day neared, she circulated through the on-campus job fair where Israel's high-tech companies vied to sign up the best of the best.

"What does your company do?" she asked, less concerned about the company and more interested in the man planted next to the poster. He sported dark sunglasses that hid mysterious eyes. His weathered skin was rough; his face landscaped with a carpet of stubble that evoked a "just woke up" GQ model. As she spoke, his ruddy lips spread into an ear-to-ear revealing a perfect set of ivory. His blue-green eyes, the color of shallow Mediterranean water, sparkled as he lowered his glasses onto his aquiline nose.

"We do a little bit of this and a little bit of that," he answered, reading her nametag. "Gittel." She loved the resonance of his voice. Her knees buckled when he touched her hand.

"Ah," she said with a knowing grin, tilting her head to the slide, and tossing her flame red mane to the side. "I've got your number. You're Shin Bet."

He feigned surprise. "Is it that obvious?"

"Israeli Secret Service? You are no Mossad agent, that's for sure. You are as transparent as the day is long."

"What about the day God made the sun stand still? That was a very long day," he said.

"That was a bit before my time. Besides, that was just a story in the Bible. Did any of that really happen?"

With exaggerated drama, he whipped the glasses from his nose and stepped closer to her. "Do my ears deceive me? Do we have a non-believer here? A beautiful one, I may add, but nonetheless, someone who questions that the stories in the Bible are true?" He turned and mockingly looked left and then right. "I need Bible security right now! Place her under arrest." He pointed to the top of her head. "Heretic here! Heretic here!"

She tapped his chest. "Stop it. You're embarrassing me." She was lollipop red.

"That's the aim. I wanted to see how pretty you get when you blush...and divert attention from exposing my secret."

She wondered how many secrets this cliché dark stranger had? In time, she would find out. What she did know was that Shin Bet had many duties. Upholding the state security against those who seek to undermine it by terrorist activity or violent revolution; exposing terrorist organizations comprised of both Jewish and Arab Israelis; interrogating terror suspects; providing intelligence for counter-terrorism operations in the West Bank and the Gaza Strip; counter-espionage; protecting the lives of senior public officials including the Prime Minister's, insure that El-Al flights are safe, as well as protecting Israel's embassies around the world.

"Which branch?" she asked.

"You know I can't tell you."

"Do you have a name? You know mine."

His name was Noam. Noam Cohen had black curly hair and an

easy laugh. In quick order he first became her sponsor and then her lover. The bloom on her life was bursting with love when Noam was shot when a meeting with an informer in the outskirts of Ramallah went bad. It was an ambush; he never had a chance. The informer needed more money and flipped sides. One other agent was wounded, but all that mattered to Gittel was that her Noam was gone.

Weeks later, security forces shot and killed two Hamas terrorists involved in Noam's murder, but that didn't bring him back. Nor did it mend the hole in her heart that would never close.

"Be alert," the commander barked into her earpiece. The Prime Minister's speech was one of many on a whirlwind tour that appealed to the Israeli people to accept the Oslo Peace Accord as their best chance to end the bloodshed and long-standing terror plaguing their country. Yes, they would have to welcome their enemies who have always vowed to exterminate them. Yes, they would have to stop building new settlements and cease expanding dozens more in planning stages designed to absorb the hordes of Russians fleeing their Motherland. And yes, they would have to give back part of the West Bank and cede Gaza to the Palestinians.

Given the choice, the Israelis would accept a Palestinian state rather than reabsorb all the disenfranchised refugees who abandoned their homes at the onset of partition back in '47. They lived side-to-side back then, Semitic cousins with a common heritage, but no one thought they could resume that in the future.

"The price we'll pay will be high," Yitzhak Rabin, the Israeli Prime Minister said into the microphone, then his voiced dropped, "it always is." He paused a beat. Then another. "But, the value of making peace, my friends, is incalculable. Our children and our children's children will not have to live in fear of rockets sent randomly through the air, or terrorists blowing up buses, or bombs detonating in cafés, killing innocents drinking coffee on a sunny afternoon.

"The Oslo Peace Accords are the first step to fulfilling the Biblical promise that Palestine will be the land filled with milk and honey for us. Up until now it has been filled with a bittersweet and endless river of tears. Time will prove that we did the right thing. For now, all I ask is your support and faith that the Accords are best for Eretz Yisrael. Shalom Aleichem."

A thunderclap of applause erupted because they appreciated and believed in Rabin more than they supported the signing of the Oslo Peace Accords two years earlier. This would always be the case. In his later years, Rabin grew cantankerous. He was stifled in his views, with little room for other opinions. Yet regardless of this beliefs and how contrary they might be, he would always be their hero.

Now, as he grabbed the handrail to descend from the podium, none could anticipate that this would be his last speech. When does tragedy ever occupy the moment? Is there that split second before something happens that one knows the moment is off kilter? That something is about to happen? Is it as simple as the calm before the storm? The smell of "impending?" A foul wind blowing?

When he spoke, Rabin had been, by turns, cheered and heckled; moments later, there would be a national tragedy. Could it have been prevented?

Gittel heard the cacophony swell as the PM's final words were carried over the loudspeakers.

Her chest pounded. Droplets of sweat formed in the small of her back; she shifted her weight and touched the earpiece to hear what she already knew: the PM had finished speaking and was approaching his car.

Her pulse quickened.

A phalanx of Shin Bet surrounded the PM; a human armada shielded him with their lives. Gittel scanned eyes. Hands. She looked for a telltale head tilting in an odd way. Her inner clock calculated the minutes and now seconds left until her "package" was safely tucked inside the armor-plated limousine.

Rabin stopped to wave to the cheering throngs. To the dismay of those guarding him, he turned to face the crowd one last time before ducking into his car.

Maybe he knew what was about to happen? Is it possible that he was tired and welcomed it? A soldier's last battle?

Those charged with security tightened the ring around him, and gently nudged him to get inside the car.

To get out of harm's way.

He obliged.

As he leaned to step over the ledge and into the limo, a shot rang out. Rabin lurched into the car. He clutched his throat. Hit once, then a second time. Blood gurgled through his shirt and gray suit jacket, soaking his back in a crimson spill.

It could have been worse. Yigal Amir planned to murder both Rabin and Labor leader Shimon Peres for their roles in making peace with Palestinians. Amir had been overtaken by religious zealotry that deemed the peace accords against divine law. When Peres and Rabin walked off the podium separately after the rally, Amir was left with one target.

*Ashdod*

She was in Ashdod.

At a funeral.

Rabin was long buried.

She was not throwing dirt onto Noam's casket.

"What's your name?" Gittel had asked.

"Yesterday, it was Moishe Schlamowitz."

"And today?"

"Jericho Glassman."

As he spit out this new name *Jericho Glassman,* daggers of anger flew from eyes, piercing Gittel with barbs of fear. Gittel saw that same hateful gaze when Yigal Amir was trapped and then caught. And in her heart of hearts, she knew that Israel had just spawned another madman fixated on the misguided concept of revenge.

Revenge in the name of justice!

Revenge in the name of right!

Revenge in the name of the Lord.

# Chapter Eleven

"Granted," Ford said, drawing out the word to buy time, sensing that he was about to hear more than *I bet you didn't know about this tidbit of information*, "there is the obvious. We're both black. We're both Americans. We both live in New York City. But from where I'm sitting, that's where the similarities end. Apart from the obvious male/female differences, you're Jewish and I'm Catholic. What am I missing?"

She muttered out loud, her internal debate surfacing. She squashed it back for the moment.

"Excuse me?" he said.

"No, no, it's nothing." She was bursting to blab what she knew.

"Have I offended you by not seeing other similarities between us?"

She had had a raging argument with herself during the length of time sitting there.

"You look like you want to tell me something, but don't know how to do it."

"Is it that obvious?"

"It's my job to read people."

His encouragement only caused her pulse to quicken. She desperately wanted to tell him what she knew about him, but was afraid she'd make a fool of herself. The story was that preposterous. If only Cardinal Ford knew part of the story, it would be easy to tell the rest.

Did she have the right to waltz into his life, regardless of how or why it happened, and do this to him? Ever since he came to New York and rose from the first black Archbishop of the New York Catholic diocese to the America's first Afro-American Cardinal, she had wanted to meet him. Tell him the things she knew about his past. And now that she was sitting in his presence, only a few feet away, did she have the courage to lay it all out for him?

What to do?

Ford uncoupled his hands and leaned forward. He scrutinized her face, waiting for her to expound upon her point.

LeShana, on the other hand, remained silent, debating issues that, for the moment, only she knew existed.

"I'm waiting," he said.

Her face crinkled in anguish. She drew in a deep breath and then exhaled with a bit of drama. No sense holding back any longer. If she did, she'd burst keeping this knowledge all to herself.

"Okay, Your Eminence. Here goes. Stories are legend on how your white American missionary parents found you swaddled in a basket in the middle of the Italian-Ethiopian War. They brought you back to the States, raised you, educated you, and here we are today." Her hand sliced through the air. "Cardinal of the New York Archdiocese. My, my. They would've been so proud of you! It's nothing short of a modern-day Horatio Alger story...Catholic style."

A flash of pain seared his face. He waved his arms. "If only they had lived long enough to see this."

"Even so, they knew you were destined for greatness." She pointed. "I'm sure they're watching from above."

"I pray they are. But I still fail to see our so-called 'connection.'" He pointed to LeShana and then back to himself.

"I'm betting that there's something your parents failed to tell you, Your Eminence. Something they didn't know how to handle, so they kept it from you. At least that's what I'm thinking."

Ford leaned back. The glint in his eye clouded over. "My parents gave me every advantage a child could wish for. I'm not talking about food and shelter, or even education. They gave me their heart and soul; they gave me their morality. And most importantly, they gave me their love and belief in the Almighty. I'm afraid you're wrong, Detective. There's nothing my parents kept from me."

At that moment, anyone else might have retreated from the gentle phrasing, with its clear meaning, by the Cardinal of New York. Not LeShana. One thing colleagues in the department knew about her was that when LeShana was on a mission, nothing deterred her from getting the job done. And Arnold Ford had just become a mission.

"There is one thing, Your Eminence. Your parents failed to give you your history. They hid your true identity. As mighty and great and brilliant as you are, Cardinal Ford, as much as you have accomplished, there is a key part of your life that I'm betting you don't know anything about."

"With all due respect, Detective, how can you think for even a moment that you know more about me than I do? Than my parents did? I know everything about my past that I need to know."

If life were a swimming pool of collected histories and experiences, LeShana had just sprung off the diving board into the deep end. "Do you know who your biological parents were?"

"I was an infant when they died, too young to remember them."

"I don't mean to challenge, Your Eminence…"

"But you are," he said bemused.

She ignored his challenge to stop, and dismissed the notion that she might be out of her league if she continued…but she felt compelled and she *was* on a mission. "What *do you know* about your real parents?"

"I'll play your game. For starters, I know I was born in Africa to American blacks that literally took the 'Back to Africa Movement' to heart. They left America and the Great Depression behind, not to mention the KKK, Jim Crow, and picking cotton. The Depression was in full force and the group of them was seeking a better life for themselves and their children. They found their Promised Land in the outskirts of Addis Abba, where they wouldn't be judged for the color of their skin or who they were. Paradise, it wasn't. They lived in mud huts built with sunbaked bricks. I was told that my father farmed the land and made a meager living. Things were just starting to get better when a plane flew down the center of our village and strafed everything and everyone in sight. My parents were mowed down, caught in a meaningless war between the Ethiopians and the Italians."

LeShana shifted her feet, and snuggled back into the straight-backed chair. "And?"

"And what?" he asked.

"That's it? That's all you know about your family history?"

"What else could I know? I was only a few weeks old when all that happened. I'm pretty certain that I didn't have any brothers or sisters. My parents were expatriates killed in a war that wasn't theirs. It's a story that's occurred to many around the globe."

"And then the missionaries found you," she said, prompting him to continue.

"Correct. Later that same day, missionaries came to the village to tend to the wounded and stumbled over me. There were no agencies like we have here; there wasn't even a hospital nearby. They couldn't just leave me there. They didn't have any children, so they took me and raised me as their own. I was the lucky one. I couldn't imagine better parents than they. That's all there is to know."

*Oh, but there is so much more.*

LeShana was in the middle tuck of a triple gainer; one more spin, arms extended and she would plunge into the Cardinal's pool of life. Here she was, sitting in front of the most important Catholic clergyman in the United States, and she knew more about his origins than he did.

His tone was clear: this topic is over. So LeShana dropped it…for the moment. Dropping it only intensified the turmoil bubbling inside her, one that would soon boil over.

"Let's get back to the business at hand," she said.

"You're done with me that easily?" he quipped.

"Let's just say that I am taking a professional break. We may very well return to this topic, even though you think you know it all."

"There you go again, insinuating that you know my story better than me."

She opted not to reply. Oh, the *yenta* in her was about to put him in his place. LeShana returned to her police face and scrolled through her electronic tablet.

A clock ticked. Neither spoke; each with their own thoughts.

If they could only read each other's minds!

No need for parlor tricks; LeShana would not let this drop. She couldn't.

# Chapter Twelve

L eShana broke the silence and recited the facts without glancing up. "The victim was eighty-two. Married. He had four children and nine grandchildren. He worked in the diamond district over fifty years."

"Assuming it was about this piece of paper," he was still holding it, "what's this codex that it was taken from all about?"

LeShana looked squarely at him. "The Codex of Aleppo. Sometimes it's referred to as the Crown of Aleppo. It's more than a thousand years old."

He turned the laminated paper over and over, as if it would talk to him and share its secrets. Why would an old man lose his life for this? Why was he, the Cardinal of New York, brought into contact with it? Was it a random happenstance? Or had Fate delivered the man and his paper into Ford's arms?

"And you're certain that this shard of paper comes from that book?"

"It would take a manuscript expert and a forensic team to verify that it's from the Codex of Aleppo, but that's my educated guess."

The Cardinal turned bemused; a smile crept across his face. "Am I to assume that this is more than a police hunch?"

"Now who's the detective? That was clever. It just so happens that over the last few weeks, there've been a number of unsolved murders circulating through the various police networks from around the world: Brazil, Uruguay, Curacao, outside of Florence, and from the US including Brooklyn and Deal, NJ. Always old men. Each a Syrian Jew. And all linked by one thing in common." She plucked the talisman off the desk where Ford had rested it and held it with a delicacy reserved for sacred treasures. "They all owned an artifact just like this one...and they all have been verified as coming from the Codex of Aleppo."

"And given what you've already said, their fragment of parchment was missing once the authorities were brought into the case."

"Bingo, again. You *are* good, your Eminence. There will always be a spot in the department for you."

Ford ignored the backhanded compliment. "Before he died, he told me that it brought him good luck."

"Every one of the victims thought the same until it was no longer so. Back in '91, I was called in on B & E. That's when I first learned about the Codex. An old couple in Crown Heights. Both of them were beaten up pretty bad. They kept a lot of money in the house. Owned a wholesale egg business out on the Island. No bills, always cash on delivery. Before Brooklyn, they had lived in Syria, although originally, they came from Iran when it was still called Persia. When I questioned them, they didn't much care about the money that was lost. What mattered most to them was losing the precious piece of parchment. It didn't matter how much they were roughed up, they wouldn't cave in and tell the burglars about their talisman. The thugs tried, but couldn't beat it out of them. They might have succeeded if it had gone on a bit longer, but the phone rang and they figured whoever was calling might get curious why the old people weren't answering. So they left without the sliver of paper."

"They came from Aleppo, too, like all the others?" Ford asked.

LeShana nodded. "Aleppo was a thriving city built on commerce. Been that way for hundreds of years. All that changed the day the U.N. voted for partition at the end of World War II. The moment that happened, the world collapsed for the Syrian Jews. Synagogues were trashed and burned, including their Torahs and precious artifacts."

"Including the Crown of Aleppo?" He pointed to the laminated fragment. "Their sacred book survived, didn't it?"

Her lips pinched upward. "That's where the story gets interesting. It seems that locals ran into the burning synagogue and managed to save a few pages. Nine sheets in all. Once they did, they cut them up into small pieces, like this one, and distributed them to lucky families. The survivors, I guess we can call them that, have carried these souvenirs ever since. Always protected in plastic. Laminated like this one. The assumption always was that the rest of the book was destroyed in the fire."

"And these people in Brooklyn? They had a part of a page from this same Codex?"

She shook her head. "Actually, they had an entire page. No one else in the world had that. Maybe that's why they fought so hard. Their page came from Numbers. Like this one."

"I'm impressed that you were able to recognize it from your Hebrew School training."

"Don't be. I'd like you to believe that I'm that smart, but I'm not. I consulted with a biblical scholar at the Union Theological Seminary. Phyllis Trumble. That's when she explained the history of the Codex of Aleppo to me and I learned about the missing pages."

"There have been important illuminated manuscripts through the ages that have been stolen, damaged, or forged. Church documents. Rare books. Each was special, but not worth killing over. What's so special about this book?"

LeShana perked up, ready to spit out the answer and be the teacher's pet. "For one, it's the single greatest copy of the Bible ever written. Second, it's the most important document the State of Israel owns, much the same as Declaration of Independence is to us, or the Magna Carta is to England. In some respects, it could be likened to the Rosetta Stone."

"And three?"

"It is part of the reason why there may never be peace in the Middle East."

Cardinal Ford frowned. "Isn't that a bit overdramatic? I could believe that this laminated parchment is important. I could believe you're able to translate the words and identify where this came from, even though you're not a scholar. You've convinced me of all that. But trying to sell me on the concept that somehow this Codex of Aleppo is an integral to the success of the Middle East peace process? That's pushing my credibility to the wall, Detective."

"I'm just repeating what I heard, Your Excellency. I'm not asking you to accept any of it. We're just talking here, right?"

*No, Your exalted Cardinal Ford, we're not just talking. We're on the precipice of something very important here…and you're about to find out just how much.*

"Why would the Palestinians care about these pieces of paper? It's not remotely connected to the Koran, right? It's from the Bible. The Hebrew Bible."

"The Old Testament."

"And it has nothing to do with Muslims or say anything bad about Mohammed?"

"Nothing bad; nothing the likes of that."

He grabbed it and inspected it for the umpteenth time. It was no bigger than a credit card, and just as thin. "And you're trying to tell me that the Israeli government is holding up the peace process because of this?"

"Here's the unbelievable thing," said LeShana. "There's a good chance that the robberies around the world, and today's murder, have been carried out by religious Jews."

"Detective, each time I force myself to accept your story, you add a wrinkle that defies belief. Orthodox Jews murdering their own? This is too much to accept."

*Wait 'til you hear the rest!*

"But it may be true," she answered.

"Something that may be true is not the same as saying it *is* true."

"I know the difference. I am a detective."

"And yet you've dismissed Palestinians as possibly being behind this string of crimes or today's killing."

"Absolutely, they had nothing to do with them."

"And the Israeli government is not behind them either?"

"Certainly not."

"Yet you're claiming that Jews are behind these crimes."

"I am."

"How can you possibly explain this?"

*I can...and I will.*

"This is not just my conclusion. My friend, Dr. Trumble, she absolutely believes that the Orthodox Jews are behind this."

"But why?" interrupted Ford. "This makes no sense."

She held up her index finger. "But it does. You see, the orthodox Jews are hellbent..." she put her fingers to her lips, "...can I say that here?"

"I've used that word myself."

"Good," she smiled much relieved. "These religious Jews want the Codex reassembled on their terms. Like I said before, only a few pages went missing back in 1947."

"What you said was that nine pages were taken and cut up, except the full sheet that found its way to those old people in Brooklyn. Then you said that it was presumed that the book was lost in the fire."

She pointed her index finger at him. "Let me back up a bit. Seems I left out the part about the book being saved and hidden for years by the few Syrian Jews that remained behind."

"Back in 1947."

She nodded. "They let the world assume the book was lost; only a few knew of its existence. And then conditions changed. The few remaining Jews in Syria felt threatened. It was no longer safe to hide it. They felt compelled to move it out of Syria and smuggle it into Israel, which did happen."

"Just like that? Something as rare as the Declaration of Independence or the Magna Carta just waltzes through the door one day. And like everything is okay except for nine missing pages? Is that what you are saying?"

"If it happened that way, it'd be a simple story."

"This is anything but simple, young lady."

"That's what I'm trying to explain."

*She did amuse*, thought Ford. "Okay, then what?"

"Skipping over the when, why, and how the book appeared, trust me that the book was handed over to the Israeli government completely intact except for those few pages taken for souvenirs. Then, a few years go by and someone remembers that the Codex of Aleppo is sitting on a shelf. They rediscover it and are shocked to find that one third of the book is now missing."

"The pages disappear, just like that? Wasn't anyone guarding them? Were they in a protective case? Everyone knows the Israelis have the best security in the world."

"Nothing like that. The book was on a library shelf just like any other book. The authorities in charge might have remembered that they had the book, but that's when Nasser decided to blockade the Suez Canal and the Israelis went to war again. Let's skip that and fast forward."

He made a face and sighed. "What's one more war in this story? What happened next?" This Detective continued to stretch his belief system. Little did he know that it would be manipulated to the extreme by the time she was finished.

"The prevailing thought, today, is that whoever is gathering up these fragments..."

"Murdering for them."

"Unfortunately. That these same people have the other missing pages. That's the only thing that makes sense."

"Little of this makes sense to me."

"I've tried to explain it carefully."

"And you have. It's just too fantastic to believe."

"Ain't that the truth!"

"And now you want me to believe that religious Jews are not only killing elderly Syrian Jews from Aleppo for these fragments, but have the missing pages from the Codex to boot. Why? To blackmail the Israeli government?"

She clapped her hands. "Precisely, that's what's behind this! See, you do understand."

"To what end? What am I missing? If *you* know these pages exist, then so do others. Why can't the Mossad find them? They've proven time and time again that nothing is beyond their reach. Eichmann in Argentina. Taking out the nuclear plant in Iran. Airlifting tens of thousands of Ethiopian Jews in the middle of the night. If Israelis want something, they get it done."

"My guess is that the Mossad has known where these pages have been for years. Given the crazy politics of their state, their hands are tied. There's no hope of rescuing the pages without causing a maelstrom around the world…one no Israeli government wants to suffer at this time."

Ford tented his fingers and then drummed them on the table.

*Take your time, she thought. Let him digest the words. Bring him along slowly.*

He chose his words. "The Hebrew Bible is a record of every word God spoke to man, or through his prophets to man."

"Correct."

"And through the ages, scribes had the good sense to write these words down so there was no mistake in what the good Lord wanted from us."

"Correct, again."

"And the importance of this special book, again? Is it a different version of the Old Testament? Some facts that are different? A hidden message?"

"Nothing like that. But it is the most important Bible we have. Here's why. The Codex of Aleppo is the first time in history that every single word of God spoken to man was put into a single book."

"And by book you mean bound and held together by two hard covers."

"Which was invented by the Romans," she added. "Think of it, Your Excellency, holding all the God's words ever spoken to man in your hand at one time. It could never have been done before this book was written."

"There are twenty-four books in the Old Testament, with the Torah being only five of them."

"It would have been impossible to hold all twenty-four scrolls in your hands at once. Lord knows that Torah is heavy enough to hold by itself."

"I'm beginning to understand this, now."

"Here's the key. Imagine a renegade group of Jews on a mission to reassemble the missing pages of this one-of-a-kind sacred book, and then hold it hostage as a bartering tool for the state of Israel?"

"Is that what this is about? Blackmail?"

"It's certainly an angle we need to consider."

"Is there anything I can do to help?"

"Can you work miracles?"

The Cardinal stood and walked around the desk.

He took her hand.

A shiver of energy coursed through her; the hair on her neck prickled.

"It just so happens" Ford continued, "I *am* in the business of making miracles. But first, tell me about my story. There's obviously more I need to know."

"You must have busy schedule."

"Detective, I have all the time you need. How else will I pull off that miracle if I don't know the facts?"

For no rational reason at all, LeShana Thompkins believed that if she told her story...his story...that something good would come of it.

And in a way, it did.

# Chapter Thirteen

Zakkarhia fired his rifle at the helicopter to no avail. He ran to where he knew a rocket launcher was hidden behind a produce market, but by the time he got there, there was nothing to shoot at except empty sky. He launched a rocket toward Israel anyway, hoping that it would find a target, any target – any man, woman, or child – and spill Jewish blood to avenge the death of the Sheik and the others.

He raised his fist toward Allah and rocked in place. He clamped his eyes drum-tight.

"I swear upon all that is sacred, upon your life, my precious sheik, that it will not have been in vain. I will make the world pay for your death and the death of my brothers and sisters. When I'm finished, my name will bring fear to their lips...and happiness to my soul. Praise be to Almighty Allah."

◆　◆　◆

Gittel returned to headquarters when the report was received: Ahmed Yassin had been neutralized. Hamas had lost the terrorist provocateur who was behind so many Israeli deaths.

Under any other circumstances, Gittel would have rejoiced. Not this time. This time, in the clutches of victory, she shuddered with the image of Judah Maccabee and what he meant centuries ago when a band of Jews fought off the Assyrians during the miracle of Hanukkah. It was as true then as it is true now.

*No matter how many of the enemy were killed, no matter how good Israeli intelligence was, war begets war. Victims beget victims. Killings beget killings. And when it came to the Israel and its neighboring countries, when it came to Israel and the Palestinians, and even Israel and the settlers insisting that the occupied lands were rightfully theirs, the killings were far from over. For both sides.*

◆　◆　◆

Weeks later, holding a tattered brown suitcase that contained all of his possessions, Zakkarhia stood in front of the kiosk outside the train station in downtown Khartoum. He had stolen his way out of Gaza through one of the many tunnels that led away from the refugee camps into Egypt. There was no shortage of *brothers* willing to aid him travel from Cairo to Sudan so that he could train for the *fatwa* and participate in the war against the infidels.

Searching for his ride, he bobbed to music. He pulled out the earphone connected to his cellphone. "Aleichem Shalom." The cab driver waved through the open taxicab window. He was light-skinned with coiled dark hair. He wore a khaki shirt that was sweat-stained, and his teeth were bathroom-tile white and perfectly formed, except for the chip on the top left front incisor. The uneven enamel made him look boyish. But all Zakkarhia noticed was his dark, feral eyes.

Zakkarhia was told to expect a special taxi, one that had normal lettering and signage, but no fare meter. He was told to trust the driver, that this man transferred most of the soldiers who came for training from any of the number of international terrorist groups that supplied soldiers: Hezbollah, the PIJ (Palestinian Islamic jihad), the Abu Nidal Organization, which was an offshoot of the PLO in the md-70s, and Hamas.

What most came to learn was that Al Qaeda had more potential than all the others, that Al Qaeda training was the best in the world.

"How far to the camp," Zakkarhia could not wait to start his training. He had lost weight since leaving home, living on the streets and begging for or stealing food when necessary. His one vice was a cigarette, which he smoked as often as he could get one. He liked the bitter sting when he inhaled deep draughts of smoke and the way nicotine made him both relaxed and his senses more acute at the same time. He never did go home, not after what his father said about the jihad and how the wrong people were influencing Zakkarhia. His father could not have been more mistaken. As much as it pained him not to see him mother and sisters and brothers, he was willing to give them up, too, in order to be a soldier of Allah.

"What's your hurry? There's plenty of time to die. I see them come and I see them go," said the cab driver. "There's no need to rush. No shortage of pine boxes for all of you." And then he gave a guttural laugh that sounded more like a hyena to Zakkarhia.

*All of you? We are fighters in the jihad. Where is the respect?*

"That's not going to happen to me."

The cabby snorted. "That's what they all say."

"It will be an honor to die for the glory of Mohammed."

"Harrumph!" the cabby snorted. "What did Mohammed ever do for you?"

"He brought me here," answered Zakkarhia.

"Ah," said the driver, "that he did."

"And you are the one driving me to the training camp."

"That I am."

"Answer me this," said Zakkarhia, "why are you cynical about us training for the jihad? Isn't our enemy your enemy?"

"I have no enemies. My God is my money. As long as they pay me to pick all of you fools up and bring them to the camp, I'm happy to defy the authorities and drive this fake cab. I make your leaders happy and that makes me happy."

Zakkarhia clenched both fists. How could any Muslim brother not think the same as Zakkarhia did? How could money be his God? No, thought Zakkarhia, this man is not a believer and therefore, he is the enemy. He's as bad as a Jew. No, thought Zakkarhia, he was worse. He was a Muslim who thought and acted like a Jew.

The camp was in sight. "Pull over to the side," Zakkarhia told the driver. Zakkarhia had noted guards posted in secreted places as they neared, making sure the cab was not followed. It never was.

"I'm supposed to bring you into the camp," said the driver, "not leave you out here."

"This is close enough. I want to walk into the camp. Feel its power enter my body. I don't want this cab to shield it and get in the way."

"As you wish," said the cabbie as they pulled to the side; he slid the car into neutral. He looked into the rear mirror at Zakkarhia with a smirk. "My job delivering another fool has been accomplished."

Those were the last words the cabbie ever spoke, as Zakkarhia, age sixteen, defended the name of Allah for the first time. Years later, after Zakkarhia committed his last act of terror, he will have defended Allah's name too many times to count.

◆　◆　◆

It didn't take more than a few days after burying his father and meeting Gittel Lasker, for Moishe Schlamowitz to claim his destiny. He shred every vestige of his life to the point that all connections to his young past ceased to exit.

He didn't deny his childhood; he obliterated it from his memory.

He didn't forget the songs sung at Passover Seders with his cousins, aunts, uncles, and parents; he branded these memories into fire-hot anger. Moishe lost his mother years earlier and, at sixteen and a half, was now made an orphan at the hands of Hamas.

He vowed revenge.

He tried to join the army, but his fake papers did not pass close scrutiny. Then he saw the sign that would make him feel alive again. It called his name.

"How old are you again?" asked the head of the ambulance corps.

"Old enough to drive," Jericho answered.

And in the slash of a pen, Moishe was approved to enter the ranks of the highly regarded ambulance corps of the city of Ashkelon, only

10 miles from the Gaza border. The ambulance recruiter turned the paper and squinted.

"Why'd you change your name?"

Moishe's chiseled face turned grave. "Because Moishe Schlamowitz died when his father was killed." He rocked back on his heels, "Jericho Glassman took his place."

"You're sure you want to this, Jericho?"

He liked hearing his new name spoken out loud.

"More than anything in the whole world."

"It could be dangerous."

"That's what I'm hoping for. Will I get to see fighting?"

"More than you would ever want. It will be good training for when you enter the Army."

"That's what I want."

"You won't be disappointed."

"Neither will you," answered the newly minted Jericho Glassman.

# Chapter Fourteen

Aaron bent closer, squinting to see the parchment in the fading daylight. A few precious moments, a few strokes more, and he'd finish for the day. He dipped his quill into the indelible black ink that was made dark and lustrous by iron. Sometimes Aaron used oil of vitriol, which dried glass-like. Not this time. As he finished a *parsha* or section from Deuteronomy with a flourish, a shadow darkened his doorway. Aaron tossed down the quill, satisfied with his good day's work. As usual, he made no mistakes, but could not relish his hard-earned daily success with a glow of accomplishment because someone dared intrude into his sanctum.

It had to be a stranger. Everyone in town knew not to disturb a scribe when he is working. One mistake, one wrong curl of a letter, and everything is destroyed.

"May I help you?" he asked the stranger who was dressed head-to-toe in black. Dressed as he was, the man was not from Tiberias.

"Are you the scribe they talk about?"

Aaron tossed his head back. "You're in the city of scribes, my friend. I'm but one of many."

The man was big. He had a strong voice, but there was an edge of kindness wrapped around it. He thrust his meaty hand toward Aaron, making him flinch.

"I'm looking for the one who wrote this?"

The scribe saw that the parchment leaves were bound by wood on either side. Aaron took the book and beckoned the man to sit on the wooden chair against the cool, stone wall.

"Can I get you some water? It's hot and you've come a long way."

"There is time for water. Did you write this *sefer*?"

Aaron ben Asher, son of Moses be Asher and great-great-grandson of Asher the Elder, the latter having lived during the early part of the ninth century by the Christian reckoning, nodded that he was indeed. "Yes, I wrote that book."

Tiberias was the intellectual center of Palestine, a worthy rival to the great learning centers in Babylonia. The Asher clan was considered not only the greatest scribes in Tiberias, but also the most accomplished in the entire Middle East. Aaron was the last Asher in the family line - he was not married - and achieved the greatest notoriety of all by writing the first grammar book for the Hebrew language. As it was, few spoke Hebrew and fewer still could read it. Arabic was the *lingua franca* of the lands surrounding the Mediterranean. By creating the Hebrew grammar book, Aaron singularly saved the written language from certain extinction.

Aaron offered the book back. Though he had written for nearly twelve hours straight, there was not a smudge of black ink on his fingers.

"Do want to buy more copies?"

Aaron was of medium height and build. Locks of hair were flecked with gray. His pallor reflected long hours spent transcribing any of the twenty-four books of the Bible into individual scrolls. Each book, some small, like the Book of Esther, or the largest like the Five Books of Moses that comprised what is commonly referred to as the Torah, was painstakingly crafted. Each word written perfectly without a misplaced stroke or an errant letter. Should ever a mistake be made, the work had to be discarded according to Jewish law, and a new version started over again.

Maybe the stranger wanted a copy of the rabbinic teachings that were accumulated centuries ago to explain how best to live by God's rules. These interpretations were accepted as law and could never be changed. Then as Jews scattered to the farthest ports of the Mediterranean, long before the birth of Jesus, more rulings were needed on how best to follow God's laws. Together, these great bodies of rabbinic interpretation were combined to form the Talmud.

Inwardly, Aaron was hopeful. The Talmud meant a large commission, which was always welcomed. Alas, this was not it.

"I want you to write me a special book," said the stranger.

"All my books are special."

"This will be your most special. I've been searching for one like you for years, waiting for one like you to come along. Now that I've found you, I need your skills."

"I'm like all the other scribes here, my friend. I'm not so special."

"But you are."

Ever since Aaron adapted the Arabic invention of dots and dashes that served as vowel sounds, also known as massoretic notes, which he inserted under Hebrew letters, the nearly extinct language of the Bible, the ancient tongue of Abraham, Isaac, and Jacob, once again became a living language. Like Latin, Hebrew was destined for the entomologic graveyard until Aaron produced his fete of brilliance.

Jews spoke and read Arabic, not Hebrew. Worse yet, the masses could no longer read Hebrew, which was only read by Rabbis during Sabbath services. The irony! God's Chosen Children, the Jews, had become illiterate to His words spoken to Moses on Mount Sinai.

How did this happen? Hebrew was a consonant language; it had no vowels. There was no way to know where a word began and where it ended in Hebrew. And there was no way to know how to pronounce it either. If that wasn't bad enough, there was no way to know if the words had syllables or which syllables should be accented. The language was a disaster. Homonyms were treacherous to decipher. Since no one could speak it, barely a handful could read it. By the tenth century, the skills needed to read Hebrew were fast vanishing. Soon, no one would be left who could read Hebrew; Jewish prayer would become obsolete. Its legacy was left to the handful of skilled scribes who faithfully copied the ancient texts without forethought that they would ever be read out loud or understood, much the way the medieval monks labored in future years, when few could read their writings.

Enter Aaron ben Asher.

The moment Aaron laid eyes on the notes the Muslims had invented to make reading Arabic easier, Aaron adapted them to Hebrew, writing the first grammar book for Hebrew. If Hebrew was in its death throe, Aaron ben Asher was the hero who thwarted the Grim Reaper of this ancient language.

"Who are you?" Aaron asked, pushing away from his writing table.

"A simple man following God's word." He told Aaron that his name was Jacob al-Kirkisani.

From the way he dressed, in all black, Aaron recognized him as a Karaite. Karaites were a peculiar sect of Jews concentrated in Jerusalem. They evolved from the same thought fabric that spawned Hasidic Jews in the nineteenth century. The Karaites were Biblical extremists who followed the teachings of Anan, a man who lived at the end of the eighth century and into the ninth. Anan believed that if the Hebrew Bible represented all of God's words spoken to man through the ages, then His teachings were meant to be a guide on how man should live. And the Biblical words were to be taken to their literal excess, and were not open for interpretation.

For instance, if God said that no kindling should be carried on the Sabbath, fires went cold. But that was the extent of the dictum for these strange believers from Jerusalem. This was diametrically opposite the rabbinic interpretation handed down since the days of Moses. During the previous two millennia, not to carry kindling on the Sabbath also meant not doing any sort of work, and that the Sabbath day was meant for rest and prayer.

The Karaites would have none of that.

Aaron rose. The wooden chair squeaked on the stone floor. "And why travel from the Holy City to speak to this humble scribe? You've seen my book. I'm glad for that, but what do you want from me? I have more commissions than I can possibly complete."

"To ask that you fulfill God's mandate."

Aaron flicked a finger toward the Torah perched on his venerated writing table first used by his grandfather. "I'm doing that already, my brother. When this is finished, it will be blessed by a rabbi and brought to a new synagogue being in built in Fez. There is no greater mandate than writing a Torah."

While most Jews did not look kindly on the Karaites because they were considered heretics, they were respected for their business acumen. It was the Karaites who controlled the businesses of Jerusalem, not the rabbinates as was typical in the other villages dispersed throughout Palestine. They were shrewd and Aaron was on his guard.

Aaron saw that the man did not know were Fez was located. As such, Kirkisani did not understand the breadth of the Jewish diaspora. Every new community needed its own Torah. A Torah and a cemetery. Two centuries later, Fez would be a journey stop for the greatest Jewish scholar who ever lived, Moses Maimonides. But to the Karaite, none of this was relevant. Only the Lord's words mattered.

"Writing a Torah is nice, but it's no substitute for what God wishes."

*Nice!* Aaron crossed his arms and rocked back on his sandals. He tilted his head, then drew in a deep breath and held it before speaking. This one, like all the others, he thought, is dangerous. A true believer of Anan's words. How not to offend this stranger? But why should Aaron care? He meant nothing to Aaron. Helping accomplish his misguided goal was not any of Aaron's business. He certainly did not feel responsible to help him.

But business *was* business, and that had a certain ring for Aaron ben Asher.

"Am I to assume you know what God's wishes are? How is that possible? Didn't Anan teach not to follow man's interpretation of what the Lord said? And here you are, interpreting what the Lord said."

Unperturbed, the man countered. "The meaning is quite clear. The Bible tells us 'To make God's words available to all His children.' And that is why I've come here. For you to do fulfill the Lord's wishes, to make all of His words available to our people. I want you to write a Bible and insert all the appropriate vowel sounds so anyone can read it."

"I've spent my life making God's words available to all His children.

We follow His teachings. We follow His rules. His laws. What else is there to do?"

Aaron spoke the truth. Jews not only read portions, or *parshut*, from the Torah every Sabbath, but they also read from the Torah on Monday's and Thursdays not to mention praying three times each day in ritual prayer. No, His words *were* available to all His children.

The bearded man waved his hand around the dimly lit room, a room illuminated by the light of a single candle. "I'm afraid you're too much the scribe, Aaron ben Asher. Your knowledge is great, but these walls that contain your skills limit your views. Are you so out of touch so as not to realize that the only ones who can read Hebrew these days are the rabbis and the ones who sing the prayers, the *hazzans*?" Jacob paused for effect, and then pointed upward for effect. "But you know that. You, more than anyone else, knew our language was in trouble. Why else would you transpose vowel sounds to our ancient language?"

"That proves nothing. The words are there for all to read and sing."

Kirkisani tapped the grammar book with his meaty finger. "It proves everything, my learned friend. If you'd only venture away from a synagogue that's filled with your scribes from Tiberias, filled with those who write words for a living, you would witness man after man stumble through the Torah blessings when they're called to the *bimah* for an *aliyah*. They stagger through the words hoping no one catches on that they really can't read. This happens in Jerusalem. In Babylonia. In Alexandria. Think clearly before you turn me away, my scribe. Even if some could read Hebrew, they still can't read the Torah. Will you concede me that point?"

No argument there, that's why Aaron wrote the grammar book in the first place. Even so, the Torah, bereft of vowel sounds, was a distant relic for most.

The Karaite, who never uttered Aaron's name, wheeled and looked through the doorway at a passing donkey bearing fags of wood. He glared at Aaron. "With your *trops* and marks, you singlehandedly saved the Hebrew language from extinction. Do it to the Bible so all can read the Torah and learn its laws and marvel at its wonders."

"The other books, maybe. But every Jew knows that it is sacrilegious to change a single mark in the Torah from what's been transmitted through the years. You know I can't do that."

"I do not. The rabbinic Jews say that you can't, not me." He hunched his shoulders. "But they're just men! Who're they to interpret God's words? To make laws for us? We need to put a stop to this foolishness," said Jacob al-Kirkisani, "otherwise, there'll be no one left to read the Torah. Is that what being a good Jew is all about?"

"There will always be rabbis who can Hebrew, and scribes who can write the words."

"Ben Asher, can you possibly be serious? The future of our people is not with the rabbis, it's with the man who herds the sheep or makes the bricks. It's with the man who pulls fish from the sea or travels east to trade for silk? When they can no longer read Hebrew and they no longer know the words the Lord spoke to Moses and all the other Prophets, then our people will cease to exist as God's chosen. That's when we'll suffer the same fate of all those who have come before us that history has forgotten and future generations will forget what it means to be one of His Chosen People."

Aaron threw up his hands; he had heard enough. "That will never happen."

"What? That our people will lose the meaning of being a Jew? Open your eyes, my friend. It's already happened. Our people are doomed without a Bible they can read."

*As much as he wanted to keep arguing and protesting, Aaron knew the man was right. Tiberias was special. Most there could read Hebrew, but nowhere else. He knew that.*

The Karaite reached underneath his robe and untied a leather pouch. He tossed it onto the table next to the partially written Torah. The thud thundered its worth. "I agree, scribe, that it will never happen because you are going to give us the Bible that God meant us to have."

Aaron considered the commission, not because he wanted to fulfill a Karaite dream, he could care less about their peculiar beliefs that flew in the face of all rabbinic teachings. No, he was about the money, and this money was chirping his name.

Aaron was nimble and did some quick calculations: how much parchment he would need to write an entire Bible that had to come from the hides of kosher animals. He would need extra iron sulfate to add to the olive oil and balsam to make enough permanent ink. He would need to craft more than one new *sargel* from reeds; the *sargel* was necessary to draw faint straight lines on the parchment that only he could see. And he would need to refresh his jar of "writer's sand." Asher liked to refer to his writing implements – the quill, the paper, and the inkwell (known as a *bet deyo*) – as his "things of honor."

Both men were about the moment. Neither considered the implication that this commission could have in the future. It was beyond both of their grasps. What was critical was whether or not Aaron would forsake rabbinical dicta and succumb to the allure of money.

Aaron picked up the purse. He felt its heft.

"There's not enough here. If you want me to write your book, you have to do better."

Al-Kirksani reached under his robe and pulled out a second purse of equal weight. "This is all I have."

Aaron studied Kirkisani. If the man looked away, there was more money to be had. A fairer commission. But the Karaite met his gaze and shrugged. "There is no more."

"Then you will get your Bible."

# Chapter Fifteen

For the next hour, she spoke without pause. And, for the first time in his life, Arnold Ford, orator extraordinaire, a man who captured the attention of his minions over the years, sat transfixed by a story spun by a black, Jewish detective who read and understood Hebrew.

And what she knew about him simply amazed.

"What do you know about Marcus Garvey?" she asked.

"That he was one of the first, if not the first, black man to give African Americans a reason to believe in themselves. A reason to hold their heads up high." Ford thought for a moment. "If I'm not mistaken, Marcus Garvey may have even been the man who coined the phrase, 'Black is Beautiful.' But I'm not certain of that."

"He's the one. And he did so much more. In 1917, Garvey founded the New York chapter of the Universal Negro Improvement Association. The only reason the local ministers let their parishioners go to these so-called Liberty Halls, was that Garvey preached solidarity for the blacks. He urged them to unite and stick together as one people."

"Like the Jews."

"It wasn't the same. After the Civil War, the blacks here had to first develop their own identity." She continued. "Garvey chastised black mothers for letting their children play with white dolls. He was the person who not only told blacks that they should work for themselves, but he created businesses for them. Grocery stores. Laundries. Truck services, too. Garvey said that if the black man didn't pick himself up economically, he would never be equal to the white man, no matter how equal he might ever feel inside himself. It was all about money and self-esteem, and those translated into equality."

Cardinal Ford raised his hand for LeShana to pause. He opened the well-worn Bible on his desk and flipped the pages until he found what he was looking for. "Psalm 68:31: 'Princes shall come out of Egypt: Ethiopia shall soon stretch forth her hands unto God.' That was the basis of his 'Back to Africa' movement."

A smile cracked across her lips. "So you do know about him, Your Eminence."

He nodded without countering.

LeShana continued her tale. "Garvey needed to give purpose to his followers. His organization took as its motto, *One God! One Aim! One Destiny!* That destiny was raising the black man's sense of self and pride to the equal of the white man. He did it with good old-fashion preaching and through black-owned enterprises. And he was careful not to compete with the ministers who were only too happy to send their congregants to him as long as he stayed away from anything that smacked of religion. To his credit, he was able to navigate those tricky waters."

"I understand Garvey's importance to our black conscience. But why tell me all of this. You were supposed to tell me things I didn't know about myself? What does Garvey have to do with me? He may have been a religious man, but like you just said, the UNIA was not a church. He didn't preach the gospel; he left that for the ministers in the local parishes. I'm not seeing the parallels here."

LeShana turned playful. "You needed to understand Garvey in the context of the times. While Garvey did his speechifying, his congregants were itching to sing their praises and hallelujahs."

"Isn't that a bit stereotypical."

She frowned. "C'mon, Cardinal Ford, you know that's what black folks do, they sing. They sing praises to the Lord all the time. They even sing here in St. Patrick's."

"Okay. Fine. I get it. I still don't see where this is going."

A twinge of strain crept across Ford's face. She had strung this out as long as she dared. She wiggled straight in the chair and leaned forward. "Where I'm going with this that those folks at the Liberty Halls needed their music. M-U-S-I-C." She spelled out each letter. "Does this ring any *bells* for you? Pardon the pun."

The power of his gaze reprimanded; she needed to end the game she was playing. And yet she wasn't ready to stop toying with him. "The UNIA had a music director. He was a *very* special man."

"I'm sure that he was very special," said Ford. "Wasn't this about the time that the Black National Anthem was written? Is that where you are going with this M-U-S-I-C stuff?"

"But you don't know who wrote it, do ya?" She pursed her lips in victory, which was akin to winning Trivial Pursuit or getting checkmate against a master of the game.

Ford shook his head. "Haven't a clue. Should I know his name?"

"How're your pipes?"

Ford's eyes widened. "Are you asking me if I can sing?"

"That's exactly what I'm asking, Your Eminence."

"I've been known to tickle the ivories in my day. Can't say that I could sing much, but I could certainly bang out a tune or two on the piano." A chime clanged somewhere in the church. Ford glanced in the direction of the bell. "A sharp."

"Excuse me?"

"I do that often. Hear a note and can tell what it is."

She marveled. "Wish I had perfect pitch."

He waved it off. "It's nothing. Let's get back to that music director. What does this have to do with me?"

"That music director for the UNIA. Garvey's handpicked choice to write the Black National Anthem..."

"What about him?"

She did an impromptu drum roll on his desk.

"His name was Arnold Ford."

That got the Cardinal's attention.

# Chapter Sixteen

ericho Glassman wiped the dust off his mirror-coated sunglasses. The sun glared white-hot, causing pain in his eyes during the few moments it took to clean them. Glasses back on, Jericho blew on a metal whistle and waved an iridescent orange baton the way airplanes are guided to the gate, only this was not about airplanes. Jericho herded retreating tanks back to Israel after years of border fights - both minor skirmishes and major battles.

Jericho turned to the soldier next to him. "I don't know what they're thinking. Unilateral withdrawal. They're going to be sorry they ever abandoned these positions. Here, we can defend our country. Giving up this strategic advantage is suicide." Jericho's unit was assigned to marshal the evacuation out of southern Lebanon once Israel had briefed world leaders that it was ending its twenty-two year occupation.

The soldier tugged on the blue bandana protecting his mouth and nose from the dust kicked up by the heavy lumbering tanks.

"This is the Army. We don't question, we do. Leave the thinking to the gray heads back in Jerusalem. Besides, it's good to bring our soldiers home. If nothing else, that should make you happy."

"What do you mean?" Jericho stepped back as an errant tank drew too close.

His comrade continued. "Jericho, aren't you the one who can't wait to get posted in the south? Now that we no longer need to protect this border to the same degree, we can turn our attention to Arafat and his goons. You've been itching to be assigned there ever since I know you."

"I'm also the one who can't stand the way this government keeps ceding land and opportunities back to the Arabs. We can't count on any other country in the world to protect us. You know that. Every Israeli knows that. No matter how good the Americans have been to us in the past, we can't count on them always being there. We've been lucky that every US President has supported us through the years. But one day, our luck will run out and there'll be one who will hang us out to dry."

"I can't see that day ever coming," said his fellow soldier.

"Don't be a fool. The Americans have to walk a fine line between standing up to the rest of the world in support of Israel and not offending the leaders of the countries who supply them with oil or buy their arms. Theirs is a two-edged foreign policy. The minute Jews stop giving money to *both* of their parties, Israel loses."

"Do you really believe that?"

Jericho answered. "In the end, it's us. Always us. To give up a defensible position is placing one foot in the grave for this country. I will never allow that to happen."

His friend sneered. "And you plan to protect our country all by yourself. That's a good one."

"Don't laugh. You don't know me that well. I'm going to make certain nothing ever happens to Israel."

His friend looked at him the way one stares at a caged lion with both fear and respect, even though you know nothing is going to change the circumstances at that moment.

His friend continued, "Well I'm glad we're pulling out. Our missile defense system is so accurate now that we could hit a shekel on top of a roof. That's the reason we can pull out and Hezbollah knows it. They're not going to lob rockets into our kibbutzim across the Lebanese border anymore."

*But not Hamas, thought Jericho. They still have rockets, and they will continue to fire them at our people.*

Jericho grew quiet. Images of his father filled his head. It saddened him that they were less crisp then they were in those first years after the suicide bombers sneaked into their village and snuffed out ten innocent lives. He tried to picture his father's smile, to hear his voice, but it was more difficult. He couldn't remember his mother at all. She had died when he was so young.

He mechanically guided the tanks along the evacuation route without seeing them. The sonic booms of Israeli Air Force planes above provided the necessary reminder to Hezbollah that Israel had the technology and the will to return at any time.

But Jericho wasn't in the moment. He was transported back to Ashdod, planted in front of his father's tool shed. Curls of smoke wafting upward. His father's body contorted; his head severed three-fourths from his neck, floating in a pool of black congealed blood. One leg was extended backward, poised to hurdle a fence, the other one missing. He remembered turning his head. There, against the back wall, he saw a swarm of flies zeroing in on the dismembered leg.

Hamas. He hated Hamas for continuing to fight, to promote chaos any way it could to keep the spark of hope alive for their people. Was it a spark of hope or a flame of perpetual Hell that served to remind the refugees that they were banished into a permanent exile?

Didn't Hamas know they were doomed to fail?

Why continue their *jihad*? What did they hope to accomplish?

His comrade jerked his arm. "That's the last of them." But instead of returning to his platoon, Jericho marched into the temporary headquarters.

"I was told that after the evacuation has been completed, I could be assigned to Special Forces. It's completed."

His commander peered at Jericho from above gold-rimmed glasses, then glanced at his watch.

"It's been over less than two minutes. Now remind me, again, Corporal Glassman, why it is that you want to transfer out of this unit?"

"I need to be closer to Gaza."

"You mean closer to the action." He leaned back in his chair and sized up Jericho. "I remember you. I've read your file. You're the one who wants to be transferred to a combat unit. You're the last person I want to send to the south."

"If you looked into my files, you would know that I finished first in my class in almost everything. And I qualified as a marksman, too."

"Look, Glassman. A few red flags popped up along the way."

He stood taller, turning his head a degree to the left. "I don't understand."

"You *were* tops in your class, but your instructors felt you had a chip on your shoulder. That you're still angry about your father's death. We can't have someone like you in key places. That's why you've never gotten the assignments you've requested."

"I admit I was angry back then, sir, but not anymore. I've channeled my energies into being the best soldier I can be. Send me south. Give me an assignment. You'll see. I'll make you proud."

# Chapter Seventeen

Zakkarhia ibn Mohammed held the match out for Walid. The two stopped to admire the gleaming white minaret that was all that remained of the Manarah Mosque. Dusk would soon creep over the ancient structure. For the moment, the sky was a darkening sea of blue, speckled with greying tufts of white. A bird spiraled into the water for a fish.

The two were standing to the windowless side of the brown-bricked court of justice that faced the minaret so that those who knelt in prayer did so without prying eyes. Directly in front of them was a garage-sized storage house, and beyond that, the great minaret. There were eighty-six steps to scale the top of the minaret. Roped off now, it offered a bird's eye view of the old part of the city built in a defunct volcanic crater. But no muezzin had graced its steps for centuries. Now it was a fixture for those intrepid few who dared vacation in Yemen and gaze at the Arabic version of the leaning tower of Pisa.

"Have you checked the weight?" asked Walid. He drew in deep and hard, filling his lungs with the burning smoke. He held it for an extra beat and then exhaled a steady stream out of his nostrils. He picked at tobacco bits stuck between his nicotine-stained teeth, spitting them out without regard for Zakkarhia.

"We can't afford to let the same thing happen when those bumbling idiots overloaded the boat last time," Walid said.

Walid referred to the aborted attempt to bomb the USS *The Sullivans* on January 3, 2000 that was part of a group of events that would be labeled as the "Millennium Plot Attacks." In addition to that mishap, plans had been set in motion to bomb four sites in Jordan: the booked Radisson hotel in Amman, Mount Nebo where Moses could see the Promised land, a Christian holy site, and the spot where John the Baptist allegedly baptized Jesus in the Jordan River. All four plots were foiled by keen Jordanian intelligence that rounded up twenty-eight terrorists once phone chatter indicated, "The time for training is over." The last Millennium target was a bombing plot of LAX airport. This, too, was thwarted by good enemy surveillance and bad strokes of luck. Having all six Millennium targets thwarted, sleeper cells planted around the world continued to wait patiently for their next opportunity.

Tomorrow was the next one.

"Zarqawi was out of the loop on this one," answered Zakkarhia, who had now matured into an accomplished instrument of terror.

"So you're assuring me that all is ready?" Walid stated it as a fact, not a question. Walid was the same Walid Muhammad bin Attash who masterminded the embassy bombings in Kenya and Tanzania two years earlier. And as soon as tomorrow's mission succeeded, he would begin interviewing candidates for al Qaeda's next attack that could be anywhere in the world.

"Checked and double-checked. My only regret is that I'm not on the boat with them."

Walid looped his hand through Zakkarhia's arm. "No, my friend, it's not your time to revel with the virgins. We have great plans for you."

Zakkarhia beamed inside, not because he would dodge death the next morning, but his calling for the holy *haj* against the infidel was greater than even he had dared to dream.

◆　◆　◆

The next day was clear and dry. Zakkarhia and Walid embraced the two Mujahedeen who were destined for Paradise in a matter of minutes. Walid kissed both men and uttered words of encouragement.

"Let those who sell their life of this world by fighting for Allah, be victorious and receive the rewards of Paradise.' May you die a thousand deaths only to return to this world and die again for Allah."

With streams of joy tearing down their pockmarked faces, the men boarded the boat as Zakkarhia untied the mooring rope.

Walid rubbed the stump of his amputated leg. He whispered to the side. "The boat sits low in the water."

"The weight's fine," said Zakkarhia. "I checked and rechecked it myself, loading it with the same weight in fish. We're good this time. No mistakes."

"After so many recent defeats, we need this victory."

Zakkarhia hefted the Kiowa highlander binoculars and followed their wake.

He had never been so proud as the boat chugged toward its target.

He focused on the shaped charges lashed to the hull of the boat; no attempt was made to camouflage them.

He saw his men wave to the sailors on board; he saw the sailors wave back.

Then the moment of impact, the explosive-laden boat plowed into the side of the destroyer.

The blast erupted in a sonic bang. Tongues of flames lapped the structure in all directions. Plumes of black smoke spiraled skyward. Metal melted. A mini tsunami rolled back toward shore.

The blast ripped a hole in the ship's galley.

It was lunchtime.

Seventeen sailors were killed, and thirty-nine more were severely injured or burned.

Later that day, in a video released on the Internet, Osama bin Laden claimed responsibility, boasting that the attack on the USS *Cole* was little more than a warning shot over the bow. The next attack, and he promised there would be more, would bring his enemies to their knees. He made his claims with a sense of impunity. The West was weak, without conviction. After all, hadn't President Bill Clinton had an opportunity to kill him and passed it up? And he, Osama bin Laden, would wage his battles with a glacial patience that was necessary to win this war, even if it stretched to eternity.

Zakkarhia lit a cigarette and handed it to Walid, and then lit one for himself.

The two slinked into a taverna and ordered a bottle of scotch. Victory needed to be toasted, regardless of rules that prohibited drinking alcohol.

"This is a good day," said Zakkarhia. "A very good day."

"It is the first of many more," Walid said, putting the amber firewater to his lips, inwardly pleased to rid himself and the jihad of the curse of the foiled Millennium Plots.

"What's next?" asked Zakkarhia.

Walid put down his glass, and stepped back, studying Zakkarhia. "Aren't we the impatient one?"

"I want to kill as many of the infidels as possible. In my mind, every second wasted is a second that I could be killing one of them."

"You will get your chances. Remember," Walid smashed his hands together, "the louder the boom, the greater their casualties."

Zakkarhia tossed back another. His throat burned, he was not used to drinking alcohol. "It will not be soon enough." Then he leaned closer. "How big will the next one be?"

Walid dropped his meaty hand on Zakkarhia's shoulder.

"This was nothing, my friend. Simply a test to see how ready they are for us." He bared a mouthful of broken teeth. "And they weren't ready at all, were they? Our enemy has grown fat on decadence; their brains are dull. They will not connect this to anything else. They'll think it a random event, like the others. We can count on the fact that each time we strike they will not be ready, that it will be unexpected. That's why we'll win this war."

"There has to come a day when they will catch on," said Zakkarhia, downing another shot.

"By then, it will be too late. May Allah be praised."

"May Allah be praised."

# Chapter Eighteen

A gavel cracked and all heads whipped to the front of the musty synagogue that was swathed with the honey hues from a rising sun. As with children fearing a stern teacher, all fell silent.

The benches were filled with townsmen all waiting for the judge to speak.

Pinchas ben Itzhak HaNagid, Tiberias's highest judge, stretched his hands upwards, as if to connect with God, not for strength but to grasp a sliver of wisdom, because that's what the judge needed at that moment: wisdom. He was about to embark on a journey fraught with obstacles and roadblocks, the likes of which he had never before encountered.

To look at Pinchas ben Itzhak HaNagid was to see an ordinary man. His parchment-paper skin, latticed with tiny blue veins, stretched across angular facial bones. He had small, sunken eyes hollowed by dark circles, hairs that sprouted from his ear rims, a sparse brow and even sparser silvering hair, at least what little was left of it. He was narrow of frame, but for all his physical shortcomings, his voice commanded.

When points of law were raised, his sallow color blossomed into a rose flush and his beady eyes bulged. When this happened, his soft voice rose into a clear, crisp pitch, his wisdom and sometime wit commanding respect.

The all-consuming issue? Working day and night, it had taken Aaron ben Asher over a year to complete the Karaite's bidding. He transcribed all twenty-four books of the Bible without a mistake; each word annotated with the dots and dashes above and below the Hebrew letters that would make for easy reading. He bound the massive tome, both front and back, with wooden covers that would protect the pages from damage or from being lost.

The Karaite would be pleased, thought Aaron. No one else could have performed such a task, and so quickly, too. Perhaps, before Aaron handed it over, he would ask for an extra commission for a job well done. *Why not? It can't do any harm to ask.*

An extra commission was not to be.

The day Aaron lay down his pen down and stretched his legs in the town square, eager to share his accomplishment with a fellow scribe, was the same day Aaron was ordered to stand trial for a *herem* before the high court. No one was certain who charged Aaron with heresy, but in time, Aaron would sense it was a jealous copyist, whose skills were mediocre compared to Aaron ben Asher's. Jealousy, it seems, trumped objectivity.

Who charged him with a crime was not the immediate issue. Avoiding banishment from the community was. The end result of a *herem* was that found guilty, Aaron had to leave Tiberias for good. This was a fate one didn't wish on one's enemies, and yet this is just what a fellow scribe hoped would befall Aaron.

Throughout their history, there had never been an excommunication in Tiberias. While all were concerned with the outcome of this trial, scribes had the most to lose. None wanted to live in fear that taking a commission to transcribe a work, any work, could result in banishment. After all, they were copyists, not criminals.

Sides were taken in a flash.

There were those that supported Aaron for putting the massoretic notes to the Bible, even when he applied them to the Torah, so that every word would be easier to read and pronounce. Some held more traditional values. They could care less what Aaron did with most of the Bible's books. But tampering with the sacred books of Genesis, Exodus, Leviticus, Deuteronomy, and Numbers was flat out heresy. There was no margin for interpretation here. Certainly the claims made by the

Karaites that they were fulfilling God's wishes to spread His words held no sway with them.

Laws were reviewed. There were countless talks in hushed whispers. Rabbis from nearby towns were consulted. Talmudic rulings were studied. It fell onto the sloped shoulders of Judge Pinchas HaNagid to create an appropriate forum to conduct the *herem*. It had been so long since there had been a *herem* anywhere in Palestine that no guidelines existed on how to conduct one.

Satisfied that all was ready, Judge HaNagid banged his gavel.

"This *herem* shall now begin. Will the accused take his place to bear witness on all that occurs here." He pointed with the gavel for Aaron to sit in the chair that faced the courtroom; the custom forced the accused to remain in front of those present for the entire proceeding.

The Judge was about to describe the ground rules of the *herem* when a white spectre floated down the center aisle of the synagogue.

Shrieks, oohs and ahs greeted the stranger; jaws dropped but uttered no sounds. Even the judge was speechless.

"It's Saadia Gaon," whispered one. "He struts like he owns the place."

"If this were Rome, he'd be the Pope," answered his friend.

"Rome is nothing anymore. The Saracens overran it and jailed Leo X. Now there's a pretender claiming to be the Pope," said another. "They're adrift. As far as I'm concerned, Saadia Gaon is as mighty as any, except maybe Abdullah al-Mahdi Billah."

"No one is as powerful as the Fatimid ruler." Abdullah al-Mahdi Billah was the first caliph of the Fatimid Dynasty who ruled all the North African and Middle Eastern lands that bordered the Mediterranean.

"Even so, no one is as smart as Saadia Gaon."

The unexpected appearance of the greatest scholar of the day baffled those present. The synagogue became a beehive of speculation. The *Gaon*, as Saadia was known, was dressed in a siglaton made of the finest Chinese silk. It was tangerine in color, with a burnt almond border. A white cloak draped around his broad shoulders which, in turn, was covered by a white shawl. The shawl was inscribed with

Arabic lettering in gold thread. It read, "May the Lord Bless You." And as he flounced before riveted eyes, Saadia fingered the fringes dangling from the four corners of the ritual shawl, a daily reminder of the Lord's commandments that was also a not-too-subtle reminder of why he was marching into these proceedings.

Saadia Gaon was born the son of a laborer in the Faium district in Egypt in 882 AD, which was near the outskirts of Fostat. In his early twenties, already a noted scholar, Saadia left his homeland and taught in Aleppo before being picked as the *Gaon*, the chief scholar of the Sura Academy in Bagdad. Though he had a humble start, he adapted the mantle as the highest authority in the Jewish world with ease. This was no small task.

Saadia was, indeed, the *de facto* Pope of the Jews. Given that the Jews owned no country or army to match the might and reach of the Arabs who ruled the Middle East, nor did Jews have a structure in place like the evolving Catholic Church had developed over the last few hundred years, the *Gaon* was the final world on how Jews lived their lives. There was no one else to turn to for settling disputes.

These rulings became necessary ever since that fateful day, August 10th, 70 AD, the 9th of *Ab* in the Hebrew calendar, when Emperor Titus burned the rebuilt center of Jewish worship, commonly known as the Second Temple, with only a single wall – the Wailing Wall – presently remaining as a testament to that once great edifice. Was it divine irony that previously on the 9th of *Ab*, in 586 B.C., Nebuchadnezzar destroyed the First Temple?

As a result of no longer having a house of worship, the Jews needed guidance as to how to follow the Lord's commandments and live pious lives from the distant shores of the Mediterranean to the four corners of the former Roman Empire to the villages along the silk trade to the ports in Yemen to as far away as China. The Gaon helped decide these matters and more.

"To what do we owe this great honor, Joseph Al Faiymi?" asked the judge using the *Gaon's* familiar name. "We all applaud your heroic translation of the Bible into Arabic which permitted the Jews around the world to be able to read the sacred words again. This feat will mark your place in history." He motioned to the assemblage. "But I must confess that your presence in our humble synagogue is a surprise."

A murmur of agreement coated everyone's lips; everyone's except the *Gaon's*.

Saadia peacocked down the aisle and stood in the front of the assemblage, next to an empty seat. Unlike most scholars bent and rounded from reading and studying from dawn to dusk, Saadia stood tall, with full shoulders that topped off a round, muscular barrel chest. His piercing blue eyes made men squirm and caused them to turn from his gaze, a gaze that washed them with the sense of guilt, a gaze that made innocents feel guilty though they were certain they had done nothing wrong. His mere look caused self-doubt.

Saadia's voice was rich in timbre. More to the point, it was full-bodied and polished and so strong that when he spoke, crystalline words darted from his tongue like biting sand in a swirling storm. The *Gaon's* words tattooed all in range.

"The only surprise," said Saadia with the slightest nod to the left and then the right, insuring that the ruby broach pinned to his regal turban sparkled from the light of the oil-burning lamps, "would be if I had not witnessed this proceeding with my own eyes. Surely you must be aware of my feelings on the subject."

The judge coughed, struggling to answer without incurring the *Gaon's* wrath. "We are all aware of your feelings about the founder of the Karaites, as the followers of Anan are known now. You wrote about the refutation of Anan's teachings fifteen years ago. Surely such a trivial…"

Saadia glared the judge to be silent. He scanned the faces of those who dared look back, locking eyes one-by-one. Deliberate, he missed no one. He strode to the rear to engage those cowering down hoping to avoid his gaze.

He approached the judge. "Are memories so short as to have forgotten that I stopped Ben Meir, the Karaite who tried to change the calendar so *they*," he hissed so there was no mistaking that he meant the Karaites, "could pick when we celebrate our holidays? You, Pinchas ben Itzhak HaNagid, and all the other judges were going to let them get away with that. I couldn't let that happen. I, alone, stood up to *them*... and prevented *that* debacle."

*The inference was clear. This herem was already a debacle in the eyes of the Gaon.*

The sum and substance of what Saadia implied was not lost on any present. He stood up to the Karaites. He preserved honored traditions. As *Gaon* he deflected challenges to Jewish law, cherished laws that enabled Jews to remain Jews no matter where they lived. Laws handed to Moses from God. Laws that prepared for the day the Messiah would return and create heaven on earth, when peace would rule the world and all would be forgiven for their transgressions.

Pinchas bowed, his head touched the tabletop. "We acknowledge your fierce dedication to our laws."

"Which is why I am here today. To make certain this fiasco ends according to the Lord's wishes." His voice softened; he turned toward the others. "After all, we are all rabbinates, are we not? Our traditions must never change. Not ever."

"Saadia, we're convened here on a single complaint, one made by another scribe, no less. While it's trivial, as *nagid* I am duty-bound to investigate the charge. I assure you that there's no substance to it."

The *Gaon* jerked his arms to the domed wooden roof. "How can you say there's no substance to it? Either ben Asher annotated the Torah or he didn't; there's no greater sin in all of our laws than changing even a single flourish of one letter. Let me see the book and I'll decide for myself."

No one spoke; no one moved. Saadia plumbed the judge's face, then Aaron's. He strutted up to Aaron. "Where's this book you've written. I want to see it."

Aaron shrugged. "I don't have it, Your Excellency. I was paid a commission and delivered it to my patron when it was completed."

"You knew this would happen."

Aaron arched his back, wanting to stand, but if he did, he'd bump into the Gaon. "You accuse me of expecting this *herem*? You couldn't be more wrong. I was asked to write a book, I wrote the book. I did nothing wrong. For me, a book is a book."

"That's for me to judge."

Now, for the first time in more than a year, with the commission completed, Aaron considered the man who had made the strange request that caused this *herem*. He thought how peculiar it was to annotate the entire Bible. Now that he had, in a curious way, Aaron related more to the Karaite, Jacob al-Kirkisani, than to his own neighbors and those he called *friends*. He pushed his chair back and stood. Though he was not as tall as Saadia Gaon, he was strengthened by the principle at stake.

"Who are you to interpret what God wants or doesn't want? For that matter," Aaron quick-scanned the synagogue, gathering power from nods of affirmation, "how can any of us truly know what God wants about anything? You're a man just like any of us." Aaron swirled, his gesture encompassing all present. "Are you better than us? Are you a prophet? Is that how you know what God wants?"

Saadia's nostrils flared, veins bulged in his neck. "This is blasphemy." He stood to his full measure, making eye contact with many; most turned away.

"On the contrary," answered Aaron, "this is a truth that must be exposed. We're a people of the book, with a long and storied history. Prophets claim they spoke to God, they gave us rules to live by, directions from God. But where are these prophets today? How come none step forth and tell us how to live? What to do? How come God doesn't restore us to our rightful place as rulers of this land? Is that why you've come here, Saadia Gaon, to lead us in a revolt?"

A murmur of approval buzzed from many.

Saadia fronted the group. "Do you hear this man? His nonsense? God will restore us as rulers of our land when He says the time is ripe."

Aaron tilted his head and leaned into Saadia. "And how do you know this?"

"Because I do."

"When the Messiah comes, is that?" said Aaron, losing control of the contempt that filled his mind. If he hated one thing in life, it was hypocrisy.

"We *will* regain the ownership of our lands," answered Saadia. "Regardless of when that happens, it will be God's will and not before. And as far as fulfilling the prophecy of the Messiah, He *is* on his way. God has promised."

"And you know this the way Christians wait for Jesus to return?"

"I know this because it is written."

Aaron wheeled and faced the assemblage. Emboldened, he said in a louder voice, "And you take the written word literally, the same as the Karaites. Perhaps *you* are one of them." The crowd erupted in laughter; Saadia stamped his foot for silence.

Saadia Gaon had met his match. This was not turning out the way he expected. He thought his mere presence at this *herem* would speed up the trial to a swift and inevitable result. He did not expect such insolence.

Saadia ignored Aaron, lowered his voice, and slumped just enough to appear humble, less arrogant yet still commanding.

"Aaron ben-Asher is a clever man who almost got away with the world's greatest sin, breaking the fundamental law we've followed for two millennia. Don't let that happen." He extended an outstretched arm toward Aaron and pointed an accusing finger. "He's a master with words. You all know that I'm the leader and interpreter for rabbinic law. Yet for all we know the Karaite in this synagogue may be Aaron ben Asher."

The room grew silent.

Saadia continued. "Such rumors have existed since the time of his grandfather, Asher the Elder. Do I need to remind any of you that this grandfather lived at the time of Anan? That they shared a cell next to each other? How simple would it have been for his grandfather to embrace the ways of the Karaites?"

No one spoke; all were afraid to utter a word.

The judge had long since slinked away from his chair, tucked behind a column, listening. He prayed this would end with Saadia storming out and letting him and the Tiberians getting on with the trial.

Saadia continued. "Regardless of the outcome of this *herem*, the book Aaron be Asher has written will be destroyed. Who will go with me to Jerusalem to find this Karaite and do God's bidding?"

There was a throb of silence, and then the timid judge stepped forward.

"Your Excellency, even if we are able to take this book away from the Karaite, how can we destroy it when the Lord's name is written in it thousands of times? Our laws forbid destroying any book that mentions God."

"This is not any book, this is blasphemy. It must be burned," roared Saadia Gaon.

Little did he know how prophetic his words were.

# Chapter Nineteen

ardinal Ford's shoulders dropped; he put both hands on his desk, palms down, and leaned forward, his back straight. His words were measured. "Let me understand this. This same Arnold Ford in New York, working alongside Marcus Garvey, was my father in Ethiopia?"

LeShana tilted her head in assent. It was clear now that his missionary parents who adopted Ford had never told him about his father. They had to be aware of who his parents were, thought LeShana. How else would they have given the child his name? They could have easily given the boy their surname. But no, they wanted him to have a connection to his biological parents, no matter how remote and vague it would be. What else had they learned about the infant baby's family? Their history? Maybe nothing else.

*From Ford's point of view, LeShana waltzes into his life as the connector of his past with his present life. Was she the messenger of some spiritual journey? Did a Divine hand, somehow, guide her?*

"Was Ford a well-known musician?"

"For a reason I don't understand, you Eminence, your father never received the notoriety he deserved. For starters, Garvey overshadowed him. Garvey not only had a Napoleonic stature, he played the part to the hilt. If you can believe it, he paraded around in a gold-braided uniform. I've seen pictures of Garvey replete with a tri-cornered hat. His was an ego that could not have been upstaged by anyone. By the time things turned bad for Garvey, your father had drifted off in a totally different direction."

"Didn't J. Edgar Hoover dirty his hands in this, somehow?"

"I'm impressed that you know even that much. As for J. Edgar, Garvey was a threat to that obsessed SOB cross-dresser."

She shot her hand over her lips. "Sorry, you Excellency."

He waved it away and urged her to continue.

"Garvey made the government nervous. He was too far to the left compared to W.E.B. DuBois. DuBois's revolution would come about through education. From the *Talented Tenth*, as DuBois called them. Educated blacks didn't threaten."

"DuBois fostered the goal of creating hundreds and then thousands of Ivy-league trained lawyers and doctors and engineers," added the Cardinal.

"Exactly," she said. "Hoover could live with a nouveau class of professionals, even if they were black. But when Garvey bought mothballed battleships left over from the Great War and created the Black Star Shipping Lines, that's when the black leader went too far for the paranoid F.B.I. head. Can you believe Hoover? He couldn't tolerate the fact that blacks could stand on their own two feet and make a buck shipping bananas. As far as Hoover was concerned, a successful black business threatened the very fabric of white society."

"How did J. Edgar bring Garvey down?"

"By a trumped up mail fraud charge. Garvey's crime was that he sold shares in five-dollar increments to raise enough money to buy the rusted ships that no one else wanted. As soon has he launched the company, J. Edgar railroaded Garvey and got him convicted. Garvey was sent to jail for five years."

Ford winced knowing Garvey was imprisoned for no reason other than another man's paranoia. "When he was released, did Garvey pick up where he left off?"

Le Shana shook her head. "When Garvey got out, Hoover had him deported. Garvey spent his remaining years in ignominy, first in Jamaica and then in London. He died just before the US entered the war in 1940, a broken man."

Ford made the sign of the cross and whispered a prayer for Garvey's soul. He looked up. "And my father? You said he took a different path."

"Indeed he did. It was a few years earlier before Garvey was arrested."

Ford wrinkled his brow. "How much more bizarre can this story get?"

"How much time do you have?"

# Chapter Twenty

T hunderous applause bounced off of the gold-gilded walls and dripped from the velvet drapes behind the rotund speaker. The speaker was fireplug-stocky, with a broad grin that masked a bushel of worries. There was no mistake about his message: Black is beautiful. Saying this when blacks could not drink from the same water fountains as whites or use the same bathrooms was considered sacrilege by most.

Sprinkled among the mostly black audience were navy blue-suited fraternity brothers. Their affiliation represented no Greek letters, though their handshake often took place behind closed doors. These were agents of J. Edgar Hoover, head of the vaunted Federal Bureau of Investigation. And did Marcus Garvey worry that he saw them from the mahogany lectern? Not in the slightest. He was used to seeing them in the back of rooms, on street corners, even close to his brick stoop when he trudged home late at night and struggled to climb the grey slate steps.

Why Hoover would waste the precious time of his overworked minions to hang around Garvey and at the back of his meetings was perplexing. There was nothing Garvey ever said, or would say, that jeopardized the status quo for the whites. Garvey was about dignity and taking care of oneself. Self-reliance. Independence. Mom and apple pie.

"Asia is for the Asians, my friends. Europe is for the Europeans. And Africa is for the blacks. Africa belongs to us," Garvey said in a loud, clear, melliferous voice. Cheers erupted. Anywhere else, especially in the Deep South, this would be heresy coming from a black man's mouth. But here in New York, here in Liberty Hall, here in front of members of the Garvey-founded UNIA – the Universal Negro Improvement Association – with its thousands of chapters and more than twenty-two million members, this was what they came to hear. This is what they wanted to believe. And he was the man who gave them hope.

When his speech ended, his musical director of the UNIA choir, Arnold Ford, greeted Garvey. "That was righteous, Marcus. A wonderful talk. More and more new members are signing up every day."

Marcus Garvey tilted his head as Nancy Paris walked past. Nancy was the main singer for the choir. "They'll be singing your song in a moment." Ford started to say something and then stopped. It would have to wait. He had an audience waiting.

Ford strode to the stage, snatched the baton and rapped the metal music stand. With a flare, he launched the orchestra into "Ethiopia," which speaks of peaceful days before cruel slave boats plied the dangerous waters snatching and shackling bewildered natives. The song stressed pride. The song praised Ethiopia as their natural homeland. "Ethiopia shall soon stretch out her hand to God (Psalm 68:3)." Garvey interpreted this to apply to his efforts. Their efforts.

And while the words did not particularly threaten, they threatened every ruler of every African colony plus ever country run by whites.

When it came to feeling threatened, add J. Edgar Hoover's United States of America to that list.

◆　◆　◆

Later that night, when the adrenaline floodgates simmered to a slow trickle, when the crowds receded and the lights dimmed, Garvey and Ford eased their way to The Hoofers Club. It was a special night. Pried away from the pool tables he so famously loved, Bojangles Bill Robinson was making a rare appearance. The small room was located in the back of a basement gambling club formally called The Comedy Club run by the proprietor, Lonnie Hicks. In one corner, sat Nora Zeale Hurston in animated talk with a fledgling poet, Langston Hughes. In another, Duke Ellington took a night off from performing at the Savoy.

"There's something that's been a plague on my heart," Ford said after the waitress served both of them sugary iced tea; the tall glasses, filled with ice chips, sweated from the humid air. Sprigs of mint clung to the glass rim.

Large fans sliced through the thick summery air to little avail.

Garvey took a long swallow. "You're not telling me anything I don't know. I've seen it in your eyes."

Ford sat taller. "You knew?"

"Not exactly," said Ford. "But it's hard not to notice you're troubled." He pointed to the nearby empty stage, its spotlights being adjusted in readiness for Mr. Bojangles's performance. "Is it time to spread your wings? Is that it? Do you want to break out and perform? Maybe at the Savoy or the Cotton Club? You're a mighty fine composer, Arnold, and I know you can play all those instruments better than any musician alive."

It was no secret that Arnold Ford was a talented musician. He had mastered seventeen different instruments and had written the Universal Ethiopian Hymnal. His music would endure.

Ford shook his head. "Local ministers and pastors let their people come to you because you don't preach religion. You're not competition to them."

"And it's got to stay that way. We've got enough mountains to climb teaching our brethren about running businesses and making black dolls and learning to stand on their own two feet. I don't like J. Edgar's goons showing up at every single meeting. I know that he thinks we're gonna raise a black-led revolution in this country, and that he and all the other whiteys in this country won't be safe."

"Let him think what he wants. What can he do to you?" Ford said, taking another sip of tea.

"No black man is safe in this country, never was. But they won't stop me. We've come too far to back down. I can take whatever they dish out." Garvey put his brawny hand on Ford's arm. "Now tell me, friend, what's troubling you?"

Ford swallowed. "You're not going to like this, Marcus."

"Til I know what it is, I'm not gonna think anything? Now spit it out, man. You've never held back when you have something to say to me. Don't start now."

"It's just that I've been thinking about this thing long and hard. Ever since I came here and been working with you. We're not Christians. You know that I was born a Wesleyan Methodist, but that's not my religion. Before our slave brothers and sisters were brought here or to the islands where my people ended up, we lived in our own land. Ruled ourselves. Back then there wasn't any such thing as Christianity. Meaning no disrespect to you or anyone else, brother Garvey, but the man folks saying is the Son of God, well, that man didn't give up his life for us. There was no Jesus for black folks."

"What are you talking about? You're sounding like a fool. Mention a word of this at one of our meetings and we might as well close up shop. And if that happens, Hoover will dance in the streets in a girly dress with crinolines. No wonder you had a hard time telling me this. You crazy. Now bottle up those fool notions in your head so that those church leaders keep sending their people to our Liberty Halls. It's our mission to give them back their pride and their heritage, not to talk about who was Jesus and what he wasn't."

Undaunted, Ford continued. "Pride and heritage. That's exactly what I'm talking about. We were never Christians, Marcus. Not ever."

Garvey turned to see if anyone was listening; all eyes were riveted towards the stage, as Bojangles was about to start performing. "I know where this is going," he murmured *sotto voce*.

"You do?" Ford turned wide-eyed, his nervousness having long-since dissipated.

"I do. You've been angling to tell me we black folk were once Jews but you don't know how to say it. Isn't that so?" Garvey smiled, comforted that he maintained an upper hand. Ford looked stunned; he neither confirmed nor denied it. "So it's true you're starting a Jewish temple. Word's been spreading for weeks. Can't keep nothing from me, you oughta know that by now."

Ford pursed his lips. "You're not angry with me?"

Garvey tossed his head back and roared. "It's a good cause, Arnold, just not mine. You want to be a Jew? Be a Jew."

"I didn't know how you were going to react."

"Don't you think I've heard some secretly call you Rabbi Ford? I got ears."

"And you don't mind?"

Again, he turned left and right and peered over Ford's shoulder to make certain no one paid them any attention. "Only thing I mind these days is J. Edgar. The man's rotten through and through. I know we're not doing anything wrong; our lawyers have made certain of that. But just the same, the man is blind to anything that he doesn't know or understand, and he sees a conspiracy under every rock. Our days are numbered, so you go and do this thing of yours."

"How can you say that? Things have been going great for you. And the UNIA."

Garvey leaned back and sighed. "I'm not going to lead my flock to any Promised Land. It looks like the mantle of leadership is going to fall to you. Can you do it?"

"Not in the way you're thinking," answered Ford.

It was a challenge Ford would take, but in a manner neither could have thought possible that night.

# Chapter Twenty-One

"**A**re you saying that my father was a rabbi? A rabbi and a musician?"

"Self-ordained. But that didn't matter to his followers. The way they saw it, Garvey was gone and your father gave them hope. He helped them shed the shackles of their white slave owners more than Christianity ever did. He helped them find a belief system that they felt comfortable with. That fit their needs. From their perspective, it was a religion that was all theirs."

"What happened next?"

"To understand that, you need to know what happened to the Bible that Aaron ben Asher had written."

"Are you going to tie that book," he fingered the ancient parchment, "and my father together?"

"In a matter of speaking. There's still more you need to know."

LeShana proceeded to explain about the *herem*, how Saadia Gaon marched in like a sand storm, blanketing the excommunication with the power of his position and previously unchallenged intellect.

"What was the final verdict at the *herem*?" Ford asked LeShana.

"It was astonishing, especially for those times. The local judge in Tiberias stood up to the great Saadia Gaon. That's like a parish priest rebuking the Pope. In any event, Aaron ben Asher was not excommunicated."

"And the book?"

"The Karaites brought it to their synagogue in Jerusalem. To celebrate, all of the Torahs were taken out of their synagogue and paraded in the streets. A holiday was declared; the entire city came out for the spectacle. Jews, Arabs, and Christians all celebrated as if a new king had been crowned. In a matter of speaking, it wasn't that far from the truth."

"That was more than one thousand years ago." He hoisted the parchment protected in plastic. "How did this end up in that poor man's wallet?"

"Your Excellency, we've only taken the first step on this journey. Tighten your seat belt because the ride gets real bumpy from here on in."

# Chapter Twenty-Two

F our years earlier, in 1095 in Clermont, France, Pope Urban gathered together three hundred bishops to implement his aggressive agenda. His first order of business was to validate the practice of the Abbey of Cluny by reinvigorating the commitment to the arts and caring for the poor. Next, he dealt with King Philip I of France, better known as the amorous king. Pope Urban excommunicated the King for divorcing his first wife, Bertha, for being too fat, in order to marry Bertrade de Montfort. This on-again-off-again battle with the monarchy and the church would not be settled until years later, but it paled compared to the Pope's agenda which he purposefully withheld until the last day of the council meeting.

Months earlier, the Byzantine emperor, Alexios I Komeneos, had journeyed to Piacenza, Italy, where the Pope held a council attended by thousands. Alexios asked for the Pope's help against the Muslims who had seized Jerusalem and were stirring up troubles throughout his lands. The Pope saw an opportunity to unite the Catholic world and bring the Eastern Orthodox sect back under Rome's fold. Ever the opportunist, he seized his chance.

"I, or rather the Lord, beseech you as Christ's heralds to publish this everywhere and to persuade all people of whatever rank, foot-soldiers and knights, poor and rich, to carry aid promptly to those Christians and to destroy that vile race from the lands of our friends. I say this to those who are present, it is also meant for those who are absent. Moreover, Christ commands it."

Huzzahs and cheers erupted from those assembled; bloodlust overcame them.

The Pope continued. "Christians, hasten to help your brothers in the East, for they are being attacked. Arm for the rescue of Jerusalem under your captain, Christ. Wear his cross as your badge. If you are killed, your sins will be pardoned."

So promised Pope Urban, calling for a righteous war that would regain Jerusalem from the Muslims. Enthusiasm ran high. Most volunteers sewed red crosses on their soiled and torn tunics. The French word "croix" means cross, and the word changed to "croisades." The *crusades* against the Muslims became a Holy War, a fight to recapture Jerusalem.

Thus the first Crusade took form; it would not be the last.

Word reached Jerusalem that war had been declared. It was the war of no consequence. Soon after being formed, the Pope's peasant army was defeated in Hungary. But defeat was not in the Pope's lexicon. This time he engaged more experienced fighters. These crusaders, led by Godfrey de Bouillon and Raymond of Toulouse, reached Palestine in the spring of 1099.

Five weeks later, they were at Jerusalem's doorstep.

In short order, calamity reigned. Fighting erupted in every corner; most hid behind locked doors.

Rabbi Tobias ben Judah pried open the door of his synagogue enough to see that the city was in flames. Screams jerked his head across the courtyard where Christian soldiers dragged family after family out of their houses. The young and strong were herded like cattle onto carts; they would be sold as slaves. The weak were slaughtered; the street turned into a congealed river of red stench. When the fighting ended, approximately twenty-four thousand would die at the hands of the Crusaders.

The rabbi touched the silver filigreed mezuzah nailed to the synagogue doorpost. He brought his fingers to his lips, praying this would not be the last time he would honor the holy prayers locked inside the sacred ornament. Wasting no time he ducked inside and bolted the synagogue door. Shuffling steps brought him to the *bimah*, the raised platform in front of the pews that contained the synagogue's sacred Torahs. He hefted the largest one and clutched it to his chest, then grabbed a second. There were more to carry: a Bible penned more than one hundred and fifty years earlier by a scribe from Tiberias, and a third Torah, smaller than the others. The rabbi shrugged. There was no way to carry all to safety. Two Torahs were all he could manage.

He shot a glance at the *Ner Tamid*, the eternal light that burned day and night in every synagogue to remind the Jews of their Lord's constant presence, wondering how long it would burn once he abandoned the sanctuary.

Just then, a ferocious boom at the front door startled him so much so that he soiled his clothing. The battering ram hit the front door again. And then it happened, a ball of fire hurtled through the red, blue, yellow, and green stained glass window. Then another. The wooden pews started to smolder and then burst into flame.

The rabbi readjusted the weight of both Torahs, and scurried toward the back door. He froze when it flung open.

Christian solders, blood dripping from their lances, blocked his exit.

He turned toward the front door but it was now battered down, the doorway filled with crusaders.

The last thing he would do was let these infidels desecrate the Torahs. The rabbi blessed God, and then jumped into the roaring flames that spit from floorboards. His robe caught fire first; he clutched the Torahs tighter to his chest.

He refused to scream in pain as the solders advanced toward him, more curious than threatening.

The rabbi's world turned red hot and then black.

Jerusalem was lost.

With Jerusalem's citizens in retreat, the Crusaders ransacked every house and building, taking all they deemed valuable.

A handful of Jews survived that were able to flee to Ashkelon, an ancient city by the sea. Most felt that remaining anywhere in Palestine was too great a risk. As a result, a reverse exodus occurred: thousands of Jews streamed ahead of the Christian menace by navigating deep into Egypt...the land where they had once been enslaved.

The land from where Moses led the their great exodus more than two thousand years earlier.

A land that now welcomed them and gave them sanctuary.

A land that would enjoy a renaissance caused by this wave of Jewish immigrants.

# Chapter Twenty-Three

"**A**re the men ready?" asked the tall, bearded man. He had a soft voice and keen eyes that missed nothing.

Walid Muhammad bin Attash did not answer. He beckoned Zakkarhia closer. Walid had made good on his promise that after the bombing of the *USS Cole* he would bring Zakkarhia to the Al Qaeda training camp in the White Mountains of Afghanistan.

Zakkarhia jogged over, an AK 47 slung over his shoulder. He bowed his head.

"What's your name?" asked the revered leader.

Zakkarhia could not believe his lucky day. He had seen Osama bin Laden from a distance and felt it a supreme honor to be close to the man's gaze. To be in his presence was almost too much to bear. This was the most glorious moment in his unworthy life.

Zakkarhia ibn Mohammed had trained hard. From the moment he arrived and was assigned a berth in one of the many caves in the Tora Bora fortress rising more than 13,000 feet southwest of the provincial capital of Jalalabad, he worked and studied to the point of frenzy. He had been a thin sinewy youth when he had arrived in Sudan three years earlier. Now at twenty, he had filled his frame with muscle and his mind with cunning. He could negotiate the overhead rungs with the ease of a chimpanzee, sprint over the narrow slats of the steeplechase – up and down – without ever slipping. He could leap from pole to pole with gazelle-like speed and best his fellow mujahedeen in hand-to-hand conflict.

He hit the bulls-eye with unrivaled accuracy.

Without raising his head and meeting Osama's stare, Zakkarhia blurted his name.

"Are you Palestinian?"

Zakkarhia nodded.

Then he turned to his trusted advisor. "You've done well. I'm satisfied. What do you plan for this one? Will he be going to the infidels?"

Zakkarhia's pulse quickened. Moisture formed on his lips. His scalp grew warm. Paradise was near.

Walid and bin Laden spoke as if Zakkarhia was not there.

"The men have been selected long ago, their tickets purchased. Twenty in all. We have a backup for each." He nodded toward Zakkarhia. "I don't want this one on the planes. This is not his time," said Walid.

Zakkarhia raised his head to speak, caught Walid's stare, and fell silent.

Osama took one step toward Zakkarhia. "I've observed you from afar. Your skills are many; your glory will be great. You will have your chance to bring our enemies to their knees, not once but many times. Be patient, my son." Then bin Laden turned and strode out of the cave. This encounter had a lasting effect on Zakkarhia, though he would never meet Osama in person again.

Zakkarhia left the cave wondering why they would need twenty men for an assignment. He thought back to the bombing of the Marine quarters in Lebanon, the misguided rental truck that exploded at the World Trade Center, the hole they blasted in the USS Cole's hull. None needed so many.

Zakkarhia would wait almost four months to find out more about the assignment that would need twenty men. And when he learned about their glorious success, Allah be praised, in spite of what Osama bin Laden promised him about his future, Zakkarhia regretted not being part of the mission that would change history forever.

# Chapter Twenty-Four

ittel Lasker and Pinchas Halevi were tired. Twelve hours after leaving Ben Gurion Airport in Tel Aviv, their connecting Delta flight from New York landed at Washington's National Airport. Each toted a carry-on and scuttled through the terminal with a white-knuckled grip to an attaché case replete with an encrypted lock. They locked eyes with two suits with cropped hair, white shirts, telltale striped ties and the obligatory beige ear buds. Credentials displayed, Gittel and Pinchas slithered into the black Escalade waiting at curbside and headed for CIA Headquarters in Langley.

"No need for credentials," George Tenet said to the Israelis, nodding for them to put away their wallets. "We knew who you were when you boarded in Israel. Now what's so important that the head of Shin Bet could not tell me on a secure phone?"

Gittel handed the CIA director a sealed envelope. "Names from German intelligence. They have uncovered a terrorist cell in Hamburg – *jihadists* – who are apparently planning a major attack on the United States. We're here to warn you."

Tenet waved them off. "We have ears everywhere. If there were any chance of an attack on our soil, we'd know about it. You can tell your director we appreciate his concerns, but we've got things covered here."

Gittel struggled to suppress her reaction to the CIA Director's impudence. Could he really be this obtuse? In Israel, when operatives have concrete evidence and ask for a briefing, senior officials receive their reports with an open mind. They don't have to agree with what they hear, but they need to listen with both ears before making an informed decision. At the least, they'd look to corroborate the intel, dig deeper to verify, before summarily dismissing it.

Gittel glanced at Pinchas for an instant; he nodded for her to explain.

"Begging to differ with you, Sir, but if you had knowledge of what members of this Hamburg cell were planning, we wouldn't need to be standing here talking about it. You'd have your country war-ready, on full alert, ready to do battle. Your President would've called our Prime Minister, and our Intelligence would be working with yours. But that's not the case, is it, Sir?"

George Tenet remained unmoved. He was not used to being addressed this way, certainly not by a subordinate, regardless of the country she represented. He knew better that to stand on principle. He needed to hear from the other Israeli.

Pinchas Halevi cleared his throat, less comfortable speaking English than Gittel. "Excuse me, Mr. Tenet, but this is not a threat. Whatever they are planning is about to happen. It will be big. Hundreds will be killed. Maybe more."

"And how, exactly, do you know this?"

"Because I am the one who befriended them at the university. We took the same art classes. They thought I was one of them. I heard them speak."

"How many?"

"More than a few."

Tenet leaned forward. "What's the nature of this so-called damage? What are they scheming to do?"

Gittel turned to Pinchas, *her look told him to let her answer*, and then turned to CIA chief. "That's what we were not able to find out. As best as we can tell, it has something to do with training flights and pilots' licenses."

"I wouldn't suppose you have any names to go along with this alleged plot?"

"Four," answered Gittel, handing him a list. "Nawaf Alhazmi, Khalid Almihdhar, Marwan Alshehhi, and Mohamed Atta. We're sure of these, but there are definitely more. Fifteen. Maybe twenty."

Tenet, who had been standing arms folded across his gray plaid suit, relaxed for the first time and edged back to his desk, tossing the paper on down. He sat on the edge, partially resting one leg on the glass top.

"You've convinced me that something is eminent. I'll give you that. But forcing their way into cockpits? That's never going to happen here. And as for pilot training, there's not a school in the US that would train Arabs. Especially those from Germany."

"I was there," said Pinchas, "when they were talking about. They were bragging how easy it was to get the training on jumbo jets. They've already tested airport security to see how lax it is. They made test runs. Getting through posed no problems."

Tenet looked at his team; all appeared stern. Straight-faced. He turned back to the Gittel and Pinchas. "You want me to believe that you've spent time with members of this group who are planning to attack the US. You have no idea when or where it will be, or what the target is."

"Targets," countered Pinchas.

"Pardon me, targets," said Tenet. "You want me to scramble my forces to a ready alert, and be on the lookout for fifteen or twenty Moslems who know how to fly planes. Not Cessnas, but jumbo jets. Is that all you have to convince me that this is a real and eminent threat? Cause if there's nothing else, I've got better things to do with my time."

# Chapter Twenty-Five

"**B**ring me the book." Blind and near death, Moses Maimonides pointed a crooked finger to the tome perched on his writing table. The room was dimly lit, though it didn't matter to the blind man. Moses was propped up on pillows filled with goose feathers.

"Save your strength, father." Abraham, the great physician and scholar's only son, eased the book into his father's gnarled hands that lay limp on withered legs. *They are twigs, thought Abraham; I hope they don't snap from the weight of the book.*

Moses grew animated. He wriggled up. He struggled to tilt the book in spite of its anvil-like weight. He pried open its wooden cover and ran his fingers over the parchment, the letters imparting strength at his touch. After weeks of pain, serenity settled across Moses's face.

"Help me bring it to my lips."

Without a word, Abraham hefted the book to his father's pale blue lips. The old man kissed the book, and then waved it away. After he replaced the book, Abraham drew a chair closer to his father, filled with a sense of comfort that his father was experiencing a few good moments.

"You should rest, now."

Moses shook his head. "I have the rest for all eternity for that. I want you to protect that book with your life, and with the lives of your children. Promise me you will." Before Abraham could answer, Moses continued. "This is a book of miracles. That scribe in Tiberias, Aaron ben Asher, should never have written it. He was wrong to do it, but he did it nonetheless. And commissioned by Karaites, no less! It should never have survived the First Crusade when they burned the synagogue in Jerusalem, but it did. It's impossible to imagine how it was brought to Alexandria, but it was. By whom? Probably by one of the few Jews who made it out of Jerusalem alive."

"Maybe it was a Crusader."

"We'll never know. But it was brought here for a reason. Imagine," Moses pointed in the book's direction, "the only one of its kind in the world."

Abraham touched his father's shoulder. "Tell me the rest tomorrow. Save your strength, father."

Moses's voice grew stronger. "There will be no tomorrow. I know that, and so do you. You need to hear about this book so generations that follow will understand why it is the greatest Bible ever written. When your son is old enough to understand, I want you to repeat what I am telling you to him. And then he will be the bearer of this amazing story and tell his son. And then that one will tell his son…and so on for all eternity. This story must never die."

Abraham plumbed the crags and lines etched in his father's face. He basked in the power of this great being that few knew the way he did. He learned to live with his father's fame and pride. It was either that or appear the "ungrateful" son. Insensitive. His father was already acclaimed the greatest Jewish scholar who ever lived. As the saying went, from Moses on Mt. Sinai to Moses Maimonides, there were none greater who had lived.

Maimonides wrote the *Mishneh Torah*. It was so comprehensive and practical in the explaining the teachings of the great rabbis that no other book was needed to define how Jews should live. His writings became the essential guide for the Jews scattered around the world, in the so-called Diaspora. They were a people who had no central government, no army, and no formal place of worship since the Second Temple was destroyed in 70 AD.

The fact that the Jews were a people without a country made them special. Laws were passed in many countries that limited what they could and couldn't do. In almost all instances, they could not own land. They could not vote. They could not be soldiers.

What was left for them? They could be doctors. Scientists. Moneylenders. Traders. If nothing else, there were trustworthy, since all knew they answered to a higher authority than a king or caliph.

Moses started speaking; Abraham leaned closer to hear. Again, he pointed to the Codex. "When I wrote my *Guide to the Perplexed*, I read from that Bible every day. When I wrote my own Torah, I copied it from that Bible. That Bible is a work of perfection, greater than anything man has ever created." Every time he described *that* Bible, he did so with a reverence Abraham had never before witnessed.

"Of course it's perfect. It contains every word God uttered to his prophets. It tells our story from the creation to when we were slaves in Egypt. It tells the stories of Abraham, Isaac, and Jacob. It defines the Lord's ten commandments of how we, His children, should live. The laws we need to obey."

Maimonides responded. "Don't forget that without the scribe's brilliance, these words would have been hieroglyphics. The Hebrew language was a step away from being declared dead."

"But it's only a book, father. You revere it like an icon...and you know we can't pray to false images."

The old man turned his head to him.

"You're talking nonsense. Icons? Images? Nothing of the sort. God meant for me to find that book in the bazaar that day. Imagine me, of all the thousands of people who lived in Alexandria and those that visit from Cairo. It was me...I was the one who found this incredible treasure. What made me stop at that stall? What drew me to that pile of books? There were other stalls and other stacks. And what made me search until I got to the bottom. My fingers stretched as far as they could and when I touched the cover I knew I had touched something special. Shocks rippled through my body. My fingers were scorched, my hand on fire. My head grew light. I fell back. My breathing turned shallow."

He motioned for water. When a few drops coated his parched tongue, he continued. "God wanted me to find that book so that I would be motivated to write all that I've written since. No, my son, this is the most unique treasure in the whole world, and it is your duty to protect it."

Abraham vowed to protect his father's precious Bible.

But Moses Maimonides never heard his son's promise.

The greatest Jewish scholar in two thousand years had taken his last breath.

# Chapter Twenty-Six

R abbi Ford and Rabbi Wentworth Matthew sat at the older man's
kitchen table, reviewing the week's Torah portion. Rabbi Matthew had
founded the Commandment Keepers Congregation in Harlem ten
years earlier after standing on a ladder and preaching to anybody that would
listen that blacks were the descendants of Abraham, Isaac, and Jacob. Rabbi
Wentworth taught that blacks had forgotten their true religion during the
Middle Passage and were simply returning to their original religion from
the Dark Continent: Judaism. Wentworth was the person most responsible
for influencing Ford to reach his personal decision about his heritage.

There was a light rap on the door. The men shot a glance at each
other and then Ford hopped up to see who was there.

"It can't be a congregant," Matthew said, "they know not to interrupt
when I'm preparing for tomorrow's sermon."

A slight white man stood at the door, with a grey fedora in hand
and a yarmulke on his head. His blue suit was two sizes too large; his
grey threadbare overcoat had seen better days.

"Excuse me for interrupting but I was looking for the black rabbi,"
he said in broken English.

Ford looked at Matthew; each erupted into a proud smile. "You
found two of them," Ford said, welcoming him into the apartment. He
introduced Wentworth Matthew to the stranger. "And you are?"

"Jacques Faitlovich."

After sliding into a tattered rattan chair, the visitor wasted no time
in explaining his presence.

"I've been searching all over for you." He looked from one skeptical face to the other. "Once I heard there were black Jews in America, I had to found you and tell you what I know."

Nothing like this had ever happened to Rabbi Matthew or Rabbi Ford. Their battle to be recognized and embraced by white Jews had fallen short, since neither had been *bar-mitzvahed* or formally converted to Judaism under an ordained rabbi's tutelage. And neither had been circumcised, which was a ritual all Jewish men experienced.

"We don't need to be tutored by anyone," Wentworth Matthew had insisted over the years. The result was that white Jews never accepted them or addressed them as Jews…until maybe now.

Ever cautious, Wentworth said, "You have my attention, Mr. Faitlovich. Why were you looking for us?"

"I'm from Poland, from a town called Łódź. My mentor was Joseph Halevy who discovered a lost tribe of Jews in Ethiopia more than fifty years ago, in 1867. When I met Halevy, I was so taken with learning more about these people that I studied their language at the Sorbonne, and then traveled to Ethiopia twenty-five years ago. I lived among them, getting to know them. They are many scattered over five hundred villages. And they are so poor. Most have nothing. As I got to know them better, I understood how special they were. Since then, I've visited every European country and most in South America"

"That's a lot of traveling," Rabbi Matthew said.

"My goal was to raise money for them. They need to be lifted from their squalor and live more normal lives."

"We understand that there are thousands of Jews scattered in villages all over the world," said Rabbi Matthew.

"What is so special about these lost Jews?" Ford asked.

"They're like you," answered Faitlovitch, waiting for them to understand what this implied.

"That doesn't make them very special," said Rabbi Matthew, already accepting the fact that a Jew was a Jew, no matter which country they came from or where they lived.

Faitlovitch's eyes twinkled before responding, enjoying the moment that needed repeating. "There *are* a lot of Jews around the world, but few are like the two of you."

Ford looked at Rabbi Matthew, then his face lit up. "Black, you mean? Yes, there are more like us in America than you think. As a people, we are only just recognizing our Jewish roots," and then added, "and we have a number of synagogues scattered through the region."

"That's why I had to find you. You see," he paused for effect, "to let you know there are more."

"More black Jews in America?" asked Rabbi Matthew.

"I don't know about that," Faitlovitch answered, "but I do know that these Jews in Ethiopia are black, just like you." Then he slid back, basking in their wide-eyed surprise.

Ford stuttered. "You mean black." He tapped Wentworth Matthew on the chest, and then touched the elder's face. Then he touched his own. "Like us?"

"Those who know them call them *Falashas*. However they prefer to be referred to as *Bet Israel*."

"The house of Israel," said Matthew.

"Exactly."

Matthew turned to Ford. "This Ethiopia...it *is* our land of milk and honey. It validates everything we've been saying and thinking for all of these years, that we were Jews in the time before."

*Before the Middle Passage. Before we were slaves.*

"What do you want from us?" asked Ford.

"I'm here in New York City to raise money for the *Falashas*. I've brought many from Ethiopia to Europe to be formally trained. Some have finished their training and have been ordained as rabbis. As a people, there're very artistic. The Ethiopian Jews are great craftsmen. They make intricate silver work. Filigree. But like many, they do not know our history and have not had an opportunity to progress over the many centuries. They've been so isolated from the rest of the world."

"How long have they been in Ethiopia?" Ford asked.

"At least two thousand years. When I heard there were black Jews in Harlem, I had to come and meet you."

"Tell me more about these black Jews." Ford leaned forward; he didn't want to miss one word. Rivulets of sweat streamed down his face.

"Scholars claim they may be the descended from the last tribe of Dan." Faitlovich shrugged. "It's possible. But what is clear that at the time of Christ, caravans were passing through Ethiopia. There was much intermarriage. Through the centuries, many Jewish merchants found the Ethiopians way of life simple and safe. They stayed and started families there."

"Can they read Hebrew?" asked Matthew.

"Only a handful. But they follow many of our customs including circumcision, lighting candles on the Sabbath, and they do have some Torahs, though most can't read from them."

Ford hesitated. "There is no doubt they are Jews?"

"None whatsoever."

It was Matthew's turn to validate his years of preaching and beliefs. He had started out a Christian with Judaic leanings, and over the years, gravitated more and more to conclusion that blacks had been Jews before they were Christians. "So it *is* true that Sheba journeyed to Palestine and married Solomon. Their son was Menelik," he said to Ford, thrusting his narrow chest out, "I told you we came from them."

Ford mused out loud. "I must go there at once. Lead my congregation to Ethiopia."

Faitlovich held up his hand. "Not so fast. Ethiopia is not the most hospitable place on earth. And it will not be easy for you, as an American, to get established there."

"I must try," Ford said.

Matthew worried; he knew that once Ford grabbed hold of an idea, it was impossible to shake loose. "You can't just pick up and leave, Arnold. Ethiopia is a long way from here. Religion aside, we're still Americans. I'm not sure we belong there, and I'm uncertain that we could be happy there. Regardless of how we came to these shores, it sounds like we'd be leaving behind a much better life."

"Life can't be good until we're accepted as a people for who and what we are, and that means living with our own kind."

Matthew knew he would lose this battle. "Maybe you can leave your apartment and the life you know. But your congregants? It they're anything like mine, they'd rather stick with the miserable lives they know then pick up and go to a strange country...even if it is the Promised Land."

"We're not Americans," Ford countered. "We were brought here against our will. And I'm from Barbados anyway. You're from St. Kitts. How are we Americans?"

Faitlovitch chimed in. "All of our ancestors have been forced to move to one place or another, either against their will or for survival. That's the history of the Jews over thousands of years. But I didn't come here to entice you to move to Ethiopia, Rabbi Ford. I came to meet you and Rabbi Matthew out of respect, and to share the good news of the *Falashas* with you."

"Don't you see that you've given me hope beyond hope? I wrote the Universal Ethiopian Hymnal years back for Marcus Garvey. I don't know why I thought about it, but it came natural to say that Ethiopia was our Promised Land. And now you're bringing me the news that it is. I tell you this is more than a coincidence, Mr. Faitlovitch, it's Providence."

Ford's baritone voice soared. He raised his hand in salute as he sung, "Advance, advance to victor! Let Africa be free!" Now, more than ever, Ford was convinced of his mission.

Faitlovitch had seen this type of determination before and knew there was no need to dampen his spirits. "Make your preparations, Rabbi Ford. Queen Zawditu of Ethiopia is ill. Her days are numbered. It is widely assumed that Negus Tafari will be the next king. Your time will come soon enough."

"Is this a good thing? Who is this Negus Tafari?" Ford wanted to know.

"He is a direct descendant of King David."

Ford clapped his hands in joy. "Then this is very good."

◆　◆　◆

"So this is how I came to be born in Ethiopia," Cardinal Ford said.

LeShana gave a partial nod, stuck her neck out, hunched her shoulders, and frowned.

"There's more to this story?" he asked.

"You can't imagine. It gets more remarkable."

"More remarkable than learning that my father was some sort of pseudo Jew? Ford did end up in Ethiopia, didn't he?"

"The short answer is 'yes.' He made contact with the mayor of Addis Abba who arranged for your father to buy a tract of land for his followers. Ford spent most of the next twelve months collecting money anyway he could. When he had enough to buy a fistful of acres, a bevy of his congregants escorted him down to the west side piers. He strutted up the ramp of the transatlantic ship, found a spot at the rail, and waved good-bye to his adoring congregants filled with hope and promise. Only…"

"Only what?"

"Only he didn't arrive in Ethiopia."

"You just said he did get there." He thought about it. Then said, almost musing to himself, "I know I was born there."

"It seems good old Rabbi Ford took a bit of a circuitous route."

"How circuitous?"

"Four or five years worth."

# Chapter Twenty-Seven

Zakkarhia was under the microscope. It had been thirty months to the day since 9/11, and during that time his limits had been tested. The challenges were not as physical as much as they were mental. Yes, he became a sharpshooter. Yes, he could detonate a bomb with a cell phone. And there was more. He could bypass virtually any security system, break the silence of the best-trained operative, and when it counted, send men to their death without whim or regret. Zakkarhia was a rising jihadist who had caught the eye of the decision makers that surrounded Osama bin Laden.

And the reward for his sacrifices, for the arduous training, for passing every challenge thrown at him was to either witness or partake in most calamities Al Qaeda tossed at western civilization. The nightclub in Bali. A suicide bomb in a Tel Aviv café. From the moment he arrived at his first training camp in the Sudan, to standing on the dock and peering through binoculars as the motorboat rammed into the *USS Cole*, Zakkarhia craved to be included in every mission. He secretly wept that he was not chosen to fly a jet into one of the hated World Trade Centers or the Pentagon. It would have been enough to be martyred in that Pennsylvania field, knowing that just being headed toward their White House was a victory in itself.

And the latest? To be part of the chaos that would occur days before the national Spanish election.

But still, it was not his time. He remained under the radar and unknown to the various intelligence agencies around the world. When not tasked, Zakkarhia continued to train. For what? He hadn't a clue. One thing was certain: he was drawing close scrutiny by the higher echelons. And now? Now, he was under the high-powered spyglass of one of the best: Mustafa Setmarian Nasar. Nasar had the pedigree of a career terrorist. Born in Aleppo, Syria of Arabic parents, he passed for a Westerner with red hair, fair skin, and light-colored eyes. He first came to be noticed by career spies when he masterminded an explosion at a military-base café in Spain. Twenty were killed and scores injured. Nasar fought the Russian invaders in the 1980s, befriended Osama bin Laden, lived in London, and masterminded a dozen terrorist acts.

While Mustafa Setmarian Nasar's intellectual fingerprints were all over the Madrid bombing, Zakkarhia was the local *capo* who delivered the message to countries that followed decadent, godless ways: we are at war with you. Zakkarhia left Spain's capital before the train bombs exploded, but not without enhancing his value to his Al Qaeda handlers. He was edging closer to bin Laden's trusted circle, one that many dreamed of penetrating, but few ever could.

Zakkarhia was that special.

◆   ◆   ◆

The Madrid plan was simple. Zakkarhia used a black marker on the white wall of an apartment the Moroccan crew had rented. The way it was set up, the crew would pick the day they'd spring the chaos, including how and where. The goal? Cause the most damage. What would come to light later, as announced by the Spain's counter-terrorism director, was that the bombings were followed by a series of suicide attacks with the express intent of increasing the body count. What spared more bloodshed was that the police cornered most of the suicide attackers before they had a chance to blow themselves up in the middle of unsuspecting crowds. Luck intervened; in each case the terrorists blew themselves up, but no one else.

The human toll was horrific. Ten bombs detonated in synchronous time killing and maiming. Limbs everywhere. The sickly smell of ripe blood filled the air.

Another victory for Al Qaeda.

*Paris, March 12, 2004*
It was the day after.

"Merci beaucoups," Nasar said to the waiter wrapped in the full-length white apron tied behind his back. The terrorist nestled the savory hot croissant next to the mocha-colored café-crème, giving it time to cool. He and Zakkarhia were seated to the left of the lacquered wood door that graced the entrance to **Les Deux Magots** on Boulevard Saint-Germain. It was a crisp day, yet fair enough to take a table outside. Each pawed a copy of the Herald Tribune.

"Can you believe this imbecile of a Prime Minister, Aznar? The fool is blaming the bombing on the Basques?" Nasar spoke in soft tones into the open paper without moving his head. An unsuspecting glance by a stranger and they'd think Nasar was talking to himself.

"It's a glorious day for brothers in every corner of the world," said Zakkarhia just as gently, "Allah be praised." He beamed rereading the body count for the fourth time: nearly two hundred killed, two thousand injured. "The Spanish national elections will be thrown into chaos."

"It is one more brick to the monument we're building to our Almighty Allah." Nasar sipped his café.

"Will we quicken the pace?"

Nasar lowered the paper. He looked to his right and waited for a waiter to enter the restaurant. He searched behind Zakkarhia and then over his shoulder behind the nearby tree that blocked another table.

He leaned forward.

"London is next."

# Chapter Twenty-Eight

Not since they had first locked eyes, LeShana glanced at her Casio with the shocking green band that was water resistant up to fifty feet. Until then, it felt like they were talking minutes. It had been nearer to two hours.

"Do you have to go?" Ford asked. There was reluctance in his voice. "You've been too generous with your time. And I can't believe the story you're telling me. I never knew these things about my," he tripped over the word, "father."

She waved her hand. "There's some wiggle room when a homicide's occurred. I don't have to leave yet."

"But we haven't talked much about," he struggled to say this, "the victim."

"He'll keep. Not going anywhere except the ME's office."

"Will they do an autopsy? You know…"

"They have to. The rabbis understand it's necessary when murder is committed. The police are very respectful of all traditions."

"All right then," he said, pushing away from his desk and stood. She watched with surprise as he stretched to reach the gold-gilded coffered ceiling first with his right arm, then the left. He squatted to the floor, twisted right and left, and then took his seat. "I get stiff sitting too long."

"Know what you mean," she answered. She took this as permission to stand, too, and move about, shaking off inflexibility that had crept over her. If you asked, she felt the same as she did when she was a rookie cop, but now her joints creaked, her muscles ached, and bending down had its challenges.

Ford continued. "We know that my father ended up in Ethiopia. I'm proof of that. But you're saying that he didn't go right away. Does anyone know where he went?"

"There's some evidence he stayed in the country," she said with a sly grin, "but we don't know for sure."

"Another mystery? Nothing's going to top finding out that my father was Jewish."

"I've learned as a cop *not* to make any definitive statements until you have all the facts."

He grabbed at her cue. "And I don't have all the facts, do I? That's what you're insinuating?"

"There's more."

"Care to share?"

"Think you can handle it?"

He glanced at the row of books on the wall, and then turned back to her. "Did he commit a murder?"

LeShana didn't see that coming. She collected her thoughts, careful how she'd answer. "Not in the pure sense of the word."

"How can murder to be impure?" He thought about what that sounded like. "I guess all murder is impure."

"It's not what you think."

"I'm too numb to think anything. I need more facts."

"Good. You're a quick learner. Better reserve judgment 'til you hear the next part."

"Will that be soon?" His eyes flickered with amusement.

She liked him more and more but was uncertain how he'd respond to this next part of the story. How could anyone comprehend what she was about to share?

# Chapter Twenty-Nine

The peddler displayed colourful silk scarves on his lank arm. "Red, yellow, green; I have more colours, madam." He stepped aside to reveal a wooden handcart piled high with colourful shawls and hats and mittens and scarves. "What can I sell the lady of the house?" he asked in a tender, yet firm voice.

Buxom, stout, wearing a grey hospital dress where she worked as an aide, Matilda Jones held onto the wrought-iron railing and strained to see the stranger's wares. She nodded toward the cart, stepping off the red brick stoop onto the concrete sidewalk. "May I?"

"May the Lord bless you. Please. Please. Make your choice." The man bowed with grace, his smile never ending.

Matilda picked a bright yellow scarf with blue swirls laced through it. She draped it over her broad shoulders, beaming from ear to ear as she saw her reflection in the hand mirror he held up to her.

"Let me," said the stranger, advancing toward her, his arms outstretched.

She inched back, clutching the scarf, clenching her jaw, exposing the whites of her eyes tinged yellow like fried eggs with broken yolks.

He paused. A chuckle rumbled from deep in his chest. "Don't fear, sister. I only wish to demonstrate how the royal Ashanti women wrap their heads with a scarf as beautiful this."

Her pudgy face crinkled in awe as deft hands transformed the scarf into a towering turban. He motioned for her to inspect what he had done in the ivory-handled mirror. She twisted her head to one side and then the other, posing this way and that.

Still admiring his creation, he said to her, "The *kente* is a handwoven Ashanti ceremonial cloth. It's always multi-colored, and represents some part of the tribe's history or moral values or religious beliefs."

She grabbed her waist with her meaty hands. "And just how do you know that, mister?"

"I know much." He reached into his right pocket. A small sculpture made of polished wood and stained black materialized in his hand. The head was shaped like a smooth disc with a high forehead, flat nose and tiny mouth. Its body, neck, and arms formed a cross.

"What you got there?" she asked.

"This is called an *akuaba*. It is a fertility doll."

"And just what am I supposed to do with this here doll?"

"Carry it with you wherever you go. It brings good luck to women who are infertile."

"You have no cause to go saying something like that. You don't know me."

"I mean no disrespect, madam. But is it not true that you and your husband have been trying to have a child for many years?"

"Now how you know somethin' like that?"

"Like I said, I know a lot of things."

"And what do they call you, Mr. Know-A-Lot-Of-Things?"

"I go by many names. Fard. W.D. Fard. Professor Ford. Mohammed Fard. Many names."

*New York*
Like a splash of cold water in his face, this got Cardinal Ford's attention. "He said his name was Ford?"

She looked away before answering, knowing that this new chapter in the story would bring a host of questions. She felt sorry for him. After all, he witnessed a tragedy that would shake anyone to his or her core. The Cardinal was a man of compassion who had seen a lot in his life, but having a man die in his arms was a severe trauma for anyone.

And on top of this, learning about his father, a man of many layers and complexities from a perfect stranger, exponentially compounded the day's ordeal. Now this!

"Among others," she said. "He used Fard more often, but Ford was definitely a name he used more than once."

"It could be a coincidence."

"Could be," LeShana said. "After all, Ford is a common name in Detroit. Easier to spell than having Chevrolet as a last name."

He was in no mood for humor. "You don't think that's the case, do you? It's not about cars in Detroit, is it?"

"Nowhere near about cars, Your Eminence. It couldn't be more serious."

# Chapter Thirty

B y the time Tamberlane had married a descendant of the great
Ghengis Khan, the great Mongol leader's empire had been carved
into independent kingdoms without any central rule. Tamberlane,
who started out as a sheep rustler and bandit, declared that the mantel
of reuniting the kingdom fell to him. To accomplish that goal he waged
one ruthless, brutal campaign after another.

Tamberlane, known as Timur the Lame, ruled from Damascus
to Delphi. He had destroyed the Golden Horde, conquered Persia
and Mesopotamia, and had invaded Russia, Georgia, India, Syria and
Turkey. No one was safe from his bloodthirsty soldiers. His atrocities
struck terror into the hearts of all. Cities would surrender without a fight
hoping to be spared a sack or from having their women swept away as
slaves. Though a Muslim, Tamerlane justified his ruthless violence as
spreading Mohammed's word against the Christians and Hindus. And
if fellow-Muslims got in his way, his orders were clear, "Slaughter them
with the other heathens, they're *bad* Muslims."

Five years before his death, Tamerlane reversed directions without
completing the conquest of India; he turned west. His new target: Syria.
His goal: to bring Cairo and the Mameluke sultans to their heels. But
first, Aleppo, an ancient city continuously inhabited for eight thousand
years, lay in his path.

When word spread that the feared Mongol horde was at their
doorstep, the chief rabbi of Aleppo herded the men, women and children
into the great Yellow Synagogue. The rounded dome, formally known as

the Joab Ben Zeruiah Synagogue, was built on top of the ancient cave that once shielded the prophet Ezekiel from harm. They prayed and hoped it would offer the same protection to them.

Deep in the underbelly of the religious building, the cave housed four sacred tomes. The most important was an ancient Bible crafted by a scribe from Tiberias, Aaron ben Asher, and brought for safekeeping to Aleppo by the great-great-great grandson of Moses Maimonides. They revered the book. They declared it a good luck talisman: from the moment the treasured book arrived in Aleppo, the city's fortunes changed. Commerce soared as the city became a major way station on the silk trade route between Europe and the Far East. The town elders put so much stock in the fact that their increased wealth and good fortune were due to this book, and that this book had been consecrated by the great Moses Maimonides, that they vowed to preserve it at all costs.

But there words fell empty at the Mongol onslaught. How could they protect a book when they had no means to protect themselves? With Tamberlane at their doorstep, there was little time to think about sacred books. The raging horde broke into the synagogue and raped the women right on the *bimah*. Then trapping all who had taken refuge inside the synagogue, they set fire to the wooden structure, burning the house of worship to the ground and all within it.

Nothing could have survived the inferno. Yet, as miracles go, ben Asher's Bible, which would one day be known to the world as the Codex of Aleppo, a book that had already survived the burning of the Karaite synagogue in Jerusalem at the hands of the Crusaders, survived yet another disaster that should have turned its four hundred and ninety-one parchment pages into ash.

Somehow, the Codex survived yet again.

# Chapter Thirty-One

It took two more years for Jericho Glassman to be assigned to special duty, but the day did arrive. Jericho was planted in an armored personnel carrier in Gaza. His orders were clear: arrest a Palestinian militant called Jamal Abdel Razeq. This was not a kill mission. No reason was given as to why Jamal Abdel Razeq was to be detained, just that he was. By all accounts, he was a senior commander in the terrorist group, Fatah.

Jamal was in the passenger seat of a black Hyundai driven north towards Khan Younis by his comrade, Awni Dhuheir. Neither man sensed that they were heading into a trap near the Morag junction. This section of the main Salahadin north-south road in Gaza went straight past a Jewish settlement, which was not, in and of itself, an unusual road to travel…even for terrorists. Nor was it unusual to see APCs – armored personal carriers - alongside the road. What was unusual, for which Razeq and the driver could not know, was that the tank's regular crew had been replaced by men from an elite Army special unit, including two trained sharpshooters.

One marksman was Jericho Glassman.

This was the team's first stakeout, their first opportunity to engage the enemy. They were trained assassins with orders to only arrest and not kill the target. This did not sit well with anyone. As they counted down to engagement, for no obvious reason the orders abruptly changed: assassinate Razeq and his driver.

Jericho touched his earpiece. "Sixty seconds 'til show time and they give us the order to eliminate." Afterwards, when he was debriefed, Jericho told the psychiatrist that the orders came from a war room. "All the big chiefs were there," he said, "including a brigadier general."

At that same moment that the Arab terrorists approached, an Israeli Defense Forces supply truck lumbered out of a side street and killed the ignition halfway through the intersection. Any possibility of Razeq's driver speeding up to escape the ambush had been extinguished. The IDF truck was filled with armed soldiers instructed to box in Razeq's car and block all means of escape.

Renowned for clockwork precision, like the raid on Entebbe or Operation Moses that sent massive cargo carriers into Ethiopia to secret out the oppressed black Jews there a generation or so ago, or the more recent "mysterious" hits on Iranian nuclear scientists, little went wrong with Israeli missions. But this day would be different. This day created a calamity for the Israeli government.

The IDF moved too soon to block the street, and the job went south as it hemmed in a taxi carrying two innocents. Frustrated, not knowing they were in the middle of a military operation, the taxi driver grew animated. He punched and punched the car's horn; the blaring jangled everyone's nerves. The passengers barked for him to do something; they were in a hurry.

The Arabs' car approached the artificial blockade that was now buttressed by the taxi.

The taxi's honking horn, though natural given the situation, raised antennae in Razeq's mind.

"Is there a problem?" Razeq asked.

"It's nothing. The truck will move and get out of our way."

"I don't like the idea of waiting even a single second. Can we swing around?"

The driver noted, without concern, the APC to the right, the truck, the cab, and a barrier to the left. "We need to be patient." Still, no thought of ambush.

Razeq snapped an order. The driver kicked the car into reverse. Wheels spun, rubber smoldered.

At that moment, the sharpshooters received their orders.

"Fire. Fire now."

Not only was Razeq killed but also his driver and the two taxicab passengers who had misfortune of being in the wrong place at the wrong time. The tally: four killed.

Miraculously, the taxi driver survived.

Inquiries were swift and many, but only for public display. The world condemned the execution when it was reported that Razeq was shot eleven times in the head. Worse yet, two civilians were killed as collateral damage. To this day, the taxicab driver who survived has never given his version of what happened.

What's known in closed quarters is that instead of a public flogging for operational flaws, Jericho's squad was told by the Prime Minister that the had "succeeded perfectly," with no explanation as to why the orders were changed.

Palestinians called the killings a "public execution" of unarmed civilians and vowed revenge. Later that day, they raided an Israeli settlement, killing two innocents.

When asked for a comment, Yassir Arafat promised, "We will burn the ground beneath the feet of the Israeli occupation and the Zionist settlers."

Secret military files later reported that one of the sharpshooters – Jericho Glassman – was left with psychological scars in this first Israeli targeted assassination that would escalate and be known as "The Intifada." In spite of his trauma, in spite of his deep-seated emotional wounds, the soldier – Glassman – would kill more and more low-level terrorists, until he received his ultimate assignment: to kill Yassir Arafat.

Detroit, 1930

# Chapter Thirty-Two

F ard bid his good-byes to Matilda Jones, promising to return in two
weeks. A man of his word, he kept his promise. When he returned,
Mrs. Jones swept the peddler into her living room, where fifteen
other women had been waiting for him more than two hours. Some had
heard about the stranger who told tales of Africa from Matilda; some
heard about him from other friends he had sold scarves and tortoise shell
combs. One had been in a neighbor's house when Fard stopped by to
hawk his wares. But when they heard Matilda's news, there wasn't a one
who would trust anyone else's eyes and ears but their own. They had to
see this stranger for themselves, and hear his words firsthand.

Matilda wagged the *akuaba*. She could not contain her grin. "My
'friend' is late this month." The gaggle of women hugged and kissed her,
wishing her well on her at-long-last good fortune. "Doctor says it don't
mean nothing yet, but it sure is a good sign. And it happened right after
Mr. Fard gave me this here doll."

A rail-thin snippet of a young woman stepped forward. With head
down and eyes averting Fard, she asked, "Can you do that for me, Mister?"

Fard didn't hesitate. He touched the top of her head. "I feel your
ripeness. Your time is soon."

She closed her eyes and prayed. "I had an infection. The doctor said
I could never have children."

Matilda grabbed her. "Child, now don't you worry your little skinny
self anymore. Good things will be happening to you real soon. Like they
done me. Ain't that right, Mr. Fard?"

Fard raised his hands; the cackling ladies fell silent. Energy filled the air.

"We are from many," he said, his voice resplendent. Strong. Giving comfort like a goose down blanket on a cold winter's night. He looked each in the eye. "Some of you are from the Yoruba tribe. The Yoruba believe that the success or failure of a man depends on the choices he made long before birth. Back in the time when he was still in heaven. So if a person suddenly becomes rich, they will say that he chose the right future for himself. If this is so, then poor people must be patient, not because good things will not come to them, but because their good fate has not yet arrived. It will."

He reached for the hand of the skinny women praying to become pregnant. Her skin was chalky; hope had abandoned her chocolate eyes long ago.

"We all need perseverance," he said, his gaze locked on hers. He held her hand longer than a stranger would, but he was no longer a stranger to any of them. Later, after she too became pregnant, this woman would tell everyone that when their hands touched, she felt a surge of energy that entered and warmed her insides. Down to her core.

Fard's reputation grew. With every house Fard called on to vend his wares, more and more waited to greet him. He told parables and recited myths of the Zulu, the Maasi, the Makongo, the small and curious Bushmen, the Anlo-Ewe People, and the Bobo People. He told the epic story of Ghasir's Lute, and that of Miseke and the God of Thunder. Word spread from house to house, neighbor to neighbor. More and more came to see and hear the silk peddler who told tales from their Mother Earth, from the Dark Continent...from the womb of their existence.

Not only women came to hear him, but men, too.

In time, the crowds outgrew the houses. The movement, that's what it had grown to be called, needed to rent a hall to accommodate the growing throng. Up until that first night that W. D. Fard stood at the lectern before hundreds of followers, he had extolled the history and glories of the African peoples. But with an audience the likes of which Detroit had never seen, his message changed. It changed mightily.

"My friends," he began, the air electric, "we have gathered here in this glorious temple to reject the Christianity given us by the white slave masters. We have gathered here in this glorious temple to tell whitey that he can no longer control our minds." Heads swivelled, eyes widened, mouths gaped at the words. But then a chorus of "Amens" and cheers erupted. Feet stomped. Hands clapped. Piercing whistles sliced the air. A black man had never talked to them like this before. Most were surprised; all embraced the power of his words.

Fard continued. "Christianity is a cudgel wielded to control the black man. To keep us at bay. To keeps us down." His voice soared. "I am here to tell you what you already know, that white people are the devils. That white folks are the embodiment of evil. Our only hope as black people is to live in separation, to be self-reliant. Who better to take care of black folks than other black folks?"

If Fard had any qualms that his message might not be received well, it was dispelled that night. He finished his revolutionary pronouncements by sharing beliefs that black men and women walked tall across the Serengeti plains, that swift feet carried them through the jungles of Cameroon, and that they trudged through the sands at the base of the Great Sphinx long before the white son of God walked the earth and died for the sins of all. He may have died for sins…but not *their* sins.

"My friends. Tonight I stand before you in this mighty temple and proclaim that we are no longer the children of the white man's Jesus. We are in the temple of OUR Lord…in the Temple of Islam."

# Chapter Thirty-Three

Gittel Lasker landed in Tel Aviv and went straight to Mossad headquarters.

"Did Blair believe you?" asked the Mossad director.

"I showed him the evidence from the 2003 bombing of Mike's Place at the beach when three people were killed. How the terrorist blew himself up. Then I explained how we traced the explosives to China and that we know the terrorists came via London."

"Did you tell him that our informants have proof that the same sort of explosives were in transit this time from China to England? That they should've arrived on their shores by now?"

"His first response was that Mike's Place was in Tel Aviv."

"And his second?"

"That if any terrorist activities were taking place in England now, they'd know about it."

"The arrogant bastard's going to pay for this."

"Would you send our people in?" asked Gittel. She knew the answer before she asked, but she couldn't let the fools make such a horrific blunder when the chance existed that the impending attack could be prevented.

"To England?" The Director shook his head. "No. We did everything we could. Let's hope their vaunted SIS accidently does their job before countless innocents are killed."

*London, July 7, 2005*

Zakkarhia's plane left Gatwick and was over Gibraltar headed for Amman when the first bomb detonated in the London Underground at 8:50AM. Then a second. Then a third. The three exploded within fifty seconds of each other. An hour later a fourth bomb detonated on the top deck of a bus in Tavistock Square.

Fifty-two killed, scores more injured.

London officials first reported that power surges in the underground power grid caused the explosions. Soon after, the British government switched gears and jumped on the terrorist bandwagon, identifying four homegrown Islamic suicide bombers who entered the Luton train station.

Zakkarhia marveled at their arrogance, the equal of the Spaniards.

At first the Blair government claimed that the bombs were crude, homemade acetone, peroxide-based devices cobbled together on a "shoestring" budget. That belief didn't last long. On July 12, 2005, the Times of London ran a report stating, "A lone bomb-maker, using high-grade military explosives, possibly smuggled into the UK from the Balkans, is believed to be responsible for building the four devices." Similar components were found at all four bombing sites, linking them to the lone bomb maker.

The flight attendant stopped at Zakkarhia's seat. "Would you like coffee? Tea? Juice?"

He looked at his watch. 8:53 AM. He turned, drew in a deep breath, and whistled through his brown teeth. "Champagne, please."

# Chapter Thirty-Four

A week after the United Nations voted to divide Palestine into two provisional states, one Jewish and the other Arabic, flames engulfed twelve of the thirteen synagogues in Syria. Holy arks and silver vessels were broken or destroyed; Torah scrolls were ripped and torched. The Great Synagogue, known as the Yellow Synagogue in the day of Tamerlane, was again burned to the ground.

Braving scorching flames and thick smoke to save the Torahs housed in the seven arks, a congregant stumbled over an iron case. He studied it. What was this doing here? He couldn't be certain if it contained its treasures, or was empty. He touched the metal box but yanked his hand back; his skin blistered.

Joab ben Zeruiah was King David's commander. After conquering Aleppo, he built a synagogue on top of the cave that had once protected the Prophet Elijah. While this original structure didn't survive, the replacement built in the 5th century BC lasted a thousand years until Tamberlane destroyed it at the beginning of the fifteenth century. Rebuilt again, the Yellow Synagogue anchored the Jewish community in Aleppo for another five-and-a-half centuries. While the synagogue served as its spiritual center, the cave, isolated in the bowels of the synagogue, served many functions over the centuries, but none more important than hiding four sacred codices from the rest of the world. The cornerstone of their prizes was the Bible annotated by Aaron ben Asher, which they kept safe in an iron box. Congregants were permitted to stand in front of it and tell the Codex his or her problems. They would kiss the box and petition God to save them, to cure them, to bring them prosperity, to make barren wombs fertile and bless impending births. And the merchants of Aleppo? They prayed for continued prosperity.

And prosper they did. From the time the great book was brought to Aleppo from Egypt, the town became the most important stop on the spice route to the Far East. The townspeople believed they owed their success to this book, and for this reason, insured that it would never be removed from its magical place by adding a curse to the inside cover.

Written by an unknown hand, it was forbidden to remove the Crown of Allepo from cave.

**Holy to God concerning the Talmudic who dwell in the holy city, it shall not be sold nor redeemed forever and ever. Blessed is he who guards it, cursed is he who steals it. Cursed is he who uses it as collateral. It shall not be sold and it shall not be redeemed forever and ever.**

◆　◆　◆

The congregant who had rushed in with every intention of saving as many Torahs as possible stood longer than he should, staring at the iron box. Which was more important? The Torahs or Asher's book?

The air was putrid.

Sirens blared from beyond the charred walls.

Timid fingers reached out; the box was cooling.

He pulled back.

He scanned the courtyard.

He was alone.

Determined, he took the biggest step of his life, he lifted the lid.

The box was empty; the Codex of Aleppo was missing along with the other three sacred books.

# Chapter Thirty-Five

Cardinal Ford again fingered the laminated piece of parchment that had cost an old man his life. "If the book was missing after the fires, where did this come from?"

"It turns out the moment trouble started, the synagogue's rabbi dashed into the cave and dragged the iron case containing the Codex up into the open courtyard. Maybe it was too heavy to carry any further. Regardless, he snatched ben Asher's masterpiece and saved it."

"You know this for certain?"

LeShana shook her head. "That's been verified by more than one witness."

"And he saved the entire book?"

"We think so," she answered. This time, the "we" didn't escape Cardinal Ford. LeShana continued. "Everything that happened next to the Codex gets murky."

"It's amazing. We know what happened to this book one thousand years ago and for most of the time in between. It was apparently saved soon after Palestine was partitioned less than seventy years ago, and then we don't know what happened to it? That's as hard to accept as the story of its creation."

"Not all of it was saved," answered LeShana.

Cardinal Ford frowned.

"Presumably unbeknownst to the rabbi, someone beat him into the cave and grabbed some pages out of the Codex and then bolted."

"Do we know how many pages?"

"Too few for the rabbi to notice in the heat of commotion. We have no clues as to who did it. What is clear is that by the time the rabbi saved the rest of the book, nine pages were missing."

"And those pages are the ones that were sliced into slivers like the one that poor soul gave me this morning."

"Yes. They are similar to the ones reported in a string of thefts and isolated murders 'round the world."

"But why cut up a valued treasure?"

"They had to figure that the whole book would be lost, and that keeping a small piece would continue their good luck. Look how easy it was to hide a fragment in their wallet. Most fled Syria to the four corners of the world. They're first-class merchants. I'm sure nearly all flourished due to their cunning and ability to survive. But in their minds, their successes could not have occurred without their precious pieces of the Codex. If nothing else, they kept the myth about the book alive."

"How many pieces do you think there are?"

"From the nine pages? Who knows how they actually cut it up? There could be a hundred? Two hundred? Fifty? I don't know."

Ford pressed the middle three fingers of his right hand to his temple.

"Excuse me, your Eminence. Is something wrong? You seem distant." His face had grown pale, he seemed removed from the moment.

He jerked his head back to her. "What?" *He just had another one.* He thought about telling her about his visions. "Please excuse me. Lately I've been having these visualizations. I mean I don't know what else to call them. They appear crystal clear, as if I were watching a private screening of a movie." He gazed directly at LeShana. He hesitated, not knowing how she'd react. "I saw the old man running from his killer before I hurried out the front of the church. I knew he was going to get shot."

"No, s..." LeShana swallowed the expletive. "What did you see just now?" She asked with all the earnest she could muster.

"Something about our Lord too horrible to contemplate."

"Do you want to tell me? It may make you feel better?"

He shook his head. "I can't. My other visions have come true; I hope I'm wrong this time."

LeShana knew to let it go. She waited for him to swallow hard.

Cardinal Ford braced himself against the desktop. "You were talking about reassembling the missing pages. Making the book whole again? To what end? Whoever they are, they're killing people in the process."

She didn't answer right away. She studied his face, his breathing rhythm, searching for any sign that he wasn't well. Someone his age, he must be in his mid to late seventies, could get into a medical crisis in a flash. Learning about his father and all that surrounded him had to be an overload of facts, facts that unleashed a torrent of emotions.

His color returned to normal and his breathing was slow and steady. If she could feel his pulse she would be more assured, but outwardly, he appeared fine.

LeShana resumed the tale, still wondering what horrible flash he had just experienced. She moved on. "You're asking all the right questions; I wish I had the answers. We know they will stop at nothing to get those fragments. Most of the time, they don't need to resort to murder."

"Do you think they've found all the missing pieces yet?"

She shrugged. "No way to know. Even if all the pieces were found, a major chunk of the book is still AWOL."

He frowned, confused.

"Vanished. Gone. Vamoose," said LeShana.

"Stolen?"

"That's another way to say it," she answered.

"The story of this book gets more intriguing by the minute. Where does it end?"

She glanced at her watch. "Do you still have time, because it gets more complicated from here?"

"This is like tracing the provenance of a Stradivarius."

"As difficult as tracing an instrument over a few hundred years might be, this story is much more complex."

LeShana was about to embark on the last part of the Codex's journey, when there was a knock on the door. It was the first interruption since she first started interviewing Cardinal Ford.

A young priest entered. He stole a cursory glance at LeShana and then scurried behind the mahogany table and whispered into the Cardinal's ear.

Ford nodded.

A bolt of pain tattooed his face.

"Make the arrangements," Ford said, gathering himself.

Once the priest left, Ford explained. "I have just received word that I need to leave for Rome. The Pope has had a stroke and is not expected to make the night. They are preparing for a conclave of the College of Cardinals."

*Is this what he meant by seeing visions? Did he know about the stroke before the aide marched in? That the Pope would soon die?*

The hair on the back of LeShana's neck stood on end.

Knowing he needed to go soon, she rose. His outstretched arm caused her to freeze.

"We have a bit more time. Don't leave me hanging because I don't know what the coming days will bring, and when we can meet again to finish these stories."

She edged back in the chair, taking comfort in spending more time in his presence. Ford wasn't the first person she had ever told the story of the Codex of Aleppo to, as the great Bible had come to be known, nor was he the first person whom she presented her thesis that Arnold Ford's and W.D. Fard's stories were so intertwined that they could be one and the same person. Could she prove her thesis? Not exactly, but there was always the chance that the implausible could be possible.

There was an aura of majesty attached to the telling this story. Recounting past events was spiritual enough, and sharing the story with the Cardinal was a religious experience in itself. But something else was going on.

At first, LeShana was unclear what was gnawing at her, what was percolating under her skin as she regaled him about Garvey and Ford, ben Asher and the Karaites, Maimonides and Tamberlane, Faitlovitch and the Falashas, the Crusades and the fires. And while she was attracted to him on many levels, what was most compelling was that the longer she was in his presence, the more she understood Cardinal Arnold Ford better than he did himself.

Ford's legacy transcended the entire Judeo-Christian experience. When she began to relate what she knew about his father, she did so to enlighten, to explain gaps in his background and heritage that he should know about. Now that she had shared this with him and heard the words out loud, she experienced a vision of her own, one where Cardinal Ford became an indispensible character in an increasingly complex story.

Regardless of how she intuited the Cardinal's role, no matter how clever she thought she was, LeShana could not imagine the twists and turns this tale was about to take.

In a way she manufactured this story, but it would soon take on an air of verisimilitude and run away from her.

# Chapter Thirty- Six

For weeks and then months, W.D. Fard preached from his new pulpit. His mission was to arouse the Black Nation within the United States and teach them that heaven already existed on earth, but not in their recent past, certainly not in the lands Columbus discovered. He exhorted all who listened that for nearly four hundred years, blacks had been living in hell, a hell created by the "blue-eyed" devils. By white slave owners.

"But there's hope," Fard announced. "In the great Islamic tradition, a savior will appear to lead our black brothers and sisters out of his abyss. This savior is known as Mahdi."

There was an audible gasp by all in earshot. Hearing this mystical name gave them chills. Many shrieked out, "Hallelujah. Praise the Lord."

Some whispered "Mahdi" under their breaths.

Fard contained himself. He wanted to admonish them that they were doing just what whitey had taught them. To be thankful to their white savior. To the Son of God. To Jesus Christ.

He raised his hands for quiet. In another time, he might have explained why their outbursts were the very things he was trying to teach them to abandon. He thought better of it. Now was not the time.

When the room quieted, he stood taller, pushing off the lectern. In a loud and clear voice, he proclaimed, "*I* am that savior."

Again they shrieked. Word had spread wide and far that W.D. Fard was a special man. He made barren women fertile with child; he healed the sick. Why couldn't he be our savior? Fard explained that the Mahdi was the instrument of redemption and that there would be time when a utopian paradise would be created in a separate territory in the United States ruled by blacks.

Fard's message rang true for most. His disciples were hungry for someone to believe in; his words pointed the way to where life would be better than in their present existence. Unlike wannabes that raised the hope of the downtrodden, spinning their stories like a spider's web that would entrap and sometimes defraud or leave them spiritually wanting, Fard had an action plan. In a matter of months he created the Fruit of Islam, which trained blacks how to defend themselves. He created a school that taught blacks their history, one that emboldened them with a rich heritage that exuded pride. If he followed Marcus Garvey's playbook, it was never mentioned.

As his movement grew. He needed to pick and train key men to become ministers and help spread the word. Jesus had his disciples; Fard needed his.

One man came to Fard's attention.

"My father is a Baptist minister," Robert Poole told Fard. "While I appreciated what I learned as a young boy, I never felt comfortable with Jesus. Jesus was a great man and all, but I kept asking myself how was it that black folks came to worship him? They said he was the Son of God, but how we do really know that? And why was their God our God? There had to be something else, I just never knew what it was."

"You have a job?" Fard asked.

Poole beamed. "Work the assembly line over at Chevrolet."

"And you want to become my minister?"

"I wouldn't know how to do any minister stuff."

"The doing part is easy, I can teach you what you need to know. It's your soul that Allah requires. That's something you have to give willingly and of your own free heart."

"Your world's better than the one we have here. Teach me. You won't be sorry."

"Then let's start with you name. It's a white man's name."

"Is my name important? I don't know no other name. "

"Your name is a leg iron to slavery. You keep on wearing it and it will always hold you back. Drag you down."

Poole scratched his head, digesting Fard's first lesson. His desire to move forward with this man wavered. Was this more than he bargained for?

Fard continued. "From this day forth, you will be known as Elijah Mohammed. In time, you will share my teachings to the flock. You will be my messenger."

*Messenger? I will follow this man to the end,* thought Poole.

Intense tutoring followed; Poole, a dry sponge, absorbed every word, every thought. By the time Poole was ready to be a minister, Poole's power and strength had grown to the point of challenging Fard. Not that anything was said by Poole to undermine Fard's control of the Nation of Islam, it was the unspoken words that caused a ripple of concern in Fard. A riptide of energy suffused the student; it was clear that he would soon surpass the teacher.

"I want you to go to Chicago. Start Temple #2. The city is ripe for our teachings," Fard told Poole one day.

"But my place is by your side," answered Poole.

"In due time, you will no longer be at side, you will take my place."

"That will never happen." Though Poole lusted to lead, it would never be at Fard's expense. He revered Fard too much.

Secret thoughts or not, Poole was armed with the pledge that one day, he would lead the Nation of Islam. That was enough for him. With a glad heart and a light step, Elijah Mohammed, a.k.a. Robert Poole, left for Chicago. Temple # 2, of the Nation of Islam, was about to be built.

Little did he know how fast his star would rise.

Little did he know how well he would learn his lessons.

◆  ◆  ◆

With a following of eight thousand strong, Fard and the Nation of Islam became more than a blip on the tapestry of religions that clothed the spiritual needs of the United States. J. Edgar Hoover and his G-men put Fard and others under surveillance.

Gaining followers at every turn, growing stronger each day, Fard's hard work was nearly destroyed by one follower: Robert Harris. Fard had renamed Harris as Robert Karriem. Karriem was an unskilled forty-four year old laborer. What attracted Karriem to Fard was his message. He had never heard a black man speak like Fard. He sat ramrod straight as Fard proselytized.

"It's not enough that we recognize that the white man captured us in our Motherland. It's not enough that we recognize that the white man burned our homes. Ripped us from our families. It's not enough that we recognize that the white man herded us into the bottom of ships and let us rot with the rats. Never gave us a chance to breathe or live. Threw us overboard to be food for sharks."

Tears flowed.

"It's not enough that we recognize that the white man turned our noble chiefs and warriors into slaves, our women into chattel."

"Amen."

"It's not enough that we recognize that the white man separated us from out women folk and children. Treated us like animals."

"Amen."

"It will never be enough until we recognize the white man for what he is: the Devil."

A chorus of cheers. Many jumped up in their seats, raising their hands upwards.

"And what do you do to the Devil, my children?"

"Kill him!" they shouted in unison.

Those words branded Karriem with a truth like nothing he had ever known to be truer. Words he had to act on. And he knew just what to do.

Karriem believed he was carrying out Fard's teachings when he built a makeshift altar in his home. In the presence of his wife, two children, and twelve other Fard followers, Karriem tied James J. Smith, a white tenant his house, down and stabbed him in the chest with an eight-inch kitchen knife. The *Detroit Free Press* reported that the police accused that the Nation of Islam was nothing more than a "black voodoo cult." To make matters worse for Fard, Police detectives found a booklet next to the bloody scene in Karriem's house written by Fard. It was entitled, *Secret Rituals of the Lost-Found Nation of Islam.* In it, Fard openly preached to kill unbelievers. More incriminating, the police found a quote attributed to Fard in Karriem's handwriting that described, "*stabbing the infidel through the heart.*"

Fard was arrested for inciting the murder. Some thought him insane. State-appointed psychiatrists performed a barrage of tests and found Fard perfectly normal. It was ruled that Fard could not be tried for Smith's murder. It was Karriem's misguided "interpretation" of Fard's preaching that was responsible for the horrific killing, no matter how much Fard's words incited. When asked, Fard explained that his words were meant only as metaphors.

Psychiatric clearance notwithstanding, the police would have none it. They made it clear that Fard would be continually harassed as long as he remained in Detroit. Fearful that police tactics would undermine the Nation of Islam, the ever-pragmatic Fard left Detroit and moved in with Elijah Mohammed in Chicago for the next year.

Fard told Elijah Mohammed everything he knew. He drilled him in the ways of the Koran and how to follow and honor Allah.

The day came when the student had learned all he could from the teacher.

That was the day W. D. Fard disappeared.

# Chapter Thirty-Seven

"**W**here did these orders come from?" asked the chief of the Mossad.

Gittel Lasker waved the secret communiqué in front of him. "From the top. And..." she paused, "from President Bush. It has his fingerprints written all over it."

"And does the PM agree?"

Gittel shook her head. "Sharon is against it."

"So? What's the issue? I say, 'No.'"

"It's not for us to say yes or no. It's our job to follow orders."

"If Sharon says no, then we have every right to say no, too. Killing Arafat is not the hard part. That pig could have been eliminated long ago. We've kept him alive all these years because he was a better alternative than anyone who would've taken his place. He's the Devil we know."

"Everyone in this country knows we must keep him alive, but Bush is searching for anything that will help his image. It's six months since the Trade Towers have come down and he needs to show the world he can to fight back. He thinks that by eliminating Arafat the Palestinians will reform their institutions and adopt democratic and free-market principles. He'll milk that for all it's worth while he gets his army ready to launch an attack against Saadam."

"What a fool. Bush is asking us to get rid of the only moderate in the Palestinian world. If Arafat is made into a martyr, a real terrorist could head the Palestinians. We'd be the loser on all accounts. What's in it for us?"

Gittel shrugged. "What else? Money…and the assurances that the US will back us up if we go into Iran. They're nuclear program is ramping up again."

"Who's our best sharpshooter?"

"Jericho Glassman."

"Have you met him?"

She hesitated.

"Which is it?" he asked. "Do you know him? Yes or no?"

"I met him year's back. He was a kid then. His father had just been killed. Palestinian rockets. I was there when he changed his name."

"Why did he do something like that?"

"Because the boy that he knew was dead."

"And now?

"He's an expert marksman."

"Can he be trusted to get the job done?"

She gave it some thought. "Give him a target and he'll get it done."

◆　　◆　　◆

Fluent in Arabic, Jericho Glassman let his beard grow. With the help of a cousin of a cousin he got a job as an electrician's assistant in Ramallah that offered glimpses of Yasser Arafat's comings and goings. Ramallah had been under siege by the Israeli government for months, during which Arafat was confined to his living quarters. Publicly, Prime Minister Ariel Sharon declared that it was not Israel's intention to kill Arafat at this time; privately, he regretted not doing so twenty years earlier when he led the Israeli army into Lebanon to wipe out the bases shelling Israel's northern settlements. It would've been easy to liquidate Arafat then, but it was not Sharon's decision. The higher-ups decided to spare the outspoken Palestinian. Sharon never got over the missed opportunity. From his viewpoint, not killing Arafat had been a colossal mistake; Arafat went on to be a perpetual thorn in the underbelly of Israel's quest for peace.

Not killing the Palestinian leader had been a mistake...until now, when it would be rectified.

Glassman's orders were clear. Make Arafat's killing look like the handiwork of Hamas. Like it was meant to be a coup. Jericho had dreamed of avenging his father's death, of paying back the bastards who sent the suicide bombers into Ashdod that day. Arafat had to be behind it; he was certain of that. And now his dream would soon become a reality.

The multi-level plan was put into high gear. First, Israel cordoned off Arafat's compound from the outside world. The goal was to exert enough pressure to make Arafat stop his vituperative rhetoric and harangues against the Israelis. Knowing he would give a bravura performance and withstand anything thrown at him, Israel sent tanks into Gaza to knock down every building that surrounded Arafat's house. The Palestinian leader was forced to live in the middle of acres of rubble. Only a few broken structures dotted Arafat's immediate landscape.

Next, and this was done purposely to "set" the stage, the Israelis sliced the electrical wires to his house...knowing that Glassman's crew would be called in to reconnect them. The complexity of this plan was made to appear simple. It wasn't. It hinged on a sequence of many things going right, and if one thing went wrong, Glassman could lose his life. And worse than that, Arafat would still be alive.

All was set. The wheels to assassinate Arafat were set in gear.

On May 2, 2002, Jericho and his crew were called to repair the cut wires to Arafat's house. Jericho staked out a vantage point to carry out the assassination when Arafat surprised the world by handing over six Palestinian terrorists that the Israelis had demanded as part of lessening its grip on the Ramallah siege.

"Abort! Abort!"

Glassman received the message minutes before he was to execute Arafat. Jericho verified it; the message was accurate. President Bush notwithstanding, now that Arafat had conceded and handed over the terrorists Israel had so identified, Ariel Sharon could not and would not make Arafat the martyr he threatened to become.

By any measure, Arafat's decision to hand over any Moslem to Israel was daring. Playing ball with Israel, acceding to even a single request of theirs, put on a target square in the middle of his back, or in the middle of his forehead, from his *own* people. For the moment, it served to keep the Israelis at bay. Arafat's so-called victory was hollow at best. He was on the downhill slide of the slippery slope of power.

◆　◆　◆

Israel's *victory* without firing a shot was Glassman's heartbreak. Jericho was ripped apart. Thoughts raced through his brain like in an IBM supercomputer, searching for solutions in nanoseconds, studying permutations that existed at the moment, only to vanish milliseconds later.

What if he ignored the message? What if he said he received it too late, that the deed was already done? Who would mourn the bastard? He'd be doing the world a favor. It took every moral fiber in his soul not to disobey the order. No matter how deep-seated his anger, Glassman was first and foremost a soldier. And soldiers obeyed orders.

This was the second time Jericho was on a mission that was aborted. The first ended in tragedy. And this time? The tragedy here was that the mission wasn't completed.

Jericho didn't know whom he was more furious at: Arafat for being behind the storm of rockets that rained terror on innocents in an undeclared war that had plagued Israel for years, killing innocents with impunity…including his father. Or maybe he should blame the United Nations, that monolithic blob without a backbone. With any guts, they could end this perpetual conflict and mediate peace without raising a sweat. Instead they'd prefer to kowtow to Arafat and Khomeni rather than shut them down. They give both a pulpit to preach their poison. Ban them from giving speeches at the General Assembly, thought Jericho, and see how fast their luster would tarnish.

How many lives did Arafat have, thought Jericho? They should call him the "cat."

Jericho was so consumed with his fury that he didn't hear the Elite Force 17 guards creep into place. He exited the kill site and that's when Arafat's personal guards, culled from the Jabalya refugee camp, surrounded him. Jericho dropped his weapon and jack-knifed his hands into the air. He stood rigid and proud.

He was about to experience an Israeli soldier's worst nightmare. What would they do with him? Take him to Arafat? Probably not, thought Jericho, because that would mean they let a sniper get too close to the Palestinian leader. They would take him straight to jail and wait for the Israelis to demand his release. Jericho, staring at his captors, knew right then and there, that his release would not be swift.

How much would he be able to take before they broke him?

No matter how tough he thought he was, no matter how much pain he could withstand, being held by the Palestinians would be the challenge of his life.

By the time his capture was resolved, Jericho Glassman would experience a life-changing event for the second time in his young life.

# Chapter Thirty-Eight

"I have to confess," LeShana smiled at Ford's choice of words, "that I never heard of two more compelling mysteries. Three, if you separate Ford in New York from Fard in Detroit, plus everything that happened to the Crown of Aleppo."

LeShana reached for the fragment with the Hebrew letters. "Don't forget the way you were drawn into these stories today."

"That poor man," said Ford. "I would never have connected the dots...what dots there were to connect. I still don't see a connection between the Bible and what happened to my father."

"I don't see that, either, but for whatever reason, you were given that piece of parchment today. Somehow, all these stories are marshalling through you. No telling how this will end."

Ford fidgeted, knowing he had to leave. "Before I fly to Rome, can you tell me what happened to the Codex? You said that when the congregant opened the iron box the book was missing. Later it was discovered that the synagogue's rabbi had run to save it. I know about the nine pages and there is that AWOL chunk. More pages missing. Do we know what happened to them? And you need to finish telling me about W.D. Fard once he left Chicago."

"Fard is the shorter answer. He lived with Elijah Mohammed for a year and tutored him to the point that Elijah was totally prepared to take over the Nation of Islam. When Fard sensed that the time was ripe, he handed over the reins to his prize student and disappeared."

"When did this happen?"

"Sometime toward the end of '33, or thereabouts."

"Fard just vanished into thin air?"

"Maybe. Maybe not. One theory has him showing up in Ethiopia."

The Cardinal raised his head, peering upward toward the ceiling. Was he praying? Seeking an answer to a mystery? Ford took his time before speaking. "So when all is said and done, this story of yours comes back to Fard and Ford. You haven't said it directly, but you infer that Fard and Ford are possibly being the same person."

"Possibly."

"And if so? What do you make of it?"

"The cop in me says that Arnold Ford, your father, hoped to give blacks an identity. Maybe he wanted to give them more than just something to believe in. Maybe he wanted them to become militant. To fight the white establishment. But the black Jews would have no part of it. Ford gave them something to grab hold of, and they did. It was a comfortable argument that they were descendants of Sheba, that maybe they came from the ten lost tribes of Israel. Regardless, they weren't angry at the whites and never became militant. When Ford saw that his underlying goals to give blacks this new identity as a cover to turn rebellious were not taking root, he disappeared from that New York dock."

"And he doesn't make it to the Promised Land."

She shook her head. "Possibly not at that time. He might've slipped off the ship before it left New York and headed for Detroit. He drops the Judaism gig, reinvents himself, and picks up Mohammed and Islam, and tries again. This time, it works. The Nation of Islam is a success. Once he finds a worthy candidate to take over in Elijah Mohammed, his job his done and he treks off to Ethiopia to end his days."

"He marries my mother and has me. That's quite a story you're selling, detective."

"I'm not selling anything, your Eminence. Just connecting the dots."

"And the Codex?"

"A Persian cheese merchant meets the rabbi who saved the Codex from the fires. The rabbi senses that the tolerance for the few remaining Jews in Aleppo is waning, and he asks the merchant to smuggle the Codex into Israel."

"When was this?"

"1956."

"And then what?"

"His instructions are to bring the book to a pious Jew."

"That's it?" asked Ford. "Find a pious Jew?"

"Not just anyone. There were no holes in the cheese merchant's thinking. He brings it to the most pious and appropriate person: Yitzhak Ben-Zvi, the president of Israel."

"How did a cheese merchant get to the president of Israel? Can you imagine someone trying to bring a book, even if it is exceptionally important and valuable, to the President of the United States? It would never happen."

She smiled. "Like dots, Jews are all connected. Someone knows someone who knows someone, and a deal is made. Whether it's to buy diamonds or to get an ancient treasure to the country's leader, Jews get it done. The compelling point here is that Ben-Zvi was a manuscripts scholar. He immediately understood the importance of the Codex. He also understood that there was no logical way on earth that this book should have survived the previous thousand years."

Ford smiled. "Maybe some higher hand was involved in saving the book."

"It's an attractive thought," said LeShana. She continued. "Ben-Zvi knew about the Karaite synagogue burning during the first Crusade, the attack by Tamerlane, and that the Syrians burned the Great Synagogue down in '47. He also knew that Maimonides proclaimed it the greatest Bible ever written, which made it the greatest Jewish heirloom in history. Ben-Zvi accepted the book, knowing this was the treasure of all treasures."

"So Ben-Zvi was able to study it?" Ford asked.

LeShana shook her head. "He didn't get the chance. At least not right away. The '56 war with Egypt and Syria broke out at the time the cheese merchant handed it over."

"What about the fire? How badly was the book burned?"

"Apparently the edges of some pages were singed but none were burned."

"Were those AWOL pages gone by then?" Ford asked.

"Nope. Ben-Zvi wrote that the book was complete except for the nine pages. But the story doesn't end there."

"No, why should it?" Ford through up his hands to accentuate how preposterous the Fard-Ford-Codex story was.

LeShana smiled, amused at his reaction to this fantastic story. She continued. "War has a way of changing priorities and everyone forgets about the Codex. Years later, when they're cataloguing books, they find the Codex sitting on a library shelf at the University of Tel Aviv. They realized what it is, and when they study it, that's when they discover that one hundred and ninety-six pages, or nearly one-third of the book has gone missing."

"As in stolen?"

"Same as stealing the Magna Carta or ripping the Declaration of Independence in half."

"Who would've done such a thing?"

She reached for the piece of evidence. "It's been postulated that the Mossad knows who has those pages, but they've done nothing to get them back. If we're able to catch the man who killed for this," she held the historic artifact in the air, "we may not only be able to solve a series of murders and robberies, we may also be able to find the missing chunk heisted from the book."

He stood. "This has been a most remarkable day. I need time to digest this. All of it." Then he muttered under his breath, "Totally amazing. Amazing." He stepped around his desk.

"Let me give you one more thing to digest."

He clutched his heart in jest. "Detective, I don't know if I can take anymore."

"I know what you mean, Your Excellency, but this is the coda to this story. The same day the Codex was alleged to have burned and been destroyed forever in '47 when the synagogue was set aflame, a shepherd boy climbed a hill and discovered the Dead Sea Scrolls. Can you imagine? The same day! It was as if God was compensating for the loss of one treasure by exposing another one to take its place."

She let the words hang in the air. She wanted to continue extolling that this was not a coincidence, but knew it was unnecessary.

He made the sign of the cross. "This humbles me," said Cardinal Ford. "That *is* a miracle."

"In ways we can't begin to imagine," added LeShana.

Neither could understand nor appreciate that the events set in motion that day would be life changing for both. More was at stake than altering lives.

Much more.

# Part II

# Chapter Thirty-Nine

t was fifteen days since the pope passed. After the funeral, the College of Cardinals met each day to discuss the direction the church was headed and where, if any, its course should be altered. During lunches and dinners, they surreptitiously measured each other's experiences, what they said, their special talents, how many languages they spoke, and noted individual characteristics that would benefit or be a detriment to the next Pontiff. There were other factors equally germane when evaluating a potential candidate: what was his style, was he a dynamic speaker or did he drone on to boredom, what doctrines did he hold sacred and what part of the world did he represent.

During the many gatherings where the Cardinals got to know each other better, some began to rise above the flock. The Cardinal from Genoa made an impassioned speech about the calamity of Italy's low birthrate, declaring, "A community without children has no future and is in a serious cultural catastrophe." He continued. "A lack of children creates not only a bleak future but also a lack of balance between generations and educational poverty." No one disagreed.

Other Cardinals spoke. The Cardinal from Milan discussed the economic problems of the Holy See. Another Cardinal headed the Pontifical Council for Culture and was a logical candidate, but he made waves when he declared that Darwinism was compatible with Church Doctrine. There was the young Cardinal from Manila that got everyone's attention when he challenged the Church to admit its mistakes and make the Church more available to the disenfranchised.

And lastly, there was the Cardinal from New York who spoke eloquently on the New Evangelization that impelled the church to think in a fresh way. He outlined a number of points that included the courage, faith and joy to spread the Lord Jesus's message. All impressed. If this were a political race, platforms and differences were now delineated.

Milling outside the Sistine Chapel, Ford overheard one Cardinal say, "Unless it's over on the first ballot, we're going to be in for the long haul."

"You don't think there's a frontrunner?" Ford asked.

"Not this time. There are many worthy candidates but the inside track usually goes to a Cardinal who has been posted inside the Vatican."

"Wouldn't they want a Cardinal who runs a diocese," asked Ford.

The Cardinal shrugged. "You would think that one who was more in touch with His flock would be a better choice. But Vatican insiders often have an advantage because they come in contact with every bishop before they're elevated to Cardinal. They gain loyalty and build allegiances early in their careers and then cement these relationships over time. They establish a broad base that is very hard to overcome."

"Still, we should pick the best person," said Ford. "I was impressed with many who spoke these last few days."

"You will soon find out that speechifying is not enough to become the next Pope, and the best person is not always picked."

As if on cue, the tall narrow doors of the Sistine Chapel swung open and the Cardinals filed in, one-by-one, finding their assigned seats.

Cardinal Ford sat near the middle. His gaze was drawn to Michelangelo's fresco of *The Last Judgment*. The colors were vibrant. Ford stared, panning left to right and then top to bottom. *The Last Judgment* depicted the second coming of Christ and the apocalypse. He focused on Christ judging the souls of humanity that rose and fell to their fates. Ford's keen eye noted that the wall this fresco was painted on canted forward, making God appear all the more powerful and the viewer, all the more humble. How appropriate. Christ in judgment. Now, Cardinals in judgment.

When the last Cardinal took his seat, a hush fell over the chamber. Awe and reverence engulfed the solemnity of the moment.

It was time. One hundred and twenty Cardinals were assembled to choose the next Pope. A majority was European, with a handful representing Africa, South America, and North America. By mandate, all were younger than eighty.

In a crisp voice, the Cardinal from Costa Rica, who served as the Cardinal Camerlengo, reviewed the values and attributes a Pope should exhibit. There was a clutch of favorites and one or two dark horses. When one person emerged with the necessary two-thirds majority, the vacant post would be filled and the church barely misses a step.

Ford leaned to the Cardinal next to him and whispered, "Have you heard of any alliances made that would insure selection on the first ballot?"

The man frowned. "There's always an attempt to influence the choice. It's human nature. But what's clear is that he who enters the conclave a Pope, leaves it as Cardinal. It will be someone no one's thinking about this first day."

Ford turned his attention back to the Cardinal describing the historic process they would follow. "All votes are secret, and there will only be one vote today. If no one gets the proper majority, we will have two ballots in the morning and two in the afternoon for the next three days until a new Pontiff is elected. If there is no selection by that time, we will take a day of rest to renew our energy and pray for the wisdom to make the proper choice before resuming with a new vote."

He waived a white ballot for all to see. "Each ballot is headed with a Latin phrase, *Eligo in Summum Pontificem*, which means, 'I elect as supreme pontiff.' Please write down your choice. Once you've written the name, fold the ballot twice. Then, one-by-one you will leave your seats and make your way to this alter," he was standing next to it, "and cast your vote."

All knew they would next hold the ballot high for all to witness and recite, "I call as my witness Christ the Lord who will be my judge, that my vote is given to the one who before God I think should be elected."

Next, as tradition had it, they would place the ballot on a silver paten and slide it into a special chalice. After bowing before the altar, each would return to his seat.

While he knew the process, Ford followed every word the Cardinal Camerlengo uttered. "When all the votes are cast, I will mix the ballots to ensure anonymity and then pick one at a time. One-by-one, each ballot is handed to the first of three scrutineers who sit in front of you." He pointed to three men who functioned as scribes. "It is the scrutineers' job to record the votes. The first scrutineer notes the candidate's name without announcing it, and then passes it to the second one, who records it again, also without announcing the name. Lastly, he hands it to the third scrutineer who both records the vote and then reads the name out loud. This is the first time you will hear a name announced. Once the name is uttered, the scrutineer plunges a large needle through the ballot and collects each one on a string."

All knew what he would say next. "If there is no winner on the first vote, the string of ballots is burned in a special stove and the black smoke will let the world know that there is no new Pope." Then the Cardinal Camerlengo smiled for the first time. "But when the needed majority is finally reached, chemicals will be added to the fire that causes the ballots to burn white. When the masses see white smoke, they will know that their new Pontiff will soon stand on the balcony overlooking St. Peter's Square. To make certain there's no mistake about the color of the smoke, the bells of the Basilica will ring at the same time to signal the new Pope's election."

Without further delay or any discussion, the first vote was taken.

Cardinal Ford sat with folded hands. He glanced about, searching for furtive looks that confirmed prearranged votes. Nothing could be discerned from the scores of poker faces.

When it was his turn to cast a vote, brisk steps brought him to the chalice in front of the rest. His choice was thoughtful and without surprise: a Brazilian Cardinal he had befriended at an ecumenical conclave. The cardinal was a noted scholar, a jurist, and a champion of moderating church practices to include the disenfranchised. Ford was convinced that his choice could make the much-needed repairs so necessary to restore the church's image.

All the votes were cast.

The third scrutineer announced the names on the ballots and how many votes each tallied.

Ford was surprised to hear his name called, even though it was close to the bottom of the dozen or so nominated. Being on the first ballot meant nothing. It was a courtesy vote to show respect or demonstrate that the Church had liberals willing to consider an American or willing to consider a black Cardinal.

No one had a majority. Before adjourning, the Cardinal Camerlengo spoke. "This, my dear colleagues, is not a popularity contest. Return to your rooms and contemplate who from among you will best serve our Lord as the Holy See."

The Cardinals shuffled out of the Sistine Chapel in silence.

The next day, a new vote was taken without preamble.

Again, no one received a majority.

It was clear by the names in the lead that the conservatives had their candidate and the revisionists had theirs. Many cardinals insisted that the Papacy be placed back in the hands of an Italian, while others didn't care so much as long as a European was elected. Consequently, the Cardinals from Milan and Genoa were in the lead along with those who held permanent posts inside the Vatican.

By the end of the second day, with five ballots taken in total, no one had a commanding lead. With each new ballot, some candidates received more votes while others received fewer. A new name was added, a couple dropped off. But not Ford's. Inexplicably, he moved up the ladder of candidates and was now nearer the middle of the pack than at the bottom.

The voting continued. Suggestions were made in the hopes of finding a compromise candidate; new names were put on the floor for discussion. Each time a new name was mentioned, that Cardinal could no longer comment on the others in contention.

Again and again, curls of black smoke wafted from the chimney over St. Peter's. Hope that a new Pope would soon be chosen evaporated as the winds blew the results to the heavens. It became evident that the majority of Cardinals, all of whom were vested with responsibility of choosing the next Pope, were entrenched in factions and dedicated to their choices. An air of disappointment hovered under Michelangelo's fresco; new names did not gain traction as a compromise. None expected a candidate to emerge any time soon.

By week's end, twenty votes had been tallied without a winner. Surely the twenty-first ballot would decide. It didn't. But before the scrutineer revealed the tallies of that vote, Cardinal Camerlengo made an announcement. It was the Camerlengo's job during the interregnum to both bury the Pope and administer the election of the new one. He spoke. "We have now had three sets of seven ballots, without a majority. In order to break this stalemate, I will now announce the two frontrunners of which you must vote for one to be our new Pontiff. No other names may be included from this point forward."

All wondered who the two candidates could be? The Cardinal from Genoa had the most votes on every ballot, so it was assumed that he would be one of the two. The other could not be guessed. By the twentieth ballot, leading vote getters included the Cardinal from Spain, who would be a welcomed candidate to have the Papacy remain with a European, a Vatican insider who knew the inner workings of the Church and could guide it effectively but had little contact with the outside world, and the Brazilian Cardinal who represented the disenfranchised and disenchanted, and was a great hope to rejuvenate the Church.

The last name still receiving a significant number of votes was Ford's. Ford had been gaining as a compromise candidate. He was the oldest of those in the running, and was viewed as a possible caretaker for the Papacy due to his advanced age. His colleagues viewed Ford as not being controversial and felt that he would not create waves or new policy. That Ford was both an American and black demonstrated the Church's willingness to open their arms and select a non-European.

The Cardinal Camerlengo announced the two top vote getters. There was an audible gasp from the Conclave; this was not expected. After a limited discussion of the merits of each, the Cardinal Camerlengo called for a vote. "Keep in mind, the next Pope must still receive two-thirds of the votes; it is not a simple majority."

With the greatest number of Cardinals coming from Europe, and the single most from Italy, including from the Vatican, most thought they knew who the winner would be.

◆ ◆ ◆

White smoke curled from the chimney. A roar erupted in St. Peter's Square. All wondered who the next Pope would be?

◆ ◆ ◆

In the Sistine Chapel, a withered man stepped forward. Emilio Rinaldi held the distinguished position of Dean of the College of Cardinals. He beckoned the newly elected Pontiff to face him. "Your fellow brothers have chosen you to become Pontifex Maximus, the Holy Roman Pontiff. Do you accept their wishes?"

"I do, Your Excellency."

"And what name do you wish to be known by, your Holiness?"

"Lazarus II."

Dean Emilio Rinaldi looked beyond Pope Lazarus, II, and eyed every Cardinal in the chapel, one-by-one. His gaze did not waiver; it lingered on some longer than others as if to say, *"Rid yourself of any stray thoughts...this is our new leader."*

"Do you, my fellow Cardinals, pledge absolute obedience to His Highness?"

A chorus of "Ayes" responded. Then the Dean, with the help of two cardinals, dressed the Pope in his white soutane and skullcap.

When all was in order, the Proto-Deacon of the College of Cardinals, Cardinal Gianni Luccarelli stepped onto the Vatican balcony, held up his hands for quiet, and declared, "Habemus Papam!"

The throngs of people, who had been waiting almost a week for this proclamation, erupted into a thunderclap of cheers. The roar was greater than when the Italian football team won the World Cup against France a few years back.

The following day, there would be a formal inauguration to install the Pope as head of the Catholic Church. At that time, a choir would chant, "Tu es Petrus," (Thou art Peter). These are the same words that Jesus spoke to Peter when He told him that he was the Rock upon which Christ would build His Church; He asked Peter to feed His sheep.

In that moment, all eyes were riveted on the figure obscured in shadows behind Cardinal Luccarelli. When Pope Lazarus II stepped forward, a still greater cheer erupted. The College of Cardinals had not only picked the first non-European in history, they had picked a black man of African origins.

The newly elected Pontiff, with hands clasped against the white frock, bowed to his minions. Again, a chorus of cheers erupted to welcome the Ethiopian baby saved by Catholic missionaries as their new *Papam*.

As he stood on the balcony basking in collective adoration of a sea of native Italians and tourists whose good fortune it was to be at St. Peter's Square when the new Pope was elected, Pope Lazarus II would have been forgiven if he had stray thoughts about the glory of leading the Catholic people.

He would have been forgiven if he had wished his missionary parents who saved him and reared him to follow this righteous path, had lived to see this day.

He would have been forgiven if he thought himself unworthy.

But would he have been forgiven if it became known that he remained perplexed about his core beliefs at that moment? Not that he had qualms about following the commands of the church and honoring the life of his Lord, Jesus Christ. Would that he could, the new Pontiff would gladly make the same sacrifice if it meant saving others. No need to overthink personal sacrifice.

His conundrum was what to do with the new knowledge gained

days earlier when LeShana Thompkins entered his life. She knew more about his father than he did. She knew about Black Jews and reading Hebrew. She knew about the Codex of Aleppo. She knew about Jacques Faitlovich, a man who had befriended his father. She knew about the Ethiopia where he was born. And she knew about W.D. Fard, alias Ford, who was the also a messenger of God.

How many messengers did the Lord have? How many prophets?

*Who exactly was Arnold Ford, and now that he was Lazarus II, what was he the Pope of? The Catholic Church or something even greater? Could he represent the entire Judeo-Christian world? Please, Lord, forgive such a grandiose notion.*

While only fleeting thoughts, Pope Lazarus II's questions would soon have answers.

A cheer brought him back to the moment. He raised both arms above his head, and then pressed his palms to his heart in a gesture showing his humble love and thanks.

Lazarus II was their Pope; they were his people.

# Chapter Forty

In the coming weeks, LeShana followed one lead after another without getting closer to cracking the murder of the old Jew. Due to the proximity to the diamond district and because the murder happened in front of St. Patrick's Cathedral and across from Rockefeller Center, there were multiple surveillance videos that should have captured the perpetrator as he hunted down the aged merchant in cold blood.

Her boss asked for a report.

"Nothing from ballistics," LeShana stated, reviewing what everyone involved in the case already knew. "The markings weren't in the system; the gun had never been used in a crime before. Every eyewitness has been interviewed and while the descriptions match, none are of any help. We've been able to capture the perps face on a close up. We distributed hundreds of flyers throughout the Orthodox communities in Boro Park, Brooklyn and in Monsey, up in Rockland County with no luck."

"You mean they won't talk."

"Their wall of silence is just as tough as ours."

"What about Israel?" asked the Chief Inspector.

"We've received major help from the Israelis. Big time. They not only checked with the Orthodox communities in Jerusalem, but helped us in Buenos Aires and Antwerp as well. This case is growing colder by the minute."

And then it happened.

LeShana's phone rang.

A break.

"Are *you* the one looking for anything connected to the Crown of Aleppo?" asked the caller.

The speaker did not say, "Hello."

The speaker did not say, "This is so-and-so."

No chitchat. Right to the point. A female voice.

"Whom do I have the pleasure of speaking with?" LeShana asked. She was certain the clipped accent was Israeli. Who else was more abrupt than one of God's chosen?

"Gittel Lasker. I'm an Israeli agent. We've had a break in the case of the missing pages of the Codex of Aleppo. I assume you know about the Codex since you're the one looking for the murderer of that diamond merchant."

LeShana's verbal gun was cocked and ready to fire.

"What do you have for me, Agent Lasker?"

"An antiquities merchant from London contacted us a couple of days ago with a bizarre story."

"Antiquities, like in selling ancient sculptures? Things like that?"

"In this case, manuscripts. Things pertaining to Judaica." Gittel continued without waiting to determine if LeShana understood the range of items this covered. "The man received a call at his home in London asking him to journey to Jerusalem to buy pages of an ancient manuscript. He tried to find out more, but all the caller said was that these pages were special and that it would be worth making the trip."

"That was enough for him to get on a plane?" LeShana asked. "What if they were bogus? He would've wasted a lot of time and money for nothing."

"When it comes to antiquities and manuscripts, collectors travel the world in hopes of scoring something others only dream about. It pays for them to take long shots. Of course, they try to verify everything as much as they can before they travel. When it comes to provenance, they must be certain of the ownership. But having said that, dealers such as the one I'm referring to, take chances all the time."

"I'd never take a chance like that."

"Detective you take the same chances following lead after lead, even if you end up in a blind alley. We all do. That's the nature of our business. Dealers are no different. What makes it worthwhile is the potential profit that he can make buying an antiquity before it's part of an open auction."

Agent Lasker was right. How many times had LeShana agreed to meet someone with the promise of information, no matter how slight or remote?

Gittel continued. "Within minutes of checking into the King David Hotel, two Hasidic men met him in his hotel room and asked if he could afford one million dollars. The dealer said he could, provided it was for the right object."

"Did they have it with them?"

If LeShana had been in the same room with Gittel, she would have seen the agent frown at the simplicity of that question.

"They came empty-handed. They needed to size him up, make certain he wasn't armed, and that he had the resources they felt this so-called 'package' deserved."

"So did this antiquities dealer from London buy the 'package?'" LeShana asked.

"They were staying in the same hotel. In minutes they returned with sheets from a manuscript. Loose pages."

"Are you going to tell me they were the missing pages from the Codex of Aleppo?"

"That's what the dealer thought. Later, when we showed him a photocopy of the original, he was certain of it."

"Wait, how'd you get a photocopy? The pages have been missing for decades."

"During World War II, the chief rabbi of the Yellow Synagogue permitted an Italian Jewish scholar to sneak into Syria and take pictures of every page. Luckily, we have a facsimile of the complete Codex."

"So you could recreate the book if you wanted to."

"We have," answered Gittel, "but a copy is not the same as the original."

LeShana thought about the merchant and what he must have felt seeing those pages up close. Her mouth went dry. Her head pounded, she spoke faster. "Were they all there? What's missing? All hundred and ninety-odd pages? Did he buy them? Have they been authenticated?" She couldn't spit the questions out fast enough. There was so much she wanted to know.

"They're authentic all right. That's why they contacted him in the first place; he's a manuscripts scholar. And they knew he had the means to pay for them."

"Did he?"

"I wish he had," Gittel answered.

LeShana's spirits sank. They were about to break an international case wide open. So close, yet not there.

"Didn't he appreciate the value of what he had?"

"That's the problem. He did. But to his way of thinking, if he spent the million dollars to buy the pages, the Israeli government would claim that the pages were rightfully theirs and confiscate them. He would be out the money."

"You're telling me that the Israeli government wouldn't reimburse him?"

"It's like a hostage situation; they're not going to buy a hostage's freedom. That's blackmail. They won't do it for a person and certainly not for a few pages of parchment."

"They swap for prisoners. This is their national treasure. How is this any different?"

"There may be more to it than we understand," Gittel answered.

"And I guess this Mr. London Antiquities dealer wasn't the charitable sort? Not willing to do a good deed and 'donate' the missing pages of the Codex to Israel, was he?"

"I guess he didn't have a spare million to fork over."

*Who does?*

"So where does that leave us?" asked LeShana. It felt good to team up with an Israeli agent, even though she had not exactly been invited. "Was the dealer able to identify either man?"

"Not by name, but we have reason to believe we know who's behind this. Or at least what group they belong to."

LeShana cut her off. *Group?* "I don't know how I missed it before, but it's so obvious who these people are. We have them here, too."

The two compared notes.

Gittel continued. "That's why I'm calling you, detective. If we're right, then it stands to reason they may behind the murders in New York, Deal, Brooklyn, Buenos Aires, and who knows where else?"

LeShana was already formulating her next steps when she asked, "Is the Mossad going after the men with the missing pages?"

"That's the strange part of the story," she said. Again if Agent Lasker and Detective Thompkins were in the same room, the Agent would have seen LeShana roll her eyes.

*Every part of the story connected to the Codex of Aleppo is strange.*

"When I informed my superiors that there's a lead on the whereabouts of the missing pages of the Crown of Aleppo, they said they would contact the Mossad. A few days later, when I followed up to see what they were doing about it, I was told to mind my own business. That there was nothing to the lead."

"And...." LeShana paused, "you think they're stonewalling you."

"Excuse me?"

"That they knew more than they're telling you. That they're hiding something."

"The Mossad is geared to solve problems like this. The fact that they said there's nothing to the lead means they're being blocked from the top."

"The Prime Minister?" asked LeShana.

"Possibly. There are powerful Orthodox rabbis in the Knesset and the PM's coalition is tenuous at best."

'That's a lot to go up against."

"That's why I'm calling. If you use your resources to approach this from another direction, perhaps you could solve your murder and, in the process, we'd get leads to the whereabouts of the missing pages."

"You'd do an end-around the Mossad?"

"Would you circumvent the FBI to solve a case?"

"Point well taken."

Even before they said their goodbyes and promised to keep in contact, LeShana had already planned her next step.

# Chapter Forty-One

ittel hung up the phone after speaking with the New York detective with the Hebrew sounding first name. She drummed her short but manicured fingers on the gray steel desktop. She reviewed the Londoner's story over and over in her mind. When she first heard about the possibility that the lost manuscript pages had surfaced, she thought it a hoax. But after drilling the antiquities dealer for more time than the poor man could tolerate, during which she had to once stop so he could take his heart medication, she was convinced he was telling the truth.

That was a week ago when Gittel was about to take a long weekend and join a team sifting through a recent discovery. A hotel started to expand their swimming pool when the backhoe hit an archeological jackpot after two scoopfuls: they had uncovered an ancient ritual bath. Gittel was on her way to the site when a call came in about missing manuscript pages. It was known in the department from the early days of their forensic training that when it came to stolen artifacts, ancient history, or studying the shifting sands of time, Gittel Lasker needed to be brought into the loop.

As was the case on any archeological dig she, an amateur, knew when to defer to experts. Her strength was to know her limitations and find out who had more knowledge than she, and who could help push an investigation or a project forward.

Enter Professor Yussif Tawil, from the University of Tel Aviv. Tawil had ringlets of salt-and-pepper hair. His forehead was lined with troughs of worry. His skin was ruddy and pitted and thick; for centuries his ancestors traded spices and traveled by camelback from town to town throughout Yemen. He was small of stature, wiry, with a spark of life that lit up whenever talk turned to Biblical history. Though it was Friday evening and he would soon go to synagogue to start the Sabbath prayers, once he heard Gittel relate the details of the man from London and the loose pages, he rocketed to Jerusalem in record time. He muttered the ritual prayers as he sped across the country; God would have to understand.

Professor Tawil asked pointed questions about the vocalization. What was on the first page? The last page? Had the man from London ever seen script like this before? Was there anything written in the margins?

It was apparent that whoever the men were, they had picked the right person. The antiquities dealer from London recited chapter and verse what was on the first page, what the trops looked like, and what was in the page margins. That the writing was identical to the sample Professor Tawil showed him...a facsimile of a page from the Codex of Aleppo. And lastly, he verified the text on the last line of the last page the men showed him. It was from Deuteronomy. The end of the blessings; before the curses. That was the clincher.

The Codex of Aleppo contained 491 pages. It had been verified by many that all but nine made it out of the fires in 1947. The missing pages were not ruined, burned or destroyed. They were taken for good luck charms. Cut up into snippets of lines. Laminated. Saved in wallets. Jewelry boxes. In blue velvet prayer shawl bags.

Professor Tawil explained. "When the Persian cheese merchant, Murad Faham, brought the book to Israel and handed it to Yitzhak Ben-Zvi, the book was virtually intact. They put the book on the shelf and lost track of it when the Sino-Israeli War, broke out in '56. By the time someone remembered the Codex, almost two hundred pages were missing."

"Wasn't the book put under lock and key?" asked Gittel.

The professor shrugged. "No one gave it a second thought. It sat on a shelf for years, untouched. Ignored, like so many other artifacts and treasures. When the Codex was finally brought to a curator's attention that was doing inventory, they ran to protect it. That's when they discovered that one-third of the book was missing."

"And the curses?"

He pointed to the ceiling. "Ah, for me that's a clue as to who took the missing pages."

"What clue?" Gittel challenged him. "What more could there be? Someone intended on taking the whole book. They heard someone coming and lifted a bunch of pages. A simple theft that fell short of being completed."

He wagged his finger; Gittel was transported back to grade school. "Agent, I'm surprised at you. You, above all people, should know that what appears simple and obvious may not be that at all. Not when it comes to the Codex of Aleppo."

"But sometimes things are what they appear to be: simple."

"Not when it comes to the Curses. Didn't you learn about them in Hebrew school?"

She blushed. "I was more interested in playing football with the boys."

He ignored her avoidance of proper schooling. "God, for all his glory, is not as benevolent and understanding as most want to believe. Deuteronomy is the fourth book of Moses that makes up the Torah. And the Torah is five of the twenty-four books that make up the Bible."

"Deuteronomy is all about the rules and laws. That much I remember," Gittel said.

His wrinkled face glowed. "Ah, so you *were* a good student."

"Not that good, professor. I must've paid attention that day."

"You underestimate your abilities." With a jolt of clarity, he continued. "Deuteronomy reminds us that we are more than disparate individuals, we are a community that needs to act as a unit. We need to follow the rules our Lord laid down in the Bible for us. Put simply, we are God's people, in God's place, expected to follow God's rules and laws."

"And if we don't?"

"The wrath of God will be unleashed like no tragedy that has ever befallen our people."

"I would remember that," she said, "but I don't."

"Few do. Everyone thinks, or at least wants to believe, that God is wonderful."

"It's assumed."

Tawil's eyes lit up the way someone is about to reveal a secret. "That's why I know that the missing pages of the Codex are not random."

She frowned. "Please explain."

"Because whoever stopped at the curses knew what they were doing. The curses are many. They outnumber the blessings maybe three to one. Remember, these blessings and the curses were handed down to the Jews who have been wandering in the desert for forty years. They left Egypt and slavery behind, and were headed to the Promised Land. Guided by Moses. God tested them every step of the way. At times they failed, but God keeps on giving them new chances."

"Like when they built the golden calf."

"Precisely. God forgave them...that time. But our God is not a forgiving God. The curses prove that. God tells them in no uncertain words that if they don't follow the rules of the Covenant, they will all suffer. They will experience poverty, be devastated and stressed in every facet of life. Women will be barren. So will their crops. They will be conquered, forced to pay tributes, enslaved. And it gets worse."

"Not nice."

"Those curses are just the beginning. God goes on to tell them that their bodies will be food for birds and beasts, that they will experience boils and tumors and scabs, insanity and blindness. Their wives will be molested, their children taken from them, and the list doesn't stop there."

Gittel gulped. Like all other Israeli children, she learned about the Bible and thought she knew all the key parts. But curses? This is the first she's ever heard about them. Wasn't God good? Sure, life's a challenge. There've always been bumps and bruises along the way. In the case of the Jews, their portfolio hadn't missed much. Consider when they were enslaved by the Egyptians, expelled from their homes during the Spanish Inquisition, burned at the stake starting in France, then Spain and Portugal and then the *auto de fer* was exported to the New World, and more recently anti-Semitism, pogroms, ghettos, arm bands embossed with the yellow Star of David, and Nazi gas chambers just to name some of the choice morsels of cruelty and bigotry that have made His Chosen People a clan bound together by centuries of persecution.

They are survivors.

Curses? In the Bible? How could that be?

"What does all of this mean, Professor?"

He grabbed her hand and squeezed; his eyes shone bright. "It means that the people who took the missing pages were learned. They were scholars of the text. At the very least, whomever they're answerable to, whoever sent them on this mission to take the pages, knew the Bible inside and out. You see, the very last page they stole ended with the following challenge:

*But it shall come about, if you will not obey the LORD your God, to observe to do all His commandments and His statutes with which I charge you today, that all these curses shall come upon you and overtake you. (Deuteronomy 28:15)*

"Am I correct in surmising that the very next phrase, the one they left began the curses."

"Precisely. Otherwise, they would have stolen the whole book."

"Who do you think stole these pages?"

"I don't know who stole them. No one does. But I know who has them. I know the sect those two men in the hotel belong to."

She nodded, curling her fingers, palm upward, cajoling the answer from him.

"The Satmar Jews."

Hearing that, Gittel was able to connect the missing pages with a report she had glanced at that had come over Interpol a week earlier. It was about a Jew in New York killed for a piece of parchment. Not just any parchment.

There were Satmar Jews in New York. And in Deal, NJ. And in Buenos Aires. And every other place connected to fragments of the Codex of Aleppo. It was beginning to make sense.

That's when she rung up the New York detective with the Hebrew name.

# Chapter Forty-Two

L eShana checked her notebook a second time. The Satmar synagogue, Congregation Yetev Lev D'Satmar, was located at Kent Avenue and Hooper Street. The address was correct, but there was nothing in the area that remotely resembled a house of worship. Across the way she noted a plain white stucco building. It had two stories with a brown fire escape leading up to the second floor. There was little else to distinguish the building.

She stopped a black-frocked man passing by. "Excuse me, but I'm looking for the rabbi."

A twinkle sparkled from his deep-set eyes, weighed down by sacs of flesh. He waved his hand. "Every man you see in this part of Brooklyn is a rabbi. That includes me," he added with a measure of pride.

"The rabbi I'm looking for is the head of the Satmar sect. Rabbi Breitstein. There's supposed to be a synagogue around here, but I don't see one."

"That's it," he pointed, "across the street. You were staring at it."

"Where?"

"There. The stucco building. We call it the 'miracle' synagogue because all 20,000 square feet were built in fourteen days."

"That's not possible," said LeShana. She didn't have to know anything about construction to know that building a structure that size would be heroic in fourteen weeks. Building it in fourteen months would be more realistic.

The man arched his back and beamed. "That's why it's called a 'miracle.'"

"And that's where I can find Rabbi Breitstein?"

"Do you have an appointment? He's a very important man. Few ever get an audience with him. Even *I* have never met him in person. I've only been blessed to see him from a distance."

She showed him her gold Detective badge. "It has to do with a murder investigation. I'm certain he can find time to give me a few moments of his time."

*Washington, DC*

The Secretary of Defense appeared by remote hookup from his office, live on the Anderson Cooper show.

"Let me ask you directly, Mr. Secretary, by all accounts, the war in Afghanistan is winding down and our troops are being withdrawn. We'll keep a maintenance force and advisors there, while the Afghans are expected to protect themselves. This follows the same pattern when we extricated ourselves from Iraq. The question I have for you: is this the best outcome we could have achieved? "

"Given the circumstances, Anderson, we're very pleased with the outcomes in both wars."

"Do you consider them victories?"

"Beyond a doubt. Consider this: if we had left Iraq before it was secure, there would've been mass carnage with the Sunnis massacring the Shiites. The Kurds would have seceded and Iran would have, more than likely, marched in and taken over the country, including Iraq's oil fields."

"And would that have been so terrible?" Anderson asked.

"Let's be clear about one thing: the Iranians would never have gotten close to those oil fields. So let's not go there. Regarding Iraq, our goal from the outset was to not only topple Saddam but to create a democratic nation with free elections. Admittedly it took longer than planned, but we achieved our goals. Since then, there have been democratic elections in Iraq and the Iraqis are now able to defend themselves."

"With our help."

"Yes, with our help, but the goals have been accomplished. The Iraqis are sovereign and we only serve as advisors."

"Like we did in Viet Nam."

The comparison caused the Secretary of Defense to bristle. "This is much different than Viet Nam, and you should know better."

Cooper moved on, undaunted by the reprimand.

"What about Al Qaeda? They've been able to test and learn valuable skills that they need to carry out their *fatwa* around the world at our expense. What do you have to say about that?"

"By that logic, you would say that we made ourselves more vulnerable by attacking our enemy."

"Is there another way to look at it?"

The Secretary squirmed in his seat, and tugged at his collar. He swallowed before answering. "I wear a different pair of glasses, Anderson. From where I'm sitting, Bin Laden's dead and al Qaeda's top echelon has been annihilated. Al Qaeda is no longer the force it was. We defeated them in Afghanistan and keep in mind that we've thwarted every effort they've made to attack us on US soil since two thousand and one. I'd say we've fought our enemy remarkably well... and have won war."

"We may be winning, Mr. Secretary, but the war isn't over."

"From where I'm sitting, Anderson, it's over. To that end, Americans can go to sleep each night knowing that everything is being done to protect their safety and freedoms."

"But can you tell American people watching tonight that our country is safe and that Al Qaeda no longer has capability to attack us again?"

"Nothing would give me greater pleasure than to answer you in the affirmative, Anderson, but I can't."

"Then by that reckoning, Mr. Secretary, no matter how many leaders we've killed, no matter how much their organization is decimated, it sounds to me like Al Qaeda has won the war and we're the losers."

"That's where you and I differ, Anderson. They've thrown their best against us and we've repelled them every time. And we'll keep doing that 'til there are none left to carry on their jihad."

"It will take a miracle to have that happen," said Anderson. "I'm not as hopeful as you are, Mr. Secretary."

"Then perhaps you should start praying harder."

# Chapter Forty-Three

Zakkarhia clicked off Anderson Cooper.

"What fools!" Zakkarhia had planned many assignments during the intervening years. Bali. Algiers. Manila. So many others. His present mission was a great challenge: organize a training camp in the hinterlands of Yemen with the goal of overthrowing the country's weak-willed leader. With a foothold in the toe of the Arabian Peninsula, it was only a matter of time before the jihad would advance to where it all began: Saudi Arabia.

Three thousand princes, all soft. The *fatwa* against them will be issued in due time. Their days as oil-rich Bedouins were drawing to an end, it would be as if their precious wells went dry. The difference would be startling. Instead of retiring to their palaces and decadent homes on the Riviera or in Bel Air, vultures would feast on their carcasses as the jihadists took command of their country.

It was only fitting. After all, Yemen was the birthplace of Mohammed Bin Laden, Osama bin Laden's father. Few would remember that the first terrorist act was the bombing of a hotel in the southern city of Aden used by U.S. troops en route to Somalia. Two civilians were killed in that attack in 1992. At the time, it was not connected to any terrorist group. Then there was the first Twin Towers. The Argentine Mutual Aid Society killing scores of Jews. The Twin Towers again, this time the final act. Bali. Madrid. London. Algiers. The hotel in Amman. The police academy in Bagdad.

Zakkarhia clapped his hands. He shuffled over to the built-in bar under the T.V. He fingered through the small bottles of liquor until he found a bottle of Smirnoff. He twisted off the cap and tossed it down. He savored the harsh burn on the back of his throat. He found another.

Thank you President Clinton, for lacking the balls to go after Osama.

Thank you President Bush. Thank you for letting us train at your expense.

Thank you President Obama for making us stronger.

Thank you for uniting the brothers around the world into a cohesive unit.

Thank you for teaching us how best to beat you.

When Zakkarhia was done thanking Presidents Clinton, Bush, and Obama, he dispatched a team to make the first kills that would undermine the latest Yemenite government. First they killed a few Japanese tourists. Next they attacked the palace and almost killed President Saleh. With a new buffoon in place, Al Qaeda had the run of the country. Let them send drones. No matter. Zakkarhia's comrades were that much closer to Saudi Arabia.

What did the fools think al Qaeda was doing in Yemen if not to undermine the Saudis?

*Williamsburg, Brooklyn*
"Rabbi Breitstein, do you know this man?"

Any number of security cameras had captured the image of the jewelry merchant's assassin, yet no one could identify him. When in doubt, go to the source.

Breitstein was not a foot from her, but continued *dovening* without acknowledging LeShana standing there. Apparently nothing stopped him from completing his afternoon prayers, not even a NYPD detective.

LeShana squashed her thoughts of Orthodox men who spent their days in worship while others toiled to support them, or those who had no shame asking for handouts. Who did they think they were, sending their wives and their children out to work so they could pray all day? Was that what it took to be a righteous Jew? Be a mooch?

She waved the picture in front of his face; the rabbi looked away from both her and the picture.

"Rabbi, I'm not leaving until you give me the courtesy of looking at this picture and telling me if you know this man or not."

"What can my looking at a picture mean to you? It's just a picture. I wasn't there. I don't even know what happened."

"It's funny how you know that something happened. I didn't mention it."

He made a gesture. "Why else would you be here? To *doven?*" The image of the black cop praying made him chuckle.

Nonplused, LeShana wouldn't give him the satisfaction of correcting him. "But you could tell me if this man is a member of your congregation. Is that asking too much?"

That challenge got the rabbi's notice.

"Why would he be? My congregants obey the Lord's laws, His Ten Commandments, which, I don't have to remind you, includes...."

*"Lo teer tsakh."*

This got his attention. Rabbi Breitstein edged his gold wire-rimmed glasses further down his nose and peered over them.

"How is it that someone such as yourself can recite the sixth commandment that forbids killing? In Hebrew, no less?"

LeShana leaned forward, allowing him to focus on the picture. Curious, she thought, he wouldn't reach out and touch it. Probably, he was fearful of touching a woman other than his wife.

She stepped in front of him. Studied his eyes, which were pale blue. In Yiddish, she said, "Are you asking if I speak Hebrew because I'm a woman? Or is it because I'm an American and not from the *shtetl?*"

*Why not have a bit of fun at the expense of this arrogant man who assumes that no, sic woman, one is as learned as he?*

Stunned at the ghetto tongue, *his* ghetto tongue - Yiddish - he pulled back.

"You're a most unusual woman. Many of our own speak Hebrew and Yiddish. The days of women remaining uneducated have long since past."

She knew that was the case, but why push him? "But it's a new day when a Jewish cop happens to also be a black woman. Now that's something new, isn't it?" she said with a warm smile. Most of the time, she was amused when others were surprised at her being a Jew and able to speak both Hebrew and Yiddish. But in front of this rabbi? She was downright pleased with herself.

*Chalk one up for black Jewish sisters!*

He nodded and then turned to the picture for a beat. "You impress me, Detective." He shot a cursive glance at the picture and then turned back to her. "He's not one of ours."

"Are you sure?"

"He's not from here."

"But he is a Satmar."

With emphasis, he said, "Yes, but from *Eretz Yisrael*." He spit the words out with venom. LeShana knew there was no love lost between Breitstein and his brother, who headed the Satmar sect in Israel.

"How do you know he comes from Israel?"

"Because he's not one of us."

"You're certain of that? Aren't there about fifty thousand members here?"

"More than one hundred thousand. And I know everyone of them. Now I have a question for you." LeShana nodded, surprised he would venture to ask her anything. "What is this man accused of doing?"

LeShana offered a quick summary, omitting any reference to Cardinal Ford. "Was the man killed a Syrian Jew? Did he have a piece of laminated parchment in his possession?"

"How'd you know that?" asked LeShana. "We kept that piece of information out of the papers."

"I hear things."

"What else did you hear?"

"I heard they would stop at nothing to find *all* the missing pieces of the Codex of Aleppo."

"Why now? These fragments have been in the victims' possession for decades."

"Because the time is ripe."

She pressed. "For what?"

"To save Israel from itself."

"Forgive me, Rabbi, but I don't understand. The State of Israel has existed for as long as these pages have been missing. Actually, since the very day these pages went missing. Everybody knows the Israeli story of how they've overcome adversity after adversity and how they've succeeded every time their existence was threatened. No matter how hard they try, the Arabs can't destroy that tiny little country. And the Iranians, in the end, know that they will never be allowed to build a bomb. Not as long as Israel continues to exist."

"Iran, I know nothing about. Israel, I do. And what I do know is that there are other ways to overthrow a government. To control what they do. It doesn't always have to come from extrinsic forces."

"Are trying to tell me there's a Fifth Column operating in Israel?"

"Detective. I'm not from your world. To me, a fifth column is used in accounting. What I do know is that radical Zionists want to dance on the grave of the State of Israel. And my brother is one of them."

"I know you sent your brother to Israel years back. Has he gone rogue? Is he connected to Al Qaeda? Hezbollah? Hamas? Is there some other terrorist organization that's under the radar that you might know about? If there is, you need to tell me."

The rabbi retreated. "My brother sees the world differently than I do. His agenda is not mine."

LeShana shrugged.

*LeShana had met this religious type before, the kind that talked in riddles, ever virtuous, never revealing anything, but posturing as if he did.*

For the first time, the Rabbi engaged LeShana, peering into her eyes. "My brother and his followers are in an alliance, Detective Thompkins, that is stronger than with any government or subversive group."

"They must be getting help from somewhere? Someone? It's a worldwide operation."

"Think of it like insider trading."

"I'll bite. So who's giving them the inside track? Organizing their activities?"

Before answering, he cleaned his glasses with his black tie that was speckled with food stains.

"They're in partnership with the Lord Almighty himself. And the Lord Almighty has a master blueprint that these people seek to carry out. You don't have to look any further than that."

That was a challenge she was revved to take.

# Chapter Forty-Four

Pope Lazarus II waved to the crowds from the central balcony of St. Peter's Basilica.

*"Dear brothers and sisters,*
*The cardinals have elected me, a simple, humble worker in the*
*Lord's service. I am comforted by the fact that the Lord knows that*
*a fallible servant can be trusted with your exalted prayers in His*
*honor. With the joy of the risen Lord, and confidence in his constant*
*help, we will go forward. The Lord will help us, and Mary his most*
*holy mother will be alongside us to give us strength in these difficult*
*times. Thank you."*

The following morning, Pope Lazarus II started his first day in office celebrating mass with the cardinals who elected him as leader of the world's billion-plus Roman Catholics. The pontiff, visibly moved and wearing the papal mitre on his head, led a solemn procession followed by one hundred-and-twenty Cardinals into the Sistine Chapel, where less than twenty-four hours earlier, they had chosen him to succeed the late Pope.

Lazarus II and the Cardinals, standing under Michelangelo's Last Judgment, began the televised mass chanting of "Iubilate Deo" (Celebrate God), with the small stove used to the burn the ballots still in the chapel. According to tradition, he delivered his homily in Latin.

With the inauguration over, Lazarus II began his day-to-day duties of papal responsibility. As spiritual leader of the world's Catholics, and as the Vatican's head of state, the Pope's responsibilities were vast and his duties many. He served as bishop of the archdiocese of Rome, providing spiritual guidance to its members; he appointed bishops and cardinals; he presided at beatification and canonization ceremonies; he spread the word of the Roman Catholic Church throughout his travels; he wrote documents that defined the Catholic Church's official position on issues facing the world; and he conferred with global leaders and politicians about these and other issues.

He wasted no time creating controversy. Summoning key Cardinals and decision makers to his office, including all who were nominated to become Pope, he announced, "I would like to hold a Vatican III conference."

To a one, they were stunned. Most were known for speaking their mind. Not this time; they were all speechless. Pope John XXIII convened Vatican II and when he did, he turned the church upside down by permitting mass to be conducted in the peoples' native languages and no longer in Latin. Vatican II went further by dispensing with the ban of eating meat on Fridays. Pope John XXIII, beloved by all, brought the masses and the church back to the people. Catholics around the world adored him for doing this, but changes wrought by Vatican II did not sit well within the church hierarchy.

And now they had to deal with this Anglo upstart? He was supposed to be a caretaker to the throne of St. Peter. Hold it without controversy for a few years and then have the good sense to die. Or, based on the Pope Benedict XVI's precedence, step down when the College of Cardinals would urge him to do so.

"What do you hope to achieve?" asked the Cardinal from Brazil, who had had Lazarus's support to be Pope.

"The Church is rapidly becoming irrelevant."

They gasped. Maybe a neophyte from the Philippines or Nigeria would say this, but the new Pontiff? This was sacrilege.

"We must find ways to engage the young, the disenfranchised. How can we remain viable and relevant if our priests continue to behave as they do? It's unnatural not to be in love, to share life with another soul."

Flummoxed, the Cardinals argued back. "We are all in love with our Lord, Your Excellency. We are wed to Jesus Christ our Savior. We have given our lives and our souls to him."

"And that, my dear colleagues, is not enough," said Lazarus II. "We must let priests marry. No, we must encourage it, so they can share in the joys of wedlock and of raising children. This will enable them to better relate to our congregants, to understand their cares and worries, to provide better for their spiritual needs."

Pope Lazarus II left the topic of molestation alone, trusting that each Cardinal present would understand that by permitting priests to marry, it would attract a different sort of person into the priesthood, it would open the door for nuns to assume greater roles in the Church, and it would go a long way to righting the course the Church had taken over these many centuries.

The Cardinals all spoke at once, chirping that his ideas were heresy and preposterous.

Pope Lazarus II raised his hands for silence. "I'm not finished. I want to discus women having the right to control their bodies. We have lost too many followers because we dictate what they can and can't do. It's time to stop preaching and start listening; it's time to give the people what they want. What they need. And when we do, they will return to the flock in droves."

"Your Excellency, do you know what you're asking?"

"Obviously, my brother. I've already made the arrangements. Vatican III will convene in three months time."

Lazarus stood, blessed them, and returned to his office. He didn't dare look back. He didn't need to; he knew what their reactions were. Inwardly, he permitted himself to glow in contentment. If they thought he was a figurehead Pope, they had another thing coming to them.

◆　◆　◆

Pope Lazarus II returned to his office and was reviewing papers in need of his attention when he stopped, stood, and then stepped toward the door without any prompts.

As he neared, there was a knock. The door glided open and a young, determined priest entered, eyes and face down, stepping briskly. He dodged to the left a split second before colliding head-on with the Pope. Was it the priest's imagination or was the Pope waiting for him? How?

The priest bowed. "Your Excellency."

"I'll see her."

The man looked up, open-mouthed. "I didn't say anything."

"I know."

The priest froze. Lazarus II waved for him to bring the visitor. The young man had heard the rumors that the new Pope had a sixth sense. To experience it firsthand on the inaugural date of his papacy was, well, not easy to describe. As time went on, the unusual surrounding Lazarus II would become the commonplace. What would become commonplace for Lazarus was extraordinary by all other measures.

The priest backed away.

"It's a gift," he heard Lazarus II call after him.

Moments later, the priest wheeled Hui Chan into the Pope's study. Hui had been acclaimed China's greatest classical dancer and was to perform at the Beijing Olympics when her career was smashed to smithereens. Two weeks before the Olympic Games were to start, she leapt toward a moving stage that malfunctioned, causing her to fall into a deep pit. She fell against a steel rod with such force that she was left paralyzed from the waist down.

"The doctors gave up on you, didn't they?" Pope Lazarus II asked, knowing they had. Hui was on course to be a national and world celebrity when the tragedy struck. Her fierce determination roared back after a period of personal mourning for her bad luck. Even though she could not stand, she used her beauty and grace to become a fashion model.

Hui whispered what he knew, that the doctors said she would never walk again. She told the Pope she still went to physical therapy each day in the hopes that a new technology would emerge to connect her damaged nerves. She had no doubt that this would happen. It was just a matter of when.

The Pope looked at the priest who had rolled Hui into the study. "Would you leave us alone, please?"

"The photographers will be here any moment. The Cardinal Camerlengo thought this moment should be preserved. For goodwill, Your Excellency."

The Pope nodded. "The world will get its photo in a few moments. For now, I need to be alone with this young lady. We have much to discuss away from the prying eye of a camera."

Surprised that the new Pope should already be so deliberate in his thoughts, the young priest exited the study and waited. He searched the halls for the photographer who was not yet in sight. He edged closer to the door, cupping his ear to pick up any utterances he might overhear. There was little chance Hui's whispers would carry an extra meter, she spoke that softly, but if he concentrated, he might catch a few words of the Pope.

An elevator door pinged open. Luigi Pitigliano, the ubiquitous papal photographer for L'Osservatore Romano, the Vatican newspaper, who always dressed in black, rounded the corner. Luigi had been the personal photographer for the previous five Popes. Lazarus II made it half-a-dozen. In close to fifty years, Luigi had never missed a day's work. His job consisted of loitering near the Pontiff for sixteen hours each day while remaining unobtrusive as he documented the Pope's every move for posterity. Luigi's job included attending every private mass, being present for every visit by foreign dignitaries, and traveling with each Pope on their many worldwide trips. He was within a few feet of John Paul II when an attempt was made on the Pope's life during a general audience in St Peter's Square in May 1981. The pictures he took dominated front pages around the world.

The young priest straightened when he saw Luigi.

"Where's the girl?" Luigi started each morning at his office. He was in the middle of culling which pictures from the day before would be preserved in a permanent file when his editor received a call that the new Pope was ahead of schedule. He was already greeting the handicapped Chinese female athlete.

"He wants to be alone with her."

"I should be in there with them."

"That's not the sense I got when he asked me to leave. He was adamant."

That stopped Luigi's momentums as he was about to thrust open the door. He wobbled and regained his footing. "He asked you to leave? He's alone in there with a young woman?"

"In a wheelchair."

"What does that have to do with anything? We can't allow that. A scandal his first day on the job? That will never do. We need to get in there right now. It will turn into *he said, she said.*"

"Luigi. We're talking about the Pope."

"And you're talking about a man who few know anything about. And he's alone with a woman. If you don't knock this second, I will."

Luigi made a fist to rap on the door when it opened. The Pope stood aside. "We can take those photos now."

And what photos they were.

The Pope said it was a matter of willpower.

Papers around the world proclaimed it a miracle.

Not only did Luigi's pictures capture the ecstasy on Hui Chan's face when she stood, but his camera captured her first steps since the accident that paralyzed her years ago.

Thirty million viewed the video on You Tube that day alone. Pope Lazarus II was no longer the *caretaker* Pope chosen to lead the world's Catholics; now all talked of the miracle. That's what they called it, *The Miracle.*

# Chapter Forty-Five

The guard passed a tray of brown gruel through the slatted steel bars.

"They're never going to come for you," the guard said. "The Israelis will never attack Gaza again. The world won't allow it."

Jericho Glassman used his fingers to shovel the food into his mouth, no utensils for prisoners.

Jericho didn't answer.

"The only way you'll get out of here alive is if those swine free at least one hundred of our people they have in their jails. And they will, you wait and see."

Jericho spooned in more. He had no idea what the vial-tasting food was. They probably pissed in it for added flavor. Let them. After he was captured, there was an outcry from the Israeli government to set Jericho free. Secret negotiations were carried out for months without result. Hamas wanted too much in exchange. Knowing they'd keep Jericho alive, the Israeli government stopped all negotiations and waited for the right opportunity to surface that would permit a realistic prisoner exchange. They didn't know when or what the terms would be, but they knew it would come about. It always did. Days turned into weeks, weeks into years. Still, no one forget he was there.

*Jerusalem*
And then it happened. The message was clear. An Israeli official stood before a herd of reporters.

"After years of restraint, Israel will no longer tolerate terror attacks coming from the Gaza Strip. Hamas, and members of the vertical axis of extremism led by Iran, have misinterpreted our patience as weakness. Recently, Israel agreed to the Egyptian-brokered Period of Calm agreement that began in June. Unfortunately, Hamas repeatedly transgressed its terms.

Hamas's deplorable posture and their unprovoked actions have forced Israel to take military action. For this reason, we have initiated Operation Cast Lead. The goal of this operation is to improve the security situation in Southern Israel and to facilitate peaceful conditions for the Israeli civilians living there. We will hit Hamas hard. We will strike at their tunnels, we will go after the terrorists hiding behind the skirts of women and children, and we will destroy their assets in order to prevent them from continuing to commit war crimes."

And hit them hard they did. One hundred and fifty tanks occupied the old settlement of Netzarin as fierce fighting erupted on the perimeters of Gaza City. As the Israeli army identified targets, it became clear that Hamas was launching rockets into Israeli territory from populated areas that would prevent retaliatory attacks; they fired from shopping malls, schoolyards, hospitals, and the like, always surrounded by women and children. Even after eight days of pummeling air strikes, Hamas was undeterred in its mission. The rocket launches into Israel continued. This precipitated a ground invasion. It wasn't lost on Israeli intelligence that Hamas's actions were calculated to provoke this response.

Without a formal army, without significant technologies, what did they hope to achieve pissing the Israelis off? World opinion tilting in their favor, that's what. Most often, it worked.

Hamas and the citizens of Gaza were notorious for building tunnels. They built all sorts of tunnels for all sorts of different purposes. There were tunnels carved underground solely to bait Israelis to rush into them to trigger trip wires. They were no different than the IEDs planted along the many roadsides in Iraq and in Afghanistan that caused so much damage and harmed so many American soldiers. There were tunnels built expressly to smuggle weapons and food in from Egypt. And there were tunnels for those lucky enough to escape the poverty and horrors of living in Gaza. These tunnels led to the Sinai and on to Egypt and beyond, such as the one Zakkarhia took years back.

The Israeli attacks succeeded for the most part, though public opinion leaned toward the defenseless Palestinians. When the smoke cleared and the political bluster died down, one objective had not been accomplished: Jericho Glassman remained a Palestinian hostage.

# Chapter Forty-Six

I t wasn't scheduled, but when his mission in Yemen drew to a close, Zakkarhia ibn Mohammed had a yearning to visit his mother, five sisters, and two younger brothers. It had been too many years since he saw them. The last he heard they were fairing well under the present Israeli siege. But how well could they be doing being bombed day and night by the infidels? Maybe he could somehow help them.

Zakkarhia made his way to the Egyptian side of the tunnels where a guard stopped him. "My friend, everyone wants it the other way; they want to escape from Gaza, not go back."

"I've been on an extended business trip for years," said Zakkarhia. "I need to see my family. See if they need my help." He put his hand on the guard's shoulder; he stared straight at him. "I am certain you can understand this, my brother." His glare did not waiver.

Undaunted, the guard's answer surprised Zakkarhia. "You can help them by staying right here and not trying to see them. The last thing they need, the last thing any of us need, is another wannabe hero."

*If he only knew who I am*, thought Zakkarhia.

"I'll let them make that decision," he said.

Zakkarhia took one step without looking back, and then another. If the Egyptian was going to shoot him, now was the time. Zakkarhia angled toward the tunnel. Could a brother shoot another for wanting to see his family?

And just like that, he entered a tunnel to see his family.

♦   ♦   ♦

Nothing was as he remembered. Zakkarhia had trouble finding his family. Buildings once familiar to him were now piles of brick. Streets were cratered. Unexpected patches of sky were visible much like entering a clearing in deforested land. After a few wrong turns and retracing his steps, he stumbled into what remained of his old house. Half of the front wall was missing; the door swung off its hinge…a broken wing.

His mother cried out in joy when she saw her eldest. She squeezed hard; he struggled to breathe. Tears coated her face. Over her thin shoulder, he waved to three of his sisters and his youngest brother. Zakkarhia was the oldest of seven – three boys and four girls. He broke away from his mother's grip and looked for his youngest sister and his middle brother.

"Where are Aliah and Marzuq? It's too dangerous for them to be out alone."

"Marzuq is fine. He has a very important job. He will be glad to see you."

"And Aliah?"

Zakkarhia's mother opened her mouth to speak, but nothing came out. Her eyes watered and then she lost it, sobbing into his hard chest. Her knees buckled; he grabbed her elbows, bracing her so she didn't fall, and guided her to a thread-worn chair.

Faridah, a year older than Aliah, stepped forward. "The rocket. It fell on her school. She was a teacher's aid. Aliah is dead."

Zakkarhia froze. He had been wounded, starved, burned, even tortured, none of which were as painful as learning his precious Aliah had been murdered. Murdered by the damned infidels. He gasped and clutched his gut, as if he were knifed. He opened and closed his fists, and then punched the wall 'til his knuckles bled. He wiped his nose in his sleeve. They waited for him to calm down.

"And father?" It was the first time he thought of his father since the day he chastised him for being influenced by the wrong people.

Time had proven that Zakkarhia's decision to leave Gaza and become a jihadist was the right one for him. Damn his father!

"Soon after you left, he had a heart attack. We couldn't get him to the hospital in time."

Zakkarhia absorbed the news in silence. He wanted to not care about his father's death, but sad thoughts crept in that he couldn't shake away.

"I need to see Marzuq. I need to see him with my own two eyes."

His mother dried her tears. "Go to him. He always talks about you."

Zakkarhia found the building. Though made of concrete, the walls where Marzuq worked were cracked and fissured, as if having survived a series of earthquakes. All knew that Israeli bombs caused the same damage as shifting tectonic plates.

Seconds later, the brothers embraced.

"I've followed every one of your missions," said Marzuq with a gleaming smile, "at least the ones I thought you'd be on." He clutched Zakkarhia's hand with both of his, afraid that if he let go he would leave for more years, the way he did before. "You're a hero here."

"There are many heroes fighting the *jihad,* my brother. You, for one. Look at how important you've become."

Marzuq feigned modesty, but pride oozed from his young brother's pores. At twenty, he had one of the most coveted jobs in Gaza. "You're too kind. What do I do? Sit here all day and watch a stupid prisoner? Anybody could do this. Even me." He let a nervous chuckle escape.

"Do not belittle what's true, Marzuq. Anyone could have been assigned to guard the Israeli scum, but you're the one they chose. Would it be all right if I saw *him*. I want to experience their smell so I will never forget the swine that they are. I want it branded in my brain so that I always remember that they killed our sister."

"You know I can't do that," said Marzuq. "No one's allowed to see the prisoner."

Zakkarhia bobbed on his toes. "Not even someone as famous as me?" He laughed. And when he realized how good it felt to laugh, he laughed harder still. He couldn't remember the last time he had such a feeling, and then he stopped when he remembered poor Aliah. He felt shame for his momentary lapse of dignity. He held out his palms open. "Five minutes. Who will know?"

Zakkarhia didn't give Marzuq time to answer. The seasoned Al Qaeda veteran trucked down the hall, rounded the corner, and then edged toward the jail cell. He stood there for quite a bit, his steely gaze taking in every inch of the prisoner.

Jericho Glassman turned his head. Their eyes locked for a second, and then Jericho turned away.

"You know," said Zakkarhia said in a whisper, "you and I are alike."

Jericho continued to look away.

"You're trained to kill. Trained to have no emotions. Trained not to care what happens to you. Ever the mission. The mission. Always the mission. We're both pawns in a giant game of chess. You know it, and I know it."

Jericho twisted to gaze at Zakkarhia.

"And what is your mission now?" asked Jericho.

"To see that you and your kind are eliminated from the face of this earth. And yours?"

Jericho shrugged, as if he didn't hear the vituperative harangue. He would not stoop to Zakkarhia's level. To any of their level. "To make certain my people can live in peace. To make certain you and I are linked in friendship, however impossible that sounds at the moment." He sat taller. "My mission is more than that."

"Tell me your glorious mission, swine."

"To do everything in my power to insure that you and I will one day live as brothers."

Zakkarhia shook his head. He tried to swallow hard. He stopped, puckered, and then spit at Jericho. "The day we're linked in any way is the day Hell rules the earth."

"Then prepare for Hell to rule, my friend, because that day is nearer than you think."

# Chapter Forty-Seven

At the same time that the two soldiers faced each other, the new Egyptian president was brokering secret negotiations between Israel and Hamas.

"If the rocket attacks continue," the Israeli said, "we will bomb your tunnels. You'll be totally isolated from the outside world."

"But those tunnels open onto Egyptian soil," said the new president from the Muslim Brotherhood. "That would be an act of war against Egypt. We would have to retaliate."

The Hamas leader had nothing to say. They had no standing army and no leverage but to jab and poke at the Israelis every opportunity they could, then skedaddle to hide behind the apron of world opinion.

"We both know that will not be an issue," the Israeli answered. He didn't have to elaborate. As in the Six Day War, Israel would employ a preemptive strike against the Egyptian Air Force and destroy it and the tunnels at the same time. For all their bluster, the Egyptians were no stronger now then they were fifty years ago.

"So what do you want?" asked the Egyptian president.

"A prisoner exchange and a ceasefire. No more rockets."

The Egyptian president spoke in Arabic to the Hamas leader, in which the Israeli was fluent.

"They're asking for very little. You'll get many soldiers back for a couple of hostages."

"That's not enough."

"They'll leave the tunnels alone, increase medical aid, and allow more provisions to be shipped into the camps. You win at every level."

The Hamas leader stroked his silvery beard. "Still not enough."

"They're being generous," said the Egyptian president. "Take it and avoid further bloodshed. It's time for your people to move forward."

"The last time they did this, they killed Sheik Yassin. How do we know they won't do the same again? When we promise to stop shelling them, they will become stronger. Build more settlements."

The Egyptian leader leaned closer. "We both know the Sheik was trouble. He got what he deserved. If any of the newly released prisoners shoot off their mouths, they'll get the same. The fools would deserve it. And as for you stopping the rockets, it's only temporary. We both know that; so do the Israelis. Stop being an ass and make the trade."

That's how Jericho Glassman gained his release.

Once the ceasefire was in place, arrangements were made for a prisoner exchange. Jericho and two other Israelis, who had been held hostage for years, were swapped for over three hundred Palestinians. These exchanges were always lopsided; the Israelis considered a single life worth hundreds of Arabs. To get three back was a major victory.

Days later, when all the details had been worked out and the papers processed on both ends, Marzuq escorted Jericho to a waiting Humvee that would transport him out of Gaza and back to Israel. Zakkarhia gloated, reveling in the coup that Hamas had extracted from the Israelis...so many *jihadists* for three Israeli swine.

Zakkarhia needed to be there when they herded the Israeli out in shackles. He plunked himself behind a Palestinian soldier.

It didn't take long for Jericho to shuffle past Zakkarhia. Jericho smiled and made an effort to raise his hand to his forehead in a tipping gesture, but the manacles limited his reach to his chin. Instead, with palms flat against each other and index fingers points, Jericho made a motion of shooting a gun at Zakkarhia.

Zakkarhia sneered back. "Our paths will cross again, my friend. Of that, it is written."

"I look forward to it, my brother," answered Jericho. "Shalom Aleichem."

Zakkarhia did not respond.

Grit and enmity aside, neither expected to see the other ever again.

But they did...and when it happened, it shook the foundation of the entire world.

# Chapter Forty-Eight

ittel had more than a nagging feeling that the Mossad could locate the bulk of the Codex's missing pages if they wanted to, but she couldn't prove it. Once the report by the London antiquities dealer was filed, the Mossad scuttled the subsequent inquiry too quickly to have seen the light of an investigation.

Something was amiss. Israelis are fanatical about their heritage. They would go to any length to secure a chard of pottery if it had Biblical importance. With the help of Professor Tawil's explanation, Gittel developed her own theory as to why the Israeli government was not pursuing the recovery of the stolen Codex pages with its usual "get-the-job-done-at-any-cost" approach. The only explanation that made sense was that the Israeli government did not want to go after the missing pages because it meant tussling with the Satmars. Could there be a better explanation? History has proven time and time again, that they would go to any length to recapture what they thought was rightfully theirs...the way they did on the raid in Entebbe.

◆　◆　◆

*Entebbe, July 4, 1976*
A week earlier, Air France Flight 139 departed Tel Aviv for Paris, stopping in Athens. What seemed to be a routine flight turned ugly when two members of the Popular Front for the Liberation of Palestine and two Germans from the Revolutionary Cells hijacked the plane as

soon as it was on its way to Paris. The terrorists ordered the pilot to land and refuel at Benghazi, Libya before continuing on to Uganda. When the plane landed at Entebbe, three more terrorists joined them. In defiance of world opinion, pro-Palestinian dictator, Idi Amin, welcomed them with open arms.

From the runway the terrorists funneled the passengers into the airport terminal. Once corralled inside the structure, the hijackers segregated those with Israeli passports or Jewish sounding surnames, and then freed the rest. The Air France crew was given their freedom but, to a one, chose to remain with the captives.

The terrorist demands were simple: release forty Palestinians held in Israel and another thirteen *jihadists* held around the world. If the hijackers' demands were not met by July 1, they would begin killing the hostages one-by-one. The Israeli government needed to buy time. On July 1, they opened negotiations, which succeeded in delaying the date when the executions would start. A rescue mission was put in place; Colonel Yoni Netanyahu was charged with bringing the hostages home.

In the wee hours of July 4, four Israeli C-130 transports approached Entebbe under the cover of darkness, carrying twenty-nine commandos, a Mercedes, and two Land Rovers. The plan was to convince the hijackers that President Amin or some other high-ranking Ugandan official was there to see the hostages.

The ruse didn't work.

Ugandan sentinels had been posted around the perimeter and recognized the ploy.

Losing the element of surprise, in swift order the Israelis neutralized the guards, stormed the building, freed the hostages, and killed the hijackers. As they gathered the hostages and scurried toward their transports, the Israelis destroyed 11 Ugandan Mig-7 fighters, eliminating any chance of air pursuit.

By all measures, the raid on Entebbe was a success, gaining the awe and admiration of the democratic world. The tally: one hundred hostages were freed with only three losing their lives in the fight. All six terrorists were killed, as well as forty-five Ugandan soldiers. One

Israeli commando lost his life: Colonel Netanyahu, who was hit by a Ugandan sniper. Years later, his younger brother would be the future Israeli Prime Minister.

*Jerusalem*

"In short," Professor Tawil explained at their last meeting, "you can find them concentrated in the Williamsburg section of Brooklyn and in Kiryas Joel, which is in Rockland County, close to the Tappan Zee Bridge. There are smaller Satmar communities in Monsey, Boro Park, Buenos Aires, Antwerp, and in Israel, they're mainly in Bnei Brak and Jerusalem."

"Are they all the same? Are there different brands of Hasidism?" asked Gittel.

"Rabbi Yoel Breitstein founded the Satmars, and the group is named after his tiny village in Hungary. He outlived his children. With no immediate heirs, his nephew - Moishe Breitstein - took over. When it was time, he handed the reins to his two sons, Rabbi Aaron and Rabbi Zalman.

"I'm sensing that brothers never played nicely together in the sandbox," Gittel said.

Tawil nodded. "Like most family issues, it boils down to real estate, power, and money. The older brother controls more of each. He thought he was clever years ago by sending his younger brother to Israel, to get him out of the way so that when their father died, there would be no denying him the leadership of the Satmars."

"Sort of like Cain and Abel."

"Only to the extent that one was sent away. The younger brother gained his own power base and money in Jerusalem, to the point that he is the equal of his older brother. The two factions hate each other."

"Which faction is trying to piece the book back together? The one here in Jerusalem or the one back in the US?"

"My best guess," began Professor Tawil, "is the group in Jerusalem. If nothing else they must have the bulk of the missing pages. Why else would they meet the antiquities dealer here?"

"Maybe it's the other way around," said Gittel. "The Brooklyn group has the missing pages, and the Jerusalem group is going around the world trying to regain the snippets cut from the original nine pages. Maybe they're trying to make the Brooklyn group look bad?"

"It's not about good or bad. It's about power. Whoever controls the missing pages has more power than the other brother." He rethought those words. "That's an understatement. Whoever controls the missing pages has untold power. My bet is that it's the Jerusalem group."

"How much untold power are you talking about?" Gittel asked. "Before you explain, what about ideology? Religious beliefs? Where does God come into the equation?"

"When it comes to the Satmars, God plays second fiddle. He enters the story when they invite Him in."

And then Rabbi Tawil explained why whoever had all of the missing pages, became a major power broker.

◆　◆　◆

Before going to Yoel Street in the Meah Shearim neighborhood of Jerusalem, Gittel considered wearing an ankle length dress that also covered her neck and elbows. Hasidic women were required to dress modestly in public, and married women covered their hair as well. She knew that female police patrolled the area in standard-issue uniforms, so she conceded to Hasidic tradition by wearing a blue business suit that she sported for state occasions. Since she was single, her hair was not an issue.

Gittel found a Satmar rabbi willing to speak with her. She waved a hotel surveillance picture in front of him. There was a clear image of two men dressed head-to-toe in black, with white open-collared shirts, and black fedoras. Each had a modest beard that belied their youth. Prayer fringes dangled down their pant legs.

"Why is it any of your business?" asked the rabbi.

"Recently these men offered an antiquities dealer from London, what we believe are the missing pages from the Codex of Aleppo. I assume you know what the Codex is?"

"Who doesn't?"

"We've determined that they're members of your sect. Do you know them?"

He didn't have to look at the pictures. "I do. And I repeat. Why is it any of your business?"

"Because if you know where the missing pages are, they need to be returned to their rightful owners."

"And who may that be? Not the State of Israel."

"Of course it is," she said. "Who else would it be?"

"The Jews of Aleppo are the rightful owners. But they're scattered all over the world."

The rabbi's arrogance and defiance were maddening, but Gittel remained cool. In one lucky meet, she found out more than the vaunted Mossad and U.S. authorities had, or had least claimed *not* to discover, during their inquiries into the murders and missing pages. Maybe they had the answers all along. Gittel was not one for conspiracies, but the more she delved into anything connected to the Codex of Aleppo, the more the facts smacked of one.

She reached into her black leather case and removed a picture. "Do you know this man?"

This time the rabbi glanced at the picture. It was from the surveillance camera on Fifth Avenue that captured an image of the old man's killer.

"I know him, too."

She didn't expect that. What were the chances of meeting a man, granted a religious Jew, in Jerusalem, who could identify someone from the streets of Manhattan with a simple glance?

At this point, she should have stopped the questioning and asked him to accompany her on a visit to the authorities. He had information about a murder in New York and stolen antiquities from the State of Israel. He most likely knew about the other crimes – the murders and robberies – that were connected to the cut-up fragments of the original nine pages. If what the man said was not bluster, and if he spoke the truth, he could direct them to the parties that perpetrated these crimes.

Following the logic tree, he knew where the missing pages of the Codex were being hidden.

*It was too easy to stumble across this man. Was this a coincidence or is this what Divine intervention is all about?*

"Would it be asking too much if you accompanied me to headquarters and tell authorities what you know about this man and the murder he committed in New York?"

Without a blink or an inflection in his voice, the rabbi answered, "I said I know him. I didn't say that I know what he did. As for accompanying you anywhere, I've been taken away from my studies much too long. I need to get back to them."

Gittel knew that Deuteronomy 6 commanded Jews to read the Torah every day. This rabbi, as did most Hasidic rabbis, embraced studying and learning all day, rather than working in the secular world. He was clear he would not give her many more minutes and she was not prepared to arrest him...at least not yet. She returned to the issue of the missing pages.

"Someone deserves to have these pages returned. They were stolen many years ago."

"When the time is right."

Gittel put her hands on her hips. "I don't know what made me walk up to you and ask you a question, but I did. And as it turns out, you have direct knowledge about the missing pages of the Crown of Aleppo and possibly about a murder in New York. Maybe you know about other murders, too. What I don't understand is why you're so glib about this? How can you be so nonchalant about the missing pages? They've been missing for more than fifty years."

"And they will stay missing."

"To what end?" She turned away, disgusted by his arrogance, challenged by his docile manner encased in an uncompromising shell. "What if I can get the government to buy the pages from you, or from whomever has them?"

The rabbi took off his gold wire-rimmed glasses, and squared to face her. "The pages are not for sale."

"But these men contacted an antiquities dealer from London. They were asking one million in U.S. dollars. I'm certain that amount of money would be available to…"

"My dear police lady. These pages are not for sale now, nor were they for sale then. The men met this dealer to authenticate the pages. We needed to make certain they were real, that they were, in fact, the missing pages from the Crown of Aleppo. Now that we know they are, they will play a crucial role for us."

"I know you have your issues with the government. But surely, you can cast them aside for the greater good of this Bible."

His tone grew acerbic. "Agent Lasker. That the State of Israel exists is blasphemy on the Lord, *baruch hashem*. It should never have been created. Not by the United Nations. Not by winning wars. Not because the Bible said there should be a Jewish state. Not for any rational or sane reason."

Veins in her forehead throbbed; her face reddened. "Centuries of persecution. Living in pogroms. Not having citizenship in any country or an army to defend us. It's been more than twenty-five hundred years since we've had our own country. Why aren't you grateful we finally have a place where Jews can live in peace again? You live here! Doesn't that make it special for you? Doesn't *that* justify Israel's existence?"

"Peace?" he sneered. "We're in a perpetual state of war. Villagers live in fear that a rocket will fall on their heads every day. Palestinians steal into the kibbutzim and kill for the sake of killing. But that's not the point."

She forced herself to open her clenched fists, flexing them before speaking. "Then exactly what is the point of any of you living here? And what does that book or any book have to do with your misguided notions?"

The rabbi lowered his voice and spoke more slowly. "Israel was created out of guilt for the six million that were murdered. You're no different than the rest of them thinking and believing that Israel's so important that it must be defended at any cost. I get it and I understand why this is so. But what is also true is that as long as Israel exists, it prevents us from our true destiny."

"What destiny is that? To keep us in a state of perpetual war? To hide a treasure that belongs to the people?"

The rabbi ignored Gittel's outburst. "Our true destiny is to welcome the coming of the Messiah."

She snorted and tossed her head back. How many times had she heard this gibberish before? She knew where this was going and knew she was up against an intractable belief system, but was willing to challenge him to say the words she had come to despise.

"Why hasn't your Messiah shown up? What's stopping him? I thought Rabbi Schneerson was the Messiah?"

The man scoffed. "Him? He was a scholar, nothing more. The day that the UN voted for partition back in '47 is the day they prevented the Messiah's return. Schneerson could never have been the Messiah."

Like most Jews around the world, Gittel was familiar with the notion that a Messiah would appear one day. When that day arrived, rabbis believed that the Messiah would restore the religious courts of justice, end wickedness, sin, and heresy, reward the righteous, rebuild Jerusalem, restore the line of King David, bring about peace, and if one was needed at the time, he could even be a great military leader. Above all, when the Messiah appeared, he would oversee the rebuilding of the temple destroyed by the Romans in 70 A.D.

Here was the rub. The majestic gold-topped shrine, the Dome of the Rock, sits on the very spot where Abraham almost sacrificed his son to God. It's the site where the Prophet Mohammed leapt to heaven. Now that it's in Arab hands, Jews are forbidden to step foot on this sacred mount. As convoluted as history could be, it gets more twisted knowing that the Dome of the Rock rests on top of the site of the both the First and Second Jewish Temples where the Messiah is charged with rebuilding the Third Temple. When it comes to massive civic projects that are logistical nightmares, even a Messiah would have a difficult time completing this task.

"And you think that by holding these missing pages from the Codex hostage, you and your group will change all that? That somehow you'll hasten the coming of the Messiah?"

"The Lord works in strange ways." His answer infuriated.

That may be true, thought Gittel, but she couldn't imagine God going along with this Satmar thesis for Jews to abandon their homeland, a homeland that He gave them, a homeland that Moses guided them to after wandering in the desert for forty years, a homeland that the Lord promised in the very Bible pages this sect held hostage.

It took time, but Gittel was now able to synthesize the importance of these missing pages. The Satmar sect needed to assemble the entire sheaf of AWOL pages, every cut up sliver, and use them as a cudgel to clear the obstructed path that prevented the Messiah from appearing. While it might be a righteous idea, the method was evil and distorted. How could they justify committing crimes in the name of religion? But then again, when didn't that happen through the centuries?

And then she remembered the curses. Whoever stole the missing pages honored and revered God's curses. Knowing that the Satmars violated this great Bible, how would God punish the Satmars?

# Chapter Forty-Nine

"**Y**ou need to go where?" asked the police chief. Frank Murphy, a thirty-year vet including timeout for a stint in the first Gulf War, sat behind his desk, toiling over a series of departmental memos, ticking off the days left until he and the missus could retire to their little house in the Poconos, when LeShana Thompkins tramped into his office. She handed him a ragged piece of paper encased in plastic.

He recognized it immediately. "Isn't this the parchment from that unsolved murder in front of St. Patty's a few months back? What're doing with the evidence? "

"That's just it. It looks like the piece the old man handed our then Cardinal Ford, but it's a replica of a different piece. I received it in the mail this morning, from persons unknown. Here's the message wrapped around it." She wagged a piece of white paper toward his arthritic fingers.

**Bring the matching piece from the old man to Jerusalem**

Murphy looked up at her. "They're delusional. You're not going anywhere."

LeShana was prepared for his response. The best way to handle the chief was to let him ramble on, ignore whatever he says, and stay on point. "They said to meet in the King David Hotel."

"Have you gone loco? The department doesn't have that sort of money. They're budget cuts everywhere. It's out of the question.

And, besides, you know I can't let you travel with an actual piece of evidence."

"Maybe this will change your mind," said LeShana. She produced the laminated talisman the dying man handed Pope Lazarus II when he was still Cardinal Ford. "See how the two fit together? They're from the same page. Consecutive pieces."

"I just said you can't travel with the evidence and here you are holding it."

"That's bull. You know we check evidence out all the time. The chain of custody will be solid. Whoever sent it knew the pieces connected like puzzle parts."

"Who knew it did what?" asked the chief, putting his pen down. It was time to pay attention.

"Someone who's willing to play ball with us. My contact in Jerusalem, Gittel Lasker, spoke with a rabbi recently that expressed knowledge about the killer. He claimed he knew the man in the surveillance photo, but knew nothing about the murder."

"Did the rabbi give him up?"

"He clammed up tighter than an oyster protecting a giant pearl."

"That's quite the metaphor given rabbis are Kosher"

She smirked. "He gave nothing else."

"Can't they arrest him? Make him sweat?"

LeShana thought of Rabbi Breitstein and how intractable he was.

"This is bigger than the one crime we're stuck with. If we play ball with them, we might get him to solve a string of murders worldwide, and possibly find the all the missing parts of an ancient treasure."

He pulled the matching pieces apart and then overlaid them together again. "And now, you're telling me, out of the blue, you get a piece that matches your parchment there, in the mail, and they want you to take a company paid vacation to the Holy Land. Roll some Easter eggs. Why can't the Mossad or Shin Bet or whichever agency they have covering these things, squeeze the blessed rabbi? I hear the Israelis are a persuasive bunch."

"The Mossad won't touch this. It's like a Watergate issue for them. The ball's in our court."

"I didn't hear any ref blow a whistle to start a game with NYPD blue? What am I missing here? The rabbi's Israeli. The book's in Hebrew. The missing pages are over there. Refresh my memory. How is this *our* problem?"

"Are you forgetting *our* murder on Fifth Avenue?" she demurred. "You know department regs: we follow leads no matter where they take us. And that includes the Promised Land."

"The only thing I can promise you is that with all the cutbacks we don't have the moola for any extravagant trips. So the answer is still, 'No.'"

"But it's our murder. Our vic."

This banter went on for a few more minutes. LeShana knew that Murphy was a softy and that he would cave in, but he had to make her think he was tough. In the end, he came through.

He held his hands up. "Enough. I surrender. Just be careful, Detective. Shalom Aleichem."

*Jerusalem*
LeShana cleared security and headed for the baggage claim area in Ben Gurion Airport. She leaned to snatch her yellow-ribbonned, black Tumi when she felt a tap on her shoulder. Her first instinct was to reach for her revolver; she left it home. She turned with caution.

"Are you Detective Thompkins?

LeShana turned to see a model-thin redhead that would be comfortable at a fashion shoot.

"Don't tell me you're Agent Lasker? You're way too beautiful to be a cop."

"And you don't look so Jewish, Detective."

"Neither do you."

At that, they both broke into a fit of laughter. Gittel grabbed LeShana's suitcase and headed for the door. "When're they supposed to make contact?" she asked LeShana.

"I'm supposed to wait in my hotel room. They'll get word to me."

"I'll wait with you."

LeShana shook her head. "No, no. That may scare them away. We can't risk that. They were clear about no one else being involved."

"We'll stake out the lobby. The surrounding streets. We need to protect you. The last thing we want is a NYC cop hurt on our turf."

LeShana stopped short. "Agent, these folks will know if your people are anywhere near the hotel. If that happens, I'll have made this trip for nothing and there'll be one nasty Police Chief back New York who's not going to be happy 'bout that. Let me do my job. I can take care of myself the same way I know you can. If the tables were reversed, would you permit a backup team to be close by and take the chance at scaring these guys away?"

"Five minutes, and you know me so well," answered Gittel.

# Chapter Fifty

U nlike his predecessors, Pope Lazarus II held weekly press conferences. This particular one drew more attention than the others. Navigated by Cardinal Scarponi, the Vatican's press secretary, the Pope made a series of announcements. The first was breathtaking in scope; Lazarus II was not waiting for the Vatican III to initiate long-needed reforms.

"I have established a committee to put in motion the manner in which women will become more involved in the Roman Curia," announced the Pope.

"Your Eminence, can you foresee the day when Roman priests will marry?"

Without hesitation, the Lazarus II answered. "While I accept the benefits of a clergy that remains pure and chaste, I can also appreciate the many advantages that married priests would benefit the church and its congregants. This will not happen quickly, but the dialogue needs to start now."

"How long in the future?" asked a reporter from the Christian Scientist.

"That must first be taken up in an ecumenical council. I have taken the liberty of informing the College of Cardinals that we will convene Vatican III in three months to explore this and other topics relevant to making the Church more inclusive for all."

With deft skills, Cardinal Scarponi deflected more questions on this controversial topic and prepared the group for the Pope's next pronouncement. He glanced at the Pope who nodded that he was ready.

Lazarus II spoke. "In the coming months, I will make a trip to China, to reach out to believers there. This, I may add, is at the request of the Chinese government."

A hand shot up. "Your Holiness. Will you welcome Chinese converts with open arms?"

"While I embrace all people who wish to accept the love of our Father, I am sensitive to the delicacy of my visit to China. As any good guest would act, I would do nothing to compromise my hosts." The Pope went on to say, "It is equally important that I do everything possible to help fellow Christians who are persecuted around the world. Now that Iraq is free of its dictator, I will work to make it more tolerant of all religious minorities, including Christians and Jews."

"What about the Kurds?"

"They are well on their way to having their own independent state. In the end, I expect they will carve out pieces from Turkey, Syria, Iraq, and Iran. It won't be popular, but it is inevitable."

*This Pope was not afraid to take a stand.*

"Will the Church support it?"

"The Church will support freedom wherever it is found."

"What about the Middle East? Will there ever be a solution to their problems?"

He tented his fingers together. "If the good Lord wishes me to help, I will be available."

"Is it your intention, Your Excellency, to mediate peace talks?"

Pope Lazarus II bowed his head. "I am a humble servant of the Lord, not a politician or a negotiator. My mission is to create an open dialogue between people who have not found the right path to discuss their differences and concerns. As such, I will open my arms to my Muslim brothers and sisters in the hopes they will leave the past behind and join the Israelis in a brighter future. A brighter future for all. After all, we all share the Holy Land. It is time we do so in peace and safety."

As he spoke these words, Pope Lazarus II could not help but wonder if he would have been as generous to offering a bridge to peace between the Israelis and Muslims before he met LeShana Thompkins.

Cardinal Scarponi, ever the diplomat, sensed the moment was ripe to end the press conference.

Always leave them on a high note.

He thanked all for coming, and said that the Pope looked forward to next week's meeting. Most journalists closed their iPads or tablets, grabbed their cases and eased out through the gilded doors.

Few thought any consequence to the tap, tap, tapping of the only blind journalist who covered the Vatican, Alfredo Francesco. Francesco approached the Pope. He had been sighted at birth but struggled through a series of operations to slow down the ravages of hereditary glaucoma. The fight continued until he was twelve, when he fell off the back of his older brother's moped; the jolt chased away the last vestiges of sight he would ever have.

Cardinal Scarponi whispered in the Pope's ear, the Pope nodded, and then Scarponi waved away a guard. "Let him approach."

Francesco stopped when the red tip of his white cane touched the base of the raised platform. His right hand reached out in space. Pope Lazarus II grabbed his hand and held it warmly in his.

Francesco felt a force enter his body. He leaned forward to plant his lips on the Piscatorial Ring, better known as the Ring of the Fisherman.

The Pope placed his right hand on Francesco's foppish head topped with premature strands of gray, and placed his left hand on the man's right shoulder. He studied the journalist's face.

Francesco spoke first. "Your Excellency, I have one more question."

Pope Lazarus II leaned close to the man's ear and whispered. "Your question has to do with the loss of your sight, doesn't it?"

Francesco nodded. A tear escaped his right eye. "I don't know what possessed me to walk up here, Your Eminence. Forgive me if I am out of line."

The Pope didn't answer. He placed both hands on Francesco's temples, his thumbs over the closed eyelids, his fingers firm and reassuring. Francesco felt heat emanate from his touch.

Time froze.

For a moment, Francesco was transported back to his tenth birthday. His mother and father were there. So was his brother. His nona, too. There were his school friends: Luca, Aldo, and Bernardo. The light was golden. And there were eleven candles on a tall chocolate cake. He held his breath and…

Two reporters had seen Francesco edge up to the Pope. No one ever had the audacity to do that. Curious as to why the blind reporter would do such a thing, they stopped to watch. Reflexly, one whipped out his camera, at the ready to snap a photo. The other, for no apparent reason, pressed the movie feature of his iPhone and recorded Francesco kissing the Pope's ring. The Pope first grasped Francesco's right hand and then letting go, the Pope placed both of his hands on the blind reporter's temples before exerting touching Francesco's clamped eyelids.

The camera shutter snapped and the phone continued recording, though little happened.

The reporter was about to put the camera away when Francesco started to weave. His hands shot up to his head and covered the Pope's. Hand on hand they stood in tandem, rocking in unison.

Francesco made strange, guttural, primal sounds, and yet the Pope continued his vise-like grip. The two swayed, back and forth, saplings whipped by the wind.

And then, like a sudden squall, it was over.

The Pope withdrew two steps.

Francesco rubbed his eyes. He turned to the left and held his head in the way a sighted person gazes. He rubbed his eyes again. He faced the rows of chairs without expression. Then his head drifted to the two reporters firing away with their camera and phone. He looked up; he looked down.

There was life in Francesco's eyes. He smiled. Then Francesco turned to the right, toward the window. He shuffled over without using his cane; he craned to look out and giggled in delight. Then he rotated to where the Pope was standing, but Lazarus II had already eased out of the room.

The reporters rushed up to Francesco, babbling at what they had witnessed, but Francesco just grinned. They fumbled for a piece of paper for him to read. He did at first, haltingly, and then grew confident and read with the same fluency he did when a boy.

Francesco kissed both men on the cheeks. They wanted to interview him, to ask him what he experienced when the Pope touched him? Did he feel something come over him? Through him? Did it hurt? Was it electric? Hot? Did he ever think he would see again?

He edged back and surveyed one and then the other before speaking in a voice filled with wonderment and belief, "In Matthew 20:34, it is written, 'Then Jesus, deeply moved with compassion, touched their eyes and at once they could see again. So they followed him.'"

# Chapter Fifty-One

Zakkarhia stood in the lobby of the Grand Hyatt, staring at the huge work of art on the wall. He sipped from a porcelain teacup.

"Look at that," he said to Walid Muhammad bin Attash. It had been a while since the two were physically in the same place at the same time, though they communicated in code via the Internet all the time. "It disgusts me."

The two stood in front of a large oval work of art. It had a blue background with blue or black connected pipes superimposed on it, turning this way and that.

"What do you suppose it means?" asked Walid. When Zakkarhia grunted but didn't answer, Walid continued. "I think they represent life, and the eternal quest to grow and evolve."

"And what about the dismembered woman made of wood?" asked Zakkarhia. "You can see every part of her. Why is she in so many pieces?" Then his eyes widened with a hint of joy. "Did a brother create this? Is it the death of a Jew?"

Walid ignored his comment and glanced down. "You have blood on your fingers."

Zakkarhia raised his hand. His right index finger was caked in blood. He licked it off. "It was from that pregnant whore." He hoisted the cup to his lips and made a slurping sound, all the while staring at the breast of the dismembered woman in the piece of art. "How do they report this in the news?"

"They've announced how successful we are. They said that the attacks were masterminded by the Lashkar-e-taib, which is exactly what we wanted. We don't need the credit for every victory. Knowing the enemy is defeated is reward enough."

"Will it accomplish our goal?"

Walid shrugged. "India knows that our people were trained in Pakistan. The lone survivor told them they were Pakistanis. He did as he was told, and led them to believe ISI was involved, not Al Qaeda."

"Why not take the credit for ourselves?"

"We're looking to promote a war between India and Pakistan. If it's to happen, they can't think we're involved in anyway."

Zakkarhia understood the wisdom of the plan, waiting for the day when he could plan every last detail of an attack with Walid's same brilliance.

Walid continued. "The Indian government will want to retaliate. If this isn't enough to provoke them into attacking, they will surely turn aggressive the next time Pakistan launches another insidious plot against them. Then the two will surely go to war. When that happens, Pakistan will pull troops out of the mountains in order to protect their borders with India. With no troops around, our people will find it easier to train and travel about."

"And what if the Indians control themselves and don't attack?"

"That's not an issue. We'll go at them again and again until they ultimately do our bidding. Remember, we have the strength to wait a year, a decade or a hundred years to defeat the infidel. Time is on our side. In the end, we will win and they will lose. So it is written."

# Chapter Fifty-Two

There was a light knock on the door. LeShana sprang up from the edge of the bed.

In the minutes before they arrived, she wondered if this was a wasted effort, if they would even show up. She paced the room, fourteen feet wide, sixteen feet across; she sat down, stood up, peered out the window, stared at the cars below, men and women on bicycles, vendors selling falafel, and as she waited she wished she could smoke a cigarette, something she hadn't done for more than twenty years.

A light rap.

Long strides brought her to the door. She peered through the peephole, got partial glimpses of two, and then turned the knob.

"Yes?" She planted her right foot and leaned her shoulder into the door, gripping the handle should they try to force their way in. Though eyeing them, she didn't feel the least bit threatened. She was cop-enough to know that looks meant nothing and at moments like this, she wished she had her gun. More to the point, she wished she had listened to Gittel and knew that backup was nearby.

Two religious Jews, one short, one taller, garbed in black, donned with felt fedoras, open-collared white shirts, frayed tee shirts, and scuffed black leather shoes, stared back at her. Both were young and lean with sallow complexions, pimpled faces, wisps of beards, and ringlets of hair coiled just above their ears that dangled below their jaws. It was a good bet that neither had ever seen the inside of a gym.

No threat here.

The taller of the two had crooked, yellow teeth, and spoke first. Polite. "We're here to meet Detective Thompkins."

"You've met her, now what can I do for you?" Ever the New Yorker.

Each looked furtively down the hotel hallway, hoping they weren't being set up.

"May we come in?" asked the other. "We need to show you something."

"Why should I let you in?"

"We're the ones who sent you the matching good piece from the Codex. Rabbi Breitstein instructed us to show you something special. Now may we come in before someone sees us standing here and talking to you?"

She stepped back and the two jackrabbited inside, peeking over their shoulders to make certain they weren't followed. The taller one drew the drapes closed, and the smaller one checked the bathroom to make certain no one was lurking there. He checked under the bed, too.

"Okay, gentlemen. You've managed to piss off my Irish Police Chief for springing for bucks the department doesn't have to fly me over here. Now would you please explain what this is all about?" While she played the innocent not knowing why they dragged her thousands of miles from home, she knew very well what this was about. The question was, *"Why her?"* Wasn't there someone else more qualified and better suited to be in this room at this moment with these men? Again, she asked herself, *"Why her?"*

They motioned her to sit on the bed.

"If you don't mind, gentlemen, I'll stand."

They didn't answer. Telepathically, they both inched to the bed. She hadn't seen it before, but the taller man had the fingers of this left hand firmly wrapped around a worn, brown leather satchel.

He held his hand out. "May I have the key, please?"

She was annoyed she missed this. Not like her. His black coat sleeve covered a handcuff that connected his wrist to the valise. He laid it on the bed and extracted a thicket of sheaves. He motioned her to come closer.

"Do you know what these are?" he asked, bent over, cradling the parchment pages.

LeShana didn't need to step closer. "I have a good idea what they are. Why show them to me? A while back, you were trying to peddle them to a London merchant."

"We only met him to verify that what we had was the real thing."

"You made him travel a long way for nothing," she said. The subtext was clear to all: did they do the same thing to her?

"We had no choice," said the tall one. "But you're different," added the shorter one.

"I thought this was more about the murder in New York than about the missing pages of the Codex of Aleppo."

"There's no way to separate the two," said the shorter man, his voice more uncertain with every minute.

LeShana marched to the door and yanked it open. *Let's see what they're made of.* "Not acceptable, gentlemen. Your note stated that you knew who the killer of my victim was. I flew here for that purpose, not to look at some old manuscript pages."

The taller man approached her with all the diffidence he could muster. "Please close the door. We invited you here for a reason. Be patient. You'll understand everything in a few minutes."

"Where I come from, we don't stand around waiting for someone to paint a picture. Takes too long. See here, I'm running out of patience. What's this all about?" As she said this, she flipped the door closed with her index finger. All three watched it arc and click shut.

She had gained a measure of control by acting out, now she was ready to listen.

The younger man picked up from before. "First, we wanted you to see them for yourselves, so you would know they were real."

"I'm no manuscript scholar."

"But we know you can read Hebrew," said the taller man. He extracted a facsimile of one of the sheaves of parchment. He tapped the pile. "We know that this needs to be verified by scholars, and they will. But for now, here's a copy of one of the pages that was photographed years ago by an Italian scholar – his name was Umberto Cassuto – who managed to sneak into Syria during World War II and photograph every page of the Codex. See how the pages are identical?"

He held the black and white photograph next to the original. LeShana peered from one to the other. Her trained eye told her all she needed to know: they matched. She couldn't wait to show it to Gittel's friend, Dr. Tawil, to verify it.

She forced herself to remain nonplused. "And second?" she asked.

"The second," he paused and looked at the taller one for support, "the main reason we needed to meet you in person was," and then blurted it out, "we need for you to bring the Pope here."

LeShana sat down on the bed and glared from one to the other. "Are you two crazy?"

"We know you know him."

"To what end?" She scoffed. "For papal dispensation for the killer?"

The taller man answered. "This has nothing to do with the killer, Detective."

"It has everything to do with the killer. The perp needs to be brought to justice."

"Detective, we've been patient with you and let you play your tough cop act. Now it's time to listen. The killer has already been dealt with."

LeShana had a twitch of new respect for these two, but it still didn't answer the question about the killer. What did they mean, *the killer has already been dealt with?*

"You know that means nothing to me."

"You'll have to take our word for it that he's in a place no one will ever find him. We're sorry for the life lost, may his soul rest in peace, but that can't be undone and we have more pressing issues to resolve."

"The NYPD is not going to drop an investigation on your say so."

The two looked at each other. "Detective, we understand your professional stance. Look for him all you want. For the moment, we need to discuss the Pope with you."

LeShana knew when to stop. "I'm listening. But I don't know that the Pope would ever grant me an audience. And if he did, how could I convince him to come to Jerusalem. Why would he listen to me?"

"Because he will have no choice."

They explained why.

# Chapter Fifty-Three

Israel took advantage of the negotiated truce brokered by the Egyptians to fortify the embargo against the Hamas-ruled Gaza strip. The prisoner exchange proceeded uneventfully: three hundred and fifty-four Arabs for three Israeli soldiers, one of whom was Jericho Glassman. The three were shepherded to the hospital for a battery of tests. Jericho was pronounced fit in body, given the length of his confinement; his mind wasn't. The doctors diagnosed him with post-traumatic stress syndrome. They asked him to remain at the hospital for some additional time.

"There's nothing wrong with me that a few weeks rest wouldn't help."

The doctor stopped staring at his tablet, and removed his glasses. "Jericho, we asked you out of courtesy. You don't have a choice. You're still in the Army and this is now an order."

*Gaza*

Zakkarhia replayed the moments he stood and watched his brother, Marzuq, cough up the Israeli prisoner for the exchange. Jericho Glassman. The infidel was named after the fabled city in the Book of Joshua, the first city the Israelites conquered in Canaan after wandering in the desert for forty years. And to Allah's glory, Israel would suffer the same fate as this ancient city had when its walls crumbed and its people killed.

Zakkarhia reflected on the chasm that separated him and Jericho

Glassman. They were both Semites. Both of the desert. Both warriors. There must be some molecules of DNA that connected them, but in this lifetime, they were far from blood brothers. Maybe in the next life. For now, they were sworn enemies. The more Zakkarhia thought about it, the more he was convinced that their paths would cross again. Why he changed his mind after watching Jericho leave the Palestinian cell in the prisoner exchange befuddled him? But now it was clear, their destinies were intertwined.

His instincts were never wrong.

◆　◆　◆

In the coming days, Zakkarhia grew restless. He had grown used to sleeping on the ground and under the stars. He had grown used to a bit of food and a little water. While it made his heart leap to be with his mother and bask under the glow of her warm eyes, and to be with Marzuq and his sisters and younger brother, Zakkarhia was no longer part of their world. He needed to be on assignment, always working for the *jihad*, to make the world pure and holy.

Just when he thought he couldn't stand another day of being cooped up in the Gaza ghetto, word came that he was needed.

# Chapter Fifty-Four

"I wasn't certain you'd give me an audience, Your Excellency." The last, and for that matter the only time LeShana was in Pope Lazarus II's presence was in New York, was when she investigated the old man's murder in front of St. Patty's Cathedral. But what a meeting! It was a marathon lasting hours. She had known that Arnold Ford, a.k.a. Cardinal of New York, was not only linked to the black Jews but there was the remote chance that Ford's father might have had something to do with the founding of the Black Muslims.

She wasn't one hundred percent sure that Ford and Fard were connected, but the timing of Ford's disappearance in New York and Fard's appearance in Detroit could not be better explained. Likewise the timing of Fard's disappearance from Chicago after spending a year with Elijah Mohammed and Ford's reappearance in Ethiopia coincided with known facts. They say timing is everything. As a detective that isn't enough to make a case, but it sure makes for a compelling story.

LeShana found herself strolling through the outer rim of the maze in the Pope's secret garden in the Vatican. When she and Pope Lazarus II approached the grotto of the Fountain of the Eagle, he pointed and said, "There's St. Peter's Basilica. Aside from the Popes, few have ever seen it from this viewpoint. Majestic, isn't it?" She followed his arm to the where the parabolic dome designed by Michelangelo was visible over the garden walls. It felt closer. Private.

"I'm honored that you're sharing this with me, Your Eminence."

With glee he added, " I discovered this only last week. No one told me this garden even existed. I find much solitude here; it gives me the peace and quite I need to reflect on my mission."

Early reports from media around the world praised Pope Lazarus II for setting a brisk pace when compared to his predecessor, Pope Urban III. In the weeks following his election, the new Pope had dedicated his papacy to embracing all Catholics around the world, especially those considered new to the church in China, Iraq, and most of the "stans" that sprung up when the USSR disintegrated: Kazakhstan, Kyrgyzstan, Tajikistan, Turkmenistan, and Uzbekistan. Clerics and lay people alike heaped praise for the major initiatives Lazarus II set in motion to rekindle the love for the church that had been ebbing away for years, especially in Europe and South America.

Lazarus II did not shy away from controversy. He held an olive branch out not only to the Muslims around the world, but to the leaders of Al Qaeda, should they be willing to meet with him. He was not afraid to utter his stance on abortion. He felt it morally wrong that it ended a life no matter how many mitotic divisions, but he shocked the world when he acknowledged that circumstances did exist that could morally justify an abortion.

"Do we really want to bring unwanted children in the world?" he was quoted as saying. "To give life is to participate in God's most precious gift. Just the same, we need to consider what it means to create a life by mistake and then be forced to live with the myriad of consequences that spill over to both the family and society." He stopped short of endorsing abortion. He didn't have to knowing that his remarks, now unleashed, would find a growing audience in the years to come.

With all that he had accomplished in a matter of weeks, LeShana wondered if the reason the Pope was unaware of the secret Vatican garden was because his confreres were jealous of his quick acceptance worldwide, or maybe it was simply a matter of color. Or that he wasn't European, or that he was an American. While not strange to her in anyway, and certainly after Obama broke the mold, LeShana had difficulty understanding why most thought a black Pope an outrageous choice for the Church. Some thought it a bad choice.

"What has taken you away from New York and your busy duties to come to Rome? I received your email when I was elevated, so it's not about personally congratulating me."

*No time for idle chitchat. Right to the point.*

She eyed a granite bench. "May we sit down, Your Eminence? I have much to tell you."

"As you wish." And then he added with a boyish grin, "You know, for me, you'll always be the lady of stories. You've already changed my life in many ways."

She was in turmoil. *If you only knew how much more I am about to change it.*

Once they were seated with her back to St. Peter's Basilica, she continued. "For starters, I didn't come from New York; I came from Israel."

He raised his brow. She could tell he wanted to ask more about the trip, but chose restraint so as not to take up valuable time. She put him at ease with the question most on his mind. "Not for personal reasons. I was on business."

He cocked his head. "Official police business? You don't have jurisdiction there."

"Most people don't appreciate that the NYPD travels all over the world on cases. So in and of itself, it's not unusual to find an NYPD officer anyplace in the world."

He spoke with understanding. "You're here with me. We met because of the murder. Were you following a lead?"

*Be direct,* she told herself.

"It's connected to that, but not in the way you're thinking. I was brought to Israel for the express purpose of being convinced that I needed to meet with you."

"As before, you have my curiosity. What's this all about?"

Ever since the meeting in the King David Hotel with the two Satmar Jews, LeShana had been rehearsing over and over how she would begin the message the men charged her to deliver. At first, she thought them preposterous. More than preposterous, they, or Rabbi Breitstein whom they were shilling for, were the epitome of arrogance. To think that their plot would succeed was something out of movie land. But here she was, trying to enlist the Pope to be the main character.

When she hesitated to begin, Pope Lazarus II prodded her. "It's not so much about that man's death but about the piece of parchment he passed to me?"

Relieved that he broke the ice, she spilled it out. "A few days ago, I received a facsimile of another laminated piece of parchment in the mail. It was the mate of the piece handed to you."

"Mate? I don't understand."

"You recall that when the fires broke out in Syria and the synagogues were destroyed, the Codex of Aleppo was saved. In the process nine pages were removed from the book and cut up into good luck talismans. The piece I received in the mail was adjacent to the one the old man had been carrying ever since that time. They fit together like puzzle parts."

"I want to be clear about this. You're telling me that someone found the next slice of the same page and sent it to you? Someone went to great lengths to discover that you were connected to that case. What were they trying to accomplish mailing it to you?"

She didn't answer right away.

He thought for a moment. He connected the fact that LeShana knew him and that they were now sitting there together.

"This is all about me, isn't it? That piece of paper could've been handed to anyone who tried to help that poor soul. I happened to be the one who got there first and held him in my arms. There were scores of people around. I still don't see the connection."

"You said yourself that everything has a reason, and that God wanted you involved."

"Are you implying that I was guided to be there at that moment by an unseen hand?"

"Weren't you? You had a vision? You told me you saw a man running and he needed your help."

"I get lots of visions," he said, trying to dispel their importance.

"And you help lots of people in ways that are not, shall I say, ordinary." Both knew she was referring to the Chinese athlete and the Italian reporter.

He moved his clasped hands up in down to show thanks. For the first time, sitting there, the man she knew as Arnold Ford was different. His face was the same, but somehow he appeared a bit more, she searched for the word, hallowed. Regal. More righteous.

She shook the thought off and continued. "Perhaps you'll understand better once I finish my story."

His eyes spoke legions about his curiosity, yet he waited for her to continue.

"The matching piece I received in New York was meant to entice me to meet with these people in Jerusalem, and it worked. It had to do with a series of murders and thefts around the world, but you know about that. Like we discussed the first time we met, someone or some group is collecting as many of those cut up good luck talismans from around the world as they can. If they can't buy or steal them, they kill for them."

"To what end? When all is said and done, they're still only paper. You can't equate that to a life."

"You and I value life more, but history has proven time and time again, that lives mean nothing when they get in the way of a cause."

"It's hard for me to grasp that concept, but please continue. What cause could possibly be so important?"

*What a wonderful man. He only sees the good in people, nothing else.*

She wanted to remind him about the Crusades and the sacking of Jerusalem and burning of the synagogues, but thought better of it. There were the Christians killed in the Roman Coliseum, the Jews in the Holocaust, the recent genocide of the Rwandans and Hutus, the Bosnians and Serbs, and the slavery that persists into the twenty-first century. How could she not remind him of man's inhumanity to his fellow man? Most of it, if not all, had been in the name of religion or a far-fetched cause.

Instead, she picked up the story. "You'll understand in a moment. Remember, when the book was smuggled into Israel back in the 50's, it sat on a shelf for a few years because the Israelis were distracted fighting a war."

"And when someone uncovered it during an inventory check, a third of the pages were missing."

"That's right. Then sometime during the Conclave of Cardinals, when you were sequestered, an antiquities dealer traveled from London to Jerusalem where certain people showed him the missing pages. Not the ones cut up, but the bulk of the pages that disappeared back in the '50s. To his trained eye they were authentic."

The Pope picked up the chain of events. "And you received the last puzzle part in the mail, to demonstrate they had made the book whole for the first time in more than half a century."

"They did pick the right man when they made you Pope." LeShana eked a smile out of him.

The Pope continued. "And all of this drama, if you will – the missing pieces, Jerusalem, beckoning you to see the pages yourself – was a deliberate staging to get me involved somehow. What do they want?"

And then she told him. He didn't flinch as she laid out the elaborate plan dictated to her by emissaries of Rabbi Zalman Breitstein, who headed the Satmar sect in Israel. In her mind, the disgorgement of the story with all its details should have made her relieved. Instead, LeShana trembled. She was frightened not for herself, but for the danger she might be unleashing. Was she singularly enlisting the Pope in a plan that could harm him? Disgrace the Church?

"Do you think it's preposterous, Your Excellency?"

"On the contrary, my child, I think it brilliant, in a most twisted kind of way."

"Then you'll do it?"

"Do I have a choice?"

"Your Excellency, everyone has a choice."

He clutched her hands in his; warmth spread through her. "That's where you and I differ. I'm merely the vessel for His love. Choices were made for me long ago, from the moment I was born. I didn't choose for those wonderful missionaries, the parents who raised me, to save me when I was orphaned. I couldn't control how I got to the United States or became a priest or ended up as a Cardinal in New York. Least of all, I could never have imagined or engineered a scenario that would have the two of us sitting here in a secret garden in the Vatican."

"It's for those same reasons that you had that vision and ran to help the man that started this whole process in the first place."

He shook his head. "As much as I often see the big picture, the relevance of how this started eluded me until this moment. Perhaps the Divine intervention had nothing to do with the man falling into my arms. Maybe the real collision of spirits was you crossing paths with me. Without you bringing my story to light, would these Satmars have ever engaged me as the instrument of their singular mission? I doubt it."

"You underestimate yourself, Your Excellency. When will you make the call?"

He grabbed her hand as he rose. "As soon as you and I can find a phone in this big house I call home these days."

"Do you think you'll get through the switchboard? It's not easy to get the President of the United States to take your call these days."

"My dear, I have learned that being Pope does have its privileges."

# Chapter Fifty-Five

"Secure the perimeter," shouted Walid. In the coming days, there would be thirty casualties in twenty countries, all protesting the release of an anti-Muslim film that was an affront to the Prophet Mohammed. While the film was insulting and heinous, the underlying unrest that followed the stunning accomplishments of the previous year's Arab spring was inspired and guided by the unseen hand of Al Qaeda. In country after country, protests were designed to undermine the newly formed moderate governments. The goal: to topple these new leaders, mute the protestors, and install religious fundamentalists that would move further away from the Western influences now that their respective dictators had been overthrown, imprisoned, or killed.

The US consulate was under fire. First reports blamed members from a Libyan Islamic fundamentalist group. Unlike Tripoli that was under the new government's rule, the militia who successfully overthrew Qaadafi controlled Benghazi.

Walid nodded to Zakkarhia. "It's your time."

Zakkarhia had waited years for this moment. He had been there when the USS Cole was attacked; he had been in Madrid, Bali, London, and so many other glorious places. He had killed that pregnant Jew in Mumbai; now it was time to deliver a direct message to the President of the United States.

Today was special.

The building still burned. Flanked by militia on both sides, Zakkarhia stepped cautiously around the smoldering white car parked in front of the US embassy. Gunshots popped from inside and from the roof. Pop. Pop. The two on the roof were neutralized.

Zakkarhia advanced, surrounded by a phalanx of snipers.

The last enemy gun from inside the compound was silenced.

Acrid smoke filled made his nostrils flare. His eyes teared.

He entered. All was quiet, but Zakkarhia new that his quarry was still alive. Hiding. Zakkarhia stalked from room to room. Then he found his prey cowering in a bathroom stall.

Zakkarhia smiled as the man soiled himself, knowing his time on earth would end in moments.

One shot, and the Ambassador was dead.

"That's for Osama," screamed Zakkarhia. He pumped another bullet in for good measure.

One more victory for the jihadists.

# Chapter Fifty-Six

LeShana was used to major city lock downs. It happened every September in New York City when the United Nations convened its General Assembly. When it occurred, everyday folks were aggravated the way world leaders and their entourages descended on the island like a plague of locusts. Streets were barricaded, traffic snarled, and restaurant reservations were at a premium. Security people sporting coiled earphones were everywhere. Savvy New Yorkers left the city the way New Orleanians left at the start of Lent, when Zulu, Rex, Orpheus and the other krewes filled their narrow streets with flocks of noisy, colorful floats. Who needed to see drunken revelers wearing feather-adorned masks, tossing purple, yellow, green, and red beads in an attempt to cajole women to bare their breasts?

Jerusalem would be different. Though all were invited, a few heads of state opted to stay home rather than witness Pope Lazarus II's big show. Balancing a ringside seat to history with prudence, some dared not risk the public exposure. It was accepted that Israel had the best security in the world. Knowing that, did not reassure. It was a given that Jerusalem would be turned into a locked fortress. No matter, this event would remain a security nightmare.

Stadium-like, metal bleachers were erected for the foreign dignitaries on the northeastern side of the square. When the proceedings started, three hundred dignitaries, including presidents, kings, Prime Ministers, sheiks, priests, rabbis, and imams from the Muslin world, would be protected by a phalanx of Israeli soldiers. Elaborate security measures not announced to the press, unseen but in place, offered a bit more comfort. For most, no matter what the plans to thwart trouble, the area was not secure enough.

Most reasoned that if it was good enough for the Pope, it had to be good enough for them. It wasn't, but that's what they said when asked by the media.

Nike provided binoculars for all; Fuji dispensed throwaway cameras to those without picture-taking mobile phones.

The main attraction was not English royalty including Queen Elizabeth or her grandson and his beautiful wife, not presidents or prime ministers, but the missing pages of a book penned by Aaron ben Asher in 929 AD in Tiberias.

The dance card for center stage was preordained. The Vatican, along with the help of the Israelis and Palestinians, orchestrated every aspect of this great event. Nothing was left to chance; nothing would be out of place.

The Secretary General of the United Nations, the president of the United States, the president of the Palestinians and the Israeli Prime Minister would join Pope Lazarus II. They would meet on the promenade in front of the Dome of the Rock.

By now the conditions outlined to LeShana by the Satmar intermediaries in the King David Hotel for returning the missing pages of the Codex were known worldwide. The success of the operation, Code name *Savior's Day*, ironically, the same appellation that recognized W. D. Fard's birthday, rested in one man's hands: Pope Lazarus II. Not only did he have to agree to receive the missing pages but to execute the conditions dictated by the Satmars to the minutest detail or the pages would be buried in an unmarked grave, never to be found again.

The plan was that simple. Jews, Moslems, and Christians alike, universally praised the core of what the Satmars hoped to achieve; the other players – the US and the UN - gave their tacit approval. What started out as far-fetched as landing on the moon in less than ten short years or eradicating polio evolved into an equally compelling turning point in recorded history.

When asked if reassembling the book was as far reaching as ending World War II or the Berlin Wall coming down, Pope Lazarus II answered, "Reassembling the fragmented Codex of Aleppo might have great ramifications." When pushed, he would neither speculate nor compare.

It was an eternity ago that LeShana met the two black-frocked Jews in the King David Hotel. Immediately after concluding that meeting, she grabbed the next plane to Rome and met with the Pope, and then flew to Washington to meet with the President after Lazarus II called the White House. Now an international ambassador without portfolio, though one could say she was traveling with diplomatic immunity representing the Vatican, she left Washington and returned to Jerusalem to arrange security details with Gittel Lasker and Shin Bet, the Mossad, and the Israeli and Palestinian governments.

All this accomplished in two weeks.

"Explain this to me one more time," she remembered asking the taller Satmar agent.

With patience, he repeated the plan one more time. "We have assembled all the missing pages and cut-up parts of the Codex of Aleppo, except the laminated segment that is still in your possession. The one the old man gave you. Well, not you, but to then Cardinal Ford. That is the lone missing piece that will complete the great book of Aaron ben Asher."

"How many did you kill to accomplish this?" she asked.

"Consider them casualties of war. Most were glad to get rid of their pieces of parchment to stop the pain. Old people cave in faster than most."

"You want me to help you knowing you or persons in your group have committed murder? How many murders?"

"You have no choice, Detective Thompkins."

"Oh, but I do."

"Zippora is such a beautiful name. Did you know it means 'bird'?"

"You wouldn't dare," said LeShana. LeShana never talked about her sixteen-year old daughter, not to anyone. Zippora was an honor student in high school. Even though she was *bat mitzvahed* three years earlier, she continued to attend Hebrew High School, which was a once-a-week class on the Old Testament. She excelled at fencing and field hockey, and had dreams of becoming an aeronautical engineer. When LeShana traveled or needed to keep long hours, Zippora stayed with her grandmother in the Crown Heights section of Brooklyn.

LeShana whipped out her cell phone. The tall man stopped her. "There's no need. She's unharmed. She's safe with you mother. We just wanted you to know that no one is out of our reach. Shall we continue?"

She could protest, she could threaten, she could challenge, and there was much to do before agreeing to work with them. But putting Zippora at risk was not negotiable. And, thought LeShana, if they have all the pieces, there would be no more killings, no more intimidating old people, so commonsense told her to play their game now and deal with past crimes later.

She pointed to the carefully wrapped sheaves of parchment that were now repackaged. The lone photocopy lay next to it. "I still need to verify that this is the real deal."

"The man from London authenticated them. You know all about him."

"He thought they were from the Codex. He wasn't certain."

"He was certain. That's why he didn't buy them. No matter. Your Agent Lasker brought a photocopy to a Biblical scholar at Hebrew University. Yussif Tawil. He was able to verify their authenticity."

"If they are the real deal, why hasn't Tawil gone public with them? Announced their discovery?"

"First of all, he only had a photocopy, and he did not have all of them. And second, we made him promised that if he didn't betray us, he could be at the big ceremony."

"What big ceremony?" she asked.

The taller of the two, who now controlled this meeting, leaned forward. "The one you're going to arrange."

He proceeded to weave a tale that surpassed anything she could ever conjure up, including the story she shared with the Pope when he was still Cardinal Ford. As fantastic as the stories about his father and W.D. Fard were, this one topped them by every stretch of the imagination. It didn't surprise the Satmars, however, it was preordained as far as they were concerned. It was always a question of *when* not *if* it would happen.

"The greatest treasure to the Jewish people is the Crown of Aleppo," the big man began.

"I know. It was so declared by Maimonides," said LeShana.

He smiled. "We're glad we've chosen you for this important task, Detective."

LeShana didn't respond.

"We want you to arrange for the Pope to come to Jerusalem and accept the missing pages from us."

"To what end?"

"To hand them to the Prime Minister of Israel, along with the Palestinian and US presidents present, and the Secretary General of the United Nations."

"Then what happens?" asked LeShana. "Why the formalities?"

"These formalities, as you call them, will be the result of Pope Lazarus II brokering a Mideast Peace Plan. The Pope will present our proposal to both the Israelis and Palestinians."

"Which is?"

"That Israel will vacate Jerusalem and move the center of government to Tel Aviv, which is technically the capital already, but the Israelis never recognized it as such."

"Why would they do such a thing?"

Like a well-greased tag team, the remainder of the story was handed off to Shorty. "For peace, what else? The Jews will agree to make Jerusalem an international city similar to the way the Allies ruled Berlin after World War II. But unlike Berlin, which was divided into four sectors ruled by the Russians, the Americans, the French, and the English, Jerusalem will be governed and ruled by the United Nations alone. There will be no interference by any of the powers. Not the US. Not Russia. Not the Palestinians, and not even the Israelis."

"Why would Israel do such a thing? How can it be in their best interest?"

"Because the Israelis and Palestinians are tired of fighting. They're tired of dodging incoming rockets and sabotage at the hands of Hamas or Hezbollah, or any number of splinter groups. They're tired of burying their young. The Israelis can't afford to remain on military alert every minute of every day for all eternity; they need to know that their borders are safe and that they can ride buses or drink at a café without a bomb going off. And Palestinians need to live without an embargo and smuggling goods through tunnels. They need to rebuild. They need to have their own country so they can stop playing the displaced refugee card and accept the fact that where they currently live is, and always will be, their home. Then there's Iran and the constant threat of them lobbing a nuclear bomb here. Remove Jerusalem as the Israeli capital and that threat disappears."

"Iran is not an issue for the Israelis. They've already demonstrated that they'll do whatever's necessary to block Iran's path to a nuclear warhead. When the Iranians get close again, the Israelis will terminate their new attempt." LeShana was referring to the Stuxnet virus that destroyed one thousand centrifuges at the uranium enrichment plant in Natanz. Natanz was only one of many such plants in Iran, but the message was clear from the Israelis to the Iranians: stop what you're doing or we'll destroy the rest.

Shorty continued. "Perhaps you're right. But the Iranians continue to defy everyone, and their research facilities are deep underground. Let's not focus on them because the rest of the world is against them a well. A greater concern rests with the new regimes that emerged after the Arab Spring. They still target Israel as an enemy. If a full-scale war erupts, and history tells us there will be another Mideast such conflict, Israel will face annihilation. Remember, the first war they lose is the last they will ever fight; the Israelis would be driven into the sea. It would happen with lightening speed so fast that no one could help them survive. It would be tragic, but it wouldn't make us that unhappy. Still..."

"What are you talking about? You're both Jews." *She wanted to add, just like me.* "Don't you want Israel to survive?"

Both men nodded. "Not in the way you think. We both live here along with our families. We're Jews first, Israelis second. To that end, we're apolitical and have never supported this country. We don't pay taxes. We don't serve in the Army. The truth is, we pray every day that Israel will fall apart. That it will be taken over by the Arabs."

The tall man nodded for his partner to reverse gears. Shorty caught the cue, collected himself, and got back on point.

"I digress. I was talking about the Israelis vacating Jerusalem and the UN taking over. What else happens? The Jews get lasting peace and the Codex of Aleppo is made whole; the Palestinians get their own state carved out of Gaza and from some areas that go back to pre-'67 borders."

"I'm no politician but there's got to be more to this than what you're saying," she said.

"We were told Americans have little patience." The tall man said, with a bit of amusement. "There *is* more, Detective." He continued. "Part of this plan hinges on the Arabs agreeing to open the East Gate of the ancient wall that separates the Old City from the Arabs. This is not negotiable. And the other part that is not negotiable is that the Arabs must let Jews enter the square surrounding the Dome of the Rock. Some call it the Temple Mount."

"Jews can't go there now," said LeShana.

"Correct."

"And the Dome sits on top of the ancient Temple."

"That's right."

"And who is going to convince all the parties to agree to this plan of yours?"

"The Pope," they answered in unison.

LeShana rose from the chair and paced to the window and back. She retraced her steps. She wheeled and faced them with a suddenness that caused them to jump back.

"And you asked me here so I could fly to Rome and convince the Pope that he was going to mediate a Mideast Peace Plan, one that's eluded every politician ever since Palestine was partitioned more than sixty-five years ago."

"Don't forget about convincing the American President and the Secretary General of the United Nations. When it comes to foreign diplomacy and matters pertaining to Israel, nothing happens without the US being involved. And you need to get the UN to agree to take control of Jerusalem."

"How'm I going to do that?"

"Because their mission is world peace, and because the US will foot the bill. Look at the opportunity: to make the cradle of the Bible, the heart of the Judeo-Christian world, a neutral city for the three major religions in the Western world. To have lasting peace in the Middle East. Do you seriously think they'd turn the offer down?"

"Do you seriously think the Pope can broker this? I only met him once," she said, "and he wasn't Pope then."

"You connected with him. You explained that although he was raised a Catholic, he had black Jewish parents. That his father may have founded the Black Muslims."

"How do you know I said those things to him?"

"Are we right? Didn't you say those things to him?"

She nodded. "But how?"

"We have our ways."

This upset LeShana. She had filed an extensive report when she returned to the station after speaking so long to Cardinal Ford that day. She had to account for the time spent, so she wrote in detail what was discussed. The only way these Satmars could have known anything about what she and Ford talked about was to have access to the police files. The thought terrified. Did they have a mole that deep in NYPD? Who are these people?

"But why the Pope?" she asked. She wanted to ask more, like who was their police stooge, but knew they would never reveal their source, assuming they knew who it was.

"Because he's the most perfect person in the world. Jews, Muslims, and Catholics accept him. Who else can say that?"

"Michael Jordan."

"Who?"

"Never mind."

Shorty continued. "Once you convince your president and the Secretary General, the Pope becomes the emissary who will accept the missing pages and hand them to the proper authorities. There's not a more perfect person on the planet. It's that simple."

LeShana rolled her eyes. "How can anything this complex be that simple?"

"Because reasonable people will do reasonable things."

She hung her hands on her hips. "Really? When did you know all these folks, these world leaders, to be reasonable? Especially the Arabs?"

"All will see the beauty and elegance in this plan. They can't afford not to."

She could see a glitch or two. "I get what the Arabs receive; they seem to be the big winners in this deal. And I even understand why the Israelis might consider doing this, but they won't buy into it. You can't summarily dismiss the wars they've already fought to capture Jerusalem and fulfill their Biblical prophecy."

"You're missing the key element, Detective. When you talk about Biblical prophecies, the biggest one of all has yet to be fulfilled. Even for the Israelis. That's why they'll go for this."

"And what exactly would that be?" asked LeShana. She vacillated between believing these characters were goons or brilliant. To her apolitical side, the plan didn't sound half bad. To her professional side, the plan was half-baked. How could anyone ever bring these disparate parties to agree on anything? Presidents and prime ministers have tried countless times. Nobel Peace prizes have been awarded without constructing a final document leading to peace.

*They think they can accomplish this when all others have failed?*

"When the East Gate is opened after being sealed for five hundred years, the greatest prophecy of all will be possible."

"Which is?" she asked.

"To allow the Messiah to enter Jerusalem."

And then she got it. "The Messiah has to enter Jerusalem through the East Gate and be able to stand on the site of the Second Temple."

The bigger man picked up the sheaves of the Codex. "And then there will be world peace. That's why we went to extremes to collect all the missing pages. So we could initiate the conditions necessary for the Messiah to save us."

"And when will this happen?" she asked.

"The Messiah will come sooner than you think. He may be among us already."

"Really," said LeShana. "You expect me to buy this? Worse yet, you expect me to sell it? If all this happens, how will you know that the Messiah is here?"

"That's something we don't need to worry about. When he comes, we'll know."

# Chapter Fifty-Seven

"I need to leave this place."

Jericho Glassman had been reading the paper in the solarium of the Defense Ministry's compound when he came across a story that described that the leaders of the Judeo-Christian world would soon descend on Jerusalem to witness the restoration of the Codex of Aleppo. This was no small matter. Using this rare, ancient Bible as a pretext for change, the Israeli government agreed to vacate the ancient city and move operations to Tel Aviv. They were tired of fighting. Tired of living in a fishbowl, being made accountable for everything they did to preserve their freedom. They were tired of burying their sons and daughters, and tired of paying high taxes to be war-ready every moment of their existence. They were flat out tired. This Codex of Aleppo gave them the pretext they needed to save face, the same pretext the Muslims needed to fulfill the Satmar requirements.

From their side, the commitments asked of the Palestinian leaders were equally extraordinary. Open up the east gate, let Jews enter the hallowed crowds of the Temple Mount, and give up claims to recapturing Jerusalem. It was no easy sell but buying it would fulfill their dream of creating a Palestinian State and becoming an equal in the pantheon of nations.

However it happened, the Satmar sword of reason turned steel doctrines into malleable ploughshares for peace.

"You're not ready," answered Dr. Lev ben Hodesh, the psychologist assigned to Jericho's case. Jericho was remanded to the Post-Traumatic

Stress Disorder Clinic, standard operating procedure for any Israeli soldier captured by any of a dozen enemies. "You've made tremendous progress, but there's still more to accomplish." While most others with PTSD were treated as out patients, Jericho was treated as an inpatient.

Jericho had received a hero's welcome when he was part of the negotiated prisoner exchange. Ensconced in the Army's care, he went through extensive debriefing during those first weeks. He exhibited signs of depression and was given a selective serotonin reuptake inhibitor to help make him feel less sad and worried. Paxil appeared effective.

During those first days sleep eluded him. He muttered to himself. Sometimes, spoke gibberish and then turned lucid for long periods of time. He made progress, albeit slow. When he was lucid and in the room by himself, he spoke to Voices. He first heard them when his father was killed. The Voices were the ones who told him to change his name, that Moishe Schlamowitz no longer existed. He listened to them then, and he listened to them now.

Dr. Hodesh suggested group therapy. It helped. In group therapy, he spoke to other soldiers who suffered from PTSD. Sharing his story about being captured and held in Gaza with others helped him deal with his anger and feelings of rage. He began to focus more on the present than the past. He made more progress. But he never mentioned the Voices, not even to Dr. Hodesh.

"I feel so much better," Jericho said after the first year. "I'd like to return to my unit."

"I'm afraid I can't let that happen," said Dr. Hodesh. "You may feel better, stronger, more clear-headed, but PTSD has a way of resurfacing when you least expect it. I can't release you, not just yet."

"Then when?" asked Jericho.

"We will both know when that is," answered the doctor.

This scenario was repeated many times and each time Jericho capitulated to the doctor...and to the Voices. They also told him he wasn't ready. As much as he wanted to stop therapy and resume a normal life, whatever that meant now, Jericho was relieved when the doctor gently persuaded him the time was not yet right. The Voices continued to approve.

Today was different. Jericho stared at the newspaper. This changed everything. There was little time to prepare.

"I feel better than ever," he told the doctor, smiling as broadly as he could.

"You've felt safe here, Jericho. You've said so yourself many times."

Jericho studied the doctor's face. It was as if he was seeing him for the first time. Dr. Hodesh had hound dog's eyes, a tight gray stubble covering his face, and stringy, leaden-colored hair pulled back in a ponytail.

"I know how much you've helped me, doctor. I thought it would be easy to adjust but it has taken time. You've given me comfort and taught me how to cope. I'm not angry anymore. I know how to control my feelings. And I haven't had a headache for a while now."

Dr. Hodesh had treated many like Jericho. He was well aware of how adjusted soldiers suffering PTSD could feel better and convinced themselves they were ready to resume normal activities. In rare instances, he cleared them to return to active duty. But there was danger in that. While they would appear fine, even normal and high-functioning, the untested issue was how they reacted when confronted by a trigger. Confronting a trigger was confronting their Devil. In time, most learned to cope. Was Jericho ready? In the doctor's opinion, Jericho would never be combat ready again. Anything could set him off.

Dr. Hodesh stared at the newspaper headlines on Jericho's lap. *Even reading the paper, the doctor knew, could trigger an episode.*

"You've come so far, Jericho. Your progress has been remarkable."

"Thanks to you."

"But there's still more to do. You need to be here a bit longer. Then you can go home."

*Home,* thought Jericho, *I have no home. No one to go back to. Whose fault is that?*

Jericho hunched over, made himself appear smaller. The Voices told him what to say. "I've been here a long time. I'm itching to have a more normal life again. See my friends. The medicine's working, you've said so yourself. I promise, I will come to every session you ask me to, but I want to leave. Try to lead a more normal life like the others in group."

"Do you think it wise to leave?"

"I do."

"I can't recommend that, Jericho."

"But you can't keep me here against my wishes?"

"If you leave now, you'll have a relapse. I can't clear you for active duty."

"I'll stay on extended medical leave; I don't want to return to my unit now."

"You won't know it's happening until it is too late. And then you'll be back."

"I have to take that chance."

"I can't let that happen, for your safety and the safety of others."

Jericho stood. "How can you stop me?"

"I don't like to issue orders, Jericho, but you leave me no choice. I outrank you. I'm a major in the army and order you to remain confined to this hospital until further notice."

The Voices spoke to Jericho. He cocked his head and listened. When they were done, he squared up in front of Doctor Hodesh. "You can only order me to stay if I remain in the Army."

"That's not true. As a licensed psychiatrist, I can keep you confined here, until I say you are well enough to leave."

"I know my rights. In order to do that, you need a court order and you don't have one. Not yet."

"A phone call and I'll have it."

"By the time you do, I will be long gone."

"You need to stay for now; the army has ordered you to remain in my care."

Jericho tossed his head back. "Doctor, as of now, I'm no longer in the army. I resign."

"You can't just do it like that. There are papers to fill out. In your case, tests you need to take."

Jericho moved toward the door. "You know what you can do with those tests, doctor. Thanks for your help. Have a good life."

Dr. Hodesh knew he was beat. Jericho had made remarkable progress and unless there was a remarkable trigger, he couldn't envision him not readjusting to civilian society. "Where will you go?"

"Not very far."

# Chapter Fifty-Eight

Regardless of where Zakkarhia was, no matter what his assignment, thoughts of Aliah came to him. How could such a young, beautiful child be killed so senselessly? If a suicide bomber had taken her with him, he would've understood; Aliah would be in Paradise now. But an Israeli rocket? Her death must be avenged.

He was at a secret meeting at the Al Faisaliah Hotel. Key Al Qaeda leaders were summoned by one of the King's sons.

"We need your cooperation," the Prince said as they sat around a circular table in a private meeting room. A haze of smoke filled the room, the lights less bright. "The King has pledged $37 billion for new spending, including jobless benefits, education and housing subsidies, debt write-offs, and a new sports channel. His generosity is in response to the recent uprisings across the Mediterranean."

"The King has always been generous," Walid said. The others nodded in agreement. Why wouldn't they agree? They had been funded by the Saudi monarchy from the start.

"That is not all," continued the Prince. "The King has pledged to spend a total of $400 billion in the next two years to improve education, health care and the kingdom's infrastructure."

None of the jihadists were comfortable being confined in a room. The elegance dripping from the crystal chandeliers, the pure gold sconces, the marble floors, the handmade teak chairs, made them squirm. And none were comfortable without their weapons that were not allowed in the hotel. No point scaring the guests.

"Your Excellency, the benevolence of the King is well known. But you didn't summon us here to tell us about his great generosities. We're all aware of his magnificence."

"Ever the pragmatist, Walid. You're right. In light of the Arab Spring, the King wanted to discuss your future plans. To make certain those so-called uprisings have ended and would never occur here."

"You've done much to buy peace from your people with these new initiatives."

"It's the right thing to do. We need to share more." Most grunted in agreement. "Again," said the Prince, "I ask, what are your plans?"

"You know that one of our conditions for staying out of Saudi Arabia is that we can pick any target we wish."

"And that won't change."

"Then what would you like to know?"

"Your immediate plans…and of course to pledge more money to the *jihad*."

Walid knew there was more to this meeting than hollow praise from Saudi King's son or more money for the jihad. "What does the King have in mind?"

"Soft targets. It is time to bring the jihad to the United States."

"Excuse me, Your Excellency, but America is your ally. They sell you weapons, buy your oil."

"Business is business, that will never change. But the Americans? They will always be our enemy, the same as yours. September 11 was a wakeup call. Even with Bali, Mumbai, London, Madrid, and all the others, Americans go to sleep at night thinking they're safe. The only things they seem to fear are natural disasters: blizzards, fires, and killer storms. In a way, our oil can be blamed for that, Allah be praised. But that's not enough. They've slept peacefully long enough."

"The King must have some ideas."

"Soft targets for a start. Restaurants. Synagogues. Jewish Centers like the one bombed in Argentina. Any of the embassies in Washington, D.C. will do. Let other countries worry that we're coming to them next."

"Create chaos and keep oil prices high. I get it," said Walid.

The corners of the prince's mouth turned up. "The King will be grateful." With that, the he handed Walid an envelope. There were checks exceeding five billion dollars. "Consider this a down payment."

◆  ◆  ◆

In the hotel lobby, Walid waved the envelope at Zakkarhia and the others. "All he cares about is that we don't cause any problems to destabilize the monarchy. Why would we?"

"Will we bomb shopping malls and attack the Jews?" asked one.

"In time. First there are governments we need to worry, and elections that need our attention."

"What's next?" asked another.

Walid held up a finger, "We have plans in motion," he said to those around him. He turned his back to the group and motioned to Zakkarhia. In a softer voice, he said, "Here's a leaflet that describes an upcoming event in Jerusalem. I need you there."

Zakkarhia scanned the dignitaries expected. It was clear what his mission would be.

"How?" was all he asked. Nothing else had to be said.

Walid thrust a second envelope into Zakkarhia's hands. "The Prince gave me this before the meeting." Zakkarhia opened the envelope.

It was an official Israeli passport.

Zakkarhia nodded.

This was the assignment of a lifetime, the one he had been working toward all these years.

And in the process, he sister's death would be avenged.

# Chapter Fifty-Nine

A fter explaining the role the Satmars envisioned for Pope Lazarus II, and then after shuttling to Washington and then Jerusalem, LeShana finally returned to New York. As the clock ticked down to "Savior's Day," she agitated to return to Jerusalem and observe the events she helped orchestrate.

"With all due respect, Detective Thompkins," started Frank Murphy, "you *do* have a job."

"Without me, none of this would've happened. The least the department can do is insure that I finish the job. That's protocol in all cases. Three days. Four at the most."

"Protocol is for you to stay here and work. Granted you set steps in motion that will have an unprecedented outcome, but they don't require your presence to complete them. Do I have to inform you that there are still bad guys in this city to catch, in spite of your masterful diplomacy?"

She knew it was fruitless to argue any further. As much as she did want to see the Codex made intact by the Pope on the world stage, she did miss her job. And there was Zippora.

"Then could I at least watch the event with my daughter? All the schools are giving students the day off."

*Jerusalem*

"It's going to be a security nightmare," said Amos Gadol, head of the Israeli National Security. "Our Prime Minister and President, the

American President, the Secretary General of the United Nations, the Palestinian President, plus the head of every friggin' country in the world. And if that weren't enough, throw in the Pope, whatever his name is."

They were in a tactical meeting. One of many.

Gittel Lasker ran the particulars through her steel trap, gray matter processor. When it came to strategic planning in order to reduce risks and improve outcomes, she was among the best. But this was a logistical nightmare that would create deep furrows that even Botox could not smooth out. Her mental clock counted down the hours and minutes until this event was over and she'd drink the elixir of comfort knowing all parties were safe. The last thing she or anyone else could even think about was a repeat of the Rabin assassination. That was then. Mistakes were made. They learned; it would not be repeated on their watch.

"Will we have access to the Temple Mount?" asked one agent. "How can we be expected to protect these hotshots if we can't get close."

"They won't let us anywhere near the Dome of the Rock," answered Gadol. "Not until the whole shebang is finished. Then we can stroll around it with a picnic basket on our arm."

"By then it could be too late. We need to protect our own Prime Minister. And I don't want to think of the consequences if something happens to the Pope on our watch."

"It's not our call. We have a back seat to the Palestinians on that one. They control the Mount; they control the security. We have to trust that their people want safety for everyone as much as we do. They have much to lose if there's a mishap on their territory, and up until the exchange, the Mount is still theirs."

"How can we trust them to protect the Prime Minister? We all know what happened when Sharon tried to gain access to the Mount."

*Jerusalem, 2000*

Ariel Sharon, the Likud party leader, marched up al-Haram al-Sharif, also known as the Temple Mount, which is the thirty-five acre platform that supports the Dome of the Rock. Sharon spent forty-five minutes there, surrounded by riot police and a number of Likud politicians.

"The Temple Mount is in our hands and will remain in our hands. It is the holiest site in Judaism, and it is the right of every Jew to visit the Temple Mount," he said after he climbed back down the stairs.

Controversy abounded. Both Palestinians and Israeli liberals denounced the visit as inflammatory. Protests ensued. But it didn't stop there. Young Palestinian turned violent at Sharon's audacity. At his violation of *their* holy site. They heaved whatever they could find at the Israeli riot forces: stones, rubbish, chairs. They picked up anything and everything loose and tossed it at the Israelis. The immediate toll: two riot police and five Palestinians were injured. The Israelis used tear gas and rubber bullets to quell the protest.

Yasser Arafat went on Palestinian television as the riot spread. "This is a dangerous process conducted by Sharon against Islamic sacred places." Fighting between the Palestinian youth and Israeli riot police worsened. Sharon was never forgiven for his role in the 1982 massacre, killing innocent Palestinians in a Lebanese refugee camp. Now, the ultimate insult: violating the understanding that Jews do not enter al-Haram al-Sharif...the Temple Mount.

Mr. Sharon was unrepentant. He chafed at critics claiming he had been on a mission of reconciliation. "How can there be provocation when Jews visit a place with a message of peace? I'm sorry about the injured, but it's the inherent right of Jews in Israel to visit the Temple Mount."

What made the Temple Mount so important to both Jews and Muslims that a single misstep would deteriorate into violence and mayhem?

According to scholars, the Temple Mount is the very spot where God gathered dust and created Adam. This was the same site that God instructed the Jews to build both the first and second Temples, and where God spoke to his Prophets, telling them how to spread His word, ordering them how to live.

God instructed that this site should be the center of all forms of national life: governmental, judicial, and religious. Rabbis interpreted that it would be the site of the Third and final Temple ever be built. Spookily, eerily, reverently, rabbis felt that the Divine Presence continued to inhabit the site. For this reason, no one should unintentionally walk where the Holy of Holies stood. The ironic translation: Jews forbid Jews from walking on the Temple Mount as much as Muslims did.

The site was just as holy to the Muslims because it was the very spot where Mohammed leapt to heaven on his white horse Buraq. Holy, holy, holy. No Jews allowed.

It may have been holy to both, but Arabs controlled it ever since the 1967 War.

And then Ariel Sharon jams his generous butt into the simmering cauldron.

Later that same day, rioting continued on the streets of Arab East Jerusalem and outside the West Bank town of Ramallah. This grassroots, spontaneous protest twisted into a deadly campaign of terrorism that targeted Israeli civilians on buses, restaurants and on city streets. Over the ensuing five years, this second Intifada, that's the name it was given, injured thousands.

Before it was over, one thousand Israelis and five thousand Palestinians died.

What was the point of all this? Sharon had an ulterior motive: deflect attention away from the former prime minister, Benjamin Netanyahu, who had returned from the US just the day before, and who was the only politician capable of challenging Sharon for the Likud party leadership.

*Jerusalem*

"What about the American president?" one asked. "We can't leave him out in the open?"

"No choice."

"Will they let him have his Secret Service agents?"

"I understand there will be some in the background. That's the best that could be arranged," said Gadol.

"Are we forgetting President Rothschild is a Jew?"

"Won't change a thing," answered Gadol.

"And the Pope is part Jewish."

"That's stretching it," said another. "Pope Lazarus was never part of the covenant. No *bris*, no bar mitzvah. He's not a Jew by our standards."

"But he is the Pope," said Gadol. "That does count. And we have to protect him, along with all the others. More than the others."

Gittel asked a question. "Is it true that the Arabs agreed to take down the bricks and open the East Gate?"

"They are tearing them down as we speak," said Gadol. "As far as I'm concerned, that's the true miracle of the day. Archaeologists are hoping to find the pillars of Sheba under it all, but that remains to be seen." Each Israeli, ever an archaeologist.

"What's the big deal about the east gate? It's been closed forever."

Gadol loved the chance to act as a professor. "That passage has been blocked for more than five centuries. A couple of weeks ago, I would've bet my pension that it would stay that way another five hundred years. Leave it to the politicians to create a miracle! Maybe it was the Pope's doing; we may never know. But it gives us a tactical problem. We won't be able to cover what happens on that side."

"What's supposed to happen there?"

"That's where the Pope will make his entrance. Before he gets to the Mount, he will hike down from Mt. Olive with the missing pages of the Codex. That's where he'll be most vulnerable."

"He'll have his Swiss Guard."

"They're no match for terrorists."

Gadol summed it up. "It's pretty simple, people. Our job is to protect the Western Wall where our people will be. We make certain no one gets hurt there and we've done our job. Keep in mind that we will be under a microscope; the whole world will be watching."

The briefing over, assignments were distributed to each agent. Gittel trudged to her spot in front of the *mechitza*, the fence that separates the men from the women by the Wailing Wall. She knew that she was one of thousands, some visible, some unseen, charged with making the day safe. Yet, in her heart and down to the core of her soul, she felt the success of the day rested with her alone.

In short order, her worst fears would come true.

# Chapter Sixty

Zakkarhia climbed the narrow stairs of the minaret that faced north. The Al Aqsa Mosque was due south of the Dome of the Rock. From here he would have a perfect view of the dignitaries gathering as they waited for the Pope to make his way down from Mount Olives with the missing pages. Built in 710 AD, the Al Aqsa Mosque was destroyed by fire and earthquakes a handful of times. The last major rebuild was in 1035. When the Crusaders captured Jerusalem in 1099, which is the first time the Codex of Aleppo should have been destroyed, the Al-Aqsa Mosque became the headquarters of the Templars.

Though blistering outside with the heat bouncing off the stones in waves, the stairwell in the ancient mosque was cool and soothing. It was fitting that Zakkarhia would avenge his sister's death from the second oldest mosque, sometimes known as the Farthest Mosque because it was two thousand kilometers from Medina. Unchallenged, he made his way to the minaret. Signs of security were everywhere. Soldiers. Police. Metal detectors. Facial recognition. Digital fingerprints. Every turn brought another challenge, another test.

In the end, being careful all these years had its rewards. Zakkarhia had remained under the radar. His face, pupils, fingerprints, and more, had avoided being collected. Given that he had been present when the USS Cole was bombed, had been in Madrid and London, trained in Afghanistan, and been involved in another half-dozen Al Qaeda ops, it was a testimony to his cunning and, perhaps, a bit of luck, that he had never left a forensic trail.

This time would be no different. Zakkarhia knew security would be so tight that a crooked toothpick would not have made it passed security checks. So two weeks before the publicly announced date, Zakkarhia made a journey to the Al Aqsa Mosque and after late evening prayers, sneaked up into the minaret, climbed a ledge and taped his favorite rifle to a rafter supporting the narrow dome, well out of sight from prying eyes.

*Gittel*

Gittel started her career being a first-hand witness to an assassination. Though it wasn't her fault, she lugged the weight of that horrible day with her wherever she went. It didn't matter which assignment, if she was out to dinner with friends or taking a much-needed day off, the day the Israeli Prime Minister was shot was a blemish on her record.

She would not let that happen again. And because she was not going to let it happen again, she walked the perimeter of the Wailing Wall, the streets leading down to the ancient structure, and then gained access to as many buildings as she could. She noted which ones gave the best view of the Dome of the Rock and where dignitaries would be waiting for the Pope when the big day arrived.

It was not possible to make it to every rooftop. She created a list with a line down the center. To the left, she wrote the addresses of buildings that were unimportant and had no sight lines worth worrying about; but to the right, she numbered buildings that required special attention. Her private surveillance yielded no planted guns or anything that gave pause to be concerned. Yet, she would not lower her guard until the Pope restored the Codex, replete with the missing pages, and all the dignitaries left town.

Every few days, she repeated the process until the day the police cordoned off every street to only those who could prove they lived in nearby homes. And even then, most would not be allowed in their own homes until the event was concluded.

Gittel checked her last building and saw that it was clear of anything suspicious. She left satisfied that she did all she could before the big day.

◆　　◆　　◆

It was twenty-four hours before the streets were blocked. For days, Jericho had hung nearby the building he knew had an unblemished view of the Dome of the Rock. He noted when those who lived there left in the morning and when they returned in the evening. He noted who kept their windows open and who played loud music. He noted the pattern of deliveries. After a week, he calculated the best time of day to gain access to the roof. That is when he could hide the telescopic mount he would need to accomplish his mission.

He squinted at his watch. It was mid-morning and a safe time to enter the building. He took a step and then jumped back. A woman stepped out the door; she was not a tenant. He had not seen her enter. She had red hair, straight posture, and strode with an official bearing. Her face was familiar, but he couldn't place it. He waited for her to turn the corner, waited another minute, and made his move. Guided by the Voices, he entered the building, climbed the stairs, and found the door to the roof locked; he shrugged at the ease of getting it open.

He found a hiding place for the telescopic mount and then quick-stepped to the roof edge, absorbing the majestic view in front of him. Before Jericho lay the Wailing Wall, the Temple Mount, and the Dome of the Rock.

"I'm ready," he said to the Voices.

They answered back.

He nodded.

He *was* ready.

# Chapter Sixty-One

Pope Lazarus II was told that two men bearing the special package would meet him on the steps of the Church of All Nations. Also known as the Basilica of the Agony, this Roman Catholic Church was built enshrining the bedrock where Jesus is said to have prayed before his arrest. The present church rests on the foundation of a Byzantine basilica built in the fourth century and then rebuilt in the twelfth century as a Crusader chapel.

The chauffeur guided the black limousine to the foot of the church steps, stopping next to the wrought iron fence. Besides a contingency of Papal Swiss Guards, four Mossad agents were assigned to protect the Pope.

The Pope swallowed, his mouth dry, as he watched the Satmar duo inch down the church steps and pass through the metal gate toward him. When they neared, by previous agreement with the Swiss guards, the Israeli agents accosted these same men who had first met the London antiquities dealer and then LeShana. They froze as the agents patted each down; neither was armed. Next, an agent tried to pry the package away from the shorter man, who had it clutched to his chest, to make certain it wasn't a bomb.

The Jews protested.

When words turned animated, the Pope pushed open the limo door.

"It's okay," he said to the Mossad agents. "They mean me no harm."

"Sorry, Your Excellency, that's not how we do it here. They have to show us what's in the package. They have no option. Now please remain in the car."

That was the last thing Lazarus II was going to do. Peace was in his grasp, all of their grasps, and he wasn't going to let an agent, even a Mossad agent, dampen its chances.

To the consternation of all, he stepped out and approached the men. The phalanx of Swiss Guards galloped to surround the Pope; two others sprinted past the black-garbed men who were still tussling with the Mossad. They bolted into the church to insure no one lurked inside that could cause the Pontiff harm. Though this was done multiple times earlier that day, and the day before, they couldn't leave anything to chance. Not now.

"Let them give me the package. I will open it and show it to you."

"What if it's a bomb?"

"It would have gone off by now. We have little time to spare; the entire world is waiting for me to bring these parchment sheets to the Temple Mount so they can be reunited with the rest of the Codex. So much depends on this reunion. We must proceed."

◆　◆　◆

Before LeShana finished detailing the events that led to her visit to Rome, she knew the Pope would accept the Satmar challenge. A chance to end the Middle East Crisis? How could he not want to help? As soon as he agreed, she cautioned.

"It will be a security nightmare. It will be difficult to protect you."

Trite as it appeared, Lazarus II pointed skyward. "I have whatever protection I need every moment of my life, LeShana. If I am the glue that can hold a tenuous peace process together, then I have no other choice but to follow their plan."

"You need to be wary of these Satmar Jews. They have killed to assemble the missing pages. They're not to be trusted."

"We share the same God. I'll be fine."

"But what if they only have some of the pages, and not every page?"

"Then at least more of the book will be made whole," he answered.

"You're not worried that this could be some sort of hoax?"

"We're too far past that, LeShana. You worry too much."

"That's my job."

"And my job is to tend my flock."

◆  ◆  ◆

Now, with the Mossad agents at the ready, the Pope undid the tape and edged the brown paper back to show them the yellowed sheaves of parchment.

"No bomb," said Lazarus II, holding it up for them to see.

An agent wriggled on latex gloves and lifted the pages with ginger, making certain a hollow had not been created to hide an explosive device. After all, if right wing Arabs could blow themselves up, so could Jews.

"Satisfied?" asked the Pope.

The Pope spun around and leaned through the open car door, easing the valuable package onto the back seat. He peaked at the top page to appreciate the neat strokes and massoretic tropes penned by Aaron ben Asher a thousand years earlier. He couldn't help but be overwhelmed by the ramifications of this simple task.

His charge? To carry these passages through an ancient stone gate, climb some steps and hand it off. Simple. Elegant. Even brilliant.

And the result of this modest task? Lasting peace in the Middle East.

Arabs and Jews, once again, living together as brothers.

An ancient treasure made complete.

Lives saved. Hope renewed.

Pope Lazarus II was humbled by the task at hand. He genuflected. "Thank you, O Lord, for I am not worthy of the task you have placed before me. May you give me strength, that I may fulfill your wishes."

The Pope turned to his Papal Guards. "Come with me. There's something I need to do before delivering this package."

Unscripted, unexpected, the guards were aghast. Popes didn't just up and take an unplanned stroll. They just didn't.

This one did.

"I need to be alone for a few moments," he said to no one in particular.

He pushed through a swinging gate and stepped into a lush garden. Drawing in a long breath of air, Lazarus II closed his eyes and wondered if it was a good idea to leave the missing sheaves in the limo. He glanced over the shoulder; the Mossad agents rimmed the car facing outward. No one was getting to the parchment.

Pope Lazarus II absorbed the immediate surroundings: gnarled olive trees, white stone paths, and rocks outlining gardens. This, thought the Pontiff, was how it must have been for the Lord, Jesus. It was the night of the first Passover Seder. Afterwards, Jesus brought Peter, James, and John with him to the Garden at Gethsemane. Jesus asked them to watch him, to pray that they would not fall into temptation, but sleep overcame them. Jesus tried to arouse them twice, again reminding them not to fall into temptation to no avail. Later that night, Peter denied knowing Jesus three times.

What went through Jesus's mind knowing his friends were failing him? Did Jesus know that Judas would betray him? He did. And when Judas kissed Jesus so the soldiers knew which one he was, Peter took a sword and cut the man's ear off. And just as swiftly, Jesus miraculously healed the man's ear. Yet this amazing feat had no bearing on what was predetermined to happen.

So many thoughts coursed through the Pope's brain. Would he have been as open to participating in this process if he had never met LeShana Thompkins and learned about his own father? Would the Satmars have trusted him if was still a Cardinal? Had Garvey thought himself betrayed, in the manner of Jesus, when J. Edgar Hoover railroaded him to prison and then exiled him from the US? And what about W.D. Fard? Did Elijah Mohammed undermine him? Force him to leave Chicago and find sanctuary in Ethiopia? Was Elijah Mohammed Fard's Judas?

Betrayal, intrigue, and forgiveness.

Are these parallels or contrivances?

And what about Jesus healing the soldier's ear? Hadn't he, as a new

Pope, healed the journalist's sight? The gymnast's paralysis? What about the visions that came to him? What did they mean?

The Pope slid across the ground, sidling into the shade of an expansive olive tree. He touched the bark. Had Jesus done the same? Had His Lord stood on this very spot? Run his hand against this same wood? Felt its life? Its strength? Its very fiber?

Had Jesus stood here knowing these were his last moments, praying to *his* Lord that even though he had lived a good and righteous life, he knew he was about to be punished and wondered why?

History has come to know that the Lord did not listen.

Jesus was told that he had pay for the sins of all people.

That his pain was their pain.

Their sacrifice.

His life…for their salvation.

The Pontiff edged over to another olive tree, another with a thick bark skin. He ran his fingers over the tree, as if touching the tree put him direct contact with Jesus.

Then it happened. Pope Lazarus II had a vision like the one in St. Patrick's Cathedral and the many since. Danger was near. Someone would get hurt. Guards. Throngs of people. Clusters of dignitaries.

His urgency to warn and protect abruptly ended his communion with his beloved Jesus.

"Tempus est de essential," he stated out loud, and then wheeled around. Brisk strides belying his age brought him to the limo.

"I must walk from here," he said to one of the Mossad agents. Without arguing, the agent opened the door and retrieved the ancient parchment pages.

Cradling the reassembled pages that would make the Codex of Aleppo whole, Pope Lazarus II took the first steps toward completing the greatest diplomatic mission in recent times.

No longer would the displaced Palestinian refugees be orphans to the fraternity of nations.

No longer would they seek handouts from the Arab world, assistance that rarely came.

No longer would Israel have to fear rockets exploding and suicide bombers tearing into the very fabric of their daily lives. Natural cousins would once again live in harmony. And the messenger for this change was Pope Lazarus II, a black Catholic who happened to have a bit of Judaism and Islam swirling in his DNA.

"Your Holiness," said one of the agents as they rounded the back of the limousine, "we need to keep a tight ring around you as you traverse the cemetery. There're too many people to pass before you reach the gate, too many opportunities for trouble."

The Pope stopped, and turned to the agent. "This is a glorious moment to be shared by all. Walk behind me, if you must, but I will not be escorted like a prisoner through that gate the way our Father was taken from the gardens we just left."

"This is for your safety, Your Excellency."

Without drama, Pope Lazarus II arched his brows. "If for some reason *He* wants my mission to end along this path, there's nothing you or anyone else can do to alter that. Please make your peace with this; I have."

The Pope wheeled and crossed the road, stopping at the rim of the cemetery. It was not lost on him that rich Jews paid hefty prices to be buried on the slope of Mount Olive, near the East Gate where the Messiah would appear and begin resurrecting the dead. They paid dearly to be first in line to be brought back to life.

The Arabs would have none of that. They extended the cemetery to the foot of the gate and for good measure, barricaded the opening with blocks of stone. By doing this, they stymied the rabbinic prophecy since the Messiah would be a priestly *kohen* who was not permitted to walk through cemeteries. In case a wannabe Messiah didn't read the Biblical fine print and had no qualms about strutting through the cemetery, the blockaded East Gate would be an obstacle none could overcome. Ergo, no Messiah.

Pope Lazarus II was not a *kohen*. Marching across a cemetery was something he had done countless times before. What did have meaning for him at that moment was having prayed in the same garden Jesus had prayed in, and before that, having walked from the same hillside where Jesus had overlooked the Old City and made prophecies that would change the world, not to mention standing where Jesus ascended to heaven. These were experiences he would never forget.

Not in this lifetime.

The East Gate did have a special meaning for Pope Lazarus II. It was prophesized that Jesus would return in the last days and pass through this same East Gate, also named the Golden Gate.

Curiously, it was also prophesized that Mohammed would return to this same gate and sit on top of it, passing judgment on all who passed through it. For Muslims, this same archway was known as the Gate of Mercy.

East Gate, Golden Gate, or Gate of Mercy. Jews, Christians, and Muslims. Were they that different that they needed to kill each other over the centuries? Lazarus was tickled he would have a hand in ending the millennia of madness.

Lazarus hiked the first step at the base of the gate. A mighty cheer erupted from the throngs cordoned off to either side.

Clouds that had blocked the sun all morning, now parted. A beam of light highlighted his path.

The Pope took another purposed step, and then another. He paused; the image of harm returned. He peered into his vision, but when he did, it dispersed like a lifting fog. Maybe it would be okay.

When the Pope reached the top step, he eased through the gateway that had been sealed for five hundred years. He stopped and turned to face the crowd held behind barriers, gazing upon a sea of hope. There were Arabs and Jews, Christians and Kurds, Cypriots and Russians, all on their knees, hands clutched in prayer. *Why were they doing this?*

Lazarus II kissed the package of parchment pages and hoisted them above his head, and a deafening roar of joy erupted so loud that it gave those on the Temple Mount a start. Soldiers, guards, and Mossad agents within earshot lurched for their weapons.

The Pope waved and turned, poised on the steps of history.

# Chapter Sixty-Two

ittel turned larger when she heard the roar. It could only mean that the Pope drew near. She looked at the agent to right and the one to her left. Like her, both felt the air change. Bolts of anticipation coursed between them. In the years since Rabin had been assassinated, she had been on many important details, protected many Prime Ministers and Presidents, but never felt the way she did at that moment.

She was in the moment, and she wasn't.

She was, by turns, alert and numb at the same time. Time was distorted. Something eventful was about to happen. Good or bad? She didn't know. But she was certain something would happen...and she would be ready for it, no matter what it was.

◆ ◆ ◆

Jericho Glassman stole a glance down at the street below. From his perch, he could see a line of agents, probably Shin Bet, maybe Mossad, mixed in with the police, forming a chain of security the length of the Wailing Wall. Behind them, stood the remnants of the Second Temple, the most holy site to Jews around the world. The fools came to pray there, men to the left separated from women to the right. None were allowed today. But on all other days, the righteous and the pious, atheists, and the secular, the sick and the weak, the aged and young, all stood at the foot of the stones and prayed. Some prayed that the world would become a better place. Some prayed for good health. To be healed from sickness. Some prayed for wealth.

They wrote their prayers on pieces of paper and stuffed them between the cracks in the ancient stones. As if God would come down from his throne and read them. Fools all, thought Jericho. Did they really think the Messiah would show up and change the world order? Make sense out of this madness? Prevent people from hurting each other?

For Jericho, the Israeli Prime Minister, the Palestinian President, the President of the United States and the Secretary General of the United Nations were four pillars. Each was a different element: Earth. Water. Fire. Air. That's what the Voices called them.

A fifth element was missing. The Spirit. The Spirit would walk through the East Gate and enter this Ring of Hope. The fifth element would lay the last cornerstone for peace, complete the Pentacle...or so they thought.

Jericho adjusted his sight. The four other pillars waited for their missing link that would make them whole.

◆ ◆ ◆

The protocol for the momentous event had been plastered on CNN, in the Herald Tribune, the Jerusalem Post, and every other form of news media – including both the Arab- and English-speaking Al Jezeera - day and night for a week leading up to his historic event.

Every school child on the planet with access to a cell phone, texting, TV, radio, or the Internet, knew the drill.

Israel had already completed the first historic phase: all governmental agencies, including the Knesset and the Supreme Court, had been removed from Jerusalem in preparation as a first step in becoming an international city. This new safe harbor, the Biblical center of the world for Christians and Jews, and as important for Muslims, would now be administered by the United Nations.

The script was set in proverbial stone.

Pope Lazarus II would hand the missing pages of the Codex of

Aleppo to the Israeli Prime Minister, Yehuda ben Moses. Then ben Moses would bring them to his lips before handing them to Professor Yussif Tawil. Tawil would authenticate them. Once verified as the long lost missing pages, the Professor would insert the nearly two hundred sheaves into their proper place in the ancient text while the Vatican choir sang Handel's "Messiah."

Next, Tawil would hand the completed book to the newly elected Palestinian president, Jabil Habeeb, keeping the delicate Middle East peace process on track. Habeeb would hold the book over his head, bow to Mecca, bow to Medina, and then, as orchestrated, lumber to his knees, lower his head, and hold out the great book in his chunky hands toward the Dome of the Rock. In turn, he would pass the great tome to the United Nations Secretary General, the honorable Naomi Soweto. She would feel its weight, hold it a throb, and then deliver it to the U.S. President, Logan Rothschild, who would return the book to the Israeli Prime Minister.

It was fitting that one Jew would hand the greatest treasure of the State of Israel to another.

That's when Jericho would pull the trigger.

◆　◆　◆

Across the way, hidden in the narrow minaret of the Al Aqsa Mosque, Zakkarhia aimed his rifle at the assemblage protected from the midday heat under the canopy that were now venturing into the open after hearing a loud cheer. He had his mission, knew his target. But how fortunate that at the same time he would exact revenge for his sister's death. In moments he would put an end to the madness centered around these absurd missing pages written on ancient parchment. In moments he would extinguish the myth that anything could be holier than the Koran, Allah be praised.

◆　◆　◆

The instant neared and the feeling returned. Pope Lazarus II reached the open area of the Temple Mount. With every fiber in his body that propelled him to deliver the missing pages, he hesitated. He knew that as he neared the assemblage, the dignitaries would leave the shelter of the canopy that was a miniature version of the Dome of the Rock and be exposed to a terror that he surely knew was somewhere close by.

The paradox was not lost on him.

He was within midst of the nation acknowledged to have the greatest security in the world and, yet, he knew no one was safe.

Lazarus II drew to his full measure; he pressed the pages tighter against his heart.

A haze of darkness hovered above the distant hills, yet brilliant sunlight shone on him. Waves of warm air bounced off nearby stone, yet a chill ran through his body.

Cameras flashed.

There was a fog of singing nearby – Handel's Messiah.

Pope Lazarus II grew disoriented. Here he was, a black man thrust in a limelight he never asked for, never wanted, and certainly never anticipated. Yet here he was. It was surreal. Out of body. He edged forward but didn't feel his feet.

Resolved that Fate was in control, Lazarus stepped toward the waiting throng. Then another. In moments, he would initiate the peace process the world had sought for these many generations. There were the 1949 Armistice Agreements between Israel, Syria, Lebanon, Jordan, and Egypt, then The Camp David Accords, the Madrid Conference of 1991, and the Oslo I Accord. All gave hope; none worked. Would a book make the difference? The world needed to achieve peace; it needed to prove its humanity, but could it?

And then he remembered something LeShana said when they sat in the Vatican Garden. "You're just like Moses."

"That's pretty good company to be in," said Ford, "but it's a bit of stretch."

"The way I see it, Moses was found in reed basket and you were discovered in a crib. Moses brought the words of God to his people and you're bringing those same words back to them in a book. Moses was the big honcho for his people, and you are the Holy See."

Lazarus II knew the world was waiting for him to take those final steps. Who could blame him for taking a few extra moments to finish his thoughts? For, unlike Moses who was forbidden to enter Israel, he, Lazarus II, was already in the Promised Land.

But was he?

# Chapter Sixty-Three

Gittel Lasker's arms ached. She stole a moment to let the Nikon 10x42 Monarch ATB binoculars drift downward, long enough to rub her tired eyes. With the cheers growing louder, and the Pope edging closer, she had been scouring the buildings rimming the Wailing Wall with a vengeance. There was no way she would let something happen in her sector. She studied every window, every alleyway. People. Vendors. Children. Baby strollers.

Her walkie-talkie crackled. "All clear." She replied in kind.

What had been a gloomy overcast day, brightened during the last few minutes.

The louder the cheers, the closer the Pope came to handing over the missing pages, the brighter the sun shone.

There was no magical rainbow; no aura that portended that a global event was about to occur.

*Just God shining a spotlight on this very important happening.*

*He was pointing the way to peace.*

*Perhaps to something greater*

Gittel drew her field glasses upward. That's when she caught a glint of sun bouncing off something metallic that wasn't there moments ago. Something that shouldn't be there. Israeli soldiers were positioned on all roofs with a direct view of The Mount. But they had strict orders not to display weapons. All knew that…except a possible assassin.

"Eleven o'clock," she whispered into the microphone that coiled from her ear, hugging her cheek like a viper ready to strike. Not a second to lose.

"I need to check that rooftop," she said, pointing to a building across the way. "Over."

♦  ♦  ♦

Each assassin needed to wait for the moment to ripen before the seeds of their discontent would burst forth like flowers blooming from a desert rain. Only theirs were black flowers. Black flowers that would bleed red. Jericho and Zakkarhia felt throbbing in their ears; their pulses announced each passing second like a countdown to launch. Triumph drew nearer, so much so that they could taste it on their dry tongues. Jericho slipped his finger off the trigger and wiped it dry on his pant leg; Zakkarhia licked the sweat off his upper lip.

Breaths shallow; senses heightened.

Jericho saw the Pope emerge on the top step above the East Gate and then halt. The Pope appeared to be gathering his thoughts, taking in the sights. Sunlight broke through the clouds. Then, as if willed by Jericho or cajoled by the Voices, Lazarus II lifted his right foot and strode toward the anxious pillars: earth, fire, water, and wind. The Spirit was about to complete The Pentacle.

♦  ♦  ♦

Zakkarhia heard the shouting but knew a few more ticks would pass before he could zero in on his target; he was at the opposite end of the Mount and needed for the Pope to close the ranks with the others.

Earlier, had he wanted to take it, he had a clear shot of the Pope when he was reveling in the aura of Gethsemane. The fool must have thought himself the next coming of his Lord. He must have savored touching the ancient olive tree thinking he and Christ touched the same bark. His feet must have tingled as they glided over the same rocks that Jesus stepped on when they ushered him to the cross. The spirit of Jesus must surely be with him, thought Zakkarhia. How poignant.

How pathetic.

As much as he wanted to pull the trigger, the time had not been right. Not then. Zakkarhia must stick to the plan. Accomplish his cherished goal. Years of training told him to exert patience. Obey his inner strength. Wait until The Pentacle is assembled in the designated order, praised be to Allah.

◆　◆　◆

Nasser Albakree, the much decorated general in the Palestinian Army, left nothing to chance. His mission was to secure the base of the slope leading to the Eastern Gate, the Gate of Mercy, through which the Pope would enter the ancient city of Jerusalem. With his back to the limestone walls, he scanned all in front of him with grid-like precision. His eagle eye followed the Pope's every step. He could not fathom how the Mossad, let along his coterie of Papal Swiss Guards, allowed the Pontiff to walk in front of them. Unprotected.

Albakree stepped forward. He barked into this walkie-talkie that all needed to be vigilante. He ignored what the rest of the world was lapping up in its unquenchable thirst for living in the moment of history with each passing second. Albakree had already searched a fruit cart, poking the barrel of his gun deep into the stacks of oranges. He made an Arab women utter expletives that would shame a camel driver as he made her undo her baby's diaper, to make certain it was not filled with C-4. As he marked the seconds and minutes, he gained a measure of confidence that all would be right in his sector, that the Pope would be safe as he passed through the holy gate in his historic quest.

Yet he remained vigilant for that isolated possibility that something might jeopardize this sacred mission.

Albakree climbed the steps after the Pontiff passed by. He knew that the moment the Pope ventured onto the Temple Mount, no amount of security would save him if someone were hell bent on causing harm – Israeli super-agents notwithstanding, and yet he felt a relief that Lazarus II had passed his station without incidence.

It had been overcast all morning. Unexpectedly, the low-lying, steel gray clouds broke open, as if shot apart by a huge cannon. Sun poured through the opening, exposing a brilliant pastel blue sky. As the Pope trudged forward, the remaining clouds dispersed, elevating an already charged atmosphere to a higher pitch of anticipation.

Albakree was ten steps behind the Pope and the children that followed him. He watched as the Pope surveyed the scene; he sensed the Pope savoring the moment. Absorbing what was about to happen. Maybe he reflected on his mortality and about his place in history? If he had such a thought, reasoned Albakree, the Pope would surely be forgiven. *He* would forgive the Pope for this transgression.

Now that the Pope was in full view, it was not lost on Albakree that his own image, albeit steps behind the Pontiff, would be beamed to the six billion plus people glued to televisions, laptops, iPads, and smartphones the world over. Saved for posterity. Even as a shadow... what a thought!

Never since Christ drew his last breath, had the world been on such a precipice of change.

Never since the Second Temple had been destroyed nearly two thousand years ago, had the Jews been given such hope.

Not since the UN voted for partition in '47 and returned the lands of Abraham, Isaac, and Jacob back to its rightful heirs, had His children felt His love. Felt this safe. He certainly wasn't there for them during the Holocaust. Seems like the good Lord was about to make amends.

And not since Mohammed had rose to Paradise from the very spot where the Dome of the Rock would be erected, had Muslims around the world had so glorious a reason to rejoice, to know that Mohammed would one day return to the Gate of Mercy.

In moments, history would set off on a new course that was calculated to bring peace to the Middle East. This course was plotted by the Trinity plus Two – The Pentacle – and endorsed by the billions of Jews, Christians, and Muslims the world over.

The brilliance of this plan was so simple, so exquisite that no soul on earth doubted its genius and the positive changes that would follow in its wake. Or its success! The rich would no longer turn away from the poor, the healthy from the sick, or the powerful from the meek. The renewable resources of faith and hope would be rekindled in a glorious rebirth of brotherhood and sisterhood.

Think of the good and bad events experienced by the various generations living today: Hiroshima, V-E Day, Sputnik, November 22, 1963, "One small step for man, one giant leap for all mankind." And today? Events on the Temple Mount. The aged counted their blessings for living long enough to experience this day, the young would remember it forever, telling and retelling what happened to their children and their children's children.

Everyone accepted the plan developed by the Satmars except two lone men who were pointing rifles at the ring of world leaders entrusted to initiate this blessed event.

# Chapter Sixty-Four

Pope Lazarus II approached the circle of dignitaries. He hesitated before handing the pages to the Israeli Prime Minister, who would then pass them to Dr. Tawil for verification. Lazarus scanned left and then right, not knowing what he was searching to find.

The dark image was still with him, though it seemed to be lifting from the warmth of the sun.

Lazarus felt a gentle breeze on his face that reassured.

It was the Lord telling him that it was okay to proceed.

He handed the pages to the Israeli PM, who handed them to Tawil.

They were genuine.

The Codex of Aleppo was made complete.

◆　◆　◆

Jericho focused with both eyes open, his dominant right eye peering through the scope.

The red laser tattooed his target.

◆　◆　◆

Zakkarhia drew in a deep, cleansing breath.

He aimed.

The beam zeroed in on his mark.

◆   ◆   ◆

Jericho marked time as the Palestinian President, Jabil Habeeb, took the book from the Professor and brought it to his lips. He bowed in the directions of Mecca and Medina, two of the three holiest shrines to the world's nearly two-and-a-half billion Muslims. Then, with an unexpected grace coming from a man who walked with a cane and was challenged getting in and out of car, President Habeeb plunged to his knees. He symbolically offered the book, his arms outstretched, toward the golden Dome of the Rock.

The Palestinian President lurched to his feet and then tendered the Codex to Naomi Soweto, the first female Secretary General of the United Nations. A pediatrician by training, a former head of Doctors Without Borders, already a Nobel Peace Laureate for improving the health of the entire African and Asian subcontinent, she extended the book to President Rothschild of the United States, uttering words that every school child would know by heart in the years to come, "Today we have peace because we remembered to love each other."

◆   ◆   ◆

Zakkarhia waited.

He waited for the son of a Palestinian grocer to kiss the thick book.

He waited for the sun to reach its midday zenith, when it would blind.

He stole a glance upward; it was time.

◆   ◆   ◆

Bells in all the churches of Jerusalem clanged, singing that *the* moment had come.

Sirens blared around the world.

◆   ◆   ◆

317

LeShana and Zippora clutched each other, their eyes riveted to the screen.

LeShana's heart was filled with happiness; her chest heaved with joy.

◆ ◆ ◆

Gittel sprinted up the stairs of the building where she had seen the glint of metal. Had it been a gun barrel? With all the security and precautions, she didn't think it possible. She had checked this roof herself the day before. Under the circumstances, nothing could be left to chance.

The door was ajar.

She nudged it open.

Halfway in its arc, after she had eased a toe onto the roof, the hinge squeaked.

She froze a split second, then slammed it open, gun in hand.

◆ ◆ ◆

Jericho heard the door creak.

It was no time to turn his head; he remained focused on his target. He could never allow Israel to abandon Jerusalem. Ever since the suicide attack that killed his father, ever since rockets rained down in a perpetual storm of hate, ever since he entered the Army, and ever since he had the time to think and plot while in the Hamas prison in Gaza and then in the army hospital, Jericho Glassman knew the day would come when he would cut down the Israeli leader. The Prime Minister was the culprit, the Voices told him so. Not the Palestinians, not the Americans, and certainly not the United Nations.

For Jericho, the biggest enemy of the State of Israel was the government that ran it. They were weak-willed goats who did not have the courage of their convictions. Signing a truce with the hated Arabs served as the death knell for the State of Israel. Exchange all prisoners. Pull back on the settlements. Revert back to old borders. Give up the high ground. Rebuild *their* infrastructure. The Israelis were soft. Too kindhearted. Too forgiving. Turn the other cheek? Ha! Jews wrote the book on it. Then again, look what happened to Jesus.

Like any other fool country that behaved this way, the Israelis opened themselves up to be attacked.

And for what?

Pages of some old book?

The Voices told him it was time for a new leader to take charge and make things right. Jericho agreed.

◆　◆　◆

Gittel shouted.

Not, again, she thought.

Twice on her watch?

Really?

She aimed for his right shoulder.

# Chapter Sixty-Five

To his right, out of the corner of his eye, Zakkarhia saw the shine of metal that could only mean one thing.

He quick-calculated the trajectory that the assassin's bullet would take.

"Shit," he muttered.

Whoever it was, was aiming at the President of the Palestinians.

Zakkarhia couldn't let that happen.

Impulse took over.

In a split second, Zakkarhia shifted his sight, caught enough of the sniper's head to have a meaningful target.

Two shots rang out.

And then a third.

◆　◆　◆

Gittel aimed her gun. There was a moment of recognition. She couldn't be sure, but there was something about the gunman that was familiar.

"Put the gun down. Hands in the air."

She fired, leveling a shot to maim his shooting arm, but was too late; Jericho pulled the trigger.

In the split second it took for Jericho to reach for his shoulder, the top of his head was blown off. Bone fragments sailed in all directions; one sliced through her cheek. She felt the sting and yanked out the shard; blood gushed into her mouth. Air whistled through the hole. The gash could be sewn later.

Gittel rushed to the ledge. She kicked Jericho's rifle to the side. It was a waste to feel for a pulse. His wide-eyed stare told her all she needed to know.

"I know him," she muttered to herself. There was no time to dwell on the fact that this was the boy in Ashdod who lost his father in a suicide attack, that he changed his name from Moishe Schlamowitz, that this nightmare was a product of all that was wrong with life between the Israelis and the Palestinians. And there was no time for her to consider where the shot had come from. Had she done so, she may have lowered herself down so as not to make a large target. But Jericho had been crouching low and that hadn't helped him.

♦ ♦ ♦

Albakree stood vigilante. Hawk eyes swept windows and rooftops. Then he saw it: a sting of light bounce off a weapon beyond the Wailing Wall. His first instinct was to yell a warning to the Pope, but nothing came out when he tried to shout. He lunged forward, wishing he had already lost the thirty pounds he had promised his wife he would do.

Pope Lazarus II stood tall, oblivious to the danger, yet he was turning his head from side to side, as if looking for something. Was he aware of a danger?

As Albakree neared the Pope, he saw a rifle barrel in the Al Aqsa minaret swivel to its left…toward the exposed weapon on the rooftop. There was no time to figure out friend from foe. Without thinking, he sprinted to the Pope who, by now, was clustered with the other dignitaries.

♦ ♦ ♦

Every step that brought Pope Lazarus II closer to the waiting dignitaries ratcheted his awareness that something ominous was about to happen.

He saw something tragic in his apparition, but the details were indistinct. Sketchy.

He approached the circle of four leaders; nothing happened. Not yet.

On cue, the Pope handed the missing pages to the Israeli Prime Minister who kissed them and dropped them to the anxious fingers of Dr. Tawil, the manuscript scholar, for verification. With a magnifying class, he studied the top page, and then the next. He lifted the stack and looked at another page randomly, then another. All good.

The pages were valid; these were the missing pages of the Codex of Aleppo. He inserted them into the original book created by Aaron ben Asher and guided the treasure into the pudgy hands of the Palestinian President.

The Palestinian President took it and held the book toward Mecca and then Medina before dropping to his knees. He extended his bulky arms toward the Dome of the Rock before lumbering to his feet and passing the Codex to the graceful leader of the U.N. who muttered something the Pope would need to hear afterwards on CNN. For as much as he wanted to savor every moment of this historic event, his keen eyes searched for that gnawing thing that was amiss, but he had yet to determine what it was.

Though all seemed in order and was following the script, Lazarus II knew it would be shattered any moment. But he didn't know how or by what.

President Rothschild received the book from Naomi Soweto. He closed his eyes and then said aloud, "Hear O Israel, the Lord our God, the Lord is One." He handed the Codex back to the Israeli Prime Minister.

One Jew to another.

That's when the shots rang out.

♦  ♦  ♦

LeShana's hand covered her mouth. "Oh my God."

◆　◆　◆

At the precise moment President Rothschild handed the book to the Israeli Prime Minister, the Pope's vision cleared and he knew who the target would be. He lunged to save the Israeli Prime Minister Yitzhak ben Moses, knocking him down, out of harm's way.

# Chapter Sixty-Six

Six billion people witnessed what was undeniably the single, most important event in the history of mankind since the crucifixion of Christ. Many thought it more important.

Not everybody saw the same thing.

When the pandemonium receded, those from afar reported that three shots were heard in rapid succession. One came from the Al Aqsa Mosque, and two from a rooftop opposite the Wailing Wall.

They saw the Pope push the Israeli Prime Minister to the ground as a Palestinian policeman, Habeeb Albakree, propelled his huge frame toward the flash that spit from the Al Aqsa Minaret. Having prayed there many times, Albakree knew the interior layout and where to stand when the shooter emerged.

But it wasn't just any shooter; it was Zakkarhia ibn Mohammed, a lynchpin in the Al Qaeda army. Under the radar, but not unknown. In the end, Zakkarhia would prove to be a trove of valuable intelligence about the inner workings of Al Qaeda. He validated what many suspected: even after Osama bin Laden had been long dead, Al Qaeda was a multi-headed hydra incapable of being killed. Cells created years back, having lain dormant for a decade or longer, would continue to plan and carry out missions, without regard to when they occurred. Time had no meaning to jihadists. Perhaps this was just the initial foray to the "Thousand Years War."

It took many seconds to peel away the layers of confusion swirling on the Temple Mount.

The moment shots were fired, the few Secret Service agents permitted to stand behind him, knocked President Rothschild down. They covered ever part of his body with theirs. Human armor worked as well as Kevlar.

The Palestinian President though short, remained erect, too scared to run, too proud to take cover.

U.N. Secretary General Soweto knelt down on one knee as Mossad agents engulfed her.

By the time the Papal Swiss guards reached the Pope, a red bloom spread across his back. Jericho's bullet meant for the Israeli President entered under between the left scapula and spine, severing the aorta.

◆　◆　◆

The Pope died instantly.

◆　◆　◆

Stories abounded. Beliefs spread virally.

There were those who claimed that Pope Lazarus II had fulfilled the Christian messianic belief that Christ, the Lord, would return and enter the Holy City through the Golden Gate. Wasn't that what Pope Lazarus II did?

Likewise, Jews believed that the Messiah would enter through this same East Gate. He would stand atop the Temple Mount and a new Temple would be built on the site of the Second Temple. His presence would usher in a new world order of peace not only for Jews to live in harmony with all others, but also for people around the globe to live in peace.

In hushed voices, whispers began to circulate that Pope Lazarus II was, indeed, the Messiah. After all, he had the heritage of being a black Jew through his father. And was not Queen Sheba, wife of Solomon, a Nubian princess? Wasn't she the matriarch to all Africans?

And then there was The Miracle. Not the miracles that had

accompanied the Crown of Aleppo, not the miracle that the book was ever written in the first place, not the miracle that it survived the First Crusade and found its way into the hands of Moses Maimonides who sanctified it as the greatest Bible ever written. Nor were they referring to the attack by Tamberlane or the burning of the Yellow Synagogue when the British partitioned Palestine or even when a cheese merchant handed the complete Codex minus nine pages to President Yitzhak Ben-Zvi after all thought it lost. Miracles all…but not the one they all claimed had happened on Savior's Day.

Pictures snapped from hundreds of cameras were uploaded onto You Tube, Facebook, Tumblr, Flickr and Instagram.

These captured a spirit hovering above Pope Lazarus II.

Transparent, with light shining through it, it had a defined shape. Some said angelic. Otherworldly. Godly.

It was thought that this was the spirit of His Holy Eminence suspended over his own body. Ready to depart and meet his Father in heaven.

♦  ♦  ♦

"Can you see it, Mama? Can you see it?" Zippora pointed to the apparition floating above the Pope.

"I can see it, baby. I can see it," LeShana answered, stunned by the horror of it all. It was Abraham, Martin, and John all over again. And Jesus. Poor, poor, Arnold Ford. What have they done to you?

♦  ♦  ♦

Optical illusion?

The sun piercing through the clouds, reflecting light off the hot stones?

Dust that kicked up?

People wanted to believe, and they went to great lengths to do so.

That was not the case with images captured by an eight-year-old

Palestinian girl, one of the children permitted to march behind the Pope. Her mother had given her a disposable Fuji 24 frame camera so she could take her own pictures of the blessed event.

The pictures were developed the following day.

These shocked the world.

There was little doubt. The first frame showed a second, larger specter floating above the first spirit.

The first was thought to be Lazarus's soul.

The second, hovering above it, was that of an older face.

Art experts said it most resembled the sculpture of Moses by Michelangelo, minus the horns of light.

Others flat out declared it to be God.

Still others conjectured that Michelangelo was God's prophet and that his works were divinely inspired. That they were messages from our Lord? Were both Lazarus II and Michelangelo God's messengers?

Debate raged. Moses handed his people the laws of God, words spoken directly to him by the Lord. But when he descended from Mount Sinai and witnessed the debauchery and the golden calf, he threw them down and broke the tablets.

Like Moses, Pope Lazarus II carried the words of the Lord to the people. And in the end, like Moses, Pope Lazarus II was denied the fruits of his own labor.

◆　◆　◆

In the wake of his death, the Palestinians and Israelis continued to negotiate the peace plan defined by the Satmar Jews in good faith.

Jerusalem became an international city administered by the United Nations.

Israel ultimately recognized and helped create an independent Palestinian State. In return, the Palestinians cast aside age-old grudges and recognized Israel's right to be a free with secure borders. Hadassah Medical Center built and operated a satellite facility in Gaza. Border crossings between the two nations were removed.

◆    ◆    ◆

But it was the last picture in the sequence the little girl shot that changed the world for good. Whether it was an image that many wanted to believe was Moses or, in fact, that of God, the bearded apparition reached down and scooped up the spirit of Lazarus.

The picture captured Moses/God cradling Lazarus II in his arms, with a single tear clinging to his cheek, his mouth open in a hollow scream.

## THE END

# Author's Notes

I always wanted to be in a dentist but my first love as a youngster was history. I read voraciously, including hundred and some odd books (for those old enough to remember) in the Landmark series. When I went to Rutgers, I began as a biological science major but switched majors to history where my grades and interest in college skyrocketed. I graduated with Honors in history and was nominated for a Woodrow Wilson Fellowship, which I declined to pursue so that I could attend dental school first at NYU and then at Columbia.

At Rutgers, I came across a book that delved into the origins of black Jews in Harlem that confused me. Every Jew I ever met was Caucasian, but here it was, in a book, that there was a congregation of American blacks (not from Ethiopia) who claimed to be Jewish. In time, I would learn there was more than one such congregation. The history of how Afro-Americans rejected Christianity and embraced Judaism was not only compelling, but made sense. Their story fascinated. I stumbled upon one sentence that not only intrigued me, but I promised myself right then and there that I would one day write about Arnold Ford, music director to Marcus Garvey's UNIA and founder of Temple B'nai Abraham in Harlem, and that he might have been the same person who founded the Black Muslims in Detroit.

One author, one sentence. Did he have concrete proof? Not at all? Do I think this might have happened? Probably not. But it is intriguing to think it possible, because that's what writers do. The timing, as described in Savior's Day, is historically accurate. Arnold Ford was to have left on an ocean liner for Ethiopia with his congregants' money to buy land to start an ex-patriot settlement for black American Jews. But there is no record of that happening right away, but there is a record of a man appearing in Detroit about that same time, calling himself Professor Ford and W.D. Fard. For those who wish to read more on this topic, I suggest starting with, "The Black Jews of Harlem" by Howard Brotz, The Free Press of Glencoe, London, 1964.

Fard did live with Elijah Mohammed, a.k.a. Robert Poole, in Chicago and did disappear, never to be seen or heard from again. His birthday, February 26th, is celebrated as Savior's Day, and this is where the title of my book came from, but it has a greater meaning in my story. And an American social worker did meet Rabbi Ford in Ethiopia in 1935. And that is where the truths of history end and where my imagination takes over. I have no knowledge of Arnold Ford every marrying or fathering a child. By all accounts, Ford did die in 1935 around the time Mussolini started a war against the Ethiopians. That event permitted me the opportunity to create an orphaned child that Catholic missionaries would find and raise, a man who would be age-appropriate for my story. This story percolated in my head for more than 40 years.

In 1993, I met Hayim Tawil, a great Biblical scholar who taught at the Union Theological Seminary in New York. Hayim was my patient and when he learned that my first novel had just been published, "Someone Else's Son," by MasterMedia, he asked if I would collaborate with him to write a book about the Codex of Aleppo. While Hayim had the knowledge, he felt he didn't have the command of English to write the story. He didn't care if the book was fiction or non-fiction, just that the story got out.

I had never heard about the Codex of Aleppo but was eager to learn more. Hayim, ever the great teacher, met with me every Monday afternoon in the lobby of what was once called the Commodore Hotel next to Grand Central Station, and is now known as the Grand Hyatt. We met weekly for two years, during which time Hayim would teach and lecture and explain the history of scribes and Aaron ben Asher, the role of Tiberias as home to the scribes of that generation, the importance of the massoretic trops, why Maimonides declared this the greatest Bible ever written and so on. It's all in Savior's Day, and to the best of my ability, I represented it as the truths that I know.

Once I had learned story about the Codex, how would I write it? My first attempt was to craft an historical fiction novel. It was miserable and I trashed it. Next I decided to write it as a non-fiction history book. A prominent agent contacted us and wanted to represent the project but asked who would write it? I said that I would. She rejected this notion out of hand. "You're a dentist," she reminded me, "and he (pointing to Hayim) can't write in English." It didn't matter that I was a history major or that my first novel had been published, nor did it matter that Hayim, an acknowledged Biblical scholar, would consult ever step of the way. To the agent's way of thinking we weren't journalists and Hayim wasn't writing it, so she couldn't sell it.

During the next fifteen years, I published a second novel while always toiling how best to tell both the story of the Codex of Aleppo and the story of the Black Jews in America. Then it occurred to me: why not meld the stories into an portrayal that tied the three great Judeo-Christian religions together. Thus, Savior's Day, my variation of it, was born.

# Acknowledgments

Hayim Tawil deserves my thanks and gratitude for being my mentor, my teacher, and my friend. He was always patient as I struggled to understand this epic story of how the greatest Bible ever written came to be, what it meant to the Jews of Aleppo, Syria, and how it fell into the hands of the Israeli government, only to have one third of the book still missing today. Is the notion that the Mossad knows where the missing pages are but chooses not to recover them true? Probably. Is it true that the Satmar Jews have these pages? Possibly. Did the London merchant see them? He did. That, my friends, is where the unfinished story of the Codex of Aleppo continues to this day. The missing pages are yet to be recovered.

I also have to thank a dear friend, Olga Vezeris, who has encouraged me to continue my writing. Olga is one of the great book editors and for a time, became my agent. While she continues to edit books, she has pushed and cajoled me to get Savior's Day published. Thank you, Olga.

I also have to thank the love of my life, Lori Rudman Blitz, who shares everything with me and this means, giving me the time to follow my passion of writing. Thank you for your understanding and this is just one more reason why you are so special.

And to those who've finished Savior's Day and made it to this last sentence, thank you for sharing this story with me. I hope you enjoyed it. This is a work of fiction, although most historical references are accurate. Any resemblance of characters in "Savior's Day" to any living person people is purely a coincidence.

For those willing to accompany me on a new adventure, I've included the Prologue for my next book here. Please look for the release of "Island Bluffs."

Alan A. Winter
Bernardsville, NJ April 13, 2013.
dralanwinter@hotmail.com
www.alanwinter.com

# Island Bluffs*
by
Alan A. Winter

# Prologue

This is anything but an ordinary story. Then again, nothing that ever occurs in Island Bluffs, one of a score of laconic towns that make up the famed New Jersey shore, is. Not now. Not long ago. Not ever. Many of the important characters in this story are already dead, yet it remains for the living to find the truths in the secrets buried in Island Bluffs.

For starters, Island Bluffs is not an island. It's a promontory that juts into Barnegat Bay opposite Long Beach Island's famed lighthouse. It wasn't that long ago that the top of the World Trade Center was visible from boats a bit off shore on sunny days. But that was before things changed.

But back to our story.

In Island Bluffs, the cast of characters, the living ones, well, most of them, anyway, are everyday folks. For starters, Gabe and Carly Berk try so hard to conceive that they need to use a renowned doctor of last resort: Dr. Isadore Teplitsky. Then there's Megan Berk, the lone child from Gabe's first marriage, who can't get past her mother's death, and still cannot embrace her stepmother after six years. And of course, quite, lovable, rock solid, Yehuda Berkowitz, Gabe's father, who has been a widower for these many years, who still does not understand why his son needed to shorten the family name. Marrying a *shicksa* was okay, but changing the family name?

Oh, there are a few more characters to toss into this cauldron of intrigue, and they will be added to this burlesque of souls when needed.

As we forge ahead, tuck in the creases of your mind that memories of dead folks will be uncovered that Island Bluffs' town elders would like sooner to forget. Truth be told, these patriarchs cocooned in their own stories almost forgot their own town's secrets. But Gabe and Carly set the hive buzzing by buying a certain house that had been off everyone's radar. That sometimes happens with abandoned homes hidden from the road by an overgrowth of shrubs and trees, especially if no one's lived in it for a generation or two.

It is the house that time forgot.

Along come the Berks and secrets buried long ago begin to surface like detritus dredged up by a sudden storm.

What kind of secrets you ask? Dark ones. The kind that makes for a tale told when the moon is full, and fires crackle, and houses creak. The kind when the wind hisses and leaves rattle, and spooks come out to play. The kind that makes the hairs on the back of your neck arch, and your heart beat quickity-quick.

So let's begin this tale of twists and turns, where lines of clarity blur, and little is, as it seems. Then again, whatever is?

Especially in the laconic town of Island bluffs, a dot of land on the Jersey coast that isn't even an island.

*To be published by the end of 2013.

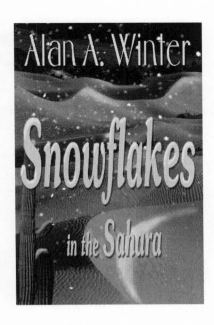

http://bookstore.iuniverse.com/Products/SKU-000550438/Snowflakes-in-the-Sahara.aspx

Set in the backdrop of the ever-worsening global warming, *Snowflakes in the Sahara* is the story of a Svengali-like mind-manipulator (Lute Aurum) who teams up with an American Business icon (Jeremy Steel) to take over the White House. When their puppet is installed as president, Aurum and Steel are poised to pull off the greatest heist in history: Canada. And they almost pull it off, if it weren't for Carly Mason, the Big Apple's tooth sleuth...A Kay Scarpetta-like forensic dentist.

One terrible day, two disasters strike America at the same time: the president's helicopter carrying him to Camp David crashes, and a bomb explodes in Rockefeller Center leaving three bodies unidentified. Carly is by turns tough and inquisitive, clever and cunning. She will need all her skills to discover the victims' names. As she gets closer to the truth, a killer is dispatched to silence her. What follows is a gripping tale of heroism against all odds. What's frightening is that *Snowflakes in the Sahara* is a tale that is only a presidential election away.

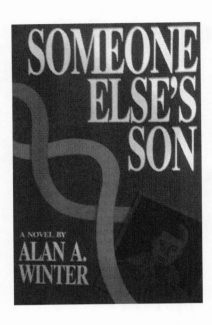

Trish and Brad Hunter are in limbo. Eighteen years after bringing their first son, Phillip, home from the hospital, they discover that they are not his natural parents. Who are Phillip Hunter's real parents? And who is Trish and Brad's biological son?

Someone Else's Son explores the host of questions, curiosities, family secrets, and changed relationships that have come with the discovery that Phillip was switched at birth. As doubts abound and relationships go awry, the whole family structure begins to shake. Every page challenges the role nurturing plays versus Nature's hidden genetic code.

Brad Hunter feels it's his fatherly duty to assist Phillip in searching for his biological parents, while Trish wants no part of it - insisting that Phillip is their son, no matter what. The escalating conflict between husband and wife, and the unfolding of Phillip's first love affair, both add emotional stress to Phillip's search for his biological parents.

Phillip questions could be anyone's - adopted children's, children from alternative forms of insemination or surrogate pregnancies, or those real-life children whose identities may have been mistaken in hospital nurseries.

At one time or another, most of us have stared into a mirror, touched our lips, our noses, or checked our smiles to see if they were similar to a parent's or sibling's. It is human nature to wonder about our origin.

Do the years spent together and the shared experiences create the parent-child bond? Or is it the genetic make-up? Which contribution has the strongest influence on the child?

www.alanwinter.com

24199619R00202

Made in the USA
Lexington, KY
09 July 2013